THE CHANGE QUARTET:
BOOK TWO

HOSTAGE

RACHEL MANIJA BROWN
AND
SHERWOOD SMITH

BOOK VIEW CAFE

HOSTAGE

Published by Book View Café

Book View Café Publishing Cooperative
P.O. Box 1624
Cedar Crest, NM 87008-1624

www.bookviewcafe.com

ISBN 13: 978-1-61138-473-4

Cover design by Cormar Covers

First printing, June 2015

THE CHANGE QUARTET: BOOK TWO

HOSTAGE

RACHEL MANIJA BROWN
AND
SHERWOOD SMITH

This book is dedicated to Judith Tarr, whose Lipizzan Horse Camp for writers inspired us in so many ways.

CHAPTER ONE
LAS ANCLAS
ROSS

Ross Juarez bolted out of bed.

His feet skidded, and he crashed into the wall. The pain came as a relief. The wall was solid. Real.

He pressed his palms against the cool plaster. He was in his bedroom, on his feet. Not writhing on the blood-soaked dirt beneath a chiming crystal tree.

The room seemed small, the walls close. He tried to focus on the stars overhead, but instead he saw the flaws and bubbles in the glass ceiling. If it fell in, it would shatter into a thousand crystalline shards.

Ross fled the house, nearly tripping over the tabby cat on the landing. He bolted across the street, and fetched up in Mia's yard.

He leaned against a barrel, shoved his sweaty hair out of his eyes, and gazed at the comforting golden glow of her windows. Mia was awake, and happily at work. Seeing her would make him feel better. But if he went in, she'd be upset because she couldn't fix his nightmares.

Ross was the only one who could.

When the blood-red singing tree had first invaded his mind in dreams, he'd had to visit it in person to establish his side of their mental link, so he could communicate with it, then learn how to shut it out.

But after the battle against King Voske's army two months ago, he had again begun dreaming of the soft pop of exploding seed-pods, of shards piercing his skin, of barely noticeable pain becoming unbearable agony as tiny needles grew into razor-edged knives and branched through his body. And always, as he lay dying, he looked up at leaves like knives and branches like swords, glittering in the moonlight and black as coal.

The scarlet tree that had grown from his blood contained his own memories, but those dark trees had grown from the bodies of Voske's soldiers, who'd worn night-black camouflage—soldiers whom he'd used his own tree to kill. Ever since, the obsidian trees had forced their way into

1

Ross's dreams to share the memories of the agonizing deaths they'd been born from.

The worst part wasn't the pain. It was waking up, and remembering his guilt.

Ross couldn't go on like this. He had to face those singing trees.

He pushed himself away from the barrel. Confronting the trees would be risky, but at least he'd be awake, not dreaming and helpless.

Out of habit, he headed toward the town hall, with its secret tunnel that led to the mill at the juncture of two city walls. But after the battle, sentries had been posted at the mill, along with extra guards along the walls. He needed a different route.

Ross hurried through the sleeping town until he came to the Vardams' orchard. He could use the fruit trees as cover, then climb over the wall in the time it took the sentries, who always looked outward, to make their fifty steps in the other direction.

He hooked his good hand around a branch and pulled himself into an apple tree. A mother raccoon hissed from a neighboring bough, then scampered across a swinging vine bridge into another tree, followed by her litter of kits. The raccoon family vanished into an elaborate two-story home of hardened mud and fallen branches.

The hot Santa Ana wind whipped stinging dust into his face. He smothered a sneeze, then checked the sentries, who did not miss a step. The rustling leaves had covered the sound.

When the sentries passed, he wedged his fingers and toes into hollows in the wall. Halfway up, he grabbed a slippery knob of stone, and set his foot onto an adobe outcropping. It broke off under his foot. Ross slid. He caught himself painfully, scrabbled for a new foothold, then inched upward until he could haul himself over the top.

He dashed into the cornfield, then crouched to catch his breath. An opossum hurried past, an ear of blue corn in its jaws.

Ross forced himself to move. He sensed his own singing tree; its chimes called to him in his mind. But he had only sight to guide him through the abandoned cornfields. Now that the area had been declared off-limits, tall weeds grew in the cracked earth and tumbleweeds rolled everywhere.

Soon he saw the jagged black fingers rising above the corn stalks, blotting out the stars. Globes of dark glass hung from faceted branches. Just one crystal shard had cost him much of the use of his left hand, and each seed-pod contained hundreds of them.

He was well out of range of the black trees. Still, he didn't feel safe. Crystal leaves should have clashed together, ringing out a threat, but the trees were silent. It was as if they wanted him to come closer.

Closing his eyes, he visualized a concrete wall with a small steel door. The door led to his own tree in the center of the obsidian grove. Ross opened the door a crack. His tree glowed a deep ruby red, an ember within coals. He gave the mental door the smallest of pushes, and—

Glass shattered and popped as every seed-pod in the black grove exploded. Needles of pain stung Ross's face, his throat, his bare hands. He'd missed one of those black trees in the dark night!

He grabbed his belt knife, knowing he could never cut all the shards out of his flesh before they took root...

Ross forced his eyes open and unclenched his fingers. There was blood on his hand, but only from where he'd scraped it against the wall. The left was unmarked.

He slammed the door in his mind. The pain vanished.

Ross bolted back to the wall, checked for sentries, and climbed as fast as he could. He caught his breath in a tree laden with pomegranates the size of crystalline seed-pods. They tossed in the wind, and one bumped against his shoulder. Ross jerked away, then fled the orchard. He didn't slow until he reached Mia's cottage, his footsteps heavy.

Before he could knock, the door popped open. "Ross! I heard you coming."

As he stepped inside, Mia adjusted a blanket she'd flung over a corner of her worktable. Sometimes she didn't like people seeing her projects until they were done.

After Ross had nearly died in the battle, Mia's father, Dr. Lee, had ordered him not to do anything strenuous, so he'd been assigned to assist Mia with engineering projects and mechanical repairs. He and Mia quickly discovered that they had to divide their working space, or he could never find his tools and she got annoyed at him for rearranging hers. His side of the table was neatly organized, hers a chaos only she could understand.

Mia's shiny black hair swung tousled against her cheek. Her glasses slid down her nose, which was smudged with the blue paint that also marked her fingers. She absently shoved her glasses back up, leaving another blue streak. Though his knees were watery and his throat dry from his run, he couldn't help smiling at how cute she was.

She didn't smile back. "You went outside the walls, didn't you? Ross, you promised not to go there alone."

"I had to go over the wall, and it's a tough climb. With one hand, I couldn't have helped you."

Mia shot a glance at the lump hiding under the blanket. Then she folded her arms. "I'll make a grappling hook for myself. For next time. If there's a next time. How did it go?"

It would only upset her if he told her how the trees had nearly tricked him into cutting into his own flesh. Just thinking about it was making his heart race. "It was fine."

"It was fine? You don't look like it was fine. It was horrible! Wasn't it?"

"Yeah," Ross admitted. "But in kind of an interesting way. They knew exactly how to scare me."

Mia grabbed his sleeve, her eyes flashing wide. "So you could communicate with them?"

"Well, they were definitely communicating with me." He breathed out. In. "Let me see if I got through to them."

Ross took another deep breath, bracing himself for an onslaught of pain and fear and nightmare images. He wished he could hold on to Mia, but, well, why shouldn't he? She already knew he was afraid, and it didn't make her think any less of him.

"Do you mind?" Ross beckoned to her.

She didn't hesitate a heartbeat—she came straight to him, her steady brown gaze so *trusting*. He put his arms around her and bent to rest his cheek against her silky hair. No matter how often they touched, the first contact always came as a shock. But he'd gotten to like that shock.

He tightened his arms, holding Mia close, shut his eyes, and stepped into the world inside his mind. There was his wall of concrete, and there was his door of polished steel. Cracks widened around the door, and dust sifted down.

But Ross could feel Mia in his arms, warm and breathing, and that gave him strength and confidence. He visualized the cracks filled in with fresh cement, made it harden in the blink of an eye, and kicked the wall to be sure. There was no response from the trees.

He opened his eyes. "Yeah. I think I can keep them out now."

"Great!" Mia squeaked, backing up a step so she could see his face.

Ross enjoyed her enthusiasm. The lingering terror faded enough for him to say, "I was thinking. Since I could talk to those trees, I should be able to talk to others."

"Really?"

"And the singing trees around the ruined city don't have any reason to hate me. I might be able to get past them to go prospecting there."

She bounced on her toes. "That's fantastic! I've wanted to get in there ever since I was a little girl. Could you take me?"

His fear flooded back. "No!" It came out more harsh than he'd intended. Mia stopped bouncing and looked hurt. He tried to speak gently. "I've always prospected alone."

"You've been taking Yuki prospecting for months now," Mia pointed out.

"I've been *teaching* him to prospect." Ross took Mia's hand. Again, the shock made his heart stutter and his breath catch. "I might be able to get past the crystal trees, but I don't know if I could protect another person."

"Your ruby tree didn't hurt me."

"Yeah, but that one's part of me. *I* don't want to hurt you. I don't know what the other singing trees will be like."

Mia squeezed his hand. "If you go alone, who's going to protect *you*?"

Ross hadn't had anyone to care for, or who'd cared for him, since his grandmother had died when he was eight.

Then he'd come to Las Anclas.

Mia had saved his life during the battle. Some townspeople said she had brought him back from the dead, though she and Dr. Lee had assured him that he'd only stopped breathing for a minute or so. He knew how much she cared about him. But like the touch of her skin against his, every new reminder came as a surprise.

He trusted her, and he trusted himself to guard her with his life. What he wasn't sure he could trust was his own strange power.

Mia was looking at him expectantly.

"I'll think about it," he said.

It didn't sound like much to him, but it seemed to satisfy her. She linked her fingers around the back of his head, and pulled him down for a kiss.

CHAPTER TWO
LAS ANCLAS
JENNIE

Jennie Riley straightened her yellow linen skirt, tucked a stray braid behind her ear, and left her bedroom.

The aroma of peaches and browning butter wafted from the kitchen, along with squeals and giggles. Her younger sister Dee and Dee's friends Z and Nhi were doing a three-day rotating sleepover, one night per house.

The night before, Jennie had spotted the Terrible Three doing the Change ritual, in pajamas, as she passed by Dee's bedroom

Dee, who had already Changed, was the guide. She stood before the kneeling Z and Nhi, proclaiming, "I lead you into the realm of the Changed! What is your desire, petitioners?"

"We wish to Change, O guide," chorused Z and Nhi.

"Hold your offering and state your heart's desire," Dee replied.

Z reverently lifted a piece of flint from a decorated box. "I want to start fires, like Grandma Wolfe! But I want to be able to control it."

Nhi took a feather from the box. "I want to fly."

The girls replaced their Change tokens in the box.

"May you be blessed with a Change," Dee said solemnly.

She opened her cupped hands and blew on the dirt they held. It rose up in a tiny dust devil, whirling before the other girls' envious eyes.

Jennie had walked on by, amused and a little sad. When she'd been their age, she'd been the guide for her friends and sibs who wanted to Change. Now she knew what being Changed really meant: a blessing from God, yes, but also an occasion for prejudice and a heavy responsibility. She'd taken children who should have been kept safe and led them into battle, solely because they had useful Change powers. And then she'd abandoned them…

Jennie hurried on. In the kitchen, Nhi was speckled with whipped cream from brown braids to bare feet, Z's auburn curls were sprinkled with sugar, and Dee bent intently over a bowl of batter that swirled furiously by itself. Dee glanced at Jennie, startled, and the batter rose up in a gloppy brown waterspout.

Nhi yelled, "Dee! Your batter!"

The batter subsided, mostly back into the bowl.

"It's to celebrate the first day of school," Z explained.

"We can't wait!" said Nhi. "The last two months have been so boring."

The kids of Las Anclas had thought that school being closed meant freedom. Then they'd discovered that they had to work from dawn to dusk, bringing in the harvest and doing odd jobs while the adults repaired the damage from the battle and rode out on patrol. It was nice to see the kids, for once, excited about school.

Jennie looked forward to her return to teaching. Every time she patrolled with the Rangers, every time she held a weapon in her hand, the memories rushed back: burning leaves swirling in the smoky air. Voske's silver hair glinting in the firelight. The smell of charred and trampled pumpkins. Sera Diaz, falling dead at Jennie's feet.

Dee poked her. "Jennie? Aren't you excited about trying the Terrible Three Triple Peach Surprise?"

Jennie forced herself not to jerk away. "Bring some to the schoolhouse for me," she said, striving to sound normal. "I have a council meeting first."

Sugar drifted down from the spoon in Z's hand. "Is something exciting happening?"

I hope not, Jennie thought. "Debriefing about yesterday's defense drill. Yesterday's terrible defense drill."

"Ugh," the three girls chorused.

Dee held out a peach. "Ma says you're not eating enough."

"Thanks." Jennie gave a mental tug, and the peach flew from Dee's hand to smack into her palm.

She headed toward the town hall.

If a teacher made a mistake in the classroom, nothing worse could happen than parents complaining or kids squabbling or someone graduating without ever really understanding fractions. It couldn't result in someone's death. And while students were occasionally injured on teacher-led patrols, in mishaps or fighting animals, none had ever died on one.

The image flashed again in her mind's eye: Sera falling, falling…

Jennie pushed away the memory. Sera was gone. Jennie couldn't fix that. What she could fix was the teenagers' performance in the battle drills. Her stomach roiled as her mind stubbornly brought her right back around again: in battle, unlike patrols, people inevitably died. And in her duty as a Ranger, when war again came to Las Anclas, she could once again find herself leading children into the fray, with their lives depending on her commands.

The uneaten peach vanished from her hand, and Jennie's fingers tightened on empty air. She looked for the squirrel that had teleported the peach out of her hand, then let out her breath in a laugh. Two squirrels were cooperating to roll the stolen fruit toward a hole in a jacaranda tree.

But her amusement only lasted until the peach and its furry thieves had vanished. She continued walking, her stomach still churning. Her hands tingled with anxiety.

She began the calming breathing exercise that Sera had taught her. Then Felicité Wolfe's voice drifted from the open windows of the town hall.

"…but, Mother, this is a council meeting. And this hat is so fashionable. As council scribe, I need to show respect for my position by looking my best."

"There is a time and a place for everything," Mayor Wolfe replied. "A council meeting is not the place for fashion, and indoors is never the place for a hat."

Framed in the window, Felicité clutched protectively at her wide-brimmed hat. "My roots will show. It'll look like I didn't make any effort at all!"

"Darling, no one expects perfection in this heat. But since it's worrying you, you may take this afternoon off to dye your hair."

Mayor Wolfe, impeccably dressed in a subdued, council-appropriate dress—and no hat—held out her hand. Felicité reluctantly surrendered the hat.

Her golden hair did have dark roots, but Jennie agreed with the mayor. No one but Felicité would care. Jennie fought the impulse to despise Felicité for her petty worries. It wasn't Felicité's fault that she had nothing worse than her hair to worry about. Felicité hadn't failed Sera.

Stop it.

Inside the town hall, it was marginally cooler. Defense Chief Tom Preston turned from his conversation with the two judges and the guild chief to give Jennie one of those narrow-eyed scans she knew from the practice field.

Or the night of the battle.

Dr. Lee gave her a cheerful wave.

"Morning, Jennie." The skin around Sheriff Crow's brown eye crinkled and the right side of her mouth curved. The skull-like Changed side of her face didn't move, but her lashless, yellow snake-eye gave Jennie a wink.

Jennie smiled back.

"Felicité?" Mayor Wolfe indicated the windows.

Felicité closed them. The hot room instantly became stifling. Jennie didn't understand how Felicité could stand the silk scarf wrapped around her throat, covering her from collarbones to jaw. Everyone else had managed to dress respectably without also risking heat stroke.

Félicité opened the book of records, dipped her pen, and poised it to record the meeting.

Mr. Preston put on his silver-rimmed glasses. "I don't need to recap how terrible yesterday's drill was. The children and teenagers were particularly unsatisfactory. That can't continue. Las Anclas nearly fell to Voske's attack. The only reason it didn't was because of Ross Juarez and his…" Mr. Preston's lip curled in disgust. "…power."

Jennie bit down hard on her anger. How could he acknowledge in one breath that a Change power had saved the entire town, and make it sound like something shameful in the next? He undoubtedly still expected her to act like a Norm whenever he was around, as the price of being the only Changed person in his elite Rangers.

"But that trick can only work once," Mr. Preston went on. "We have to be better prepared."

Jennie's chair creaked as she braced for the reprimand she deserved. Maybe Mr. Preston would take over the training, and she could bury herself in lesson plans—

"Jennie, we don't blame you. It's only been two months since we began training like this. And so we have decided not to re-open school today." Mr. Preston smiled at her. "We don't want you teaching anything but fighting."

Jennie's stomach roiled again. Until that moment she hadn't realized how much she wanted to be reprimanded, to be removed from battle training altogether. When she'd dreamed of being a Ranger, she'd thought only of risking her own life. Not even her most frightening experience on patrol, when teenagers had been injured fighting giant rattlesnakes, had prepared her to lead children into war.

She had to talk them out of it. "As the teacher of Las Anclas … I mean, speaking as the teacher *and* the trainer of the children, the teenagers, and the Ranger candidates…"

Jennie turned to Mr. Preston. "You said yourself that Ross saved us. You didn't mention that he almost died doing it. The only reason he stayed in Las Anclas long enough to get to know us—long enough to be willing to risk his life for us—was to get an education. We're all here today because Ross wanted to learn how to read. Do we want to become a place where that wouldn't happen?"

The ensuing silence had a distinctly puzzled quality.

The mayor smiled. "Jennie, very well put. But you misunderstood. School will resume next week. We will rotate the job among qualified elders, until my mother is able to…"

Control her fire-starting Change power, Jennie thought. Would the mayor say that aloud, in front of her prejudiced husband?

"… return to teaching," the mayor continued smoothly. "And Ms. Lowenstein has agreed to train the young ones. We put too much on you, Jennie. We need you to focus on being a Ranger and on training the Ranger candidates."

Mr. Preston nodded. "Sera valued your ability to train a group. In fact, she said that despite your youth, you were the best trainer of all the Rangers. Jennie, you don't have to worry about teaching school any more. You're a Ranger, and that's all you have to be."

The entire Council nodded their approval.

Jennie should have felt honored. Instead, she felt trapped.

She loved the Rangers—she loved pushing her body to its limits—she loved the camaraderie, the jokes—she was delighted that her ex-boyfriend Indra had finally recovered from his wounds enough to at least warm up with them.

She loved the idea of being a Ranger, but there was a Sera-shaped hole in the Rangers' drills, their camaraderie, even their jokes. When Jennie was away from the Rangers, she could imagine that Sera was out on a mission. But when Jennie was with them, she could never forget that Sera was dead.

Or that she'd died because Jennie had failed to save her.

CHAPTER THREE
LAS ANCLAS
YUKI

Yuki Nakamura knelt on the beach, examining the intricate construction of twigs and pebbles and wire that Ross had assembled on the damp sand. The "artifact" gleamed in the center: a steel bolt. Ross sat cross-legged beside him, head bent, giving him no clues.

The first time Yuki had tackled the exercise, the "ruined building" had collapsed when he'd removed the second twig. Though he'd gotten better at gauging what was supporting what, in two months of prospecting lessons, he hadn't safely extracted the bolt yet. His only consolation was that in two months of giving Ross riding lessons, horses still walked him into low branches.

But Yuki's frustration was mingled with anticipation. Soon he'd be a full-fledged prospector, and finally—finally!—travel again.

His gaze drifted to the open sea, which he'd once sailed as the prince of a ship the size of a town. Then the *Taka* had been captured by pirates, leaving Yuki the sole survivor of the raft that washed ashore in Las Anclas. He'd lost everything: his home, his family, his friends, his position, even his culture. And for a long time, he'd thought he'd lost his future, too.

But Ross had offered him a new future. Yuki would never again explore the deep sea, but he'd explore the land instead. His breath caught with excitement at the thought of how close he was to once again spending every day in new territory. And he wouldn't even have to do it alone—his boyfriend Paco had promised to come with him.

But first, he had to get that bolt.

He visualized the model as the size of a house. The twigs were beams, the pebbles bricks, the wedges of bark concrete slabs. He eased out three pebbles and a precariously balanced twig, then used them to brace a piece of bark.

Yuki bored a tunnel into the sand with his pocket knife, keeping it only large enough to fit the bolt through. The bark quivered, but nothing fell

11

down. The last time he'd dug a tunnel, he'd hit a buried "girder" and a wall had collapsed. His heart pounding, he eased the blade up and cut out the other entrance.

He pulled the knife back, slowly removed the sand, and threaded a string loop around a stiff wire. Barely daring to breathe, he pushed the wire through the tunnel, caught the bolt in the loop, and tugged it safely through.

"Good job."

Yuki had gotten so absorbed that he'd forgotten Ross was there. He pocketed the glasses that enabled him to see up close and wiped the sweat from his eyes.

"Seriously," Ross added. "It took me months, too."

"How long after that before you got to do any actual prospecting?" Yuki asked.

"I was already prospecting."

Yuki stared at Ross, annoyed and frustrated. "You told me it was too dangerous to prospect until I could get the bolt ten times in a row!"

Ross began neatly disassembling the structure. "It *is* too dangerous. The guy who taught me that exercise figured if a building was going to fall on someone's head, better mine than his."

"His name wasn't Mr. Alvarez, was it?" Yuki asked wryly.

Now that Yuki finally had someone trustworthy to teach him, he didn't feel quite so bitter remembering the prospector who had taken him on as an apprentice, then drugged him, stolen everything he had, and ditched him in the desert.

Ross smiled. "I was thinking about your sea cave, Yuki."

Yuki glanced toward the rippling sea below the cliffs, where an earthquake had exposed an underwater entrance into an ancient building. He'd extracted an artifact from it, but he'd also stirred up a blinding cloud of silt, gotten disoriented, and almost drowned.

Though Ross had picked up swimming much better than riding, he couldn't hold his breath as long as Yuki. Ross hadn't managed more than a glance into the cave before he'd had to surface, but he'd seen enough to call it a death trap.

"I don't know how to prospect underwater," Ross went on. "So we both need to learn. We can practice in safer caves, setting stuff up for each other. Like an obstacle course."

"That's a good idea. Thanks."

Ross scooped up his wires and bolt, and stood up. "Okay, see you tomorrow."

Yuki scrambled to his feet. "Wait, what about the ruined city? You'll take me now, right?"

Ross shook his head. "I'm going alone."

Yuki gritted his teeth in frustration. Once again, the opportunity to leave Las Anclas and explore had been dangled in front of him, and once again, it had been snatched away. "But I got the bolt. And I wouldn't so much as breathe on anything without your go-ahead."

Ross twisted the bolt between his fingers. "I know that. It's because of the singing trees."

"What do you mean? You can control them, right? I'm not afraid."

The afternoon sunlight illuminated the shadows around Ross's eyes, as if he'd been up all night. "You should be."

Ross had spoken so softly that Yuki had strained to hear him. But at his words, memories flooded Yuki's mind:

The pop of a seed-pod, followed by the dying scream of a rabbit.

On a long patrol, his rat Kogatana had squealed a warning from the saddle. Mom shot an arrow into what looked like a shimmer of heat rising from the desert floor. It bounced off a singing tree as clear as glass. Eerie chimes rang out, and continued ringing until they were out of earshot.

After the battle, Yuki had listened incredulously to babble about Ross making a singing tree kill Voske's soldiers; later, while walking the wall as a sentry, he'd looked out over the now-abandoned corn fields at the jagged-edged forest, black as a mussel shell, surrounding a single blood-red crystal tree. Each of those new trees had risen from the corpse of a human being wearing black.

"Hey!" came a familiar voice.

Ross spun around, his right hand flying up in a block. Then he relaxed, looking embarrassed.

Yuki's boyfriend Paco Diaz ran up, sand flying behind his heels. Droplets of sweat gleamed on his face, emphasizing the sharpness of his bones, and glistened on his muscular arms.

"Hi, Ross," said Paco. "Yuki, did you get the bolt yet?"

"I did. Tunneled in," Yuki said with a grin.

Paco clapped him on the shoulder. Yuki leaned into the heat rising up from Paco's body.

"I came to fetch you for Ranger candidate practice, Yuki." Paco turned to Ross. "You can do the training even if you don't plan to try out. That's what Yuki's doing. Why don't you join us?"

Ross gave Paco a furtive glance. "Dr. Lee hasn't cleared me to train yet."

"What, still? And you plan to go into that city alone?" Yuki exclaimed.

Ross edged back. "Dr. Lee's just being cautious. I'm fine now."

But Yuki saw him wavering. "How much concentration does it take to use your power? Can you control those trees and fight at the same time?

Anything could be in that city."

Ross rubbed his left arm. He wore long sleeves, but Yuki had seen the scar from where Ross had cut out a shard from a crystal tree. He looked as if it still hurt him.

Finally, Ross said, "You're right. But ... I want ... I need someone who's done this with me before."

"Prospecting?" Yuki asked, irritated. "That would be me."

Ross shook his head. "I'll take Mia."

"Mia Lee?" Yuki said incredulously. "Instead of me?"

"I'll take you next time." Ross crammed his wires into his pockets and took off.

Yuki sighed as he and Paco headed back to town. "The first trip into dangerous, unknown territory, and he'd rather have a mechanic than the only other person in town who knows anything about prospecting."

Paco's slanted eyebrows flicked upward. "I wouldn't take it personally. Ross obviously has stuff going on that he doesn't want to talk about. At least, not in front of me."

"Not in front of me, either."

"Mia's his girlfriend." A smile—too rare these days—lit up Paco's fox-like face. "If it was me, I'd want you."

"And I'd want you."

They were standing still now, gazing into each other's eyes. If they'd been alone, they would have kissed. But Yuki hated having busybodies watching him while he was doing something intimate. Or worse, commenting. No one in Las Anclas had any proper sense of privacy. He glanced around.

An old woman using her Change power to levitate razor clams out of the sand and into her basket, a fishing boat hauling in its catch, two boys and a girl playing jump-rope, the entire Tehrani family having a picnic... Yuki would have to get Paco alone later.

Paco laid his hand on Yuki's cheek. He'd been so distant and sad since the battle, when his mother Sera had been killed, that Yuki didn't have the heart to pull away. Yuki closed his eyes, tried to forget about the nosy onlookers, and let their lips meet.

When he opened his eyes again, he *had* forgotten about the onlookers. The razor clam woman gave them a benevolent smile. Before she could make any embarrassing comment about how sweet they were, Yuki pulled Paco away.

As they walked on, Paco said thoughtfully, "But you're right, Yuki. Ross can't use his power and fight at the same time."

"How do you know?" In the two months Yuki and Ross had been teaching each other, that morning was the first time Ross had so much as mentioned his power.

"Mia told me." At Yuki's surprised glance—he hadn't known that Paco had any particular interest in Ross or friendship with Mia—Paco added, "I wanted to know more about the battle. Mia didn't mind telling me what she saw, but she wasn't in the right place."

"The right place?" Yuki echoed, bewildered.

"Where my mother died." Paco's dark gaze was fixed on some distant point. "I wanted to know exactly how it happened. But Jennie won't talk about it, and the other Rangers said they didn't see who shot her."

"Paco..." Yuki reached out to comfort him.

Paco stepped aside with a brusque shrug. "But it doesn't matter who pulled the trigger. Voske gave the order. That's all I need to know."

Before Yuki could figure out how to respond, Paco was walking again, his lips pressed tight together. As silence fell between them, Yuki thought that Ross wasn't the only person with a lot going on that he didn't talk about.

CHAPTER FOUR
LAS ANCLAS
MIA

Mia recognized Ross's quick steps outside her cottage. He'd put away the demolition gear faster than she'd expected. She cast aside her polishing cloth and flung the door open.

"I have something for you!" Fizzing with joy, Mia made a grand gesture toward the worktable.

Ross stepped inside, brushing off cement grit from the afternoon's explosion, then stood gazing at her gift—a steel gauntlet.

She'd measured his hand for it before the battle, but kept her progress secret as she made sure it was sturdy but flexible, strong but relatively light. She'd meant to give it some decorative inlay, but once it was done, she saw that its clean lines were what made it beautiful. She was certain that Ross would feel the same way.

She held her breath as he fitted it over his left hand and flexed his fingers experimentally. The shining steel and his brown skin set off each other beautifully, and the swell of his triceps was echoed in the curve of the armor.

It looked magnificent on him, but what did *he* think? She'd nervously started counting once he'd slipped it on, and an entire thirty-nine seconds had passed in dead silence.

She couldn't stand it anymore. "Does it fit? Is it comfortable?"

"It fits perfectly." Ross's serious expression didn't change as he made a fist. Though the fingers of his bare hand couldn't close enough to make a tight fist, the thickness of the padding and metal allowed him to do so in the gauntlet.

"The bars brace your wrist," Mia explained. "And you use the sliding lever to lock your fingers in place."

Ross flashed his rare grin. "Yeah, I remember from the diagram you showed me."

His cheekbones darkened, and Mia knew exactly what he was thinking.

That diagram had brought about the first time they'd ever kissed. After she'd given up on the whole idea of kissing and dating, let alone falling in love, let alone anyone falling in love with her, she'd met Ross.

If she'd drawn up a blueprint for the perfect guy, she wouldn't have come up with anything half as wonderful as him. And he liked *her*. So much for everyone who'd said Mia was a weird loner who would never have a relationship with anything that didn't run on electricity!

She took a step closer, and he pulled her in against his chest. That was another thing she wouldn't have imagined when he'd first come to town, skittish and thin as a feral cat. Now he reached out to her, and he'd even gained a little weight. She happily snuggled in close. Her head fit against his shoulder like a ball in a socket.

"This is better than anything I imagined," he said. She loved the way his voice rumbled through his chest. "I can't wait to try sparring with it."

"I wanted to test that—that is, I thought of having Jennie test it, her hands are about the same size as yours—but she was busy."

Ever since the battle, Jennie never seemed to have any free time. But Jennie had been busy since she was six, and she'd never before been too busy to have time for Mia.

"Is Jennie..." Ross flicked the gauntlet's lever off and on, testing his hand in different positions.

Mia reveled in his appreciation of its workings. But then he started moving the lever without changing the position of his fingers. Like he had something else on his mind.

"Ross?"

His glance was furtive, like the old days. "When you both asked me to the dance. Before the battle. I thought... I mean... You both liked me, right? And you didn't mind that I like you both?"

Mia couldn't help laughing. "It took you two months to ask that?"

Ross ducked his head and fingered the lever.

"Jennie and I talked about it before we asked you to the dance," Mia explained. Poor Ross, wondering all this time! "We've been best friends since we were little girls. There was no way we were going to get in some stupid fight and break up our friendship over you. So yeah, it's fine that you like Jennie, too. Sorry! I thought you knew that I knew that you... well, you know."

His shoulders jerked in an awkward shrug. "Every time I see her, she says she has something to do and runs off. If she did like me, she must have changed her mind."

So it wasn't only Mia. That didn't make Mia feel any better. "She's been avoiding me, too. And I don't think it's because of you and me. That wouldn't be like her. I think she's grieving over Sera Diaz."

Ross's eyebrows pulled together. "She was the Ranger captain, right?"

Mia nodded. "Jennie says you always love the person who trains you, if you love martial arts. It was like she had two mothers: Mrs. Riley, and Sera."

When Ross looked away, Mia said, "When my mom died when I was little, I didn't want to talk to anyone for months. I was afraid if I did, they'd mention her, and then I'd start crying and I'd never be able to stop."

Mia felt Ross tense. She wondered if he was thinking of his own parents, who'd died when he was four. He hardly ever talked about them. She decided to change the subject.

"Will you take it to the ruined city?" she asked. "The gauntlet, I mean."

"Sure."

Ross's response was so prompt and so enthusiastic that Mia couldn't help herself. "Did you think about taking me? *Will* you take me? I've always dreamed of getting in there—think of the ancient machinery lying around, just waiting to be picked up!"

Ross's muscles tightened even more. Then he took a deep breath, and slowly relaxed. "Yes. I'd like to have you with me."

A shriek of pure joy burst from Mia's lips. Ross jumped.

"Sorry!" she said. "I mean, great!"

CHAPTER FIVE
LAS ANCLAS
JENNIE

Jennie's fist slammed into the pad of the schoolyard punching post. It reverberated, a solid hit.

"Two hundred twenty-three," she muttered.

Sera had told Jennie to hit the post fifty times daily for practice. "It's relaxing, too," she'd said. "If you're focused on the one perfect blow, you can't have anything else on your mind."

Jennie must not be focused, or she wouldn't be thinking about Sera at all.

She punched again. "Two hundred twenty-four."

As she drew back her fist, she noticed blood on her knuckles. Her hand throbbed in time with her heartbeat. Maybe she was overdoing it. She dropped her fist and looked up.

Ross stood at the edge of the yard, eyeing her cautiously, glossy black hair ruffling in the wind and dust swirling around his feet.

Mud had splashed around him when he'd fallen in the battle. The memory was so vivid: Ross lying still as death at Mia's feet, the blood around his mouth obscenely bright in the pale dawn light, while Jennie counted the breaths that she took and he didn't. Even though he had lived, even though he was here with her now, the grief and helplessness she'd felt then hit her so hard that she couldn't bear to look at him.

She recoiled, then caught his hurt look. "Hi, Ross." She forced a smile, but when she saw his left hand, the smile became more real. "Mia finished your gauntlet! Did you come to try it out?"

A pang of guilt knifed through her chest when she saw his unmistakable relief. "Yeah. Are you done training, or can I join in?"

The images rose up again, blotting out the dusty schoolyard. Ross falling. Mia laying her palm on his still chest. Ross falling…

Jennie blinked hard and put all the enthusiasm she didn't feel into her voice. "Sure!"

The smile Ross gave her seemed genuine. "Thanks. You're running Ranger candidate training after this, right?"

Jennie nodded. "Are you interested?"

"I don't want to be a Ranger. But I'd like to get back in shape, and I convinced Dr. Lee that I won't drop dead if I do a little sparring."

"Great! Come along." As soon as the words were out, she regretted them. Today was also her ex-boyfriend Indra's first day back in training.

She hadn't been together with Indra and Ross since the dance before the attack. How awkward was that?

Only to me, she thought. Indra was jealous of Ross when Indra and I were still dating, but now we're just friends. And Ross and Indra don't even know each other. I'm the only one who knows what I really feel about them both. So long as I hide my emotions, no one will notice a thing.

"Want to stretch first? I'll do the see-saw with you." Jennie sat on the ground and forced herself to beckon cheerily to him.

Ross dropped down lightly and extended his legs in a V. Jennie placed the soles of her shoes against his. Ross's fingers closed around hers, his right warm and callused from his years of training, his left supported by smooth metal. They shifted, stretching each other's legs out, until their faces were only a few feet apart.

One thing hadn't changed: their chemistry. His touch sent a wave of heat through her body. She could tell he felt it, too, the same way they could read each other's intentions when they sparred. Some people just fit together, like two pieces of a puzzle.

Jennie pulled Ross forward as she tilted her body backward. He grimaced.

"Tight hamstrings?" she asked.

"Yeah. I've been stretching by myself, but it's not the same."

She held the position, then straightened up. "How's Mia? I saw the dust rise from a nice explosion yesterday."

Ross leaned back until his hair brushed the ground, and the muscles of Jennie's thighs burned.

"We blew up some of the old cement road," he said, his eyes closed against the sun. She enjoyed the long sweep of his lashes on his lean cheeks. "To get raw material for repairs."

"Bet she loved that."

He nodded. She pulled him forward, slowly increasing the stretch as she wore down the resistance in his stiff muscles. Ross gave a long exhale, and she was able to go lower. He winced.

"Up?" Jennie asked.

It was hard to keep that slippery grip on his hands. She used her stomach muscles to haul herself upright. They sat still, breathing hard. Wet strands of hair clung to his forehead, and his shirt revealed rather than hid the muscles of his chest. Jennie felt her shirt clinging too, and had to resist the urge to look down.

"You must be excited about the trip to the ruined city," she said.

"Yeah." He sounded doubtful.

"Or are you worried about it?"

"I can control those singing trees." He spoke so softly that she had to lean in even closer to catch the words. Then he looked straight into her eyes. "Mia said she's wanted to get into the ruins since she was a kid. What about you? Want to come with us?"

Jennie let go of his hands, closed her eyes, and elaborately stretched out to give herself some space to think.

It had obviously been hard for him to ask. Just because of that, she wanted to say yes. It would be a day to get there, probably a day inside the city—if they could get in—and a day to get back. Three days with Ross.

Ross sprawled in the mud, chest still, hands slack...

"I wish I could," she said.

His hurt was as easy to read as the alphabet book she'd given him on the first day they'd met.

"I mean it. I wish I could go with you." Jennie *did* wish she could; more, she wished she wanted to. "But I've got too much work to do."

"We're not going right now," Ross said. "Mia's busy, too. Remember the crossbows from that ancient book I found, the ones that shoot six arrows at once? Mr. Preston is having her install mounted versions on the walls. The council didn't want her to leave town at all. It'll be at least two weeks before we can go."

Though Jennie hadn't done anything strenuous, she felt as dizzy and short of breath as she had fighting Voske's soldiers among the burning trees. She could smell the smoke now.

She fished for a different topic. "Did the Council give you a hard time about leaving, too?"

Ross shook his head. "I'm not important."

He spoke without self-pity, merely stating a fact. It made Jennie want to contradict him more than if he'd been bitter. "You—"

You saved the entire town, she thought. And he nearly died. She couldn't bear the thought of reliving those memories for days on end.

"You can take me next time," she said. "This time, have fun with Mia."

CHAPTER SIX
LAS ANCLAS
ROSS

Ross wondered what he'd done wrong.

When he and Jennie were sparring at the schoolyard, they'd begun moving together like they used to, reading each other's intentions in the subtlest movements. Laughing together. But when she refused to go with him to the ruined city, her expression had gone strange and distant, and she'd barely spoken on their way to the Ranger training grounds.

"Jennie," he began.

"I'll get your gear." Jennie dashed off toward the supplies.

Ross stood alone, taking in the area: obstacle course, training equipment and weapons laid out and waiting. His left arm ached from the unaccustomed weight of the gauntlet, but it was great to be able to make a fist again.

The Ranger candidates were warming up. Henry Callahan held a pad for Tommy Horst to punch, making faces of exaggerated agony at each blow. Brisa Preciado threw rocks at a target, the ribbons on her pigtails fluttering. Jennie's foster-brother Jose crouched near Brisa, palms on the ground, moving ripples of earth toward her feet to test her balance. She picked up a pebble, clenched it in her chubby fist, flicked it at him, and snickered when it exploded in a bang and a puff of dust.

The scene reminded Ross of the schoolyard before the battle. All it needed was Felicité Wolfe strutting around in a giant hat, taking notes for the archives.

But other people had changed. Sujata Vardam, who had once minced beside Felicité in embroidered dresses, wore rugged training clothes. She was doing light sparring with Meredith Lowenstein, keeping the smaller girl at bay with her longer arms and legs—with difficulty, as Meredith was tough and fast.

Paco and Yuki were also sparring, but not lightly. Ross had seen them spar before, but though Yuki had approached each match with the intensity of a real fight, Paco had treated drill with absent-minded competence, physically adept but saving his enthusiasm for drumming. Mostly, Ross remembered him relaxed and smiling. But Paco was serious now, his sharp features intent. His loose clothes snapped and popped as he punched and kicked, and he was moving so fast that Yuki seemed hard-pressed to keep up.

Henry collapsed in mock exhaustion, letting his blond hair flop in the dust, then spotted Ross and scrambled to his feet. "Ross! You're gonna train with the Ranger candidates?" When Ross nodded, he let out a loud whoop. "Yeah!"

Everyone turned, even Paco and Yuki. Just before the battle, the townspeople had finally stopped staring at Ross for being a stranger, but afterward he'd become a center of attention all over again. He couldn't wait for some trader to appear and draw away their interest.

Henry feinted a punch toward Ross's shoulder. "You'd make a great Ranger. It was so *cool*, what you did in the battle. I was guarding Mr. Preston, so I got to see you wipe out that entire squad of elite assassins."

Crystal chimes rang. Ross flinched.

"...I counted the bodies. Thirty at one blow! Pretty amazing. I only shot twenty-six, and not all of them croaked."

Ross wanted to tell him to stop talking, but the chimes were so loud that he wasn't sure Henry would be able to hear him.

"...one guy was still running when black branches poked right out of his back—did you see it?"

The door in Ross's mind swung wide open. From the perspective of a quickly growing tree, he saw a black-clad man fall to the ground, bloody hands scrabbling in the mud. The blood crystallized and darkened, and the man's fingers took root and began to grow into the earth.

Ross slammed the door.

"Shut up!" Ross shouted. "Shut up about that!"

Henry's blue eyes widened. "But it was cool. *You* were cool!"

Ross clenched his fists. The chimes had stopped, but his ears were still ringing. The air seemed thick and hard to breathe.

A shadow fell as someone stepped between him and Henry. Ross slid backward, guard up, and then recognized the tall guy with the long blue-black braid: Indra Vardam, the young Ranger who had been wounded in the battle. Ross dropped his fists.

Indra wasn't smiling. "Henry, you're talking about killing people, not about some game where the person with the highest score wins."

"What's wrong with being proud of defending the town?" Henry protested. "Everybody knows, if it wasn't for Ross, all our heads would be on pikes on the walls!"

"It isn't wrong to be proud of defending the town," said Indra. "But Sera taught us that killing is something we only do when we don't have any other choice. There's nothing cool about it."

Jose spoke up. "Pa Riley says that every one of those soldiers of Voske's had a family who mourned them."

Meredith nodded vigorously, her red curls bouncing. "This is Ranger training, Henry. Not psycho killer training."

Several of the teenagers laughed. Henry grinned and shrugged. "Sure. I get it." He wandered off and began hitting the punching post.

Indra flicked his hand at the crowd, and they dispersed across the grounds. Ross wiped his sweaty palms on his pants. He couldn't get the picture of the fallen soldier out of his head. Those fingers, taking root...

Jennie approached, carrying a load of gear. "Thanks, Indra. Henry needed to hear that." To Ross, she said, "Have you two met?"

"Not exactly," said Ross. "We were in the infirmary at the same time."

Jennie's hands flexed.

Indra smiled at Ross. "Doc Lee cleared me to get back in training. But I'm on light duty for a while."

He seemed like a nice guy. More, he seemed to understand.

"Thanks for stepping in," Ross said.

Indra glanced at Henry, who was still pounding the punching post. "No problem. It's about time he realized that not everything is a joke."

Jennie cupped her hands around her mouth. "All right, people! Line up!"

The candidates instantly formed a line by height.

"Let's warm up with the obstacle course," said Jennie. "Go!"

The first obstacle was a set of rope monkey bars suspended between wooden frames. Ross slowed as he cupped his left hand into a hook and locked the gauntlet into place. He leaped up and caught the first rope with his left hand. The gauntlet worked perfectly as he swung hand over hand, easily passing first Brisa and then Meredith, whose short arms had so little reach that she had to set her entire body swinging to catch the next bar.

By the time Ross reached the stone wall, he was at the head of the pack. He got halfway up the wall before he hit a spot where he needed his left hand. The hook slid off the hold. Yuki and Paco passed him, followed by Sujata and Tommy. Ross tried to balance with his feet, so he could free his right hand to adjust the gauntlet. His left foot slipped, and he fell off the wall.

Ross landed in a crouch, unhurt but frustrated. He released the lock and tackled the wall again. But even with his fingers free to move, the smooth metal prevented him from getting a grip on anything. He should have taken the gauntlet off, but he couldn't remove it without falling again.

Meredith, Jose, Henry, and plump, short-legged Brisa swarmed past him. When Ross got to the top of the wall, he saw that he was last. He jumped down, landing with a knee-jarring thud.

Ross ran full-out for the mud pit, air burning in his lungs. Yuki leaped over it, his long legs clearing it with ease. Sujata seemed to float across, landed gracefully, and pelted after him. Brisa and Meredith didn't attempt the jump, but slogged side by side through the mud. Brisa kept a protective hand over her ribbons.

As Ross came up behind Henry, the blond boy swerved off to the side and kicked out. Ross saw the rock skidding into his path, but too late to avoid it. His foot slammed into it, and he went flying into the pit. Ross threw his left hand high as he splashed into the slimy mud, desperately trying to stay upright.

Henry sailed across in a flash of yellow hair. Brisa glumly patted her mud-soaked ribbons.

"Sorry, Brisa," said Ross.

"Done!" Paco's voice rose up. Yuki finished right behind him, closely followed by Sujata.

Ross hauled himself out of the pit and ran through the final set of obstacles, trying not to care how badly he'd done. He'd known that using the gauntlet would take practice, and he'd rather have Henry tripping him than congratulating him on killing people.

Ross finished the course two steps ahead of Brisa, dripping mud, his scar a line of fire down his arm.

Jennie's gaze slid past him. He wished he knew what he could do to make her see him again, instead of staring past him with that blank gaze, like she was a thousand miles away. It chilled him.

Yuki stepped up in front of Ross, folded his arms, and deliberately looked from Ross's left hand to the muddy water puddling at his feet. There wasn't a drop of mud on Yuki's clothes, and not a hair had escaped from his sleek black ponytail.

"Take me to the ruined city. You don't know what sort of backup you might need. And Kogatana can scout for us." Yuki held out his hand in the 'deal' sign.

Ross knew how frustrating it had to be for Yuki to be denied the chance to explore the ruined city—a prospector's ultimate dream. But Yuki was so cool and collected, easily accomplishing everything Ross struggled with, that being around him made Ross intensely conscious of all his own weaknesses. The last thing Ross wanted was to have Yuki's critical gaze on him when he went to confront those crystal trees.

No, the last thing he wanted was for Mia to get hurt or killed because of his pride.

Ross laid his palm against Yuki's. "Deal. You're right, you should come. But don't bring your rat. I don't know if I can protect her."

Yuki's expression eased. "Deal."

CHAPTER SEVEN
LAS ANCLAS
MIA

Mia was so excited over the trip to the ruined city—tomorrow! —that she couldn't concentrate. She picked up tools and put them down randomly, knowing there was something she'd forgotten.

A scrape of metal on metal startled her as Ross turned a screw in a half-repaired engine.

His gift! She patted her pocket, making sure it was still there. She loved making things for him. This weapon might be exactly what he needed.

She'd meant to give it to him after dinner, but Dad had brought out his own surprise, cornmeal cakes and five tiny jugs of flavored syrup. The lemon-rosemary was good, but the honey-lavender tasted like soap, the tomato-basil was not a dessert, and she'd refused to try the horrifying olive oil-rose petal. Even Ross hadn't managed more than a taste of that one. His favorite had been the prickly pear-chili pepper, which would have been better without the chili.

Would now be a good time? She stole a glance at him. He was completely absorbed, his eyelashes casting shadows across his cheeks. Mia hated to disturb him, and she loved watching his hands moving so confidently over the engine.

"It's so hot," he muttered. He pulled off his shirt and draped it over the back of his chair. Then he bent over the engine again.

Mia couldn't believe he'd relaxed enough to take his shirt off in front of her. No, he'd obviously forgotten that she was there. She smiled. He'd never think she was weird to get completely engrossed in a good repair job —he did, too.

She surreptitiously eyed his bare chest. She'd always loved seeing the muscles in his shoulders move under his shirt, but she could see them much better now. And she'd never seen the muscles in his back at all. She leaned out to get a closer view, wondering what his skin felt like, so smooth and brown between his shoulder blades…

Ross jerked his head to get his hair out of his eyes, then caught her staring. Mia jumped.

"Am I doing this right?" he asked.

Mia managed to swallow past the boulder in her throat. "Sure. Looking good." She grimaced. *Looking good?* But Ross had already gone back to work.

A couple turns of a wrench, then he smiled. "There. How's that?"

"Perfect. The engine's perfect. What you did. It looks great." She was babbling. Her teeth clicked together as she snapped her mouth shut.

Ross yawned. "I should go to sleep. Yuki wants to leave at dawn. I think that's a good idea, don't you?"

Mia managed a nod.

He put away the tools, then walked up and kissed her. His hand caught on a rip in her shirt, just above her left breast, and he ran his finger along her bare skin. His own bare skin was pressed up against her body, so hot and alive...

With his shirt off, he was technically *half-naked*. She was kissing a half-naked guy. She froze.

Ross broke off the kiss, gave her a puzzled look, then backed off. "Don't stay up all night working."

Once he was out the door, Mia wished she could reverse time, the way Dad sped it up when he used his Change power to heal people. She should have grabbed Ross and kept that kiss going. She'd been so distracted by his shirtlessness that she'd barely even kissed him back. And it wasn't as if they'd get any chances to kiss on the expedition, with Yuki coming along. Even if Ross wasn't embarrassed, Mia would be.

She stared gloomily out the window. If only Jennie had agreed to come. If only Jennie would talk to Mia like she used to. When they returned, Mia vowed, she would corner Jennie and talk to her, even if Jennie wouldn't talk back.

She was distracted by the sight of Ross hurrying back out of Dad's house. Maybe he was coming back to kiss some more? She left the window and hopped over engine parts to her door to greet him.

But he didn't come in. She counted three breaths—ten—then hopped back to the window.

He had curled up in a secluded corner of her yard, by the sheet metal. Poor Ross! He must have been dreaming about the black trees again, or was afraid that he would if he stayed inside. He had to be so uncomfortable on the bare ground. She wished she could go out and...give him a pillow? Give him a kiss? Return his shirt?

What she wanted to do was curl up next to him. The impulse made her palms prickle, and she rubbed them down her thighs. What would he think? What if someone walked by her yard, looked in, and saw them sleeping together? What if he wanted to have sex with her? Wasn't that what sleeping together meant?

Her heart raced, but with nervousness rather than excitement. Now she was being a freak again. People were supposed to want to have sex with their boyfriends, not be petrified at the thought.

Then she remembered how long it had taken Ross to touch her, and how difficult it had been for him to let her touch him. If he thought she was about to pounce on him for sex, he'd probably jump up and run. In that case, she definitely shouldn't go to him.

She wasn't even supposed to know that he was there.

Frustrated, she sat down on the floor. Her surprise dug into her hip. She'd forgotten *again*.

CHAPTER EIGHT
LAS ANCLAS
YUKI

Yuki hefted his backpack—heavy, but he'd rather be over-prepared than under—and set it on his bed with a thump. Kogatana, who had been napping in Paco's lap with her bare pink tail curled around her furry gray body, woke with an indignant squeak, jumped off the bed, and retreated into her rat house.

"That's it. I'll carry my weapons." Yuki indicated the sword, crossbow, and knives that he'd placed on the bed.

Paco hefted a dagger. "Nice balance. I didn't know you could throw knives."

"Ross is teaching me. Who taught you?"

Paco's head bent, so Yuki couldn't see his eyes. "My mother."

Yuki grimaced. *I'm an idiot. Who else could have taught him?*

"She taught me when I was a kid," Paco added. "I never practiced."

He handed over the knife. Yuki sheathed it carefully before he looked up. Paco was staring at the worn rug. "Are you okay?"

Paco blinked and stirred. "I'm fine. All done?"

You're not fine, Yuki thought.

It was natural for Paco to grieve. But was grief supposed to change you this much? When had Paco ever cared about weapons? Last night, when he'd played with the Old Town Band at Luc's, his drumming had sounded perfunctory instead of passionate.

Paco sat silently, twisting a bit of the blanket. A few months ago, he'd have drummed on the bed with his fingertips.

Yuki used to like that Paco didn't fill up every pause with pointless chatter. It reminded him of the tranquil quiet in his first parents' chambers on the *Taka*. But this silence felt tense.

Night had fallen, and the room was lit only by the yellow glow from a terrarium of bright moths. He and Paco had spent the night a couple of times before the battle, but not since then. Before, it had been easy. Paco

30

was so light-hearted that Yuki had felt like even if he had said no, it wouldn't have been a big deal. Now it seemed as if anything he said carried an enormous weight.

But he wanted to ask, and so, when Paco finally stood up, Yuki put out a hand to stop him.

"Come back safe." Paco skirted his hand and walked out.

*

The impending dawn was a pale glow along the eastern foothills when Yuki set out. The opening door disturbed a flurry of bright moths. Colors flashed, then winked out as the moths returned to the eaves for the day.

At Mia's cottage, Ross was helping her put on an overstuffed backpack with a pouch for her flamethrower and straps for her crossbow and quiver. It all fit neatly against her back, though Yuki wondered how long she'd be able to walk carrying all that weight.

"What do you think you'll need a flamethrower for?" Yuki asked.

"You never know." Mia buckled an unnecessary number of straps around her chest and shoulders, then exclaimed in dismay. "I forgot *again*!"

She snatched something from under her pillow, then tried to cram her fist into her pack. It didn't even begin to fit. Mia flung herself at Ross, opened his pack, and shoved the thing deep down inside it.

Yuki hated it when people messed with his belongings without asking permission, but Ross didn't seem to mind. Even Ross, who'd only lived in Las Anclas a couple months, fit in better than Yuki did after five years. A pang of loneliness chilled him.

"Here," Mia said to Ross. "So I don't forget *again*. It's for you, so please don't look at it! I mean, it's a surprise, so don't look at it until we camp, and I'll explain. I made it for you. I think you'll really like it."

Ross smiled at her. "If you made it, I'm sure I'll like it."

They set out. A quail bobbed its way across their path, followed by eight downy chicks. One glowed like a bright moth, casting a halo of green.

"A new mutation!" Yuki exclaimed.

"I've seen that before, but it was yellow," Ross remarked. "You see a lot more mutations in the desert. I guess because you see more animals. Lots of creatures never go near the towns."

Yuki watched the bright chick until it vanished behind a hedge. It felt like a good omen for the trip. Maybe he'd discover an entirely new *species!*

A kid shuffled to the bell tower, yawning, and began energetically yanking the bell rope. Grandma Riley left the tower to get her rest.

On the walls, the night watch stashed their weapons and armor as the morning watch took their places. Henry's blond hair caught the light from the edge of sun cresting the foothills.

"Bye, guys!" Henry called down to them. "Have fun grubbing for tin foil! I'll think of you while I'm defending the town."

Yuki's back stiffened, but he ignored Henry. Mia let out an angry snort. Ross walked on as if he hadn't heard, which was what that unfunny joke deserved. It was idiotic of Henry to act like the attack drill Mr. Preston had planned was real fighting, or more important than exploring new territory.

But not even Henry could dampen Yuki's excitement. He was getting out of town, finally; he was going prospecting where *no one* had been. Tomorrow Henry would have all the fake fighting he wanted, while Yuki would be making the discoveries of a lifetime.

Yuki smiled as he left the walls behind him.

He could hardly wait.

CHAPTER NINE
RUINED CITY OUTSIDE LAS ANCLAS
ROSS

The stars had traveled across the sky, paling at the eastern rim of the world: dawn was three hours off. Time to waken Mia for her watch. At first light, they'd venture into the crystal forest surrounding the ancient city.

If Ross could get them in.

He knelt in the cold sand and listened to Mia's breathing, then laid his hand on her shoulder. She didn't stir.

Maybe he should let her sleep. He was too tense to close his eyes, worried that he'd get himself killed, he'd get Mia and Yuki killed, he'd be unable to convince the singing trees to let them in and they'd have to return to Las Anclas empty-handed, or the trees would overwhelm him with the memories of the deaths they had been born from, and he'd pass out or cry in front of Yuki.

Ross opened the narrowest of cracks into the door in his mind. In the distance, he sensed a multitude of crystal trees, shining like stars and chiming out notes both delicate and strong. He'd have no trouble talking to those trees. The question was, would they listen to him?

He closed the door and came back to himself. His fingers were digging into Mia's shoulder. She fumbled her glasses on, and closed her warm hand over his cold fingers. He wished they were alone under the stars. He could lie down beside her, and—

She stroked his hair. "My watch?"

"I could take it. I'm not tired."

Mia gave him a gentle shove. "Go to sleep. You've got a long day ahead of you."

At least he could kiss her. Her lips were warm and soft. Then he lay back down, not bothering to take his boots off. He'd be up in a couple hours anyway.

She buckled on her flamethrower and crossbow, which meant she also had to wear that huge backpack. Noticing his gaze, she said, "Design flaw.

When we get back, I'll make them detachable."

Ross closed his eyes. He'd rest, even if he couldn't sleep.

*

"Ross!" Mia screamed.

Ross rolled to his feet, knives in both hands. Five silhouettes charged over a dune in the pale pre-dawn light, weapons brandished.

He threw a knife at the foremost, but it bounced off the man's chest: armor. Ross raised his left hand. His arm and shoulder tightened for a throw, but his fingers couldn't close. The knife slipped, and he slapped it into his right hand.

As he cocked his arm back, a blast of fire roared from Mia's flamethrower. The attackers scrambled out of range. She swept the flame back and forth, keeping them at bay.

Yuki stood barefoot, long hair loose and sword in hand, ready for the next charge.

Ross dove for his pack, yanked out the gauntlet, jammed it on to his left hand, and locked it into a fist. The flamethrower sputtered and died: out of fuel.

He bolted for Mia's side as a pair of attackers closed in, a middle-aged woman and a younger guy.

"This is the one," the woman said calmly, holding her fighting sticks ready. "Take him."

The man rushed in, feinting with his staff, then swinging the other end down to sweep Ross' feet. Ross leaped over the staff. His jump carried him to within striking distance, and he brought the knife up in a slashing arc toward his enemy's throat.

Ross's gaze shifted. The guy he was about to kill was his own age, eyes widening, mouth falling open. Ross knew what that expression meant. When he'd made his singing tree kill thirty of Voske's soldiers, he'd felt those same emotions through his mental link: shock, terror, and the hopeless inevitability of death.

Ross turned his hand and smashed the hilt into his opponent's collarbone. The bone snapped audibly. The guy dropped his staff with a yell and fell to his knees, doubled over in pain.

Ross darted back, dodging high and low strikes from the woman's sticks, then found himself blocked by a green-haired man. He slammed his elbow into the man's temple and kicked the woman in the stomach, knocking her backward. In the breathing space he'd gained, he looked for Mia and Yuki.

Yuki was covering Mia as she struggled to unbuckle her backpack. He blocked a man with a sword and feinted at a slim girl whose bare brown hands were wreathed in lightning.

Ross had seen that girl during the battle at Las Anclas. She'd backed him up halfway to the wall before Mia had shot her in the knee.

These were Voske's soldiers.

Behind Yuki, Mia stumbled backward, desperately wrenching at her buckles. She'd managed to undo one of the straps holding her backpack on, but the other three were still tight across her chest.

Ross leaped over the fallen green-haired guy, but the woman closed in, her sticks whirling.

Ross slid aside, glancing back at Mia in frustration. She'd managed to get her crossbow out, but the fighting was too close for her to use it, especially hampered by her pack. She swung out wildly with the crossbow. A man snatched it out of her hand, then hit her in the chest with a palm-heel strike, knocking her down.

Ross raised his knife. Before he could throw it, the woman's stick rapped his ribs, quickly followed by a strike to his elbow that sent a lightning bolt of pain through his arm. His fingers opened by themselves, and the knife spun away. Ross bent to snatch another knife from his boot.

Fingers touched the bare skin on the back of his neck. Everything went black.

He swung his gauntlet behind him. His fist collided with something soft, and he heard a yelp of pain. Ross frantically rubbed his right hand over his face. There was nothing over his eyes, but he couldn't see.

Someone swept his feet. He slammed to the ground. A knee drove into the small of his back, and someone else dropped onto his shoulders, forcing his face into the powdery dirt. Rough hands twisted his arms behind his back. He blinked furiously, but the darkness was so complete that he couldn't even see the after-images of light.

At least three people were holding him down, and he was blind.

"Ross!" Mia shouted. She sounded frantic, not hurt.

The last he'd seen, they'd been outnumbered five to three. More attackers must have snuck up behind them.

"Run!" Ross yelled, then choked as he inhaled a mouthful of dust.

There was a crackle of electricity, a yell of pain, and a girl's jeering laugh.

"What about the others?" a man said breathlessly.

A woman replied. "Get rid of them."

Kill them? Ross forced his head out of the dust, sending pain shooting through his neck. He made a tremendous effort, using every muscle in his body, and struggled upward as he shouted, "Mia! Yuki! Run and *get help!*"

"No!" Mia shouted. "I won't leave you!"

More bodies piled on Ross, slamming him down.

"Mia!" Yuki yelled, his voice tight and strained.

Ross heard a scuffle. Grunts. Mia and Yuki shouting, then footsteps running away. As they faded into the distance, so did Mia's anguished cries. Yuki must have dragged her away. Though he was still trapped himself, Ross had never felt so relieved in his life.

Ross heard the rustle of cloth and the crack of a knee as someone hunkered down near his head. A male voice spoke. "The blindness isn't permanent. It's my Change power, and it wears off in five or six days. That'll be just in time to get you home."

"Where's home?" Ross forced the words out. The more he learned, the better he could plan an escape.

"Gold Point."

Voske's kingdom! Ross began struggling again.

"Simmer down, youngster," the man said. "We're not going to hurt you. And we didn't hurt your friends."

"Where are they?" Ross asked.

"Took off down the arroyo. The girl didn't want to go, but the boy made her. She your girlfriend?"

Ross pressed his brow into the sand to hide his relief. He'd already known, but it was good to get confirmation. No one had died on his behalf.

The man went on, "King Voske wants you to work for him, looking for treasure."

Someone pulled Ross upright, and fingers touched his face. He tried to flinch away.

"I'm not going to hurt you." The man tied a strip of cloth over Ross's eyes. "This is so you don't accidentally look at the sun. Don't take it off. You could blind yourself for real."

Someone patted him down for weapons. There was a tug at his waist as his prospecting tools were taken away. He hoped they wouldn't think to check his boots, but a pair of small hands slipped in and confiscated his knives. Then they unsnapped the clasps of his gauntlet and yanked it off.

"Hey," Ross said. "Let that alone. It's not a weapon."

A scornful girl's voice retorted, "Do you think I'm stupid? What else would it be?"

Ross hated the thought of Voske's people prodding at his arm or even looking at it, but he was desperate to keep the gauntlet. He'd lost everything else. "I can't use my hand without it. Look at the scar."

His left arm was released, and Ross turned his forearm over.

A man asked, "Knife fight?"

If they didn't know, Ross wasn't going to tell them. "Yeah."

A strong hand stretched out his fingers, then tried to force them into a fist. His fingers locked out, and a stabbing pain shot from his palm up to his elbow. A film of cold sweat dampened his face. Ross clenched his jaw, then wondered if he should have gone ahead and screamed. But the person let go of his hand.

"Sorry," a woman said, "I had to know. You going to hit us with that thing if I give it back?"

"How could I? I can't even see you," Ross said.

A girl snickered. Ross pulled his arm tight against his body.

"Leave him be, Bankar," the woman said. "Charles, give it to him. He's not going anywhere."

The gauntlet was pushed into Ross's hands. He strapped it back on, then rested his head in his palms. He had to come up with a plan, but all he could think of was how Mia had refused to leave him. His eyes stung, and he was glad that the blindfold hid them from view.

"Want some water?" It was a young guy's voice, breathless and tense.

A canteen sloshed near Ross's head, reminding him that his mouth was as dry as an old boot. He held out his hand experimentally, wondering if the canteen would be snatched away. That was the sort of game that Voske's lieutenant and his gang had played when they jumped Ross's claim before he first came to Las Anclas.

But the canteen pushed against his fingers. Ross sniffed at the water cautiously. It smelled slightly stale, like canteen water always did. He supposed if there was anything wrong with it, they could pin him and pour it down his throat anyway.

He took a gulp, and then another. Then someone took the canteen away.

"Santiago, is that sling okay?" asked the woman. "Can you ride?"

"Yeah. I'll be fine." It was the same voice that had offered Ross water. No wonder he'd sounded so strained—he must be the guy whose collarbone Ross had broken.

"Charles, you take our guest," the woman called.

Guest? Ross grimaced as he was pulled to his feet.

"This way." Ross recognized that voice, too. Charles was the man who had blinded him. With a firm grip on his elbow, Charles led Ross to a place where he could hear and smell horses.

"Can you ride?" Charles asked.

"No," Ross said. That might delay them.

He was flung across the shoulders of a horse. When he tried to sit up, his foot got tangled in a piece of tack, and he began to slide off.

"That part's true," Bankar taunted.

"Bankar," the woman warned.

"Okay, okay, Greta."

As Ross scrabbled to get back in the saddle, someone mounted behind him. The horse took a step forward, knocking Ross off-balance again. He grabbed desperately at the coarse mane. It was hard enough to ride any time, but he'd never realized how much balance depended on sight.

A strong arm pulled Ross upright and held him firmly. "I've got you," Charles said.

Ross tried to move with the horse's gait as the animals galloped. Every step took them farther away from Las Anclas. Yuki and Mia wouldn't get back until the day was done, and even if a rescue party set out immediately, it would take them another day to get as far as the ruined city. If Ross was going to escape, he would have to rescue himself.

He couldn't fight the whole gang, but they'd have to camp sometime. He might get a chance to slip out while they were asleep. Then he'd have to cross the desert without even being able to see if the ground in front of him was solid, or a pit mouth's funnel trap, or the edge of a cliff.

But he'd seen Gold Point, and he'd seen the heads of Voske's enemies stuck on poles along the walls. Maybe walking blind through the desert wasn't as crazy as it sounded. He'd traveled on moonless, foggy nights. He knew the desert through the soles of his feet, and by its smells and sounds and textures. He was blind, but that didn't mean he was lost.

He opened the door in his mind, to seek out the crystal trees. His own tree, back in Las Anclas, must be too far away. He couldn't sense it. But the trees around the ruined city were bright in his mind. If he were free, he could feel where they were and walk toward them. Once he got to the ruined city, he should be close enough to Las Anclas to sense his own tree, and use that to navigate back home.

The horses alternated between a gallop and a fast trot until the sun beat on the top of his head: noon. They'd set out before dawn. Horses from Las Anclas would have been exhausted by now. These horses were obviously bred for endurance.

Greta called, "Bankar, pass out lunch."

The horses slowed to a walk. Charles pushed a lump into Ross's hand. It turned out to be a dry cornmeal cake, nothing like the nice moist ones that Dr. Lee baked. Ross forced it down. He'd need the energy. After that he got a piece of jerky, more salt than meat and tough as his saddle. To his relief, when everyone finished choking down the jerky, the canteen was passed around again.

Horse hooves clopped up, accompanied by clinks and rustles.

"Anything interesting in the guest's pack, Bankar?" Charles asked.

"No... Wait. Wait." Metal rattled fiercely against metal, then Bankar asked, "What's this thing?"

"Part of a pipe," Charles said.

Bankar replied, "It's solid."

Ross didn't have anything like that in his pack, so it had to be Mia's mystery gift. It had only been a few hours since he'd last seen her, but he already missed her. Whatever she'd given him, he wanted to snatch it out of Bankar's hand.

"Hey! You!" A finger poked Ross's arm. He barely stopped himself from slapping it away.

"What's this metal cylinder thing?"

"No idea. I found it on the way here." If Ross said it was a tool, they'd examine it until they figured out what it did, and then they'd steal it. Mia had made it, so it must do something.

"What does it do?" Bankar asked.

Ross shrugged. "I don't know what half the stuff I find does. I just find it and trade it."

"You must get ripped off all the time," jeered Bankar. "How do you sell your finds? 'Here's a valuable, uh, I have no idea! I'm asking a sack of flour for the whatever-it-is.'"

"Break's over," Greta announced. Ross wondered if she was as sick of Bankar as he was. "Let's get moving."

The horses broke into a trot. Ross lost his balance and grabbed for the mane. *They already think I'm an idiot. Good.* He deliberately exaggerated the lurch, almost sliding out of the saddle. Charles grabbed him by the shoulder.

Once Ross got used to the rhythm, he reached out with his mind again. His sense of the singing trees was getting faint with distance. If they went too far, he wouldn't be able to feel them at all. He had to escape tonight.

*

The heat had faded into evening cool when the horses began to descend, making Ross clutch at the saddle. The air smelled more of minerals than of dust, and sounds echoed slightly. They were heading into a canyon.

Greta raised her voice. "Let's dismount and walk. The horses are tired. And so am I."

"I'm not!" Bankar piped up.

"Santiago?" Greta asked. "How's your arm?"

"I'm fine." Santiago sounded like he barely had enough energy to get the words out.

"We'll camp soon," Greta said as they pulled up. "No, Santiago, don't dismount by yourself."

If they decided to tie Ross up, it was over. His only chance was to appear so helpless that they didn't need to bother. Hearing Greta help Santiago down from his horse gave Ross an idea.

Charles dismounted, then tapped Ross's free hand. "Here, take my arm."

Ross gripped Charles's arm, then dumped himself out of the saddle like a sack of beans and collapsed on the ground. When Charles tried to give him a hand up, Ross let his knees buckle and sank back down to the canyon floor.

Charles pulled him up. "We're all tired. Just a little farther, now. You can do it."

"I can't see. How can I walk?" Ross threw out his right arm, and was relieved when he touched stone. "Oh. I can lean on this."

He spread out his fingers. The stone was grainy and hard. Granite. When he brushed his palm upward, he hit a seam of crystalline rock, smooth and faceted. Quartz, probably. He'd bet the entire canyon was striped with seams of different types of stone. The cracks under his hand were barely big enough to get his fingers into, but he knew this type of canyon. There would be bigger cracks and fissures all over.

"We're losing the light. Let's get a move on." The speaker was one of the people whose name Ross hadn't figured out yet.

Ross needed to figure out the size and depth of any Crevices he might find without making it obvious what he was doing. Also, he had to make sure no one wondered why he was walking so close to the wall. He deliberately stumbled over a rock, and fell flat on his face. He let out a yelp.

Bankar laughed.

"You'd better lead him," Greta said.

"I can manage." Ross got up and pressed his body into the side of the canyon. "If I stick close to this wall."

No one argued. They plodded on. He found several cracks and caves big enough to fit into, but they were either too shallow for concealment or so large that they were obvious hiding places. A couple emitted the dank, nasty smell of bats, which wouldn't put him off, or the sharp chemical odor of tarantulas, which would.

Then he found the one. It was a narrow Crevice, so small that no one would think he could fit into it. But he'd gotten into tighter places than that. Better yet, the floor was lower than the entrance, no doubt gouged out by water ages ago. If he lay down in it, anyone glancing in by flickering torchlight would only see a shallow crack and the back of the cave wall.

Ross began counting his strides away from the Crevice.

CHAPTER TEN
LAS ANCLAS
JENNIE

Jennie picked up her wooden practice sword, wishing she'd gone to the ruined city with Ross and Mia. What was wrong with her? Why did she keep pushing them away?

She wished she was doing anything but preparing to play an attacker in the battle drill that Mr. Preston had promised would be "the most realistic one yet."

Jennie tapped the sword against her nails, reminding herself that it was only wood. Realistic didn't mean real.

Indra waited at the front gate with the other Rangers, dipping his cloth-wrapped sword into a bucket of red dye. His black braid slithered over his shoulder as he waved at her.

Jennie's chest tightened with emotions that didn't make sense: she was glad to see him, but she was afraid to look at him; she was thrilled to be training with the Rangers, but she couldn't stand the thought of another battle, real or false.

Mr. Vilas loomed over them, his eyes shadowed under his hat as he rubbed his sectional staff with chalk. He looked as sinister as ever. Jennie still thought of him as the bounty hunter. Though Julio Wolfe had officially taken over Sera's position as leader of the Rangers, it was the Defense Chief who gave the orders, and Mr. Preston's real second in command seemed to be the bounty hunter.

Sera would have kept Jennie by her side, so Jennie could hear all the details of her plan. Sera would have moved little, spoken softly, and missed nothing.

Julio, bouncing from toe to toe, began giving a pep talk to the townspeople he would lead in the attack, then broke off and started another pep talk, this one directed at the Rangers. When the townspeople began to chit-chat, Julio returned to exhorting them. The bounty hunter stood alone, ready and alert, but ignoring his supposed comrades.

Neither of them could ever take Sera's place.

Indra beckoned to Jennie, the orange light from the setting sun catching in his long eyelashes. "Don't forget to dip your sword."

A flash of gold scuttled past Jennie's ankles, making her jump. Then she recognized Felicité's rat, with Felicité close behind. Jennie couldn't decide which was most inappropriate for a drill: Felicité's frilly dress, feathered hat, long scarf, or high-heeled shoes. Probably the shoes.

Even in the battle, Felicité had been dressed for a party. Jennie had watched her running along the ridge, her lace veil floating around her face, just before Ross had fallen...

Ross, falling...

Jennie bit the inside of her cheek to distract herself.

"Indra, is there anything you need?" Felicité asked. "Wu Zetian could run a message."

Henry elbowed past Jennie to stand beside Felicité. "I can send one of the brats, if you forgot your equipment, Indra."

Ever since they were little kids, Henry had always worn a grin. Sometimes it was a small grin, sometimes a wide one. But he wasn't grinning now as he flung an arm around Felicité's shoulder. "You don't have to waste time on his errands, Felicité. You or your rat. You have more important things to do."

Indra shot Jennie an amused look. "I quite agree."

Felicité and Henry walked off, Felicité laughing. "Henry, this is a drill, not a dance. You can't be jealous!"

"Does anyone appreciate you like I do?" Henry retorted.

A flash of anger burned through Jennie. Sera had died when Voske had attacked Las Anclas. Indra and Ross had almost died. How dare those two treat battle preparations like a joke!

Jennie took a deep breath, willing her anger away. Felicité had been trying to be helpful, and Jennie needed to be calm and focused. She motioned the Rangers, the Ranger candidates, and Julio's squad into a huddle.

Mr. Vilas stood aloof, listening. Mr. Preston had given him a solo assignment, but hadn't told her what it was.

Conscious of Sera's example, she said, "Let's review the plan."

"Me and my team attack the armory," Indra said.

Jennie nodded. "Then my team fights across the square to the north granary."

Julio turned to his team of townspeople, flashing his broad smile. "We're attacking the front, where we'll encounter a fierce defense! But when the granary goes up in smoke, drawing off the defenders—"

Jennie continued, "—we come around to the back of the town hall."

"Where we join you, and attack from the rear," Indra said.

Julio clapped his hands. "Trapped between us! Then we capture the town leaders. Got it, everybody?"

Jennie glanced at Mr. Vilas, and noticed the other Rangers doing the same. The bounty hunter stood silently, tall and menacing.

She raised her fist to signal Ms. Lowenstein on the wall, silhouetted against the sunset. The archer's yellow cat eyes gleamed in the dimming light.

"Okay, Brisa," Ms. Lowenstein said. "Blow out the gates."

Grinning, Brisa tossed two rocks high into the air. They exploded with loud bangs, sending dust and gravel raining down.

"Let's go!"

Jennie's team moved into position. To her relief, Mr. Vilas took off in the opposite direction.

*

It was dark by the time Jennie and wiry, silent Frances got past the last roving patrols of defenders. Jennie crept behind the surgery while Frances snuck up on the bell tower. The granary was in sight. When they reached it, they'd send up one of Mia's skyrockets, indicating that the building was on fire.

Jennie's grin of anticipated success faded when she remembered what it meant: the townspeople had once again failed to protect Las Anclas.

At this rate, Preston will have us drilling every day for the next ten years, she thought. Jennie joined Frances in a dash across the last open space.

Paco straightened up from behind a trellis of ripening squash, sword held high. Another head popped up, and Tommy Horst charged Frances with a yell.

Paco gave his sword a threatening swing. "Surrender?"

"No chance." Jennie launched herself at him.

Two months ago she would have flattened him in three moves. Today Paco stood his ground, meeting her attack with a blow so fast that she had to leap back. He followed up, trying to drive her backwards.

She smiled to herself. Teacher after teacher had uselessly tried to get Paco to do more in training than going through the motions. It looked like he had finally found his warrior spirit.

As she slashed to force him back, she lifted her left hand and mentally yanked his sword. His swing broke from its smooth course, and the tip of his sword dipped.

Paco jerked up the blade up, stepping into a pool of light from a hanging lantern. Every sharp angle of bone that he'd inherited from his father cast shadows across his face: Voske. Jennie stumbled back, recoiling from the memory of Voske, silver hair glittering, signaling to his soldiers in the firelight…

It's Paco, Jennie reminded herself. *He doesn't know who his father is, and he never will. He's Sera's son, and that's all he'll ever be.*

Paco pressed his attack again, his sword a blur. There was no trace in his intent expression of the dreamy musician she'd grown up with.

I made him into this, she thought. *I didn't protect his mother. Sera wanted him to live his own life. If I'd saved her, he wouldn't even be fighting now.*

A sharp pain lanced across her wrist, and she gasped.

"Oh. Sorry," Paco said breathlessly, his sword lowering. "I thought you'd block that."

From the back gate rose a hubbub of voices amid bobbing lanterns and torches. It had to be a diversion created by the defenders. Jennie kept her weapon up.

Paco's head jerked. "Tommy, they're attacking at the back!"

The crowd parted. The floodlights revealed Mr. Vilas carrying a body.

Tommy's voice cracked. "It's Yuki!"

Cold shock ran through Jennie's veins. She bolted toward the bounty hunter.

"I can walk," Yuki said faintly. His shirt was soaked through with blood. Mr. Vilas ignored him.

Jennie looked around wildly. "Where's Mia? Where's—"

"Here." Mia stumbled out from behind Mr. Vilas. She, too, was splashed with blood, and tears ran in twin tracks down her dirty face.

Jennie caught her shoulder and steadied her. "You're hurt. I'll carry you."

Mia shook her head. "It's Yuki's blood. One of them attacked him from behind."

There was no sign of Ross. Jennie heard her own voice as if she was another person speaking from a very long way away. "Was Ross killed?"

"No! They took him. It was Voske's soldiers. I recognized a girl from the battle. She could generate electricity." Mia straightened up, shaking off Jennie's support. "We have to go after him."

Jennie's thoughts slogged as if she were stuck in mud, as Mr. Vilas carried Yuki into the surgery. Paco ran in after them.

Dr. Lee rushed out, shouting, "Mia!"

"I'm fine, Dad!" she called. "I'll be right there."

Dr. Lee vanished inside. A crowd was already gathering.

"We're being attacked!" Mrs. Callahan yelled shrilly. "Why isn't the bell ringing? It's another war!"

"No one followed us." Mia's voice wavered.

"No one followed them!" Jennie shouted. "There is no attack!"

Mr. Horst's voice boomed, "Everyone, go back to your stations and finish the drill!"

The hubbub continued unabated. Mr. Preston emerged from the crowd, kicked off his boots, and hurried into the surgery.

"Come on, Jennie!" Mia said impatiently. She scrubbed her filthy sleeve across her eyes, smearing tears and dust into muddy streaks. "We have to get Mr. Preston to send a rescue team."

In the surgery, they found Yuki lying on the examination table, the upturned soles of his feet blistered and scraped raw. Dr. Lee was sponging a long sword cut on his back. A strand of bloodsucking ropethorn vine ran from a basin to Yuki's wrist, to suck the saline solution from the bowl and transfer it into his veins. The sharp smell of alcohol filled the air. Paco leaned over him, his palm against Yuki's cheek.

The blood, the black hair, the stillness … like Ross, lying dead on the ground. Like Indra, when she'd uselessly struggled to lift him. Jennie closed her eyes, but that only made the images more vivid.

Mr. Preston's voice jolted her. "Mia, I want to talk to you. Jennie, you can stay." He raised his voice to carry outside of the room. "But no one else comes in here!"

Yuki's adoptive mother, Ms. Lowenstein, pushed past him, her yellow gaze fixed on Mr. Preston as if daring him to object. His sister Meredith followed at her heels.

"Nobody but family." Mr. Preston gestured to Mr. Vilas, who shut the door in the faces of the crowd and stood with his back to it.

"He's not badly hurt," Dr. Lee said. "But he's lost a lot of blood."

"I did my best to bandage it," Mia said unhappily. "But it opened up every time he moved."

"Actually, Mia, you did a good job," Dr. Lee reassured her. "Without you, he might not have even made it back."

Dr. Lee's timid apprentice, Becky Callahan, hurried up with a jar filled with sea water and writhing strands of fine-sliced seaweed. Dr. Lee began to stitch Yuki's back. The seaweed sutures would adjust themselves to Yuki's movements, stretching or tightening as required. Dr. Lee had used them on Jennie a few times. They burned like fire while they were still wet with salt water.

Yuki didn't flinch. Jennie wasn't sure if he was being stoic, or if everything hurt so badly that he didn't notice. The surgery was quiet except for the harsh sound of Yuki's breathing.

Mr. Preston stepped forward. "Can you tell us what happened?"

"We were attacked," Yuki said, the words coming with difficulty. "I left Ross. I ran away."

Jennie winced at the bitterness in his voice.

"Yuki, don't talk," Mr. Preston said. "Mia, report."

Mia gulped and clenched her fists as she gave a report that was so concise Jennie suspected she had rehearsed it for the entire journey back.

"…I couldn't get my pack off," Mia confessed at the end. "Ross and Yuki were distracted trying to cover me. If I hadn't had my *stupid* pack on, maybe Ross would have gotten away."

Mr. Preston made a dismissive noise. "Fighting eight soldiers, at least two of them monst—two with Change powers? You're lucky you aren't all dead."

Jennie's jaw clenched. Two monsters. Could they have won if she had gone, and there had been a *monster* on Ross's side?

Mr. Preston went on. "Or more likely, luck had nothing to do with it. Voske's team didn't let you go, they *made* you go. It's something he does to win people over. Not you two: Ross. Voske shows them what he could do to hurt them, like kill their friends. Then when he doesn't do it, they're grateful."

"We have to rescue Ross." Mia's voice rose to a squeak. "Now. This minute!"

"I'll go." Jennie's anxiety vanished: she had a clear goal.

"I will, too." Yuki struggled to raise his head. "Heal me now."

Dr. Lee pushed him flat. "You know that my power takes time off your life. I don't use it unless it's a life-threatening emergency."

Paco took Yuki's hand. "It's okay, Yuki. You don't have to go. I volunteer."

"No!" Jennie was startled when her exclamation was joined by several others, from Mr. Preston, Ms. Lowenstein, and Dr. Lee.

"Hold on," Mr. Preston commanded, and swept the room with an intent gaze.

Jennie shivered. Voske could be spying on them at any time, though no one knew how. Maybe he really did have an invisible son. Or did Mr. Preston know?

Mr. Preston let out a short breath. "No one is riding out tonight."

Paco frowned. "Why not?"

"It's dangerous at night. We're already a full day behind them, and the least of their mounts don't need as much rest as our fastest horses do. There's no way we could catch them before they reach Gold Point."

"We should go *now*!" Mia shouted. Everyone turned to look at her, and she took a nervous step backward. "Ross could have escaped. He's really smart, you know. He could be halfway to Las Anclas, with all those soldiers chasing after him."

Mr. Preston gave her a look of total disbelief. "I don't think so."

Dr. Lee cleared his throat. "I do. People tend to underestimate Ross."

"I'll go," Jennie repeated. Why hadn't she gone on the expedition in the first place? She had a Change power. She was one of the best fighters in town.

"We'll send a mission. But later." Mr. Preston turned to Mr. Vilas. "With you, Furio. You know the way."

"Understood," Mr. Vilas replied.

"We'll discuss the details later." Mr. Preston gave the bounty hunter a quick, meaningful look.

The bounty hunter's black brows lifted slightly. Jennie's belly tightened. That was a signal between people who knew each other well. She and Mia had exchanged them all their lives. She remembered how Mr. Preston had plotted with the bounty hunter when Mr. Vilas had first come to town in pursuit of Ross. They'd known each other when they were young.

Mia tugged at Jennie's shirt—her own secret message. "When you do go, I have a new weapon I designed..."

As Mia spoke, she led Jennie into the hallway.

"They're plotting something!" Mia whispered angrily.

"They're going to talk somewhere private," Jennie whispered back. "If we can get there first..."

"The infirmary!" breathed Mia. "There's no one there now."

Mia led Jennie to the dark room. They ran barefoot to a curtained alcove, sat on the bed, and closed the curtain. Soon the infirmary door opened.

Mr. Preston said in a low voice, "Vilas, let's make this quick. Bring the boy back alive if you can. But if you can't, I don't want him alive for Voske to use."

"Got it," Mr. Vilas replied.

The girls waited for a few minutes after the men left, then dashed into the crowded waiting room.

"What's going on?" Mrs. Callahan demanded.

"Ask Becky." Mia shoved her feet into her shoes.

Jennie picked hers up and ran outside in her socks.

Inside her cottage, Mia kicked tools and papers out of the way as she paced in agitated circles. "This is my fault."

"Oh, Mia—"

Mia went on as if Jennie hadn't spoken. "I couldn't get my pack off. I got disarmed and knocked down. It's my fault for not training harder—my fault for my terrible backpack design—my fault for letting Yuki drag me away—my fault for not going back!"

"Stop it. Stop, Mia. If it's anyone's fault, it's mine. I should have been there."

"Whoever's fault it is, now that bounty hunter is going to kill Ross!" Mia kicked a stray bolt across the room. "Let's tell the whole town what Mr. Preston is plotting. Then the bounty hunter won't even get to go on the mission. I hope he gets kicked out of town. Again."

Jennie's thoughts raced. Mia's plan might work. But it depended on the rest of the town cooperating. It would be safer to handle this on her own.

She caught Mia's elbow, halting her in mid-stride. "There's too many townspeople who'd be happy if Ross never came back. People who are prejudiced against the Changed, and think what Ross did in the battle wasn't that important."

"Especially everyone who's mad about singing trees taking over the southeast cornfield," Mia added glumly, then brightened. "Let's go by ourselves."

Jennie hated having to shake her head. She wouldn't have thought it was possible for Mia to look more miserable than she already did, but Jennie's refusal obviously hurt her even more. "We can't see anything, and everything out there can see us. We could ride straight into a pit mouth. No one travels across strange country in the middle of the night."

"Ross is, right now!"

"No, he's got to be camped with Voske's soldiers. Ross is one of the best fighters I've ever seen, but even he can't fight eight to one. There's no way he escaped. *I* couldn't have escaped. It won't help him if we go rushing off and get ourselves killed."

Mia folded her arms. "Okay. Then what's your plan?"

"I'll talk Mr. Preston into letting me lead the mission. Then I can keep watch on Mr. Vilas. If I have to, I'll stop him myself."

Mia gave her a watery smile. "Do it. Go now, before he lets the bounty hunter pick the rest of the team."

Jennie hugged Mia. "Good idea. I'll bring Ross back. I promise."

She ran out into the town square, where Sujata and Brisa were fighting with wooden swords, brightly lit by flood lights. Jennie had completely forgotten the drill.

"Time out!" Brisa declared. "I need a drink of water."

Sujata pressed her attack. "There's no timeouts in a battle!"

Brisa plonked down on the pathway. "It's a drill, and it's over."

Sujata's sword drew a line of oily red dye across Brisa's throat. "It's over for you," she said with satisfaction. "You're dead."

Brisa grinned. "Yes, I am. And that means I'm going home."

The rest of the square was empty, except for the knots of people—defenders and attackers both—chatting outside the surgery.

At the town hall, Jennie found Mr. Preston getting a report from the sheriff's mothers, Trainer Koslova and Trainer Crow, who were flanked by six rats. Kourtney, a black and white rat, sat up on her hind legs, begging for attention. Jennie scratched behind her ears.

Trainer Koslova said, "Nobody's at the west wall but the sentries. Everyone else thought the drill was cancelled."

Mr. Preston scowled. "They know perfectly well that the drill isn't over until the bell rings Stand Down. Trainer Crow, what's your report?"

Trainer Crow petted Ruki, the brown rat on her shoulder. "The defenders at the front gate are squabbling with the attackers over who's dead and who isn't. They want to know if one drop of dye to the chest is a scratch or a fatal wound."

Trainer Koslova added, "You might tell Julio that a blow to the throat is always fatal. He's been killed at least three times tonight, and he's still fighting."

Mr. Preston raised his gaze to the sky. "Thank you. Will, give the signal to end the drill."

Will Preston bolted toward the bell tower. The trainers and their rats followed in his wake.

Before Jennie addressed Mr. Preston, she made sure she had control of her own temper. "About that mission to rescue Ross. I'd like to command it."

Mr. Preston's thoughts were clearly elsewhere. "I've got someone much more experienced than you already assigned to it."

"I've been training with Mr. Vilas for months now. He's great on solo missions, and he's all right in a team. But he's a tracker and a fighter, not a leader."

Mr. Preston's wire-rimmed glasses flashed as he turned to Jennie. "What makes you think *you* can lead this mission?"

"I've been leading missions for months. You know that. You gave them to me. I brought the school patrol back safely from a rattlesnake attack. Tonight my team would have burned the granary if we hadn't been interrupted."

Mr. Preston said slowly, "You seem to be leaving an important one out."

Jennie swallowed. She'd hoped he wouldn't make her brag about her biggest failure, the mission where she'd failed to save Sera and abandoned her own team. She tried to make herself sound proud. "And during the battle, I picked my own team and led them to blow up Voske's ammunition. We succeeded without a single casualty. On my team."

Mr. Preston put his hand on her shoulder. She made herself hold still, though she wanted to jerk away. "That's what I was looking for. Jennie, you should be proud of your accomplishments. Being a leader doesn't mean that you can save everyone."

Being a leader was *exactly* that. But she wasn't going to blurt that out to a man who would cold-bloodedly sacrifice a citizen of Las Anclas.

Mr. Preston continued, oblivious to her feelings, "I like seeing you embracing your potential. Yes, you can lead the mission."

Jennie's nails bit into her palms. She pried her fingers open and made them hang loose, forcing her voice to come out calm. "May I pick my team?"

"That's part of leadership. Furio Vilas goes, of course. You'll need him to show you the way. And he can describe Gold Point's defenses. Beyond him, I'm afraid I can't spare more than three people. And only one Ranger."

He doesn't care if Ross gets back or not. And he probably thinks teenagers won't be able to stand up to Mr. Vilas.

"I want Indra." Jennie could trust him. And Indra wouldn't let Mr. Vilas intimidate him.

Mr. Preston nodded in approval. "Good choice."

While the bell rang out the end of the drill, Jennie considered her options for long-range fighters. Meredith was more disciplined, but Jennie might need Brisa's power. "And Brisa."

Mr. Preston raised his eyebrows, no doubt thinking of Brisa's Change. But what he said was, "That girl needs to work on her attitude."

Jennie made sure she sounded respectful when she said, "I agree, but I can talk to her about it. When can we leave?"

"Wait a week. If you go now, Voske will be expecting you. If you wait, he might not be. He won't harm Ross. He's obviously taken him to make use of his…" Jennie watched for that disgusted look, and wasn't disappointed. "…power."

She had expected the wait, too. "In that case, I'd like to take Yuki and Kogatana. If he's up to it by then." Yuki would also back her against the bounty hunter. And though he wasn't a Ranger, he fought as well as one.

Mr. Preston nodded. "Certainly. Now, there's a second objective for this mission. After Gold Point built a power plant that uses energy from its dam, they became almost totally reliant on electricity. If we could sabotage the plant, Voske would have his hands so full trying to restore power to the town that he wouldn't be able to invade anywhere for a while. Maybe years."

Jennie hadn't heard that before. "Have you ever sent the Rangers to try?"

"Several times. But the area's so heavily guarded that they could never get anywhere near it. It'll probably be the same now, but check. If you can get in, sabotaging that plant is a higher priority than rescuing Ross."

Jennie gritted her teeth, then took a deep breath. It made strategic sense. If they could take out Gold Point's electricity, rescuing Ross would be a lot easier.

"Absolutely," Jennie said. "You can count on me."

CHAPTER ELEVEN
DESERT
ROSS

Ross counted his steps from the Crevice. Fifty-seven…fifty-eight…

"Let's camp here," came Greta's voice.

Ross had to stay by the wall, or he'd never find his hiding place again. He collapsed with an exhausted groan.

Someone prodded him with a foot. "Hey. Desert nights are cold. Move closer to the campfire."

"I don't care," Ross mumbled. "My legs hurt. I can't move."

"Have it your way." Someone dumped a heavy blanket over Ross.

Sticks clattered together, and a match was struck. Pans rattled and water sloshed. The horses clopped away in a string farther down the canyon. Wood smoke tickled Ross's nose, followed by the delicious smells of frying bacon and corn cakes. His stomach growled. He hoped his kidnappers wouldn't force him to choose between staying where he was and eating dinner.

"Wake up," Charles said. "Here's your dinner."

Ross slowly pushed himself up. A plate was placed in his lap, and a cup nudged up against his thigh. He fumbled in case someone was watching, but decided not to go so far as to drop anything. He quickly ate and drank, then flopped down and pulled the blanket over his head. It smelled of horse.

"The others have the animals, so it's us for camp guard duty," Greta said. "Let's divvy it up. Santiago, I'll take your watch."

Santiago replied, "I'll take the whole night. I won't be able to sleep anyway."

Bankar's voice came from farther away. "Santiago, I've been meaning to ask, how exactly did that pathetic kid get the drop on you? Asleep on your feet?"

"You wouldn't have done any better," Santiago said.

Bankar laughed. "I did do better! I defeated the tall guy, and I didn't break a sweat, let alone a bone."

"You didn't see him fight. He was fast."

"You mean, you were slow," Bankar retorted.

"Shut up, Shanti."

"Don't call me that," snapped Bankar. "I hate that name!"

"You want to go by your surname, you act like an adult."

"That's enough, *children*," Greta said. "Santiago, take first watch. Bankar, second. I'll take third." She paused. "On second thought, Bankar, I'll take you out of the rotation. You used your power a lot today."

Bankar's voice rose. "I'm not tired. I can pull my own weight. I could take your shift, too!"

Greta sighed. "Just take your own."

Then came the noises of people settling down for the night. Ross's heart lifted when he heard the unmistakable sounds of horses snorting and shifting weight some paces away, further down into the canyon. He would not have to try passing them when he tried his escape.

If he got a chance to escape. Waves of exhaustion tugged at Ross, coaxing him to close his eyes and rest. Under the blanket, he pushed the blindfold up and lay with his eyes wide open, listening to the others breathe. One by one, they changed rhythm from uneven to long and deep. All except Santiago, whose shallow breaths hissed in pain. Gravel crunched as he shifted around, probably trying and failing to find a comfortable position. It crunched more as he began pacing.

Ross waited, hoping his guard would settle down and fall asleep. He didn't. Now Ross was afraid that the pain of his broken collarbone would keep Santiago awake all night. Ross hoped he'd at least rest with his eyes closed once the watch switched.

By the time it did, Ross was digging his fingernails into his arm to keep himself awake. A crackling hiss startled him. "My turn," whispered Bankar.

Santiago's footsteps retreated. Gravel rattled, followed by a few harsh exhalations and a muffled groan, and then his breathing slowed.

Footsteps paced around, accompanied by the occasional crackle of Bankar's lightning, and a faint smell of singed air. Then the footsteps stopped, though the crackles didn't. Ross hoped she'd sat down. He wondered if she was creating the lightning to keep herself awake. That might not be too smart. Greta had implied that using it tired Bankar out.

Sure enough, the crackling stopped, and Bankar's breathing began to deepen and slow. When it fell into an even pattern, Ross eased the blanket from his body. With a snort and a gasp, Bankar's uneven breathing resumed. Ross went limp. Then her breathing slowed again. This time, the rhythm stayed unchanged.

Ross replaced the blindfold around his eyes so he wouldn't lose it. His heart pounding, he cautiously stood up. There was no outcry. He ran his fingers along the rough stone wall, found cracks that would bear his weight, and inched upward, taking care not to make a sound.

Staying a foot or so above the canyon floor, he climbed sideways, counting each time he shifted his right foot across. He kept his left hand at his side. A single clank of metal against stone might wake someone up, but he was afraid he'd lose his gauntlet if he took it off.

When he reached thirty-five, a loud snort nearly scared him off the wall. He froze, waiting for hands to seize him. Nothing happened. Blood hammered at his temples. Then he identified the sound: the thud of a horse shifting its weight, the sound amplified by the stone walls in the absolute quiet. No other sounds.

He let out his breath in a trickle of air—and for a horrified moment, he couldn't remember where his count had left off. But when he moved his foot again, the number came back: Thirty-six.

When he reached fifty-seven, he slowed down. Could he possibly have gone in the wrong direction? Fifty-nine…sixty-two… Sick with worry that he had managed to turn himself completely around, he gave himself to seventy-five before he'd have to decide.

He almost fell when his reaching foot encountered air. There it was. He'd climbed upward an extra couple of feet without noticing.

With excruciating care, though every muscle trembled, he eased himself down. Ross felt his way into the Crevice, squeezing his shoulders together and wriggling under the overhang until he had wedged himself into the scooped-out bottom. If anyone shone a lantern into it, so long as they didn't stick their head in and look down, they'd see nothing but the bare rock of the back wall.

Ross lay still, trying to breathe quietly. The stone was pleasantly cool, the air scented with earth and lichen. He could sense the weight of the cliff above him, but at least he didn't have to see it looming over him. Caves bothered him less than man-made structures, anyway. He'd never had a cave fall in on him.

A feathery tickle brushed at his ankle, and then a scratchier one skittered along his neck. It was almost impossible not to kick out and brush himself off, but he forced himself to stay still, even when something like a centipede eeled its way into his shirt and marched all the way up the length of his spine. He held his breath when it reached his collar; it crawled up through his hair, then fell off. He heard its little claws ticking over the stone as it scuttled away.

A noise startled him. He almost jumped up—he'd fallen into a doze.

"Where is he?" The voice echoed up the wall. "Bankar, how long were you asleep?"

"I wasn't asleep! I just rested my eyes for a second!"

"So the prisoner—" Santiago began.

"The guest," Greta corrected.

"The *guest* teleported out of the canyon?" Santiago asked sarcastically, as voices exclaimed and cursed.

Greta's voice rose over the commotion. "Everyone, be quiet. Bankar, you have to answer this honestly. How long were you asleep?"

Bankar answered, almost tearfully, "I don't know. It really felt like seconds."

"All right," Greta said. "It can't have been that long, because it's not time for my watch yet. And he can't see. I don't think he can have gotten out of the canyon yet. Any footprints at the far end?"

A chorus of "no" echoed back.

"There's so many around the campfire, it's impossible to tell if any of these are his." Greta sounded brisk and competent. They were all definitely awake and alert now. "You three, go search the far end. The rest of you, come with me."

Footsteps started approaching. Ross breathed as shallowly as he could, pressing himself down into the floor. A crackle sounded almost in his ear, but he held himself still.

"No one could fit in there," Santiago said, not too far away.

"Just checking," Bankar replied.

Someone yelped, followed by a clatter and hiss—probably a dropped torch.

"What was that?" someone exclaimed.

"It scuttled so fast, I couldn't get a good look at it," someone else replied.

Bankar asked nervously, "Where is it now?"

"Um…" someone said. "I'm not sure. It went that way."

The footsteps and voices hastily receded.

Ross wondered how long Bankar had been asleep. His entire plan depended on his kidnappers leaving the canyon to search the wrong area while it was still dark. If he didn't get a chance to leave the Crevice before dawn, they would easily spot him.

Footsteps converged from both ends of the canyon. That's when the arguing started.

"I'm telling you, there were no footprints leading out of the canyon. None!"

Someone else retorted, "Well, you must have missed them, because there were no new ones coming down toward camp, besides the ones we made last night. I counted."

Another person broke in. "Didn't Santiago say he teleported?"

"I was joking," said Santiago.

Fingers snapped. Bankar exclaimed, "But maybe you were right. He disappeared in a second. I bet he did teleport!"

"We already know what his power is," said Charles. "Nobody has more than one power. He walked out."

Bankar exclaimed, "Or maybe he does have a second power, but it's not teleporting. What if he walked out without us seeing him? Like Prince Sean —"

A chorus of voices rose up.

"Bankar!"

"Shut up!"

"Don't talk about him!"

Bankar scoffed. "The king can't hear us all the way out—" Her words were lost in a mumble, like someone had put a hand over her mouth.

Greta said ominously, "Do you really want to test that?"

There was another muffled sound, then Bankar said clearly, "No."

"I think he climbed out," said Santiago. "I think he's a lot stronger than he looks. I told you, when he fought me, he was much faster than I expected. He could have killed me. I don't know why he didn't."

One of the older people said, "Charles, are you sure you blinded him?"

"I've had this power since I was thirteen." Charles sounded annoyed. "I promise you, he can't see."

That same voice snapped, "Then you were an idiot to tell him that it would wear off by itself. If you'd said you had to take the blindness away, he'd never have tried to run."

Someone clapped their hands, then Greta spoke. "Enough second-guessing. We're wasting time. I agree with Santiago. If the king's guest climbed straight up from where he was lying, he's on the plateau. Let's get the horses and go find him."

The words 'the king's guest' silenced them all. Soon the thud of hooves died out into the distance. Ross gave them enough time to be sure they were out of the canyon before he squeezed out of the Crevice.

Out of habit, he closed his eyes. The bright lights of the singing forest around the ruined city shone in his mind like stars in a night sky. *That way.*

Ross set out back the way he'd come. If he stuck to the interconnected maze of canyons and arroyos, he couldn't fall off a cliff. More importantly, no one would be able to see him unless they happened to look down from directly above. And the floors of those canyons tended to be rock or gravel, so it would be easier to avoid leaving footprints.

Every few steps he bent down and felt the rocks around him, hoping to find something he could use as a knife. His back was beginning to twinge from all that bending when he found a sharp wedge of quartz. He stuck it in his pocket.

Grateful that he could move a bit faster, he picked up his pace, his right hand trailing the canyon wall. He needed to find food and water.

Between one step and the next, his fingers met only empty space. The canyon had branched. He groped until he encountered the new wall, paused to listen for the singing trees, then started off again.

Three canyons later, the ground began to soften underfoot. He felt around for a plant to use as a broom, but found nothing. So he took off his shirt and tied it around his left ankle to rub out any prints he might leave. Despite the awkward newness of the gauntlet, it was a lot easier to tie a knot with it than without it.

Weeds crunched underfoot, releasing brief, sharp scents. His forehead felt warm; the sun had topped the eastern mountains. It would get hot soon. He had to find something to drink.

His ankle collided with something heavy that flipped over. Blunt claws scraped along the edge of his jeans. Ross bent down and felt the frantic scrabblings of an overturned desert tortoise. He picked it up. He'd eaten them occasionally, when he could find nothing else, but he liked watching them amble across the desert, and preferred to leave them alone. Besides, he wouldn't be able to cook it.

He righted the tortoise and listened to it creep away, then straightened up. Since he'd given up one meal, it was time to find another. If there were little weeds, there were probably big weeds. Ross zigzagged across the canyon, feeling in front of him, until his fingers touched a stem as thick as his wrist, covered in small, stiff hairs. The plant trembled, and high above, he heard a rattle. It was a sunflower. A ripe one!

He used his quartz to saw through the stem until the flower toppled. If anyone came across it, it should look like it had fallen naturally. He sawed off a length of the stem to use as a stick, making ragged cuts as if an animal had gnawed it, then stuffed the seeds in his pockets. He'd wait to eat them until he found water.

The sun now baked the top of his head. Without plastic to make a solar still, he'd need to find edible cacti or else chance upon a stone tank where rain had collected. In this heat, he'd be lucky to survive two days without water. Already his mouth was dry. Feeling ahead with the stick, he encountered several cacti whose spine patterns told him that they weren't edible varieties.

Then his stick splashed into water. Amazed, Ross crouched down and touched the edge of a pool. Though he should be thrilled, he hesitated. He didn't hear any insects. Drinkable water should be swarming with life: flies, dragonflies, frogs, water skaters, beetles. Ross ran his fingers through the vegetation growing around the edges, trying to recognize the plants by touch. They were all weeds that could survive growing near an alkaline lake. Just to be sure, he dipped his fingers into the pool, then rubbed them together. The liquid was slightly slippery, more like oil than water.

Poison.

With a sigh, he continued on. But his luck turned when his stick snagged on the curved spines of a fishhook cactus. Ross carefully untangled the stick. If the cactus was jarred or shaken or uprooted, its roots would release acid into its reservoir of water. He knelt down and positioned his quartz at the base of the cactus. With a quick slash, he sliced through the thin roots that anchored it to the earth. Now it was safe. He flipped it over, cut through the membrane at the bottom, and drank half the tart liquid within.

He set out again, walking faster until the stick bumped into a cactus with tear-shaped lobes. Prickly pear! He used his gauntlet to harvest the succulent fruit, then peeled and ate them as he walked, stuffing the spiny peels into his pockets.

He'd found two more prickly pears when the sun's heat on one side of his body indicated it was late afternoon. He was so tired that his bones ached, but he couldn't stop to rest. He should be about a day's walk from the ruined city.

Ross hoped that Voske's gang was still wandering around in circles. With any luck, something would attack them. Predators started coming out right about now, as the sun went down. Only humans and reptiles walked the desert in the heat of the day.

He was on his second handful of sunflower seeds when the yodeling cry of a coyote echoed along the canyon. Ross hastily stuffed the seeds and shells in his pocket and held still, listening for the unique call of the leader of the pack. He hefted one of the rocks he'd put in his pocket.

The coyote followers yipped excitedly, signaling that they'd found prey. Then the deeper tone of the pack leader rang out. Ross forced himself to wait until the pack leader was close enough for him to hit, though his heart thumped as he heard the soft patters of the coyotes encircling him.

The animals yipped again, and there was the leader, barking the call to close in. Ross threw the rock as hard as he could. The call broke off in a shrill yelp of pain. He followed up by slinging a handful of cactus spines in a circle around him. With a chorus of yips and moans, the pack scattered. The sounds of their calls faded into the distance as they sought less dangerous prey.

Ross continued walking. He had a pattern by now: bare right hand up against canyon wall, hand with gauntlet holding the stick. One wave sweeping the air in front of him, then a couple of taps—not enough to leave distinctive prints—on the ground.

Maybe tomorrow night he'd be back in Las Anclas. He might walk to the Ranger training grounds, where Jennie would be drilling the candidates. Mia would be in her cottage, drawing up the blueprints for some new weapon. Her windows would be open, so she could smell the dinner her father was cooking. Maybe Dr. Lee was making a hot pot, with three kinds of fish, mussels, clams, and a kimchi-based broth. And for dessert...

The stick caught in something. Ross tugged, thinking it was entangled in a cactus. It gave a bit, then was slowly sucked back in, deeper and deeper, pulling him toward it. An odd smell arose, like sour beer.

Ross came as wide awake as if he'd had a bucket of ice water dumped over his head. He leaped backward, letting go of the stick. That smell, that suction—he'd nearly stepped into a jelly trap!

The fungus grew in translucent sheets, easy to spot in the day but nearly invisible at night. Anything that stepped into it was caught fast, then engulfed and suffocated in a surge of gelatin. They dissolved and digested flesh and bone, but Ross had occasionally seen metal belt buckles and weapons embedded in them.

He edged backward, then headed toward the opposite side of the canyon, cautiously scuffling with the tips of his boots as he went. If he climbed across the other wall, he could avoid the jelly trap, even if it was spread across the entire canyon floor.

Before he reached the other side, the hairs on the back of his neck stood up. He was sure something was watching him. Then a sound reached him from high above. It was the distinctive cough of a cougar.

Ross gritted his teeth. If he yelled to scare off the cougar, he might alert Voske's people. Sound carried a long way in the desert.

The cougar coughed again, this time closer. It was stalking him.

Ross grabbed a rock, knowing that it wouldn't put off the big cat for long. There had to be crevices large enough for him to hide in but too small for the cougar. Afraid of setting off the cougar's pouncing instincts, Ross forced himself not to run. He quickly walked away.

A soft chuff a few meters away had to be the cougar leaping down to the canyon floor. Then millions of lightning bolts needled Ross from head to toe. He gasped and stumbled backward. The pain was agonizing. He dropped the rock and patted at his face and arms. He'd walked straight into a stand of jumping cactus.

Ross held himself still, though his breath came in ragged gasps. Segments of jumping cactus broke off and leaped at you if you came too close. Then the hook-shaped spines dug in and sucked your blood. When the segments were full and fat as a tick, they leaped back to their parent plant. Struggling only made the spines dig deeper. The last time Ross had gotten stuck by a segment, he'd had to pull the spines loose with pliers.

There was a soft padding sound: the cougar was loping away. Ross must have walked into a huge patch, if the cougar wasn't willing to risk getting closer.

Then he realized that it wasn't the cactus that had scared off the cougar.

The thump of hooves grew louder than his heartbeat.

A girl's mocking laughter reached Ross. "Need a hand?"

It was Bankar.

CHAPTER TWELVE
GOLD POINT
KERRY

Kerry Ji Sun Voske, crown princess of the Gold Point Empire, joined her father on his private balcony.

"Here they come," Father said.

After all she'd heard about Ross Juarez, who had ruined the conquest of Las Anclas and killed thirty of Father's private guard, she'd expected him to be seven feet tall and big enough to lift an ox. But the boy riding with the dust-caked scout team was no older than she, and so scrawny and unimpressive that Kerry wondered if the team had grabbed the wrong guy.

He rode in front of Charles, whose dark face looked tired and somber as he kept a firm grip on the prisoner's shoulder with one hand. His horse uncoiled her prehensile tail and tried to smack the prisoner across the face. Charles batted the tail away.

If Ross even noticed, he didn't react. His unkempt black hair hid his face, but Kerry caught a glimpse of bony shoulders beneath a ratty old shirt. The only eye-catching thing about him was the beautifully made gauntlet on his left hand.

The scouts saluted Father, Santiago dropping the reins to do so. He'd been hurt—he wore a sling. Kerry leaned anxiously over the balcony. He gave her a reassuring smile, then faced straight ahead. Oh yes, riding right behind him was a loathsomely familiar skinny form, round face smirking proudly: Shanti Bankar. The scouts vanished beyond the guest house.

Father turned to Kerry, smiling. "Want to hear the report?"

"Of course!" Kerry replied eagerly.

"It will be a good test for you," Father said. "First, what did you see just now?"

Kerry knew better than to blab her first impression. The prisoner had to be the right one, or Father would have said something. "Santiago was injured. I'm surprised the team let the prisoner keep his gauntlet, since they obviously fought with him."

"Or with his companions. Is he what you expected?"

"I know better than to be fooled by appearances."

Father laughed. "Young Ross doesn't look very formidable, does he? Come on, let's hear what Greta has to say."

Kerry happily followed him out. She loved it when Father included her in private interviews.

He paused halfway down the hall. "Where are we going?"

The chamber closest to the royal bedroom was her favorite, with its cherry wood walls and rich tapestries. But Father only used it to reward people who had performed exceptionally well. Given that the scout team was a day late and Santiago had been wounded, Kerry wasn't sure the mission had been exceptional. For a failed mission, Father might choose the smallest chamber, which only had chairs for Father and her. But the team had succeeded, though not perfectly.

"The inner interview chamber," Kerry said confidently. "It's comfortable, but not too comfortable. And it's more private than the outer one."

Father's smile was Kerry's reward. "Correct."

The hall guards opened the chamber doors. Kerry took her seat in the richly decorated chair between Father's throne and the table with the model of Las Anclas. Her future kingdom! She glanced at the tiny clay houses, wondering which one Ross had lived in.

Father sat down. "What's the main thing we need to learn about our new guest?"

Kerry was a little disappointed. It was such an easy question. "What motivates him."

"What do we already know about that?"

Kerry considered the miniature Las Anclas. "Prospectors usually want to get rich."

"Too general," said Father. "He's not just a prospector, he's an individual."

She didn't know much about Ross as an individual. "He fought for Las Anclas. Maybe he's tired of wandering around, and he wants to settle down."

"Let's find out."

The scouts were waiting in the hall with the honor guard. Father waved Greta inside, followed by Charles and Santiago. Kerry was annoyed to see Bankar tagging along as well. The scouts looked tired and grimy, but saluted crisply.

"You may be seated," Father said. "Your report?"

Greta's voice fell into the formal rhythm of a mission report. "The trip to the ruined city of Las Anclas was accomplished without incident. We took a position out of sight and watched the road with field glasses. That evening, he and two companions, a boy and a girl, arrived and set up camp. We waited through several watches, until he and the boy who looked like a fighter were both asleep, and there was enough light for us to see. Then we moved in."

"Santiago was dropped by a guy who wasn't even awake yet," Bankar jeered.

Santiago looked embarrassed. To Kerry's pleasure, Greta gestured to shut Bankar up. Kerry wished she could use her power on Bankar. Just enough to make her squeal.

Greta turned to Santiago. "Tell the king about your fight. Exactly the way you told it to me."

Santiago shifted, as if uncomfortable. "I tried to sweep him with my staff, and he went for my throat with a knife. He moved faster than I expected, and he got in under my guard. If he'd wanted to kill me, he would have."

Kerry was shocked. It hadn't occurred to her that her boyfriend had been in serious danger from that skinny little guy. Santiago was one of the best fighters of the guys his age. That was why he was one of the king's scouts. She restrained the impulse to run up and put her arms around him.

Santiago went on, "Then he flipped the knife around and broke my collarbone with the hilt. I think he'd meant to cut my throat, but he changed his mind. I don't know why."

Father looked intrigued. "What happened immediately before he turned the knife around?"

Santiago's black brows pulled together. "I was trying to bring my staff up and move back, but he was too close. I looked right into his eyes, and I knew he was going to kill me." He shrugged. "But he didn't."

Father nodded, as if that explained everything. He glanced at Kerry, obviously expecting her to understand.

But she was too angry at Bankar's smirk, as if she thought she would have done better. Crunch! Kerry looked down. She'd crushed one of the fragile Las Anclas figurines.

Greta picked up the report. "Ross's companions didn't go until he shouted at them to run and get help, even after we wounded the boy. The girl wouldn't leave at all until the boy dragged her away."

Father leaned forward. "Out of duty? Or a personal relationship?"

"Relationship," said Greta. "I saw them kissing earlier."

"You should have taken her, too," Father said.

Greta's eyelids flicked up in alarm. "I'm sorry, sir. If I'd known that was what you wanted…"

Father waved his hand dismissively. "Never mind. I didn't give you orders for that contingency. Go on."

Greta continued, "Charles used the touch to blind Ross—"

"He says," Bankar put in, rolling her eyes again.

Charles spoke for the first time. "He was blind."

"Was there any doubt about it?" Father asked.

"*I* think so," Bankar said, arms crossed.

Santiago snorted. "You just don't want to admit that you let a blind prisoner escape on your watch."

Kerry blurted, "Ross escaped?"

There was a dead silence. The scouts glanced at Father, then stared at the floor.

Greta's usually calm voice was nervous and hurried. "We camped in a narrow canyon and set up tripwires on both ends. We also had a watch on him. In retrospect, we should have tied him up, but at the time it didn't seem necessary, given that he was *blind.*"

Greta glared Bankar's way. "On Bankar's watch, she fell asleep for a few minutes, and Ross disappeared without a trace. He didn't set off the tripwires, and there were no footprints leading out of the canyon. After a thorough search, we decided that he must have climbed out."

Kerry couldn't help it. "*Blind?*"

Father gave her an amused glance, then said calmly, "How long did it take you to find him?"

"All day," Greta admitted. "When the sun came up, we could see that he wasn't on the plateau. We employed the standard spiral search, and finally we found a footprint."

Bankar grinned. "When we caught up with him, the idiot had walked straight into a huge jumping cactus."

"Proving my point," Charles said. "If he could see, he would have avoided it."

"It took half the night to pry out the spines," Bankar said. "I still think we should have left them in him."

Father laughed, to Kerry's annoyance. She wished he'd be more selective about his pets. Sure, Bankar had a valuable Change, but it didn't make up for being an immature little brat.

"Why didn't you confiscate his gauntlet?" Kerry asked Greta, to cut off Bankar.

Greta turned to Kerry. "He can't use his left hand without it. Really. His arm is badly scarred. I couldn't force his hand into a fist. The king said to treat him like a guest, and taking the gauntlet seemed cruel."

"Did he tell you how he escaped?" Father was leaning forward, hands clasped. Kerry hadn't seen him so interested for a long time.

"He didn't say a word for the rest of the trip," Charles said.

Father put his hands on his knees. "Perhaps he'll talk to us. Bankar, you let down the team."

Bankar scowled. Had she really thought she'd get away with almost ruining an important mission? Kerry pressed her lips together to hide her pleasure.

"Ten lashes," said Father. "Then wall duty with the regulars for a week, while you reflect on the responsibilities of the elite force."

Bankar looked glum. But if she hadn't been Father's pet, she'd have gotten a much worse whipping and demotion for a month, or even permanently. She ought to be grateful for her ridiculously light sentence. Kerry hoped the sergeant on punishment duty wouldn't slack off.

Father addressed Greta. "If Las Anclas sent soldiers in pursuit, they should be right behind you. Tell the watch commander to extend the perimeter to half a day's ride, triple patrols in line-of-sight. If they attempt a rescue, we can expect it within the next few days. Perhaps as early as tonight."

"Yes, sir." Greta saluted.

"Good work," Father told the scouts. "Take your liberty. You've earned it."

As the scouts left, Bankar taunted, "Skin heals faster than bone. You'll be out of the scouts for longer than me, Santiago!"

Kerry shook her head. Being a brat would never get Santiago's attention. She remembered when Bankar had Changed, and her family had been moved to Palace Gardens. Whenever she had a crush on someone, she'd run up, hit them, and run away. All that was different now was that she used words instead of blows.

"What do you think of our guest now?" Father asked.

That was the third time Ross Juarez had been referred to as a guest. That meant father had something special in mind for him.

Kerry tried to go beyond the obvious. "He protected his companions, but he didn't kill Santiago when he had the chance. His friend and his girlfriend were loyal to him."

"How can we use that to our benefit?"

"If he made friends with people in Las Anclas and fought for them, we could have people here befriend him, so he'll fight for us. Too bad Greta didn't bring his girlfriend."

Father nodded. "Yes, that is too bad. We could have made use of her. But, Kerry, you always use the carrot *and* the stick."

"I don't think the stick will work on him. A guy who was willing to run blind into the desert?"

"You fit the stick to the individual, just as you do the carrot. From what we've heard, I agree that he's not motivated by fear. At least, not fear for himself. I was thinking about your mother."

"What about Mom?" Kerry hid a grimace at the thought of Min Soo. She didn't dare call her mother by her given name—so disrespectful! But she could at least think disrespectful thoughts.

"Opportunity Day. There haven't been any volunteers for the next one, so it would be by lottery anyway."

Kerry was confused. "You want to make Ross volunteer? But he's already Changed. Mom's power won't work on him."

"No, no," Father said. "I'll invite Ross to choose which candidate your mother tries to Change."

"What would that do?" Kerry instantly worried that she'd said the wrong thing. Maybe she should have speculated instead. She didn't want to seem unimaginative.

But Father was obviously in a good mood. He leaned back in his throne, ready to explain. "How did you feel when you chose?"

Kerry thought back to the three times when she'd chosen among the candidates. "It was an honor. I felt proud that you let me choose. But it was a letdown when none of my candidates got a good Change."

Father looked disappointed. "Didn't you feel powerful? You were deciding someone's fate. This will tell us if Ross has any interest in power. If he doesn't, it'll depend how it goes. If it goes well, it'll be a carrot. He'll be grateful to me that nothing bad happened. If it goes wrong, he'll feel guilty and blame himself. There's the stick."

"That's so clever, Father." It was always fascinating to hear him explain how people worked. Kerry felt like she was getting smarter just listening to him. "I can't wait to see what happens."

"Nor can I." Father got to his feet. "Kerry, don't forget that Las Anclas might send soldiers. If you ride outside of the gates, take an honor guard. Or check first."

Kerry knew what that meant. "I will."

She hurried out of the palace. Servants were watering Min Soo's rose garden. Kerry wondered if the servants tending those stupid roses hated them as much as she hated hearing her mother drone on about all their dull varieties.

She cut across the punishment grounds and skirted the whipping post, idly imagining Bankar's upcoming flogging. The girl had no proper dignity. There was no way she'd make it through without squealing—in fact, she'd probably start yelling at the first cut, hoping to make the sergeant pity her and go lighter.

Kerry picked up her pace, nearly skipping past the execution platform, lost in happy daydreams of her reunion with Santiago.

At the infirmary, she heard Santiago's voice through an open door.

"Can I take a bath?"

Kerry stepped up to the doorway. The doctor had his back to her, tossing old bandages into the laundry basket. "You can, but have someone help you."

Santiago met Kerry's eyes and smiled. "That won't be a problem."

The doctor turned, then saluted. "Princess! May I help you?"

"I'm here for Santiago," Kerry said. "Shall I walk you home?"

Santiago jumped up and formally offered his hand, as if she had requested a dance. They both laughed.

A hot flush of happiness welled up in Kerry as she walked with him, holding his hand. It was so nice to see his brown eyes, his snub nose, his bright smile. Her sister Deirdre used to sneer at Kerry's "common" taste, meaning that Santiago didn't meet her shallow standards of handsomeness. But Kerry loved his pleasant, blunt-featured face. It looked friendly and warm and straightforward, which was exactly what he was.

They disengaged their hands simultaneously, reaching out for each other.

"Jinx," said Santiago.

Kerry laughed as she put her arm around his waist, and he put his around her shoulders. Now they were even closer, pressed together side by side.

The lead trumpeter on the palace guard watchtower blew the watch change. The trumpeter from Garrison West picked up the chords, and as the fanfare died away, Kerry heard the soft strains of Garrison East's trumpet, carried on the hot winds.

Soldiers marched past, saluting when they saw Kerry. She waited for them to get out of earshot before she spoke. She was sick of having her every private moment reported to her mother for her to critique in detail.

"You don't have to report to the barracks, do you?" she asked.

"No, I'm on medical leave." Santiago grinned. "I can go home for that bath. And by the way, my family won't be there."

She laughed as they passed the barracks, then headed toward officers' quarters. The squads reporting for duty vanished along the ridge in a swirl of dust. No servants were visible in the officers' gardens.

"Where did you stash the prisoner?" she asked, now that they were free of listening ears.

"The cubes."

Kerry knew the rooms where soldiers were locked up after fights or drunk and disorderly rowdiness, to cool off or sleep it off. There were no windows or breakables, but they had a clean cot and room to stand up, which was a lot better than the hell cells.

Santiago went on, "I thought he'd be happy to get a real bed, but he made a break for it. It took Charles and a couple others to boot him through the door."

"What did he expect? A house of his own?"

"No, it wasn't like that. Maybe he thought…" He glanced around. "We did tell him that he was a guest and no one would hurt him."

Unless he needs some stick, Kerry thought. She'd find that out for herself when she got to interview him with Father.

They ducked under the flowering purple bougainvilleas that divided the compound from the officers' gardens. The sun was disappearing behind the hills, haloing the house's peaked roof in red-gold light.

"If no one's around, want to take your bath in the courtyard pool?"

"That's exactly what I was thinking," Santiago said.

Kerry tipped her head back, inviting a kiss. After two weeks apart, she wanted to sink into it, like a hot bath. He bent toward her…

"Princess! Princess!"

She leaped back.

A disheveled servant rushed up, her face crimson. "Princess, her highness summons you."

Kerry was tempted to order the servant to return and say that she hadn't seen her. Another ten seconds, and it would have been true.

"Don't," Santiago whispered. "You're not the only one who would get into trouble."

The servant sent Santiago a pathetic look of gratitude, then fled.

"I'll see you later. Like tomorrow." Kerry saw in Santiago's face the same frustration she felt. She gave him a quick kiss. "Get some rest."

She was certain that Min Soo had sent the servant specifically to foil their reunion, as yet another infuriating, pointless "lesson" in self-control.

Kerry walked as slowly as she dared. She had to get her temper under control, or at least her face. The smallest sign of impatience or what Min Soo called pouting, and Kerry would get an extra lecture.

Inside her mother's suite, Min Soo's attar of roses hit her like a punch in the nose. She slipped off her shoes and stepped onto carpets so thick that they squelched like quicksand. If quicksand could be dyed a delicate pink.

Min Soo wasn't in the reception chamber. Oh, great. That meant she was in her frilly bedroom. Sure enough, her mother lounged on the silk coverlet, being fanned by a maid. She smiled and patted the bed.

Kerry folded her arms. There were no chairs, but if it was sit next to her mother or stand, she would stand.

With a frown, Min Soo dismissed the maid. As the door closed soundlessly, she offered Kerry a delicate saucer heaped with candied rose petals. "I saved these for you, my darling."

"You know I don't like those." Kerry loathed the perfume-tasting things.

"Even a crown princess must have good manners," Min Soo said in her sweetest voice. "If someone offers you food, especially a delicacy they might prefer to eat themselves, you always graciously accept." She extended the dish again to Kerry. "Let's try that again. Please, my dear, have a sweet."

"Thank you." Kerry boiled with anger as she choked down the smallest petal she could find. It stuck in her throat.

"That's better. At your age, and with your responsibilities, perfect manners should be a habit. Now, sit beside me and tell me about your afternoon."

Kerry knew what her mother really wanted. Father obviously hadn't filled her in about the prisoner. Kerry was once again stuck between the two of them. But that didn't mean she had to give in.

She leaned against the bed, hoping that would be close enough to satisfy her mother without having to sit on silk when she was hot and sweaty. "My tutor set up a military problem for me. I have to take a guarded dam on a mountain river. They have a force of sixty, no horses. I've got a team of—"

"I'm sure you will do admirably, dear," Min Soo interrupted. "And what else did you do? Outside of your lessons?"

"I got in some good training. We're doing night maneuvers next month, so I've got to practice moonlight orienteering." Kerry stopped there to force her mother to bring up Father.

Min Soo helped herself to a pink rose petal. "And in the interview chamber? Did you learn anything new from your father?"

"You know I can't talk about that."

Min Soo made a reproving click with her tongue. "Ian shares everything with me. There are no secrets between us."

Hot blood rushed to Kerry's face. "Then he can tell you himself. Why are you asking me?"

Min Soo's voice was calm and sweet as always. "For your perspective. And further, it's a matter of trust, darling. I would never interfere in your relationship with your father. That's very important, and it fills me with pride. But you seem to assume you have nothing to learn from your mother. What I teach you is just as important as what you learn from your father. But you are going to have to show some respect for the niceties of life before you can be trusted with more dangerous knowledge."

"Who cares about niceties?" Kerry burst out. "Those are for weak people. Followers. It doesn't matter if people *like* me, when I can have them executed."

Min Soo shook her head. "Darling, you must never rest on the assumption of power. Ian was not the only potential ruler of his generation. The princes and princesses whom he *liked* are ruling towns in his empire. The others are dust and bone."

Why did Min Soo have to bring that up? Father undoubtedly had his reasons. They were probably traitors. "Then you should be teaching my half-sibs how to make *me* like *them*. I'm the crown princess. There's no one above me."

Min Soo held up a delicate fist. Opening one finger, she said, "Sean."

Kerry snorted with contempt. "He'd never hurt me. Anyway, he's never coming back."

"You don't know that. On both counts." Another finger opened. "Francisco Diaz Voske. The one they call Paco."

Kerry laughed. "He's been raised by the enemy. Father would never trust him. Anyway, I've heard the reports on him. He doesn't care about anything but his silly drumming."

"Any boy would like to wake up and find himself the crown prince of an empire. Darling, you'd be amazed at how quickly allegiances can shift." Her hand opened. "Now back to you and your behavior. If Deirdre were still alive and, God forbid, something happened to your father, how long do you think you'd outlive him?"

Kerry squirmed, hating her mother's sweet, cool voice.

"For that matter," Min Soo added, "if your places had been reversed, how long would you have let her quarrel with you before you had her put to death?"

Kerry, irritated, was about to snap that she wouldn't have executed her own half-sister, no matter how much Kerry disliked her.

But Min Soo didn't wait for an answer. "Let us begin again." She picked up the dish of candied rose petals, and gracefully offered it to Kerry. "Good morning, darling. Would you care for a sweet?"

Kerry had lost this round. All she could do was try to keep this interview as short as possible. She forced herself to smile. To take one. To put the nauseating thing in her mouth, chew, swallow, and look like she liked it.

"Thank you, Mother. How considerate of you to save them for me."

*

The only thing that calmed her down after her mother's lessons in weakness was a good ride alone. Kerry loathed being slowed down with honor guards and Pru had returned from Las Anclas two weeks ago, so she decided to take her father's other option and *check*.

Kerry hurried to the royal library, which was empty. Or so it seemed. She looked around, consciously thinking, *Is Sean here?*

He'd been gone for three years, but she still searched for him: sometimes out of habit, and sometimes in the hope that the rumors were true, and her half-brother hadn't run away, but was lurking in Gold Point, using his "don't notice me" power to escape detection. But she didn't believe it. He would have let her know.

Kerry was alone. She bolted the hall door, but didn't touch the door to Father's suite. From a bottom shelf, she pulled out the most boring book ever prospected, a battered blue tome with faint gold lettering reading *Estate Tax Law, Volume XLVII*. Kerry ran her fingernails down the shelf until they snagged. She pried the hidden panel open and flipped the latch behind it, then sprang back as the bookcase swung out.

She replaced the book, slipped into the passage, and hit the switches to turn on the lights and make the bookcase swing back. It was cooler than the library. She ran down the stairs, crossed under the garden, then took the stairs three at a time until she reached the door.

Pru answered her knock. "Kerry. Your father send you?"

Pru was shorter than Kerry, a wizened old woman with a face so wrinkled that it was hard to see her expression unless she laughed. She wore the worn cotton shirt and blue jeans she preferred, no matter how much scrip Father gave her. Her callused feet were bare as she led Kerry across carpets as soft and deep—and pink—as those in Min Soo's rooms. It always amused Kerry how two people as completely different as her mother and Pru had such identical taste in furnishings.

Kerry shook her head. "I want to go riding. Can you check for enemies outside the walls?"

"Have a seat." Pru indicated a leaf-green armchair. "There's cucumber water in the jug."

Kerry poured out a mug as Pru plopped down on a mauve silk cushion and closed her eyes.

"Ah. My old friend the peregrine is circling the Joshua Tree forest." She paused. "He sees the sinkhole in the middle. It's rippling. A frog jumped in. He's diving to catch it. Oh! He got it!"

Kerry sipped her cucumber water as Pru's gruff voice reported everything the hawks outside of Gold Point saw and heard.

"The only humans the kestrel at the south gate sees are the sentries, the patrols, and the pickings on the wall." Pru opened her eyes. "Go riding. My hawks see no one approaching. You can tell your father there will be no attack before sundown."

CHAPTER THIRTEEN
GOLD POINT
ROSS

Ross huddled in the corner of the windowless room. His chest hurt as if it was squeezed in a vise. No matter how he gasped for breath, he couldn't get enough air into his lungs.

I'm not here, he told himself. *I'm in Mia's cottage. The windows are wide open, and flies are buzzing in circles. Mia's sitting next to me, so close that I can see the rip in her shirt, and her skin showing through.*

The door creaked open. Ross didn't move. People had opened it before, to give him food he couldn't force himself to eat, but there was no sunlight or fresh air, just a windowless corridor. He'd stay where he was, and think about Mia again—

A girl's voice startled him. "Is he faking? He tricked the scout team."

A man said, "I don't think so." Footsteps came closer. "Look how the sweat's pouring off him. He can't fake that."

Ross heard the shift of fabric as someone crouched next to him. He curled tighter into his ball.

"What's the matter, Ross?" The man sounded friendly. "Are you sick?"

Ross tightened his arms around his head.

"Come on. I can't help you if I don't know what's wrong."

Ross opened his eyes, peering past the crook of his elbow. He couldn't see much. He uncurled his right arm. A man with silver hair knelt beside him, smiling. Ross focused on his sharp-featured face to avoid looking at the ceiling.

"Talk to me," the man encouraged.

"Can you get me outside?" Ross forced the words out.

The man glanced around the room. "Oh." He hauled Ross to his feet.

Ross shook the hands off. The man stepped away, leaving Ross standing. "Follow me."

Ross glanced at the girl as he went into the corridor. She was his age, her steady gaze curious. He looked past her to memorize the layout before they locked him back in: two guards outside the room, two more at the end of the corridor. They all had rifles as well as batons.

The man opened a door and let Ross step outside. The sun was bright, the air moved. He shut his eyes against the glare off the pale dirt and just breathed.

"What did you see in there, Kerry?" the man asked.

Nothing, Ross thought. *Nothing but walls closing in.*

The girl, Kerry, said, "He's scared of us."

"But we're still here," the man replied. "What do you see now?"

Kerry's voice was precise, like she thought about every word. "You're right, Father. He's not afraid of us. It was something about the room. I'm not sure what."

"Ask him," the man said. Ross could hear a smile in his voice.

A foot crunched the gravel beside Ross. He resisted the urge to move away.

"What was wrong with the cube?" Kerry asked.

Ross didn't answer.

"You weren't put there as a punishment, Ross," the man said. "It was meant as a quiet place to rest after a tiring journey."

Ross's right hand flexed. He couldn't help it.

The man went on, "If you don't tell us what was wrong, we won't know how to fix it. Where would you like to stay?"

"Somewhere with windows," Ross said reluctantly. But now that he'd spoken, he added, "Whatever you want me to do, I won't do it. So you might as well let me go."

"I'm not going to hurt you. I just want to make a better offer for your talents. My daughter can show you around. Kerry, not the guest quarters. I think he'd prefer Deirdre's old room."

Ross opened his eyes in time to see the tall, silver-haired man walk back inside. He wore a fancy uniform and polished riding boots. Ross didn't need to see how fast the two guards saluted to know that if the man wasn't Voske himself, it was probably his second in command.

Kerry had the same angular features and slanting eyebrows as the silver-haired man, making her face more striking than pretty. Something about them both seemed familiar, but he couldn't figure out why. Maybe it was only that they looked so much like each other.

She was a bit taller than Ross. Long black braids coiled around her head like a crown, and she wore well-woven riding clothes with fine embroidery. Her new boots didn't have a single wrinkle across the uppers or sag at the ankle, and the earrings that swung glinting at her cheeks were made of gold.

"This way." Kerry indicated a gate across the plaza. Or maybe a parade ground, as only soldiers were in view: a pair on the wall either side of the gate, and a squad marching in. They spread out in lines and started exercising. If Ross made a run for it, he'd be jumped or shot in seconds.

He walked beside Kerry, taking her in. She had no visible weapons, but since her father had left her alone with him, she must be a good fighter. She moved like one. But Ross was a good fighter too. If he could get her alone, he'd try to take her by surprise.

They passed through the gate to a tree-lined path leading upward.

Kerry broke the silence. "How did you escape from the scout team?"

He shrugged, peering between the trees. No soldiers in sight—so far.

"You have nothing to fear. My father won't hurt you," Kerry said.

The huge city walls rose up on their left. He didn't see any sentries on the wall. Scrubby hills rose up behind it. If he knocked Kerry out and climbed the wall, he could make a run north for the Joshua Forest. He'd crawled through it the last time he'd been in this territory, with the bounty hunter in pursuit.

"You remember Charles?" Kerry went on. "He was recruited, just like you. He and his husband have a fine house nearby. They met each other here."

Ah. Here came sentries from both directions.

"...Father said it took Charles a while to adjust, but that was years ago. He's perfectly happy now. We make a point of rewarding people for good work, here in Gold Point."

I remember what I saw on points, Ross thought, throwing his head back.

The palace that loomed beyond the trees was so startling that he almost missed his step. It was the biggest building he'd ever seen, more than twice the size of the Las Anclas town hall.

"And that's the royal palace," Kerry said. "You're the first...guest I've ever seen Father invite to stay there. You should feel honored."

So that silver-haired man *was* Voske. And this girl was his daughter. Ross tightened all over. He had to get away.

Guards passed in pairs along the towering roof. In the time it took to walk five steps, he counted four pairs. There must be three times that many on the ground.

"You'll like Deirdre's room. She loved pretty things, so it's full of artifacts. Perfect for a prospector."

If Ross was going to make a break for it, it had to be now, before he got any closer to all those guards.

"Do you like to read?" Kerry asked. "There's—"

Ross had casually stepped within striking distance. He shot his fist at her jaw. His knuckles slammed into what felt like a steel wall. He staggered backward, bringing up his left hand in a block. Kerry stood still, with her left hand held palm out. She brought up her right hand as if she gripped an invisible sword. Something sharp pricked Ross's throat.

He froze.

"I won't hurt you." She smiled just like her father. "But don't try to run."

CHAPTER FOURTEEN
GOLD POINT
KERRY

Kerry let her sword vanish, though she kept her shield up.

"I thought you'd try that," she said, trying to hide her exultation. "I even guessed where. But you're faster than I expected."

A dark flush began at Ross's ears and slowly spread across his entire face. It was kind of cute. *He* would be cute, if he wasn't so silent and scrawny. Not that she would mention that to Santiago.

"Is your hand okay?" she asked.

"Yeah." He wiped his bleeding knuckles on his pants. "I wondered why you didn't have any weapons. That's a cool power. Can you make anything? Or just the sword and shield?"

Kerry didn't see why she shouldn't tell him. Everyone in Gold Point already knew. Besides, her power was what had gotten him talking. "Any weapon I can hold in my hands. But nothing with projectiles, like a crossbow. I have to keep touching it." She created a whip and cracked it at a low branch. A shower of leaves and twigs rained down.

"Wow." Ross looked impressed. "How far can you reach?"

"That's about my limit—six feet or so."

He was terrible at hiding his thoughts, so she could see how he considered jumping her again, then decided not to try. Her mood brightened even more. Father would be pleased at how she'd passed his test with the prisoner. The *guest*. She'd foiled Ross's escape, but without making him hate her.

"Come on, I'll show you your room. And I bet you're hungry."

He shrugged, but couldn't help swallowing. Elation tingled through her. Father was right, as always. Noticing details as revealing as an interrogation.

They passed the Japanese garden, where Ross gave a curious glance at the shrine and orange torii gate. Kerry liked him a bit more when he ignored Min Soo's stupid roses. Instead, he was clearly counting the guards and memorizing their patrol routine.

She wouldn't tell him that the routine changed every day. Nobody Father had recruited had ever escaped, though some hadn't worked out. She restrained herself from eyeing the northwest sentry tower. She wouldn't tell Ross why those heads were there. If necessary, Father would inform him.

She took Ross to the front entrance, so he could be impressed by its magnificence. The guards sprang to open the doors. She walked him through the throne room, with its beautifully laid wood floor and throne of prospected white marble.

Kerry noted what he looked at, knowing that Father would ask. Most people stared at the throne, but he seemed most interested in the crystal chandeliers. They were beautiful, too, of course.

Victory bloomed inside her again when he was the first to speak. "Is the whole palace lit with electricity?"

"Don't you have that in Las Anclas?" She'd been certain that they did.

He looked at the floor, but not as if he was admiring the hardwood. He seemed to have shut down because she'd mentioned her future town. She'd have to remember not to do that until he'd gotten more accustomed to Gold Point.

She led him up the stairs. All the way up, he seemed fascinated by the electric lights. Probably his own home hadn't had them.

"Almost all the houses in Gold Point have electric lights," she said. That clearly caught his interest, so she went on, "The main streets do, too. Hardly anyone uses bright moths or oil lamps."

He listened to her explain electric fans until they reached Deirdre's room, where the workers were finishing welding. Then his gaze went straight to the new bars across the windows.

"You can still open the windows," Kerry said. "Deirdre picked this room because she loved the wind."

The workers packed their tools and left. They stood in silence while Ross watched the floor and Kerry watched him. But she could outwait him.

She sat on the bed. The mattress was softer than her own. Kerry hadn't set foot in the room for over a year, since Deirdre had volunteered at Opportunity Day, and changed in more ways than one. Her books filled the shelves, with the few she'd last read still stacked on her bedside table.

Apparently Deirdre had never stopped loving those silly ancient novels about haunted houses and handsome, dangerous men. If the cover had a terrified woman fleeing a house, Deirdre would read it. Kerry wondered what Ross would make of *The Specter of Blackraven Manor*.

"Who's Deirdre?" Ross asked at last. "Where is she?"

"She was my half-sister." Kerry hesitated. "She won't be coming back."

Strange, how Kerry couldn't bring herself to say, *She's dead.* She had never liked Deirdre, and that had turned to hate after Deirdre got her power.

Now that Ross had managed to pry his gaze off the floorboards, he caught sight of his backpack. He dug through it, his face reflecting disappointment when he found that his weapons had been confiscated.

She opened the clothing trunk. Sure enough, Father had provided clothing approximately in Ross's size. "You can wear this training gear for now. We'll have the tailor measure you for regular clothes."

"These are fine." Ross patted his worn jeans. "Does that mean you'll let me train?"

"Do you want to?"

Ross shrugged his bony shoulders. She could tell he did, though. It would be another carrot she could offer. And how he fought would tell her a lot about him.

It was time to remind him how successful Gold Point was. How powerful. She opened the bathroom door. "You have hot and cold running water." Since he was so fascinated by electricity, she added, "They finished the power plant by my sixth birthday. It took almost twenty years to build."

His gaze shifted to the window. She wondered if he could have climbed out, if Father hadn't put in the bars. It would take a lot of skill....

"Did you climb out of the canyon?" Kerry asked. "Or did you hide in it until the scouts left to look for you?"

She was sure Father would have been able to read the truth in the way Ross blinked, but all she could see was a boy keeping his face carefully expressionless.

Someone knocked. Since Ross stood like a lump of stone, Kerry opened the door to Santiago's round face and clipped black hair.

"Santiago," she exclaimed with relief. It was exhausting trying to make conversation with a lump.

Santiago gave her the private, special smile that he saved just for her, then looked past her. "Hi, Ross."

Ross didn't reply; all she could see of his face were his eyelashes against his cheeks. It was obvious that he was waiting for everyone to go away and leave him alone.

Santiago grinned at Kerry. "Let's get some breakfast."

Ross clearly didn't care about grandeur, and just as clearly didn't like company. The royal dining room would probably make him withdraw even more.

On their way out, Kerry snapped her fingers to a servant. "Have hot food brought to the staff dining room."

The plain room was empty, as the staff breakfasted at sunup. Santiago helped himself to sausages and hash browns with cream gravy. Ross, showing some enthusiasm for the first time since she'd demonstrated her power, methodically piled his plate with some of everything, all the way down to the sickeningly sweet birds' nest pudding.

She and Santiago got a limping conversation going with each other. They couldn't talk about anything important, but she didn't want to sit there in gloomy silence.

In desperation, Kerry asked, "How's your collarbone?"

As soon as she said it, she couldn't help glancing at Ross. So, she noticed, did Santiago. Ross stared at his plate. Several beats too late, Santiago said with exaggerated cheerfulness, "It's fine."

The doors banged open, and a kitchen servant brought in a tray of scrambled eggs, their savory steam still rising.

"Eggs!" Ross exclaimed.

Eggs? Kerry and Santiago exchanged glances.

Santiago put his fork down. "So, Ross, what's your favorite way of fixing eggs? I like them fried over medium. My mom pours a little milk into the pan."

That caught Ross's interest. "Milk? What does that do?"

"It makes the whites creamy. You should try it."

Kerry added, "I like them poached."

"Fresh." Ross watched the servant spoon the eggs onto his plate. He swallowed again. "I like them fresh."

Kerry wondered what not-fresh eggs tasted like. From the way Ross watched that ladle, he knew.

The door opened again, revealing Father. Santiago's chair scraped as he leaped to his feet to salute.

Ross froze, his fork midway to his mouth, then warily set it down, his shoulders bracing tight.

"Sit down, Santiago. Enjoy your breakfast," Father said.

Ah. So Father had sent Santiago.

Father dismissed the servant, leaving the four of them alone. He helped himself to bacon and waffles before sitting at the head of the table, opposite Ross. Kerry didn't remember the last time he'd eaten in the staff dining room, much less served himself. He seemed determined to set a friendly tone for Ross.

Still, no one else ate until he gestured. "Enjoy."

Santiago stuffed a forkful of eggs in his mouth, and Kerry pulled apart a biscuit. She'd eaten earlier, with Father. But he obviously wanted them giving Ross a pleasant breakfast.

Ross folded his arms.

"Did you try the waffles, Ross?" Father asked. "They're my favorite."

Ross gave a wary nod.

"I like them with blueberry jam," Santiago said. "When the trader from the North Road comes around, my family buys five jars."

Kerry tried to continue the conversation. "Have you ever tasted blueberries, Ross?"

"No." His arms stayed tight across his chest.

She hoped Father appreciated how hard she and Santiago were working to befriend the guest. It wasn't easy.

Father dipped a piece of bacon in mesquite syrup. "You might get a chance at the potluck for Opportunity Day."

"Everyone brings their favorite dishes for Opportunity Day," Kerry added, seeing where Father was going.

She waited for Ross to ask what Opportunity Day was, but one look at him made it clear she'd wait forever. Kerry kicked Santiago in the ankle.

"I remember my Opportunity Day," Santiago said immediately. "Best day of my life."

Father smiled at him. "Ross, the first day of every month is Opportunity Day. Kerry's mother, Min Soo, has a remarkable power. She can make the Change happen to people who have that potential. Because we value Changed people in Gold Point, we let one person per month have that opportunity."

Santiago spoke so quickly that Kerry knew he'd been rehearsed, "I volunteered as soon as I turned eighteen, and I knew it would never happen naturally. My aunt Maria-Luisa is the only person in my family who's ever Changed, but I always dreamed of having an amazing power like Kerry's."

Kerry chimed in, "You wanted to have a fire power, didn't you?"

Santiago grinned. "Fire, explosions, anything cool I could use in battle."

Ross didn't speak, but he did look interested. Kerry wondered why Father hadn't mentioned Santiago's role in his plan, then gave an internal shrug. Santiago was an excellent choice to get Ross relaxed. He was so friendly. Most boys were so intimidated that they didn't dare address her, let alone flirt with her. Or they made fools of themselves trying to impress her. Only Santiago was his natural, wonderful self. She reached for his hand under the table as Father addressed Ross.

"Each of the five provinces of Gold Point offers a candidate. On the day itself, there's a lottery to select which one gets the opportunity to Change. Min Soo takes their hands, and even if nothing visible happens, they always know if they've Changed. What they don't know is what their Change is. Go ahead, Santiago, tell Ross about your day."

Santiago tensed under her hand. Maybe his collarbone hurt, but he wouldn't want to show weakness in front of Father. "There's a table set up on the stage, with a bunch of different things on it: a chunk of wood, a bowl of water, a dish of soil, a rock, a plant in a pot, and a live mouse in a cage. The moment her highness touched me, I could feel that I was different. I marched up to that table, ready to burn that wood or blast that rock into smithereens. When I saw the rock, I knew I could do something to it."

Kerry had to laugh. Because Father was smiling, she took over. "It was the funniest thing! He walked up to that table looking so determined. We were all sure something spectacular was about to happen. He stretched out his hand and held it over that rock…and stood there…and stood there… and we all stood there…for fifteen hours. No, it was fifteen minutes, but it felt like fifteen hours. I thought Mom had turned *him* into a rock."

Santiago shook his head. "I had no idea that much time was passing. When the rock started to glow and the table started to smoke, I was so excited. And then I looked up, and saw the entire crowd asleep on their feet."

"That's your power?" To Kerry's amazement, Ross was talking. "You can make rocks heat up in fifteen minutes?"

Santiago gave a wry shrug. "That's it. The most useless power ever, but hey, my parents appreciated the reward the king gives to volunteers' families."

Ross didn't seem interested in rewards. "It sounds useful to me. Why didn't you use it when we were in the desert?"

Santiago lifted one shoulder, and his face tightened. Kerry could tell he was trying not to wince. "Flint is faster."

Father had finished his breakfast. He rose to his feet. "The next Opportunity Day is tomorrow. You'll be our special guest, Ross. I'm sure you'll enjoy it."

Santiago had shot to his feet again. Father waved at him to sit down, and went out.

Kerry pushed the mesquite syrup toward Ross. "Finish your breakfast."

"I know the king can be intimidating, but he's very fair," Santiago said. "All the soldiers love him."

Ross slumped deeper into his chair. Kerry kicked Santiago again. He gave her a *What did I say?* look, but he dropped the army talk. Ross began eating again.

Kerry was starting to relax when a servant came in. It was the same one who had dragged her away from Santiago yesterday. Not twice in two days!

"Her highness summons you and the guest," the servant said.

Ross's fork clattered to his nearly empty plate.

"I'll be at my house." Santiago flashed a private grin at Kerry. "Taking a bath."

"Ready, Ross?" She wished she could warn him, but she wasn't sure what to say other than, "Don't eat the rose petals."

Mother met them in her formal sitting room. Not a good sign, but then nothing with her was a good sign.

"I'm delighted to make your acquaintance, Ross. I'm Kerry's mother, Min Soo Cho." She indicated a chair with a lavender silk cushion. "Please sit down. Has my daughter been making you feel welcome?"

Ross muttered something completely unintelligible.

Min Soo offered him the dreaded porcelain candy dish. "Candied rose petals, Ross?"

To Kerry's surprise, Ross popped a few in his mouth. His eyes widened in what appeared to be sincere pleasure. "They're good. Thank you."

Min Soo looked annoyingly pleased. "Have you ever tasted such a delicacy, Ross? I would be surprised if they have such things in Las Anclas."

When he didn't answer, she pushed the dish forward again. "Do have more. Nothing gives me more pleasure than to see my precious roses enjoyed. These are specially bred for flavor."

Ross helped himself to a handful. Kerry wondered if it was so he wouldn't have to talk.

"So, tell me about yourself," Min Soo said in the Encouragement Tone that she claimed made people want to talk. Kerry doubted it would work on Ross. "You are a prospector?"

Ross nodded.

"How fascinating! I adore prospectors, such interesting people. We have one living nearby. You must meet Prudence."

Like that's going to happen, Kerry thought. Except when she was reporting on her hawks, Pru was the only person Kerry had ever met who talked less than Ross. Which was just as well.

"I understand that you planned to breach the ruined city north of Las Anclas," Min Soo said. "We have one here, too. Not as large as yours, but also surrounded by singing trees. The legends say that it was abandoned completely intact and that to this day, it's full of artifacts just waiting to be picked up."

"How far is it?" asked Ross.

Kerry couldn't believe that he was talking of his own accord. Maybe there was something to the Encouragement Tone.

"One day's ride." Min Soo pointed southward, her gold bracelets rattling. "Any prospector who finds a way in will be set up for life. We have fine rewards for prospectors. Prudence found a very valuable artifact for the king. Now she has her own beautiful home, with velvet carpets, a staff to take care of it, and complete freedom to come and go. She no longer needs to work, but she still prospects for her own enjoyment."

The way Ross's gaze had flickered when Min Soo mentioned the valuable artifact had to mean that rumors about Father's "spy device" had reached all the way to Las Anclas. It was one of Father's cleverest ideas, to divert attention away from Pru herself and onto the nonexistent artifact. Though Min Soo had always claimed it was *her* idea.

"Tell me about Las Anclas." Min Soo again offered the dish to Ross. He'd already eaten half the candied petals. "How long had you lived there?"

"Couple months."

"It sounds like a fine town. Though I understand that it can be a difficult place if you are Changed. I hope no one gave you any trouble about yours."

Ross almost choked on a petal. Min Soo had clearly struck a nerve.

"I can guess whose influence is behind that. I know people your age have trouble imagining that their parents were ever young." Min Soo looked straight at Kerry as she spoke. It was true. Kerry could not imagine her mother as a teenager.

Min Soo continued, again to Ross, "When we were your age, Tom Preston and the king—he was Prince Ian then—and I all knew each other. Even then, Tom tried to ignore the king's Change, minor as it is. As for me, he pretended I didn't even exist."

"Vo—uh, the king is Changed?" Ross asked. "What's his power?"

Min Soo laughed. "His hair went silver when he turned thirteen. Nothing so dramatic as your Change, Ross. You must be very proud of it."

Her words acted on Ross like salt on a slug. He hunched his shoulders.

Min Soo leaned back, making herself non-threatening, and again deployed the Encouragement Tone. "How old were you? Did anyone in your family have a similar Change?"

Metal scraped against metal. Ross was clenching his fists, the one bare and the one encased in steel.

Min Soo said soothingly, "I know it can be difficult. Not only how people treat you. Sometimes powers themselves can be hard to adjust to. But here, we understand that. You'll see on Opportunity Day." She smiled. "Enjoy your day, Ross. We will talk again."

Kerry leaped to her feet. Ross didn't know how lucky he was to have been spared a lesson on social skills, followed by an excruciating role-play. But he looked more disturbed than he had since they'd pulled him out of the windowless room.

As soon as they were safely outside, Kerry said, "I could use a workout. Want to spar?"

Her reward was a fleeting moment when Ross's black eyes met hers, and a hint of a smile. "Sure."

CHAPTER FIFTEEN
GOLD POINT
ROSS

A guard escorted Ross to his room after the most uncomfortable dinner of his life. The food was wonderful, but he couldn't enjoy it while he was trapped between Voske and Min Soo. The more they pretended to be friendly, the more Ross worried about what they wanted from him.

He closed the door, relieved to finally be free of spying eyes. Or was he? Well, Voske was welcome to watch him sit on the bed. Ross hoped he'd bore the king to death. As for the bars, he'd test them when it was dark.

A new shirt and pants waited on the bed. He'd been measured before his sparring session with Kerry, but he hadn't imagined the clothes would arrive this fast. He'd never owned new clothes, much less ones made specifically for him.

The shirt was fine cotton, dyed red. The color reminded him of blood, of the crystal shard he'd cut out of his arm, and the scarlet tree it had grown into. The trousers were black linen. Without even holding them up to himself, he knew they would fit better than anything he had worn in his life. He wished he had Dr. Lee's old shirt and jeans back.

He concealed the blood-red shirt underneath the pants, then surveyed the room. It was decorated with framed pictures—every one an artifact—of huge towers of glass and metal, and metal carriages on wide, smooth roads. Two whole cases were filled with as many ancient books as they had in the entire library at Las Anclas. They were held in place with wooden replicas of the prehensile-tailed Gold Point horses. The tails curved upward, forming holders for jars of potpourri. The scent of the dried flowers and spices reminded Ross of Jennie's room. Jennie would have loved the books, too.

He had a sudden, overwhelming sense of something missing. Like there was a hole inside him, and he was falling into it.

He took off his gauntlet and laid it on the table. Since he'd convinced his captors that he needed it to use his hand at all, he had to wear it all the time. He let his left hand hang limp as he walked to the electrical switch and turned off the light.

Hoping the spy thing couldn't see in the dark, Ross pushed and twisted at the bars on the windows, careful not to make a sound. Unsurprisingly, they didn't budge.

He returned to the bed, wishing he was in Las Anclas with Jennie and Mia. One girl on each side, the way they'd walked into the town square for the dance. Where were they now? Jennie would probably be with the Rangers, and Mia? Ross liked to think of her in her cozy cottage, working on some weapon from his ancient book.

Mia! Ross remembered the mystery tool she had dropped into his backpack. Though his weapons had been taken, the tool was still there. Voske's people must not have known what it was, either. In the one glimpse Ross had gotten of it, it had looked like a chunk of steel bar.

Ross tiptoed to his backpack and took out Mia's tool. The days he'd spent blind had given him lots of practice in memorizing locations.

The tool had a hairline seam, as if Mia had joined two pieces of steel. He tried to twist it apart, but it didn't budge. Maybe she had intended it as a weight so he could punch harder when he held it. But he couldn't close his fist over it. When he gripped it like a club, it fit perfectly. But a club that small would be less useful than a rock picked up off the ground—which was undoubtedly why Voske had let him keep it.

But it fit so well. And Mia had measured his hands for the gauntlet. She'd obviously made the tool just for him. Experimentally, he held it as if it was a club, and swung it lightly. It wasn't quite as heavy as it should be if it was solid steel.

He stepped to the center of the room and swung the tool as if he was trying to hit someone with it. With a soft snick, something snapped within the rod. A set of hidden segments slid out and locked into place. Ross ran his free hand along the steel baton that Mia's weapon had become. It was as long as his forearm, giving him much more reach than he would have with his fists. He wished Mia was there so he could kiss her.

He gave it a few practice swings, then collapsed it against his palm. The segments slid neatly into place. Ross gave it a twist until it heard a click, and it returned to its original state.

Ross returned it to his pack. He was still smiling when he fell asleep.

*

He awoke to sunlight warming his face. For a glad moment he thought he was back in Las Anclas, under his glass ceiling. Then he saw the bars across the windows.

He pulled the covers over his head. He'd rather go hungry than have another meal with that smiling king who put people's heads on poles, and Min Soo and her sweet-toned questions prying into things Ross didn't want to think about.

Someone banged on the door. Kerry called, "Ross? Breakfast is ready."

Ross was tempted to ignore her. But what would it prove if Voske sent somebody to haul him out of bed? He might as well pretend to cooperate while things were easy. It surely wouldn't be easy for long.

"Be right there," he called.

He changed into the new clothes, trying not to look at that blood-red shirt.

Ross opened the door, then froze. Kerry wore the same colors he did, but her outfit was fit for a princess. Her high-collared scarlet blouse and black pants were heavily embroidered and tightly fitted, and she wore high-heeled black boots. A gold tiara encircled her crown of braids, and her ruby earrings sparkled like his crystal tree.

She laughed, gesturing at her clothes. "Do you like them? I designed them myself."

He'd been staring. His ears burned. "They're nice," he muttered.

Her parents were terrifying, but Ross didn't mind Kerry. Other than the food, the only thing he'd enjoyed in Gold Point had been sparring with her. She was as almost as good as Jennie, though her style was completely different. Jennie liked fancy techniques; Kerry liked simple ones that only worked if they were done perfectly. As long as they sparred, he could almost forget that he was a prisoner.

In Las Anclas, everyone dressed up for dances. "Do you dance at Opportunity Day?"

Kerry's brows shot up. "Dance?" she repeated, like she'd never heard the word before. "No. Oh, we have our fair share of dances, but those are…other festivals."

Ross knew he'd said the wrong thing, but had no idea why.

In the royal dining room, Voske sat at the head of the table, wearing a long black silk tunic slit up the sides and embroidered in red. His trousers were also black with red embroidery, vanishing into glossy high boots.

Min Soo wore a high-waisted full skirt of floating white silk and a short, wrapped white blouse edged with red. Her bun of black hair was pinned with a gold clip. Three women sat with her. Two wore red trimmed with white. The third was in a military uniform and wore her hair like Jennie did, in short black braids tipped with beads. Every bead was red or white.

There were seven children at the table, all in red trimmed with black. The oldest three, two girls and a boy, were around eleven or twelve. They stared curiously at Ross, and the smaller girl waved. The younger children didn't pay Ross much attention after the first look. Ross was hoping he could sit with them when Voske indicated a chair near himself. Kerry sat between them.

Ross wondered uneasily why he'd been given the same colors as the royal family—and even the same split of red and black as Kerry, the crown princess. Voske couldn't possibly mean to put Ross on the same level. Maybe it was another fake-friendly thing.

"Ross, meet the rest of my family." Voske introduced everyone not only by name, but by Change. All four of his wives and the three oldest children had powerful Changes, though the toddler girl only had feathered eyebrows and a little boy could make flowers bloom. Two of the younger kids got a fond, "Not Changed *yet*."

The table setting had no sharp knives, nor was any food served that would have required one. Everyone had a fork with blunted tines, except for Ross, who was only offered a spoon. Voske wasn't taking any chances on being attacked at the table. Ross had spent half his life without tableware, so he had no trouble eating. While he dug into the pancakes, he thought up ways to kill Voske with a spoon.

The soldier woman kissed Princess Fiona, the one who had waved at Ross, and stood up. "Enjoy Opportunity Day. I'm off to the garrison."

"Float me!" squeaked the little princess, who had the same rich brown skin and huge brown eyes as her mother. "I want a float before you go!"

With a laugh, her mother took her hand. Fiona floated off the ground and rose as high as her mother could reach, flapping her free arm and making bird calls. Her braids stuck straight out, as if she were underwater. Her older half-siblings rolled their eyes as if they were far too mature for flying. Ross couldn't help thinking that it looked fun.

Fiona's mother deposited her back on the ground, straightened her blouse, and left with a wave.

Voske turned to Ross. "Min Soo has offered to give you a tour of the palace."

Min Soo beamed at him. "The tapestries in the ballroom alone are worth an hour's contemplation."

Voske continued, "Or you could accompany Kerry to her tutors. Which lessons are you having today?"

"Public speaking," Kerry said.

Ross would prefer the tapestries—but not Min Soo. Maybe *he* wouldn't have to do any public speaking.

"Or you could explore the town," Voske said. "We want you to see what it has to offer. Think about how you'd like to fit yourself in."

Ross's anger must have showed. Voske's lips twitched, but he opened his hands in a friendly gesture. "Yes, you had a rough start, but you have everything you need to be happy here. Don't worry about the people you left behind. I specifically ordered my scouts not to kill your friends."

Ross thought bitterly, *Am I supposed to be grateful?*

Voske went on, "They fought hard to save you, and their loyalty should not be rewarded with death, don't you think?"

He does expect me to be grateful. Ross wanted to get as far away from Voske as he could, but he forced himself to speak calmly. "I'd like to explore the town."

"You may ride one of the royal mounts." Voske lifted his hand casually to a servant. The man vanished out the door.

Horses were almost as bad as public speaking. "I don't mind walking."

"Gold Point is far too big to walk through," Voske replied. "You have to be back in time for the ceremony."

"How far can I go?"

Voske smiled. "The walls. If you see anything you want in a store, just take it. We know you have nothing to trade. Yet."

A guard escorted Ross outside. There a servant held the bridle of a shimmering silver horse, like a metal statue come to breathing, tail-twitching life. Ross didn't much care for horses, but this was the most beautiful animal he'd ever seen. So that was what Voske had meant by the *royal* mounts. Like the other horses in Gold Point, it had a tail like a cat.

The silver horse tossed its head as he approached, then laid back its ears. Yuki had told Ross that horses did that when they were angry. Hoping that this horse wouldn't be a repeat of Old Betsy, who had walked him into a saguaro on his first ride at Las Anclas, Ross approached cautiously.

He tried to remember Yuki's lessons as he swung up into the saddle. But before he could sit down, a glittering silver tail wrapped around his ankle and tried to yank him down the other side. Ross clutched the saddle.

The servant yelled, "Sally! Stop it!" To Ross, he said, "I'm so sorry, sir. She never does that."

Sir? The guy was his age, but he sounded so anxious that Ross's shoulders tensed. Remembering something Yuki had told him, he said, "She probably knows I don't like riding. It's okay."

He took the reins in his right hand and tried to close his legs around the horse's barrel with a sense of authority. Sally snorted and sidled. He wasn't fooling her any.

Ross tightened his legs. Sally's ears twitched back, then forward. Ross let his breath out as she began to move forward amicably enough. The servant turned away.

Whap! The tail smacked Ross between the shoulder blades. But he'd been expecting something like that. He ignored it.

Sally broke into a trot. Ross picked up the rhythm, settling into the up-and-down. Sally seemed to sense that he was more comfortable, and didn't hit him again.

Though he was alone, he had to assume that Voske was watching him somehow. At the very least, anything he said would surely be reported back.

He'd already seen the heavily guarded main gates when he'd arrived with Greta's kidnap team, but he wanted to see the rest of the walls, and try to sense the singing trees around the ruined city south of Gold Point. But if he rode straight south, Voske would guess he was thinking of climbing the walls.

So he picked a random direction, riding past whitewashed wooden houses with porches and vegetable gardens. Many were bordered by picket fences, all exactly alike. The people seemed ordinary, until they spotted him and gave him a forced smile and a salute. It was as if they knew they were being watched, too. It was eerie.

Ross entered a wide street full of shops and people. A teenager whose skin glowed in patterns like a butterfly's wings stood with his arm around a girl who looked like a Norm. They were eating tacos and chatting with another teenage girl. If she'd worn bangs, they would have hidden her Change, but her clipped hair exposed a ridged forehead like an iguana's back.

No one stared or glared at the Changed teens and their maybe-Norm friend, but the teenagers all stared when they spotted Ross. Then they saluted him, with grins that switched on like electric lights.

Ross wanted to run. But where could he go? He waved awkwardly, then guided Sally across the street. Was everyone acting so weird because he wore the royal colors? Or had some order been sent out in advance? He glanced back. The teens had returned to their conversation, but the butterfly boy spotted his gaze. Dropping his taco, he instantly saluted again. The girls followed.

Ross turned hastily away, trying not to look at anyone. The shop windows were a trader's dream: bales of wool, linen, cotton, and even silk; furniture; leather goods, furs, pots and pans, porcelain and crockery in a vast array of colors; paper goods of all kinds. The only place he'd seen paper for sale in Las Anclas, it was half a shelf at the general store. Here, he saw three shops selling nothing but paper and books.

A stream of kids ran out of a candy shop, sucking lollipops. One had bright orange hair that rippled of its own accord, like the sea anemones in the tide pools at Las Anclas. It took Ross a moment to figure out what was odd about the middle-aged woman who followed them, munching sweets from a paper bag. She walked normally, but her feet hovered several inches above the street.

There seemed to be more Changed people in Gold Point than in Las Anclas—definitely more people with visible Changes. And there wasn't any blatant prejudice against them, or against Norms, either, as far as he could tell. He shifted uncomfortably in the saddle, disliking the idea that anything could be good about Gold Point.

Sally's tail whipped out and smacked him across the ear.

Ross dismounted by a bookshop. The front window held an ancient book, opened to display a colored illustration of a horseless carriage. There was no hitching post, and he wondered what he was supposed to do with Sally.

A soldier hurried out of a dry-goods shop and saluted Ross. "Shall I hold her for you, sir?" the woman asked.

Ross's neck tightened at the word *sir*. "Sure. Thanks."

As he surrendered the reins, he became aware of every single person on the street watching him. Smiling. The soldiers saluted him. The back of his neck crawled.

He usually avoided fancy shops—the shopkeepers always eyed him like they expected him to steal something—but he had to get away from all those smiles. He hurried into the bookshop.

An old man with a pair of feathery antennae stood behind the counter, talking to a customer. Then Ross entered and everyone fell silent, even the customers who'd been chatting with each other.

The old shopkeeper bustled forward. "May I help you, sir?"

Ross edged up to the book in the front window. "Just looking."

The man carefully lifted the fragile book. "It's yours, sir. Shall I wrap it up for you?"

Ross backed away. "No!"

The old man's antennae twitched in dismay. "There's no charge. It would be an honor for you to have it. Or any other books you might want."

Ross knew the value of that book. And Jennie would love it. But tempting as it was, he didn't want to be beholden to Voske. Besides, the bookseller obviously had no choice. It might as well be armed robbery.

"No, thanks. I—I don't have anywhere to put it." Ross fled the store before the man could push the book into his hands.

The soldier waiting with Sally saluted him again. The passersby froze again, staring and then giving him those awful fake smiles. Ross ducked into an alley, then another, until he spotted a park with concealing shrubbery.

He plunged into a ring of tall bushes. To his relief, no one else was there. He sank down on a wooden bench beside a dry fountain. His vision was swimming— no, patches of the ground actually were blurry green spots instead of real grass. Ross smiled. The patches were too small to conceal rabbit burrows, so they must be gopher illusions.

Sure enough, a few fat gophers popped out and scampered right up to him, then sat up and begged. They seemed completely tame, like the rats in Las Anclas.

"Sorry." Ross held out his empty hands. "I don't have any food for you."

The gophers looked up hopefully at him, noses twitching.

"Next time, okay?"

They waited a while, then gave up and trundled back into their hidden homes.

Ross took a deep breath. It felt good to be alone. No mysterious shadows crept along the bushes, and all he saw overhead were tree branches, rustling with nothing but the breeze, and a few hawks making lazy circles in the sky.

He wondered how far Voske's spy thing reached, and whether the king was using the artifact Min Soo had mentioned, or the invisible son that Ross had heard rumors of before he'd come to Las Anclas. Or both. Whatever it was, the king couldn't possibly watch everyone, all the time, in all situations, or he wouldn't have time to do anything else.

On the other hand, Voske had known when Las Anclas was holding a dance, and when Ross planned to visit the ruined city. But he hadn't known that Ross's singing tree even existed, or he wouldn't have sent his men right past it at the end of the battle.

Maybe the mystery artifact couldn't see, but could only hear voices.

One thing Ross was sure of: it couldn't see in the dark.

Ross forced himself to return to the main street. He thanked the soldier waiting patiently with Sally. The woman saluted again. When Ross mounted Sally, she made a grab for his ankle. This time he was ready for it, and simply reached down and unhooked her tail.

They ambled down the street, then followed a canal into farmland, until they came within sight of the town wall, topped by marching sentries. Beyond the walls, mountains loomed, bisected by a deep valley.

At the top of the V, he could barely make out the dam Kerry had mentioned, surrounded by tiny twinkles of light. Gold Point's main power source! Those glints of light had to be sentries with field glasses, sweeping constantly.

Ross was within sight of two sentry towers, both decorated with a pair of gleaming white skulls. Wishing he hadn't seen those, he rode up a hill. Let the sentries watch him tie the reins to a tree branch and sit on the grass.

He closed his eyes and reached out with his mind, searching for singing trees. At first he saw nothing but the red glare of sunlight against his eyelids, and heard nothing but bird calls and the rustle of leaves. Then chimes began to tinkle and ring. A forest of singing trees grew in the distance, too far for him to catch more than a sense of their presence. But five trees grew closer, their music bright and clear in his mind.

Five singing trees in a clump near Gold Point. That was odd. Ross decided to take a quick look. It was the deeper memories that were dangerous. He made sure the wall in his mind was secure, then cracked open the door.

He saw Voske's face.

The image was as vivid as if the man were standing over Ross. Then the color shifted to red, the image blurred, and Voske became a silhouette of heat, seen as a crystal tree sees. The image repeated from slightly different perspectives, four more times. Voske had been present at the birth of each one of those trees.

Ross had to know what happened. He'd risk a peek into the last memory of one tree. Bracing himself, he opened the door in his mind a little wider.

I'd been so sure it would work for me. The surgeon was standing right there, holding my hand, scalpel ready.

The dying woman stared down at her arm. The bone within had turned to scarlet crystal.

Ross tried to stay clear of the pain of her last moments, and only hear her thoughts and see what she had seen. She was picturing the moment when she'd raised her hand and volunteered, and wishing she could take it back. She looked up at the sun, which splintered into a thousand facets of liquid light. The whole sky turned to brilliant crimson before pain overwhelmed her.

Ross had to get out before he fell any farther into memories. He couldn't breathe or see or feel the ground beneath his feet. Then he brushed up against the cool steel of the door in his mind. He threw himself through, and slammed it behind him.

He looked up, gasping for breath. The sun dazzled his eyes, which were blurred with tears. He rubbed his hand across his face. His cheeks were wet.

As his vision cleared, he saw that he was surrounded by soldiers. Ross stared in horror. They knew!

One of them laughed, but another punched him in the arm. The laughing man instantly sobered.

They had no idea what he'd been doing. They must have thought he was sitting there feeling sorry for himself. The captain saluted Ross as he defiantly scrubbed his crimson sleeve across his eyes. They could believe whatever they wanted, as long as they didn't know the truth.

"We were afraid you were lost, sir," said the captain. "We've come to escort you back to the palace."

Ross had a splitting headache, and his legs wobbled as he stood up. He wished he had Dr. Lee's headache elixir. More than that, he wished he was back in Las Anclas with Mia. He imagined her arms around him, holding him tight…

"Do you need help mounting, sir?"

Ross gritted his teeth and hauled himself onto Sally, hoping she wouldn't try to unseat him. He'd probably fall off if she did. She flattened her ears, but the captain gave her a warning smack on the nose before she could try anything.

As they rode past the garrison, he wondered how many people knew about Voske's experiments.

The parade ground in front of the palace had been transformed. A platform had been erected in the center, with a table holding the objects Santiago had described. The royal family sat on a dais at the palace terrace, their table set with golden dishes. Decorated tables were scattered around the perimeter, occupied by people in fine clothes. The scene reminded Ross of the dance at Las Anclas, when Jennie had worn that tight red dress. Here, only the royal family—and Ross—wore red.

Kerry ran to Ross's stirrup. "Did you have a good ride? I love Sally."

Ross slid down, trying not to lean against Sally for support. She'd bite him for sure. Sally gave him what he could swear was a contemptuous glance, then nuzzled Kerry.

Kerry's smile vanished as she inspected him more closely. "Are you all right?"

"I'm fine."

As Ross slumped reluctantly at Voske's right hand, he thought grimly, *He can kill me, but he can't make me do anything.*

A servant piled pork ribs and gravy-drenched mashed potatoes on his plate. The sight and smell ought to be tempting. But he already felt sick, and that made it worse. He edged his chair back.

Voske was watching him. "Drink up, Ross. Something cold will do you good."

A golden goblet stood by Ross's golden plate. He picked it up. The cold metal sides were beaded with moisture. He had never seen so much gold in his life, much less touched it. But all he wanted to do was press it against his forehead. The liquid inside smelled like strong alcohol. He put the goblet down. The last thing he needed was to have his reflexes slowed and his mind clouded.

Kerry spoke softly to a hovering servant. A few minutes later, a mug was placed before him, and a familiar, astringent scent wafted up.

She nudged the cup toward his hand. "You rode too long in the sun, didn't you? It's so tempting to do that with Sally. She rides like a dream. Have some willow bark tea. It'll make you feel better."

Ross sipped the bitter brew gratefully, not minding the heat, and soon his headache lessened. But he couldn't stop picturing bones turning to scarlet crystal. His gauntlet weighed on his left arm, and the scar pulled and ached.

Voske's voice made him jump. "Not hungry yet? Take a walk with me. It'll wake up your appetite."

Ross followed Voske into the throne room. It was much cooler than the terrace, which had been baking in the late-afternoon sun.

"Let me make sure you're prepared for Opportunity Day." Voske leaned against the white marble throne like a black-clad silhouette, the light glinting in his silver hair and on the silver belt buckle at his waist. He wore no weapons that Ross could see, and he stood a bare step outside of Ross's striking range.

Ross ground his teeth. Voske was *deliberately* out of range. The man thought like a fighter, he moved like a fighter, he gauged distance like a fighter. By the time Ross could close with him, he'd have shouted for his guards. They'd pull Ross off before he could do more than bruise the king, and then Voske would have his head chopped off.

The king eyed Ross knowingly, then smiled. That same watchful expression, that same expectant smile, had been the last thing that five people had seen before they died. Voske's face dissolved into a heat image.

"Ross, this is important," Voske said. "Are you listening?"

Alarm flashed through Ross. "Yes."

Voske lifted a casual hand as if that unspoken exchange had never taken place. "You heard what happens when Opportunity Day goes well: a candidate gets a power, even if it's not quite the one they wanted. Sometimes they don't have the potential to Change, and nothing happens. But we hold Opportunity Day every month, and about once or twice per year it doesn't go well."

Was this how Voske meant to threaten or bribe him?

"I'm already Changed," Ross said. "You can't Change twice."

Mia and Dr. Lee thought his ability to communicate with singing trees wasn't a true Change, but maybe Voske didn't know that.

Voske laughed. "I wasn't going to ask you to volunteer. You already have an extremely valuable Change. Your role in this will be different. As I was saying, sometimes it doesn't go well. We don't know why, but every now and then, a candidate dies. The family still gets the volunteer reward, plus compensation, but it can be quite a shock."

Ross blurted out, "People die twice a year, and you still do it?"

"The risk is worth it. Many more people die in battle."

Ross didn't think that dying in one of Voske's battles, invading some other town, was any better.

"I've chosen you for a particular honor," Voske said. "As I told you, each Opportunity Day, five candidates are presented. Usually we draw straws, but today, you will choose the candidate."

"I won't do it." Every muscle in Ross's body tensed.

Voske's gaze was unsurprised. "Normally, the candidates who weren't selected go back home and are exempt forever after. But if you don't pick one, all five of them will go through it. It's up to you."

Ross stared at that smiling face, sick with anger.

"Why don't you take a stroll around the ground?" Voske went on. "Get to know them. Make an informed choice." He straightened up, still out of striking range. And still smiling. "But you will choose."

Ross almost ran Kerry down as he rushed outside.

"I'll introduce you to the candidates," she said.

"You knew," he said bitterly, following her. "You knew he was going to do that."

"You don't want to choose?" She watched him like her father had watched the dying woman, like she was curious to see what would happen. "Don't you feel powerful?"

In his entire life, Ross had never felt more powerless.

When he didn't reply, Kerry went on, "It'll be interesting to see how you do. Only one of my picks Changed, and it was nothing special. What's the use of levitating three inches off the ground? She got stuck like that, too—never did learn to control it. But maybe you'll have better luck."

He couldn't believe that Kerry simply didn't care. She didn't even seem to understand why anyone would. "Did you think it was bad luck when your father killed five people with crystal shards?"

Kerry stopped short. "What are you talking about?"

"Five people. Five trees. On a hill south of your city walls."

"No, those grew from a coyote pack." She seemed to believe it.

He yanked up his sleeve, pulled off his gauntlet, and showed her the scar that ran the length of his forearm. "I was hit by a single shard, and I cut it out before it could kill me. That's how I got my power. Your father tried to give my power to five people, but they didn't get the shards out in time. They all died." He caught his breath, remembering the stabbing pain of crystal twining around bone. "In agony."

"Who told you that story?" she demanded.

Ross knew he should keep quiet, but he couldn't help himself. "Nobody told me. I saw it. That's part of my power."

"You're lying. Nobody would do that."

"Five people must be missing. Three men and two women." He thought back to the flood of memories he'd received. Everything those people had thought of as they were dying had been imprinted into the trees that grew from their bodies. "There was a Changed woman. She could make plants grow. She had a toddler." He thought again. "A son. With dark hair."

Ross watched Kerry's face closely. When he mentioned the woman's Change, her lips twitched.

"She died on patrol." Kerry sounded angry. "Come on. You have to meet the candidates."

Ten people sat at the richly decorated table, five dressed in white, and others in colors. As Kerry approached, nine of them stood and saluted. One of those dressed in white sat head down on the table, sobbing, as an older woman in blue tried to console the dark-haired figure.

Ross thought, *Not that one.*

As Kerry introduced the candidates, Ross tried to figure out how to decide between the four others. He supposed he should pick the one who looked toughest, best able to survive whatever would happen.

"I'll leave you to get acquainted," Kerry said icily.

She walked away, leaving Ross with the candidates and their companions: loved ones, Kerry had said.

Ross cleared his throat. "Please. Sit down." He dropped into a chair, his knees watery.

The candidate nearest to him was a woman with a gray braid that fell to her hips. She looked tough, come to think of it. Actually, she reminded him of his grandmother.

He couldn't pick her.

Ross felt sick. He'd left the throne room certain that he wouldn't cooperate, and here he was, deciding people's fates. He couldn't let all of them risk death.

He looked past the old man sitting with the grandmother to the next candidate, a woman in her mid-thirties cuddled up with another woman of the same age. They wore steel wedding rings. The candidate was thin and pale, with a drawn look to her face, as if she was recovering from some illness. Her wife had her fists clenched, almost vibrating with fury, and wouldn't meet Ross's eyes. Ross wished he could tell her she had nothing to worry about. There was no way he'd choose anyone who looked that fragile.

The remaining candidates were his age. Luis, the boy, was tall and muscular. He wore white, but he bore himself like a soldier. The strong-looking girl with him, who had her hand on his thigh, wore a military uniform.

Andrea, the other candidate, sat with her identical twin. Both were plain and weedy, with long sand-colored braids, and they held hands so tightly that their knuckles were blotched red and white.

"Did you come from the coast, Ross?" Luis asked. "What's the ocean like?"

"Big," Ross said. "Really big. Blue all the way to the horizon. In all directions."

"That sounds spooky," Andrea said. She tossed her head so her sandy braids flapped; she was trying hard to sound brave. Her twin giggled, a high, nervous sound.

"I think it sounds cool," Luis said. "Though I'm not sure I want to try being in a boat." He laughed. "I've never even seen a boat."

His girlfriend gave him a smacking kiss, then said, "And you never will, if I have my way. I was in a rowboat once. I've never been so sick in my life!" She stroked the back of his neck, and he twined his arm tightly around her waist.

Ross couldn't decide between Luis and Andrea. Would it be worse if something terrible happened to your lover or your twin? He ground his teeth, hating Voske for forcing him to make that decision.

"Did you guys volunteer, or were you—" *Forced?* "Picked?" Ross asked.

There was total silence. Even the head-down candidate stopped sobbing.

Luis's girlfriend said quickly, "It's an honor to win the lottery. Especially if you're in the army. Even if you don't get a good power, or any power, you've shown courage in front of *him*." She touched two fingers to the hair at her temple in an odd, ritualistic gesture.

Luis made a forced shrug. "If I do get chosen, I should get a good power. My grandmother could lift little objects, and one of my uncles can predict the weather. They're not spectacular powers, but they're useful."

Andrea's twin said, "The only person in our family who ever Changed was our aunt Julia, when she got pregnant. Her hearing got so sharp that she could hear conversations three blocks away. Everyone had to tiptoe around the house, because any noise louder than a whisper gave her terrible headaches. Then she died in childbirth."

"Shh, Amber! Don't talk about that." Andrea added mechanically, "It's an honor to be chosen."

"An honor," her twin agreed, bobbing her head so vehemently that Ross's skin crawled.

A flicker of white and red approached. It was Min Soo, walking at a stately pace.

She stepped onto the platform, then gestured toward the candidates' table, her long sleeves fluttering. "Who has the honor of being chosen?"

Ross wanted to shout, "I won't do it!"

Voske smiled straight at Ross. It was a cool smile, with no mercy in it. Ross knew Voske meant what he'd said. If Ross didn't choose one, all five would have to take the risk.

It hurt Ross, how fearfully everyone watched him. He wanted to explain, to apologize, but the words couldn't get past his throat.

"Luis," he said.

Luis met his eyes. He was scared. But he was going to try to look brave. Ross could feel it as if the thoughts were his own. Luis kissed his girlfriend. Their hands tightened, then dropped.

"It's okay," Luis whispered as he passed Ross. "You had to pick someone, and I'm the toughest."

Then he marched to the platform and leaped up.

The crowd cheered. Luis held up his arms, turning in a circle. The shrill cheers of the little princes and princesses rose up, then died away as a military band began a drum roll.

Min Soo had her palms pressed together. She pulled them apart in a slow, ritual gesture, then held them out to Luis, palms up. He laid his hands on hers, and she gripped them.

Ross closed his eyes, hoping that the absolute worst that would happen would be an unimpressive Change that people would tease Luis about later.

A shriek of pain shocked his eyes open. Min Soo jerked her hands away, her fingers splayed apart. Blood ran down from her palms. Everywhere she had touched Luis, her skin had been ripped away.

She swayed. Luis moved to catch her, but she backed away, screaming, "Don't touch me!"

Luis stared from her to his blood-stained palms. He wiped them down his white shirt, leaving red smears. His own hands were unharmed.

Voske vaulted past Luis and caught Min Soo, then settled her down on the platform. "Where's the surgeon?"

"Right here, your majesty," an older man called, pushing through the gathering crowd.

Ross recognized the man from the memories of the five trees. Looking from Voske to the surgeon, to Min Soo's bleeding hands and the growing terror on Luis's face, Ross felt as if he was trapped in a nightmare.

Soldiers started waving the crowd away. Luis's girlfriend tried to dodge around them, yelling, "Let me through! Let me go to Luis!"

Voske gestured to the soldiers to let her pass. She leaped up on the stage.

"Wait," Voske ordered. "Luis, don't move. You should be able to control this, like Min Soo controls her power. Remember how it felt a moment ago, and don't do that. Concentrate on not hurting her."

Luis slowly stretched out his hand, his brow tense, his fingers trembling.

"Careful, Sophie. I don't know if I can…"

Sophie glanced at Min Soo, who was being bandaged, then stepped firmly up to Luis, holding out her own hands. "I'm not afraid. I know you won't hurt me, Luis." But her voice was quick and tight, and Ross knew she was as scared as he felt.

Voske spoke quickly. "Not like that. Sophie, touch his cheek."

Sophie stepped confidently forward and brushed two fingers over Luis's cheek. She jumped back with a yelp. Blood dripped from her fingertips.

Luis closed his eyes.

Guards led Luis toward the palace, careful not to touch him. Sophie was escorted off in another direction. Ross heard a sob, quickly muffled.

Voske stepped down and joined Ross. "Well done, Ross. Very well done."

Ross stared at him in horror. "I ruined his life."

Voske glanced after Luis. "It'll take some getting used to, but that is a very valuable power. Even if he never does learn to control it, can you imagine how terrifying he'd be in battle?"

A dizzying rage rose up in Ross. Voske was standing close enough that if Ross moved fast and caught him unaware, he just might be able to kill Voske with his bare hands before anyone could stop him.

The nearest soldiers stepped forward, weapons raised.

Voske held out a hand to halt them, his stance easy but ready. Ross breathed out. His chance was gone—if he'd ever had one.

"Go to your room and get some rest. Take another ride tomorrow. Clear your head." Voske gave Ross another of those cool, deliberate smiles. Ross's skin crept at his next words. "But next time, take some bread for the gophers. You should always keep your promises."

CHAPTER SIXTEEN
LAS ANCLAS
MIA

Dad always told Mia that cooking was scientific. If you do each step in an experiment in the same order and the same way, the results are always the same, no matter who conducts the experiment. So if Mia followed Grandma's dumpling recipe exactly, it should produce dumplings exactly like Grandma's.

Mia peered at the crumpled, grubby paper. Step fourteen: add a quarter cup of cream, beating at a medium speed. Mia hoped one-fourth was right. It had been hard to get Grandma to be more specific than "a dollop" and "beat it."

Mia poured the cream into the bubbling sauce, and began to beat at a medium speed. Whatever "medium" meant. The sauce broke into disgusting lumps floating in a nasty liquid. Mia beat harder, trying to squish the lumps. The sauce sprayed up, as if in revenge, splattering her glasses and stinging her face. Mia jumped back with a yelp, and her whisk caught the handle of the pan and flipped it off the stove.

Dad opened the door, then skidded back from the wave of curdled glop. "What is that? Or should I say, what was that?"

Mia groaned. "It was supposed to be Grandma's cream sauce for dumplings."

Dad gave a doctorly prod to the plate of objects the size, color, and consistency of rocks. "May I ask what inspired this?"

"I thought learning something new might take my mind off things," Mia said glumly. "I will never again make fun of anything you cook, I swear. Even if it's avocado-flavored vinegar-soaked oatmeal."

"Ugh." Dad tipped the petrified dumplings into the compost bucket. "Some experiments are too cruel to contemplate. Let's eat at Jack's. I know you've been training hard. You need to feed those new muscles."

Mia prodded her bicep with her forefinger. Was the weight-lifting paying off? "I don't just want to be stronger, though. I want to fight better."

"If you want to improve your skills at anything, you have to practice."

He had a point. Mia needed someone to fight with. Someone who wouldn't make fun of her. Ideally, someone her own size…

"I'll be right back." Mia swept the glop-soaked rags into the laundry bin. "Actually, don't wait for me. Say hi to Anna-Lucia!"

Mia didn't stop running until she arrived at the Lowensteins' house. There she counted her pants per minute, hoping they'd be fewer than the last time she'd run that distance. Instead, she counted three gasps *more* than her usual average.

Still, she'd only been training for two weeks. If Jennie were here, she could tell Mia how long she'd need to exercise before she saw consistent, measurable results.

Jennie and her team would reach Gold Point tomorrow night, if they hadn't been delayed on the way. Tomorrow night, they might set Ross free!

Or the bounty hunter might kill him.

No, Jennie would stop him. But what if Jennie had to kill the bounty hunter to save Ross? What was Voske *doing* with Ross? Was he torturing him? Had he killed Ross and stuck his head on a pole? What if Ross escaped, with the entire Gold Point army after him, and then Jennie's team missed him and ran into the army?

Mia's thoughts ricocheted around her mind like a swarm of trapped, angry bees. She flung open the Lowensteins' door. Meredith and her mother sat at the kitchen table, two coppery heads lit by the slanting rays of the westering sun. They looked up in surprise.

"I forgot to knock," Mia explained. "I mean, hi!"

Ms. Lowenstein indicated a noodle casserole. "Have you had dinner?"

"It's on the floor." Mia wiped the sweat off her glasses, then replaced them just in time to catch the mother and daughter exchanging puzzled looks. "Meredith, can I talk to you? I need some help."

"Sure. An explosion?" Meredith asked hopefully.

Ms. Lowenstein picked up her plate. "I'm going to eat on the porch. It might be cooler. But girls. Much as I'd love to see Preston's house blow up and give him something other than drilling to occupy his time, promise me that at least no one will be inside it."

Mia raised her hand, palm out. "I swear."

The door closed, leaving Mia with Meredith. Mia instantly felt awkward. Meredith was Jennie's friend, not hers. She'd always liked Meredith, but they hadn't been alone together since they were ten. The explanation she'd planned went out of her head.

Meredith broke. "Did you want to go look for your flame thrower?"

"No, it's about me. I mean, about me and you."

Meredith stared at her.

That had come out all wrong. Mia hastily continued, "You've always been so good at physical things, especially shooting, but really, everything. And I'm not, except for shooting, a little bit. I never cared before, but I do now, so what I was wondering was…would you mind training with me? When you're not with the Rangers?"

"Sure, I'm always up for more training. But a group is better than two." Meredith tapped her spoon on the table. "I'll ask Paco. He's been great in Ranger training. Jose, too. Yolanda is too young to be a Ranger candidate, but she's pretty good. And she's just your size."

"She's your size, too."

"Oh yeah," Meredith said. "I always forget."

Mia wondered what it would be like to not even see yourself as small. Was that why Meredith was so confident? Or did she not see herself as small *because* she was confident? If Mia started imagining that she was Jennie's size, would she—

Meredith snapped her fingers. "I know! I've got one more person. I'm not sure if she'll be interested. We used to not get along. But she's been serious about Ranger training, she's good enough to challenge me, and if we could practice on her family's land, no one would bother us. Okay. I'll ask Sujata."

*

Dry leaves rustled in the Vardams' orchard. The last time Mia had been there—

"Oh no," she breathed.

Months ago, she'd made a deal with Mr. and Mrs. Vardam to keep the raccoons out of the water supply. Then Voske had attacked, and Mr. Vardam had been killed. Mia had forgotten all about the raccoons. But the raccoons hadn't forgotten about the water. They'd once again dug a canal to divert the Vardams' stream into their little city. Mia mentally reorganized her schedule for the next day.

Everyone Meredith had mentioned was there, with the exception of Paco and a surprising addition. If anyone liked training less than Mia, it was shy Becky Callahan. But there she was, shrinking behind Sujata as if trying to hide, her pale hair lifting in the hot breeze.

"Becky wants to be in the group," Sujata announced, stepping aside.

Meredith raised her eyebrows at Becky. "You realize that you'll have to hit things."

Becky looked horrified at the thought. Meredith's red eyebrows went even higher.

"Tell Meredith why you're here," Sujata prompted.

Becky indicated the pink ribbon tied around her wrist. "My mom wants me to stop dating Brisa. She was okay with Brisa being Changed when Brisa was a friend of Felicité's. But after the battle, Felicité called Changed people monsters, and she and Brisa stopped talking. Then Mom said I wasn't allowed to date, um—" Becky glanced nervously at Yolanda and Jose, and mumbled, "She called them mutants."

Meredith snorted. "Your mother would let you date a girl with three heads if her parents were rich enough, and lived on the Hill."

Becky nodded sadly, cradling her ribboned wrist against her. "Mom said I had to take off Brisa's ribbon. And I wouldn't. Every time she sees me, she starts yelling at me. I just want to get out of the house."

Meredith patted her shoulder. "You're in. Let's stretch."

Mia automatically started for the back of the group. But Meredith arranged them in a circle, where everyone could see exactly how clumsy Mia was.

Meredith dropped into a runner's lunge. "Left foot forward."

Mia hastily got into position, only to hear Meredith say, "Other left, Mia."

Her face burning, Mia quickly switched feet. She couldn't believe she'd managed to mess up *stretching*. Even six-year-olds could stretch. Three stretches later, Mia again heard, "Mia! Other right."

When Meredith finally had everyone stand up, Mia was briefly relieved. Until Meredith brought out the punching pads. Mia skittered over to pair up with Becky, who probably wouldn't hit her too hard.

"Oh, no, you don't." Meredith grabbed her wrist. "Becky, you're with Yolanda. Mia, you're with me."

Mia backed away. "You'll knock me over the town wall!"

Jose and Sujata laughed.

"If you have a good stance, Sheriff Crow couldn't knock you down." Meredith sounded irritated.

In a panic, Mia couldn't even remember what a stance was, let alone a good one. She planted her feet firmly into the ground. Meredith gently kicked at one of Mia's ankles. "A front stance, Mia. Left foot back."

Mia looked helplessly at her feet. Was her left the one that worked the treadmill? It was so hard to remember which was which when she used both her hands interchangeably. She never thought about left and right in her workshop.

"Other left, Mia." Meredith sighed.

"Sorry. Sorry." Mia was already regretting her 'bright idea.'

"Am I annoying you? Get some revenge! Hit me as hard as you like!" Meredith swung one leg back like she always knew which was which, and held the pad close to her chest. "Punch!"

Mia flung out her fist as hard as she could. Pain shot up her forearm, but Meredith didn't even blink.

"Ow!" Mia exclaimed, wringing her fingers.

"Keep your wrist straight." Meredith adjusted Mia's arm like she was a doll. "See? Forearm level with the first two knuckles. Try again."

Meredith proceeded to criticize the angle of her elbow, the proximity of her elbow to her side, the angle of her knuckles, and the motion of her hips. About the only thing Mia seemed to be moving right was her nose. And if they'd done one more drill, Meredith probably would have criticized that, too.

Every muscle in her body ached when Meredith said, "Take a water break. Then we'll spar."

Mia shakily slurped down two cups of water. All the skin had been knocked off her knuckles. Meredith, Jose, Sujata, and Yolanda looked refreshed and cheerful. Becky's lips were trembling as if she was about to cry, which was how Mia felt.

"Sorry I'm late," came a new voice.

"Paco!" Meredith exclaimed. "Perfect timing. We're about to start sparring. Let's give them a demo, then we'll pair everyone up."

He and Meredith squared off, Meredith bouncing lightly, full of energy. Cloth popped as they struck and kicked, beads of sweat flying off them. Mia couldn't believe how happy they looked. At least, Meredith looked happy. Paco looked...*intense.*

Mia could train every day for the rest of her life, and never be anywhere near as good as either of them. She could train every day for the rest of her life, and never be any good at all. She'd drilled thousands of times, and she still couldn't keep her wrist straight.

What had she imagined, anyway? That if she trained hard enough, it would magically bring Ross back? That if he did come back and she could fight, she'd never let him down again? That she'd be like Jennie, strong and trusted— and trustworthy?

Ross was gone. She'd already let him down. No one had even considered sending Mia with Jennie to rescue him, because Mia would have been nothing but a useless piece of luggage. All the training in the world couldn't change the past. It wouldn't change the future, either. Terrible things could be happening to Ross and Jennie right now, and Mia was completely powerless to help them.

With all her strength, she hit out at the punching post Meredith had set up. And missed.

CHAPTER SEVENTEEN
GOLD POINT
KERRY

Kerry loved having breakfast with her father, just the two of them, in his private dining room of polished oak, golden and mellow and easy on her eyes, unlike Min Soo's headache-inducing pink.

She glanced out the window as she sipped her coffee. The trees were bare, so she could see the guest house where they'd put Luis. She wondered if he'd learned to control his power yet.

Father opened the door. "Good morning, darling. Sorry I'm late." Over his shoulder, he said, "Let's fall back to the inner perimeter. We can safely assume that no one is coming from Las Anclas to disturb our guest. I want South Company Three pulled off patrol and sent to reinforce Captain Flores at Lake Perris."

He shut the door on the aide-de-camp and sat across from Kerry. "I hope the pancakes are still hot."

"They are," Kerry said. "Did you send Pru to check on Lake Perris?"

"Yes, she left last night on 'a prospecting expedition.'" Father picked up his coffee mug. "I gather our guest is still sulking in his room?"

"After three days, I was sure he'd be hungry enough to come out. I knocked on my way here, but he wouldn't even answer."

Father helped himself to the crispy hash browns. "What's the next step?"

Kerry put down her cup. "We can't let him sit in there until he starves —he's only useful if he's alive. If we wait too long, he might figure that out and try to bargain with us."

Father smiled. "We will not permit him to build a citadel within our citadel. He must come out and engage with the world. That is your job this morning, Kerry. Bring him out, make him eat something, and get him ready to ride out with us to the ruined city. I'll be waiting at the garrison at seven o'clock."

Kerry could tell that Father was annoyed, though it was difficult to say how she knew. He rarely got angry, but when he did, he didn't stamp or curse or yell. If anything, his voice got softer. Maybe that was it: his voice was too soft.

She finished her breakfast as fast as she could without letting Father see that she was rushing. It was hard to be around him when he was angry, even though he barely showed it. It was as if he had a force field like the ones she could make, only his could kill with a touch.

"See you at seven," she said, trying to sound confident and in control. "With Ross."

She headed to Deirdre's room and knocked on the door. "Ross?"

No answer.

"Ross, I need to talk to you." It was humiliating to have to shout through the door at a *prisoner*. If Ross made her walk in, he would have won this small battle of wills. And the guards would see her lose.

She knocked once more. "If you don't answer, I'm coming in."

No answer. In three days, there had never been any answer. Fine. She'd let him win this battle. Once she got inside, she'd win the war.

Kerry went in.

Ross sat in a corner, his head resting on his knees, his face hidden. She wondered if it would seem more powerful to stand over him, as if he were a child, or if she should sit on the bed, as if she didn't particularly care about the outcome. She decided to loom.

"Ross, you've got to eat something. You must be starving."

He didn't move.

He'd cooperated, more or less, till Min Soo had Changed Luis. Sure, it had been bloody, even frightening. But nothing had happened to warrant shutting himself in a room for days, refusing to eat or speak. It seemed cowardly. Weak.

She'd seen how frightened he was of enclosed spaces, and heard the patrol captain's report about him crying by himself beside the wall. Yet he'd escaped the scout team and evaded them all day, alone in the desert. Blind! He'd fought at Las Anclas, and used his Change power to kill thirty of Father's elite soldiers. When she'd sparred with him, he'd seemed fearless. Disabled hand and all, Ross was a better fighter than Santiago, and Santiago had won division medals.

Father said that the key to true power was understanding other people. How could she exert true power over someone she didn't understand?

She'd start with basic power: the threat of force. "You have to come out sometime. It may as well be now. Do you want to sit here, starving, for three more days, and then be dragged out and forced to eat?"

His right hand clenched, just enough to whiten his knuckles. Ah. Threats were good.

"Three things are going to happen," Kerry said. "You are going to get up. You are going to eat breakfast. And you are going to ride with Father and me to the ruined city."

"No, I won't." He was barely audible.

"Yes, you will," Kerry said. "It's happening whether you cooperate or not. If you won't get up, I'll have the guards drag you up. If you won't eat, they'll pin you down and cram food down your throat. And if you won't ride by yourself, they'll tie you up and throw you over the horse."

"Let them."

She could hear the effort it took for him to speak, and felt defeated by him again. He'd maneuvered her into making threats that she didn't want to carry out. Before he'd made those ridiculous accusations about Father turning people into singing trees, she'd liked Ross a bit. He was a great sparring partner. In a way, she even respected him for sticking it out for three days.

But Father had given her orders.

She crouched down. "You're not the first person to try this. I was serious about the force-feeding. It's painful and humiliating. And dangerous. You could choke. But Father told me to have you ready by seven, and it's already after six."

She sat on the bed, which didn't seem to have been slept in. She counted slowly to three, then to five. Then she sighed aloud and stood, making sure the bed springs squeaked. If that didn't get him, she'd call the guards.

Ross dropped his hands to the floor and lifted his head.

He looked awful, ashen and drawn. She'd won, but it wasn't the satisfying victory she'd expected. It was more of a relief.

"We've got scrambled eggs," she said. "I know you like those."

"If you eat rich food after you've had nothing in days, it makes you sick. I'll just have some bread." Ross was obviously speaking from past experience. Kerry didn't know why, but that made her feel off-balance, as if she'd missed a step in the dark.

She escorted him to the royal dining room, where he took a piece of toast. She slid some bacon on to his plate, but he ignored it and her. As he slowly ate half a piece of toast, she couldn't help wondering how often he'd gone without food for days on end. She felt vaguely guilty, which made no sense. *She* hadn't starved him; she was trying to get him to eat.

The uncomfortable sense that she'd stepped wrong turned to triumph when he took one bite of bacon. She could barely see his downcast face, but his color looked a bit better.

I won, she repeated to herself. *I'm stronger than Ross. It's exactly like Father said.*

As they headed outside, she racked her mind for something, anything to talk about. Nothing came to mind.

To her immense relief, Santiago was waiting. "Hi, Kerry. Hi, Ross."

"Morning, Santiago." Kerry wished she could steal a kiss. But it seemed best to keep Ross between them. "How's the collarbone?"

"Oh, it's fine," Santiago said absently, as they headed for the palace garrison. His attention was fixed on Ross. "I'm still on liberty, but the sling comes off next week. Not a moment too soon! Yesterday I made the mistake of telling my mother I was bored, so she put me in charge of the Brat Patrol."

"No!" Kerry said, laughing. Now that Santiago was here she could at least pretend Ross was part of the conversation. "The Brat Patrol is what we call Santiago's cousins, baby brother and sister, and nephews and nieces. There's seven of them under the age of six, so they're not in school yet."

"They're underfoot." Santiago pretended to shake a little kid off his leg. "My baby cousin, Maria-Elena, decided to make a mud pie. Which would have been fine, except she took out the bread out of the oven while it was still doughy and substituted the pie...."

At the palace garrison, guards readied the horses, checking cinches and bridles and packs. Her father's silver hair shone in the crowd.

The guards backed away, saluting Kerry. She smiled at them. Min Soo harped far too much on politeness, but she was right that if you were pleasant to the people you ruled, they went away happy. A glance at Father made it clear he had seen and appreciated. She basked in his approval.

He took out his gold pocket watch, clicked it open, and smiled. "Six forty-six. Excellent." He turned his smile to the boys. "Good morning, Ross."

Ross's shoulders jerked up and his head dropped. Kerry wanted to smack him. That wasn't how you acted around a king.

"Ross, if you're that unhappy, tell me what we can do to improve your stay." Father said gently. "Is it loneliness that troubles you? I'd be happy to send a team to fetch your girlfriend."

Why didn't I think of that? Kerry thought.

Rather than looking gratified, Ross stiffened as if Kerry had jabbed him with one of her invisible knives. Steel scraped as he clenched his left hand, and his knuckles paled at his right.

"I don't have a girlfriend," he told the ground.

"We'll have to find you one, then," Father said, laughing. "Mount up." He swung onto Coronet, his magnificent silver stallion.

Kerry mounted her own stallion, Nugget. He tossed his head, sending his glittering mane flying, like strands of spun gold. She hoped he wasn't in one of his ornery moods. That was the trouble with stallions: you kept having to remind them who was in charge. But he settled down when she stroked his neck.

"I picked Sally for you," Santiago said to Ross. "You seemed to get along with her. My Aunt Maria-Luisa bred her. She let me watch the birth —well, it wasn't so much that I wanted to watch, as she needed someone to fetch buckets of hot water. But it's pretty amazing to watch a foal take its first breath, and to hear it and its mother whicker at each other."

Though Santiago was presumably talking to Ross, he wasn't watching him. Instead, he glanced toward Father as if to say, 'Am I doing it right?'

Father nodded in approval, then rode past to take his position at the head of the column. Santiago rode up beside Ross, leaving Kerry behind. With no introduction whatsoever, Santiago launched into a long tale about the time Bankar had carved soap and coated it in sugar, then swapped it for real sugar skulls on Day of the Dead. Santiago's younger brother Diego had retaliated by filling her sleeping bag with slugs on a class overnight trip…back when they were all ten and eleven.

Father had clearly ordered Santiago to befriend Ross, but Santiago was trying too hard. He should start up a real conversation, giving Ross plenty of chances to respond, not keep up a constant stream of random anecdotes. And why this obsession with stories about family members Ross had never met? Ross couldn't possibly be interested.

Kerry tried to indicate to Santiago that he was doing it wrong, but he gave her a quick shake of the head, then continued telling Ross about his cousin Maria-Luz's elaborate plans for her upcoming quinceañera.

Irritated, Kerry gave up. If Santiago was that set on boring Ross to death, she would leave him to it.

She caught up with Father and the guard captain. Father gave her a smile, but continued his conversation with the captain about taking pre-emptive action to crush signs of incipient rebellion at Lake Perris. To her disappointment, he said nothing about his orders to Santiago.

The evergreens were the only spots of color in the bright air. She resigned herself to a dull ride. When they finally stopped for lunch, she dismounted and threw her reins to a waiting cadet, then set out in search of Santiago.

He was still babbling, his voice as husky as if he'd been talking nonstop for the entire time.

"…and that was when my youngest sibling was born. But we couldn't agree on a name, so my mother had everyone put their favorite name on a piece of paper, and we held a lottery. She drew Maria-Delia's paper: San Ramon-Nonato, the patron saint of children. But we just call him Ramon. There's four of us now—isn't that lucky? What about you, Ross? Do you have any siblings?"

He took a swig from his canteen, obviously not expecting any answer.

Now that she saw him, Kerry was no longer annoyed. Instead, she wanted to laugh. What a horrible morning he must have had!

"I don't know," Ross began.

Water spilled down Santiago's chest. As he gazed at Ross in surprise, Ross hastily backtracked. "I mean, no. Everyone's dead."

"I'm sorry," Santiago said.

Kerry was amazed that Ross had actually spoken. "Where were you born?"

Up came the shoulders in a shrug. Kerry bit back a sigh of exasperation. She and Santiago waited hopefully, but Ross had his arms crossed, his mouth tight. He was clearly done speaking for the hour. The day, the month, probably the year.

Kerry's annoyance returned. Father had loaned Ross a royal steed, housed him in the palace, even dressed him in the royal colors, and his response was to act like a spoiled, ungrateful brat.

Father's voice made her jump. "Don't bother with the chow line, Santiago. A cadet is bringing us our lunch."

"Thank you, sir," Santiago said.

Cadets put up a canopy to give them some shade. Father stepped into the protection of two huge boulders before he shooed away his bodyguards. He sat on a flat rock as large as a table, and gestured for them to join him.

Santiago usually came straight to her, but this time he waited for Ross to sit, then dropped down beside him. So Kerry moved to Ross's other side.

Father nodded approvingly at her, past Ross's bowed head. "About that power of yours, Ross."

Ross flinched, his arms tightening across his chest.

Father went on, "I understand that you can walk right up to those singing trees and put your hand on them. Have you ever tried picking a seed-pod? Imagine what a weapon that would make."

Ross lifted his head and looked directly into Kerry's eyes. He spent so much time avoiding eye contact that his gaze was like a slap in the face. She knew he was remembering that awful thing he'd said about Father killing his own people with singing trees. Could that have actually been true?

The moment stretched out horribly. Then Ross stared down at his hands. "They break if you touch them."

"We shall experiment with that," Father said.

Kerry glanced away. She was afraid that if Ross looked at her again, her face might betray her. She had never told Father about that conversation on Opportunity Day.

A clink of metal told her that Father had picked up his utensils. "We'll talk more at sunset, when we reach the ruined city. And the singing trees."

CHAPTER EIGHTEEN
GOLD POINT
YUKI

Yuki watched in amazement as Mr. Vilas transformed himself into the most unthreatening person in existence. All he did was take off his coat and hat, put on a wool sweater and a pair of glasses, and stoop a little. Then he collapsed his staff and hid it in a basket of carrot tops that he'd picked when he'd slipped over the Gold Point wall to make a quick scouting foray.

Mr. Vilas said, "If anyone looks at you, just keep walking as if you have somewhere to go."

Jennie had unbraided her hair so her beads wouldn't click, and folded two of their blankets to carry. Yuki took two carrot tops to stick out of the backpack that concealed his sword.

"Ready?" Jennie asked.

Mr. Vilas nodded along with the rest of them. Yuki had spent the trip waiting for the former bounty hunter to attempt to usurp Jennie's leadership. But to Yuki's relief, all he'd done was guide them and scout. He'd even gone hunting for them.

They'd surveyed the dam and power plant from a distance, but each was guarded by at least a company of soldiers. Brisa had been left to guard the horses and Kogatana on the other side of the Joshua Tree Forest. Now the real mission would begin.

Indra put his hand on his machete. "If I hear a commotion, do you want me to fall back or come help?"

"See what's going on *if* you can evade detection," said Jennie. "Otherwise, fall back to Brisa."

Indra didn't look happy with that. The Rangers never left anyone behind.

"If we get captured, we need you both free to rescue us," Jennie pointed out.

Mr. Vilas gave a short nod. Yuki suspected that if they were captured, the bounty hunter had a plan for saving his own skin, never mind the rest of them.

Jennie turned to Mr. Vilas. "Over to you."

"Like I said," Mr. Vilas said. "This wall is near the palace and the south garrison. Fewer sentries here, but that's because of the heavy defenses of the garrison and the palace. We're moving directly into danger. Don't let down your guard."

Everyone nodded.

"The palace farm is beyond this wall. We head straight east till we hit the 'guest quarters' where Voske keeps his important prisoners. *Quietly* take out the guards."

"I've got rope," Yuki whispered.

"No rope. Slit their throats." Mr. Vilas seemed to sense Yuki's sickened reaction. "It'll be more merciful than Voske will be. The guards get flogged if a prisoner escapes. Losing an important prisoner means flogged to death."

No one spoke. Yuki had been prepared to kill in battle. He'd done so before. But in cold blood, by stealth...

I abandoned Ross, he reminded himself. *I left him and ran. I have to do whatever it takes to rescue him.*

"We get Ross, and come straight back," Mr. Vilas concluded. "If we're fast and quiet, we'll be gone by midnight."

He turned to the stone wall, which towered ten feet higher than the walls of Las Anclas. Mr. Vilas had said earlier, "Five years ago, we couldn't have gotten over the wall anywhere. But Voske is fighting on three fronts, not counting Las Anclas, and he's constantly in need of soldiers. So sentries are thin on this particular stretch of the west wall."

Yuki was sure that any invasion coming over the wall would be annihilated in minutes. But Gold Point apparently assumed that no one would infiltrate so close to the palace and the garrison. Maybe no one had ever dared. Or...

Mr. Vilas went on, "Just stay away from the towers and watch the timing of the sentries."

Yuki couldn't help wondering if Voske's spy device had been watching them the entire time. The instant they climbed the wall, they might be met by a hundred soldiers. It was far too easy to imagine Mr. Vilas leading them into a trap.

Yuki had never trusted the bounty hunter, who captured or killed people for money. That distrust had strengthened after Jennie told Yuki, Brisa, and Indra about Mr. Preston's secret orders. Not only did Yuki have to watch for enemies, he had to be ready to stop one of his own teammates from assassinating the person they were supposed to rescue!

As Mr. Vilas swung up the padded grappling hook, Yuki watched him for a signal to the enemy. The Ranger candidates had done plenty of rappelling, and though the healing scar on his back pulled and stung, he had no trouble climbing the wall. What he wasn't prepared for was his first glimpse of Voske's city.

The city below lay in a shallow bowl, glittering like a night sky spread out along the ground. The houses had electric lights. The *streets* had electric lights. Golden light streamed from every window of the palace.

It reminded Yuki sharply of the floating city he'd been meant to inherit, before it had been taken by pirates and he'd been cast adrift. The *Taka* too had been lit like the Milky Way. The name came to him in Japanese, his mother tongue: Ama no Gawa, the River of Heaven.

Jennie elbowed him in the side, and he dropped down swiftly. They followed Mr. Vilas through the darkened orchards.

Yuki's thoughts circled back to Ross's kidnapping. If Yuki had done better, they wouldn't be here now: if he'd woken up faster, if he'd grabbed his crossbow instead of his sword, if he'd spotted the attackers sneaking up behind them.

If he hadn't left Ross behind. He'd thought he was saving Mia's life. Instead, Mia had saved *his* life, dragging him through the desert after he'd collapsed from loss of blood.

Yuki had been meant to become a king. He couldn't make the excuse of not having been raised with a sense of responsibility. He knew his duty, and he'd failed.

Mr. Vilas scouted ahead, then returned, strolling casually. Yuki walked with him, hoping they'd look like two carrot farmers. Jennie trailed well behind. Three older women walked by, carrying push brooms. They barely glanced at him. In Las Anclas, a stranger would have been noticed immediately, but Gold Point was so big that people lived among strangers.

The palace loomed ahead. Yuki had never seen such a gigantic building, not even on the *Taka*. At least twenty guards patrolled it, with more on the roof and at the stairwells. Yuki forced himself not to count guards, or check to see who might be watching them. "Don't give the sentries any reason to want to check you out," the bounty hunter had said. "Gold Point citizens are used to the palace. They won't be staring like they've never seen it before."

Yuki forced his eyes down by imagining the weight of all those alert gazes. It was a relief to get past the enormous building.

He hoped Mr. Vilas was right that the 'guest houses' only had six guards each. It would be impossible for each of them to take out—kill—more than two guards without risking noise.

At least they shouldn't be seen. Mr. Vilas had said the 'guest houses' were walled with shrubbery so Voske could interrogate prisoners in private. Until Voske began using them to house his special prisoners, they had been kept for rebellious members of the royal family, with no one allowed to see in or out.

They walked by the narrow entrance to the first house. It was unguarded, the windows dark.

As they approached the second guest house, Yuki saw light through chinks in its leafy wall. He tightened his hand on his backpack, then released it, trying to look like a normal, non-suspicious passerby. He and Jennie kept a lookout while Mr. Vilas peered between the waxy leaves.

Mr. Vilas beckoned to them. They followed him through the bushes and into a garden behind the house. To Yuki's surprise, there were no guards in sight. But light shone through the open windows.

Yuki met Jennie's wide gaze. It seemed too easy. Jennie gestured to him to join her as they crept toward the back porch, leaving Mr. Vilas on lookout.

A girl's voice carried on the night air. "He should have chosen Andrea. I could tell it was between her and you. And her family needs the reward."

A boy responded, "I don't blame Ross for picking me. I would have, too."

Yuki was so startled that he missed the next few words. Jennie slithered up behind a flowering bush to peer through the window. Yuki followed her.

The girl sat on the arm of a sofa. She wore a military uniform, and both her hands were bandaged. The boy was dressed far too warmly for the night, with barely an inch of skin showing. He even wore heavy gloves and a scarf around his neck. He stood behind the sofa, his arms held tight to his chest, as if he was trying to put a barrier between him and the girl.

"I could see how bad Ross felt," the boy went on.

Yuki wondered if it was the same Ross. Why would a prisoner be choosing anything? Yuki glanced at Jennie, who put her finger to her lips.

The girl stood up. "Let's try again. I'm not afraid."

The boy skidded backward until he fetched up against the wall. "Don't come near me!"

The conversation made more sense now—the boy must have some destructive, out-of-control Change power. Yuki waited for another mention of Ross.

The girl looked hurt. "At least let's try. I can't stand not being able to touch you. And you'll never learn to control this unless you practice."

The boy began to shout, "I'll never learn—" He stopped, then said in a low, forced voice, "I'll never control it. Every time I've practiced at the slaughterhouse, it's only gotten worse. If I put a finger on you, I could kill you."

"Luis," the girl began, extending a hand.

Luis lunged toward the door, his face twisted in misery.

Yuki and Jennie bolted out of the garden. A door slammed behind them. Jennie gestured Yuki and the waiting Mr. Vilas into a huddle.

"Ross isn't there," Jennie whispered. "The people inside mentioned him, I think. But they didn't say where he was." She looked at Mr. Vilas. "Where else can he be?"

"He could be in the garrison prison, or the hell cells. Or the palace, being interrogated. Or…"

"We can't comb the entire city for him," Jennie said. "Where's the best place to eavesdrop on people who might know where he is?"

"The path from the palace to Voske Village," Mr. Vilas said. "If anyone knows where Ross is, it will be people with palace business. Let's get some gardening tools."

He led them to a gardening shed, where they switched their baskets of carrot tops for pruning shears, a broom, and a watering can.

They passed a garden with an arched bridge and artistically gnarled pine trees, larger versions of the ones that Yuki's father had grown in pots on the *Taka*, carefully trimming them and shaping their growth with copper wire. In the heart of the garden, bright against the dark leaves, were two orange pillars topped with an orange beam. Yuki hadn't seen one in five years, but its name and meaning came immediately into his mind: a torii, the gate that separated the ordinary world from the realm of the spirits. Beyond the torii rose a beautifully carved shrine.

The electric lights, the pines, the shrine, and the torii called up an image of his father bent over a favorite bonsai. If the scent of pine had been mixed with salt air and ocean brine, Yuki could have almost believed that he was home, floating on the ocean—except for the sharp pang of grief.

There was so little in Las Anclas that resembled anything on the *Taka* that Yuki was rarely ambushed by unexpected recollections. Now memories washed over him in waves, making him stumble on even ground.

He wrenched his attention away. This was no time to be distracted. But it didn't seem fair that this enemy town had so much of what Yuki had lost.

They took up stations by a flower-lined path. Yuki crouched behind a jasmine trellis, occasionally snapping the shears. He hoped no one would come along who knew anything about clipping jasmine, because he certainly didn't. Mr. Vilas was right about one thing: it was a popular path. He heard one conversation about farming, two about family problems, and one break-up. No one gave Yuki a second glance.

Maybe he could build a shrine and torii in Las Anclas. The sea caves had always felt like a sacred space to him, inhabited by some spirit of ocean and sand. His first mother had an ancient picture in her throne room of a huge torii on a beach, half-submerged in a high tide. Mia would probably know how to build a gate in sand so it wouldn't topple when the tide came in.

Teenagers' voices caught his attention. He raised his shears to a tendril of jasmine as a slender girl and a young guy came up the path.

The girl poked the boy. "Come on, Diego. Santiago and I are on the same team! All I want to know is what he's doing with the prisoner. And how come he got to go and I didn't."

The guy stopped short. "You don't want to go, Bankar."

Bankar put her fists on her hips. "Don't tell *me* what I want to do. Of course I want in on the fun. And the chance at promotion."

Yuki peered through the trailing vines. The light from the palace reached the two, revealing the flash of fear that widened Diego's eyes. Then he scowled at Bankar. "Shut up."

Kids' voices echoed through the trees.

"If you're smart, you'll drop it before you win another ten." Diego ran down the path.

Bankar called out to his back, "I'm not afraid of anything!"

As three kids appeared, accompanied by a pair of bodyguards, Bankar chirped, "Hey, Owen. Fiona, Bridget." She clapped each kid on the back as she said their names. "How was the party?"

Though the kids' hair and skin were different, they were clearly related, with the same prominent cheekbones and sharply pointed noses and chins. Yuki wasn't sure why, but they all looked vaguely familiar.

"It was great. We had cream puffs," Bridget, the tallest, said cheerfully.

"What's up with Diego?" Owen asked, peering down the path. "Did you have a fight?"

"He's being a snot," Bankar said. "Just because his brother got to go with the king on that special mission with the prisoner. Hey, do you guys know what that's about?"

Bridget nodded. "They've gone to the ruined city."

Fiona, the smallest, bragged, "We've seen more of the prisoner than anyone. Bridget spotted him trying to pry the bars out of the windows."

"He was using that gauntlet," Own said. "But he broke something on it."

Yuki froze, then snipped randomly at the jasmine. White flowers fell at his feet.

"What's he like, Bankar?" Bridget asked. "You caught him!"

"Is he a good fighter?" Owen asked.

"Nah," Bankar scoffed. "I could take him out easy. I don't know why he got special treatment. A room in the palace!"

"*I* know *that*," said Fiona. "He's afraid of rooms without windows."

Bankar threw her arms out wide. "Then why doesn't the king give him a dose of Sergeant's Aid and throw him in a hell cell? He'd be doing anything we want before the scabs fell off his back."

"That's not how it works," began Owen. Before he could continue his lecture, Fiona picked up a pebble, which popped out of existence and then in again, dropping onto his head. "Ow!" He clenched his hand into a fist.

One of her braids yanked by itself, and Fiona let out a squawk. Owen grinned.

"Stop that, or I'll make your shoes rot off your feet," Bridget said to the two younger kids.

She turned to Bankar. "Father says that torture makes people so desperate that they'll say whatever they think you want to hear to make it stop. So you can never tell whether or not they're really telling the truth. You can make them say they're loyal, but if they get a chance, they'll turn on you."

Owen spoke as if reciting a lesson. "Torture is for prisoners you don't need any more, so you can use them as examples to intimidate other people."

Yuki wasn't sure whether to be relieved that Ross hadn't been tortured, or horrified at what might happen if Voske decided to make an example of him. And the casual way those little kids talked about torture made his skin crawl.

"Uh-huh." Bankar had clearly lost interest. "Gotta catch up with Diego." She ran off, leaving the kids and their bodyguards to continue on to the palace.

Jennie, who'd been sweeping up fallen leaves, signaled to Yuki and Mr. Vilas. They quickly retraced their steps back to the wall.

Indra's relief was plain in the moonlight when they rejoined him, then turned to disappointment. "You didn't find Ross."

Jennie shook her head. "He's at the ruined city, with Voske. And they're keeping him in the palace. It looks impossible to break into. I think our only chance is to catch him at the ruined city before he's brought back."

And maybe they'd get a chance to take out Voske himself, Yuki thought. It would protect Las Anclas, and Paco would probably feel a lot better if Voske was dead and his mother was avenged. As for Yuki, he'd love to get revenge on the man who had taken the joy out of Paco's eyes.

Jennie nudged Yuki. "We have to ride all night. We'll need Kogatana to scout."

Yuki abandoned his bloodthirsty daydreams. They weren't on an assassination mission, and Voske would undoubtedly be surrounded by bodyguards. If they could just rescue Ross, Yuki would be satisfied.

CHAPTER NINETEEN
RUINED CITY OUTSIDE GOLD POINT
KERRY

Kerry woke before sunrise. She loved sleeping under the sky. Her sleeping bag was warm, the air still and cool. Stars still twinkled above the jagged silhouettes of the mountains, but the night sky over Gold Point had lightened to the shade of her sapphire earrings.

She leaned on her elbow, careful not to disturb Santiago. He looked so sweet as he peacefully slept, his eyes moving under his eyelids. She wondered what he was dreaming about. The strengthening light outlined the contours of his face, and caught on his sparse whiskers. She extended her finger and gently caressed his stubble. Without waking, he turned toward her, cradling his forehead on her hand. His skin was so soft.

Ross slept on Santiago's other side. His face was half-hidden by the fall of his hair. He looked so relaxed that he was almost unrecognizable, his strikingly long eyelashes feathering one cheek. He didn't even have stubble yet.

As if he'd felt her watching him, he awoke with a start. The wary, unhappy expression Kerry was used to instantly tightened his face. She turned back to Santiago, but the peace she'd enjoyed was gone.

The camp was astir. Somebody laughed, and a horse stamped at the picket line. Santiago's eyes flicked open. He smiled up at her, but as she smiled back his gaze drifted up to the open sky. Then, like Ross, his expression changed to one of wary tension. What was going on with him?

"Are you okay?" Kerry leaned down to kiss him.

He kissed her back, but she could tell that his heart wasn't in it. His gaze shifted to the grand tent where her father slept.

Kerry was about to ask if he needed the medic to check his collarbone when a guard offered her a steaming mug of coffee. She handed it to Santiago. As she accepted her own cup, Father emerged from his tent, fully dressed. Six guards immediately flanked him. To her surprise, he gestured for Kerry to join him.

Kerry set her untouched coffee down on a rock and pulled on her boots. She straightened out the traveling clothes she'd slept in and grabbed her gold hair clip to pin up her braids. They felt fuzzy. This part she didn't care for: no maid to brush and braid and pin up her hair.

"Walk with me," Father said.

The guards closed around them as he led them to a fall of giant rocks, the granite glittering as the edge of the sun appeared. When they were safely enclosed between walls of stone, Father dismissed the guards.

Kerry waited eagerly for him to explain how he'd make Ross prospect for him. She wished she knew, to impress him with her insight. But a stupid guess was worse than no guess, so she kept quiet.

"It will be fascinating to finally learn what's inside that city," he said.

She couldn't wait any longer. "How can you trust Ross to not just walk into those singing trees and out the other side, back to Las Anclas?"

Father gave her an approving smile. "I'll never trust him that much. That boy will always need a minder. Santiago is perfect for the job."

"Santiago?" Kerry struggled to hide her horror. "You're going to get Ross to take Santiago into the forest with him? But there's nothing to stop Ross from having the trees kill him!"

"I've studied Ross," Father said, his eyes narrowing. Kerry breathed in slowly, determined to control her voice, her face, as he went on, "I know his weaknesses. The most striking one is sentimentality. Santiago will walk into the forest, and Ross will follow him to save his life."

The emphasis on 'weaknesses' was not Kerry's imagination. Father would hardly stake her boyfriend's life on a prisoner's sentimentality. "This is a test for me, right? It's to figure out that this isn't your plan, and come up with a better one? Ross would never give up a chance to escape for the sake of someone he barely knows."

Father's smile faded. If it was a test, she'd failed. "No, Kerry. Number one, he knows Santiago very, very well by now."

So that was the point of Santiago's babble about himself and his family and even his relationship with her.

Father went on, "Number two, if you give him power over others, he'll try to protect them. We saw that when I dressed him in the royal colors and gave him the run of the town, and when I set him to choose a candidate on Opportunity Day."

"But if he can get away—"

Father continued as if she hadn't spoken. "Number three, he's weak. He couldn't bring himself to kill Santiago once he'd looked him in the eyes. I gave him the opportunity to take anything he wanted, and he went off by himself to cry. He's afraid of everyday things, like rooms without windows. You broke his will in fifteen minutes. But then, you're strong. Don't worry,

Santiago is in no danger."

Kerry burst out, "But why Santiago? We've got plenty of cadets here. Use one of them."

There was a long silence. Father leaned against a boulder. "Don't you trust me?"

That was the test for Kerry.

Memories battered her like sand in a storm: Santiago's hoarse voice as he told Ross yet another story about the family he loved; Ross shouting at her that Father had killed his own people with crystal shards; blood dripping from Min Soo's hands; Ross looking away from the skulls on the palace garrison gate; the girl Sean had chosen for Opportunity Day, falling dead on the stage.

Sean had been so sure that anyone he selected would get a wonderful power that he had picked the candidate he liked best. His crown had fallen off as he'd flung himself at the dead girl and shook her, crying, "Wake up, wake up!" Father had patted him consolingly, saying, "Next time you'll have better luck."

Would Father say that to her if Santiago died in agony, his strong body devoured by crystal? *Next boyfriend, you'll have better luck.*

"Kerry?" Father was still waiting for her answer.

Forcing herself to sound calm, she replied, "Of course I trust you."

Once the words were out, she knew them for a lie.

But she had control of her face. Her voice. "Are you going to send them in now?" That came out properly casual, the way a crown princess would speak.

"No, we'll wait until Santiago has his arm out of the sling. Next week. And don't mention this to Ross, Kerry. He isn't to know Santiago's role until then. This trip was just to get Ross used to the idea of prospecting for me."

And me used to the idea of you risking Santiago's life. Kerry's heart was hammering so hard that she felt as if he could hear it.

She had to get away, to get on her horse and ride and ride. That's what she always did when Min Soo upset her. But she expected that from Min Soo. Being angry with Father, lying to Father, having reason to lie to Father: it was as if the solid earth had shifted under her feet.

She couldn't let him see her stumble.

"Then do you mind if I ride back by myself? I haven't had a good gallop for days."

Father patted her shoulder. "Not at all. Would you like a bodyguard?"

Kerry shook her head, like the strong heir she was. "I can protect myself."

At last came his smile of approval.

For the first time, she was too angry to care.

CHAPTER TWENTY
RUINED CITY OUTSIDE GOLD POINT
JENNIE

Jennie took the binoculars from Mr. Vilas and peered down at Voske's camp in the pre-dawn light. Relief washed over her when she spotted Ross climbing out of a sleeping bag. He didn't seem to be injured, but he looked thin and tired and miserable. She wished she could run down, hug him, and get him out of there. Or at least let him know that she was near. He must feel so alone.

She swung the binoculars, taking in the forty or so guards. She saw no way to even get a message to Ross, much less rescue him.

A girl wearing a crimson shirt headed for the king's tent.

"Is that the crown princess?" Jennie asked. "The girl in red?"

Mr. Vilas nodded.

Brisa nudged Jennie. "I want to see the princess. I've always loved princess stories."

"Hold on." Jennie squinted down at the camp.

She could make out the silvery glint of Voske's hair. He was surrounded by bodyguards, just like he'd been when she and the Rangers had fought him, and Sera Diaz had been killed. Sera had said, *Take him down. They'll all fall apart.*

Jennie handed Mr. Vilas the binoculars. "If we got closer, could you get a shot at Voske?"

He laid his rifle on a rock and took the binoculars. After a long scan, he passed the binoculars back to Jennie. "I doubt it. See how he always keeps a crowd of guards around him?"

Jennie peered downward. Voske leaped into view. She flinched, remembering that face from the battle, lit by the fire that she and her team had started when they blew up his ammunition. The princess had the same sharply pointed nose and chin, and high, prominent cheekbones—a face like a fox—though her hair was black.

Mr. Vilas was right. With all the bodyguards surrounding the king, you'd never get a clear shot.

Voske and the princess walked behind some huge boulders. He was obviously always aware of the danger of unseen enemies.

Ross sat on a rock, ignoring a plate of food. Another boy sat beside him, gesturing as he talked. Soldiers stood nearby with their rifles pointed downward but in Ross's direction. They were guarding Ross, not protecting him.

Mr. Vilas nudged her. "I was wrong. I might get a clean shot from that hill." He pointed fifty feet below, where a jumble of pine grew on a cliff overlooking the camp.

Jennie brought the binoculars up. Voske and the princess were nowhere in sight. The only person the bounty hunter could get a clean shot at would be Ross.

Jennie put down the binoculars. "You're not going anywhere."

Mr. Vilas raised his eyebrows, as if she was inexplicably doubting him. "I could get that shot. Five minutes down this slope. Perfect cover all the way."

Brisa leaned out. "But…" She broke off.

Mr. Vilas reached for his rifle. "It's a clear shot."

Jennie put her hand on her pistol. She would shoot him before she would let him kill Ross. And she could draw faster than he could get his rifle. "Don't move."

He stared at Jennie, eyes narrowed, the corners of his mouth quirked.

"Something's happening down there," said Yuki. "Give me the binoculars."

Jennie held them out to Yuki, but kept her other hand on her pistol and her gaze on the bounty hunter.

"The girl in red is Voske's daughter?" Yuki muttered incredulously. "She looks just like Paco. *Just* like."

Brisa gasped. "How could she? Paco isn't…" There was a long pause. "Oh."

Leaves crunched as Yuki shifted position. "I should have known when I saw those kids of Voske's. They seemed familiar, but I couldn't think why." Jennie felt his questioning gaze. "Jennie, did you know?"

Jennie kept watching the bounty hunter. "We'll talk about this later."

"Let me see," said Indra.

Though Jennie and Indra had never discussed Paco's father—Jennie hadn't wanted to think about it, and Indra had never brought it up—she knew from the lack of surprise in Indra's voice that she wasn't the only one who'd gotten a good look at Voske's face during the battle at Las Anclas.

Indra said, "Jennie, the princess is at the picket line. Alone."

Jennie grabbed the binoculars from Indra. If the bounty hunter moved, she'd use her power to snatch his rifle from his hands.

The shimmering golden stallion the princess had approached laid back his ears and lashed his catlike tail. Jennie wouldn't have wanted to ride that horse in that mood, and neither, apparently, did the princess. She turned to a placid gray mare, swung into the saddle and rode off, alone. She was heading northward, back toward Gold Point.

That meant she'd pass directly below Jennie and her team. Alone.

An entire plan leaped into Jennie's mind—a plan that would keep the bounty hunter away from Ross, and maybe even get Ross back.

"We're going to capture the princess," Jennie said. "We'll take her back to Las Anclas and exchange her for Ross."

Nobody spoke. She lowered the binoculars to find everyone staring at her, Indra doubtful, Brisa astonished. Yuki's gaze strayed toward the camp. He looked like he was in shock. The bounty hunter's brows lifted and he gave a slow nod. He was the only one who approved.

That made Jennie a little sick. But she tightened her resolve. "Come on. We have to get into position."

"We're kidnapping her?" Indra asked, incredulous. "We don't do that. Voske does that."

Jennie kept her voice low, but put all the authority she could muster into her words. "We're not going to hurt her. We're only going to capture her. And we won't have her for long. Voske can't want Ross more than his own daughter."

Indra looked away, his mouth a tight line. Yuki stared blankly down at the camp. Brisa's eyes rounded in surprise.

Frustration boiled in Jennie's stomach. One more comment and she'd tell them all what she thought of this mission, of the Rangers, of everything. She was sick of horrible dilemmas. No matter what she chose, it always seemed to be wrong.

I hate secrets. I hate the Rangers, she thought, scowling at Indra's disapproving face, his tense shoulders. Oh, it felt so good to think that!

This will be my last mission. I'll rescue Ross, and then I'm done.

Jennie looked directly at the bounty hunter, not Indra, as she spoke. "This is for Ross."

Indra followed her gaze. Mr. Vilas still had his hand stretched out toward his rifle.

"Understood." Indra's brow smoothed, and she knew he'd remembered Mr. Preston's secret order. "Jennie, you're in command."

CHAPTER TWENTY-ONE
ARROYO OUTSIDE GOLD POINT
KERRY

Kerry guided the mare down the red rock canyon. She'd galloped halfway around the mountain, but even the magic of riding had failed to calm her. Nor was she any closer to figuring out whether Father was right to believe that Santiago would be safe. But she had to get the better of her anger. Of course she trusted Father—nobody was smarter, more determined, more successful. *Nobody.*

He had to be right.

But Ross had killed thirty soldiers in the battle at Las Anclas. Why would he care about one more? Much as she'd like to imagine that he could be happy in Gold Point, she knew that he was desperate to escape. Nobody would turn down their heart's desire to save the life of an enemy.

Think of it as a test, she told herself. *Come up with a better plan.*

She could persuade Father that Santiago was too valuable to risk. No, nobody was too valuable. Certainly not a mere scout with a useless Change power. Even family wasn't too valuable. Deirdre's death had proved that. Refusing to risk even the most precious people to achieve one's goals was weakness.

What about locking Ross in the hell cells until his will was truly broken? Nausea curled in her stomach. Anyway, that would only make him even more desperate to get away. Or he'd sit there until he starved himself to death. She wouldn't put it past him.

I could run away, she thought. *Like Sean. And take Santiago with me.*

She was weak *and* stupid if all she could come up with were childish fantasies. She needed a real plan.

This is a test. I can't fail now.

The mare's forefoot slid in rubble. Kerry guided the mare around a rock fall, then pulled up before an enormous boulder. She dismounted and went to see if there was enough room to squeeze past it. A fist-sized rock clattered down the side of the narrow arroyo. Kerry jumped back.

The stone exploded in a burst of flame, sending sharp fragments into Kerry's face. An ambush!

She spun around and flung up her hands, creating a shield. A staff whistled down toward her head, swung by a tall man in a long black coat. It bounced off her shield, jarring her entire body.

It was that traitor bounty hunter! She kept her shield up with her left hand, and shaped a sword in her right. Furious, she swung her sword with all her strength, slicing halfway through the staff.

Two people tackled her from behind. The sky and the cliff whirled as she crashed to the ground. Her concentration broke, and her sword and shield vanished.

Two enemies fought to pin her hands: a strong-looking girl with near-black skin, and a tall boy with braided hair. Kerry kicked the girl in the stomach, formed a pair of knives, and slashed out at them both. The boy stepped on her forearm. Kerry dug in her heels and yanked her arm, trying to dislodge him. He didn't budge. Turning the knife into a whip, she snapped her wrist upward. The tip of the whip opened a long cut across his cheek.

He recoiled, off-balance. Kerry rolled to her feet and got her back against the boulder. Loose braids swung across her eyes, half blinding her.

She saw five enemies now, including the traitor. Even with Kerry's weapons and skills, those were bad odds. If she wasn't so far away from camp, she'd have screamed for help.

Kerry could surround herself with a shield, but she'd quickly run out of air. All they'd have to do was wait. She dismissed that possibility. It was pointless and undignified.

She lifted her head proudly. "I am Kerry Ji Sun Voske, crown princess of the Gold Point Empire. Run away now, or I'll have your heads mounted outside my bedroom window."

Kerry materialized a sword in each hand. The dark girl jerked up her empty left hand and made a gesture with it. Kerry flinched, expecting some Change power to strike her, but nothing happened. The dark girl looked surprised.

The bounty hunter, whose coat was falling off his shoulders, signaled to the dark girl. The girl raised her sword and charged. As Kerry spun to face her, a black cloth fell over her head. Kerry swung out her sword blindly, and started to reach up with her left hand to yank off the leather coat the bounty hunter had thrown at her.

Two bodies slammed into her before she could get her hand up. She fell hard, her face shoved into the dust. Several sets of knees thumped onto her back and legs. She got one last swipe with a sword before her palms were smashed into the ground and pinned there.

A girl chirped, "I've found her hair clip! Don't want to leave any evidence. Oooh, it's real gold."

Kerry hadn't told anyone her exact route. If these kidnappers brushed out their tracks, no one would know what had happened. With the coat still over her head, she jerked her ear against her shoulder. Her face was quickly shoved back down, but not before her earring tore out. Her earlobe stung, but triumph was sharper. She'd left a clue.

The gravelly voice of the bounty hunter interrupted her thoughts. "Her Change weapons come out of her palms. Tie them together."

As strong hands dragged her arms behind her back, Kerry managed to get her mouth out of the dirt. "How dare you try to kidnap me! My father will kill you all."

Her palms were squeezed together and tightly wrapped with cloth. Then the pressure on her left leg lightened. She lashed out and connected with someone's shin, winning a satisfying grunt of pain.

Someone yanked the coat away. Kerry was hauled her to her feet. She cast her gaze down till she spotted a glint of gold and ruby, then set her foot over her earring and glared.

Finally, she got a good look at her enemies. She had no idea who they were, except for the bounty hunter, but she could give them suitable nicknames until she learned their real ones.

The dark girl was big and lumpish as a steer, with a scowl fit to strip paint. *Ox*, Kerry decided. The boy with the ponytail was pale as a ghost, and far too lanky. *Beanpole.*

The boy with the braid didn't have as obvious and glaring flaws as the other two, but... Kerry's critical gaze traveled from his face to his body, then back to his face. Nothing jumped out at her. She supposed his ears stuck out a bit. He could be Jug Ears.

Kerry was pleased to see that both Ox and Beanpole were bleeding from her knives, Ox from her right hand and Beanpole from the shoulder. Kerry's whip had cut open Jug Ears' face.

The other girl, whom Kerry was sorry to see was unhurt, had her hair tied up in babyish ribbons in a shade of pink Min Soo would love. She was fat enough to remind Kerry of the round dumplings Min Soo also loved, filled with sickly sweet bean paste. *Dumpling.*

To Kerry's disappointment, she'd also failed to wound the traitor bounty hunter. But at least she'd destroyed his staff.

"Let's go," said Ox.

With none of the respect due to a princess, they roughly grabbed her, flung her over her horse, and led her away, never spotting her earring. Kerry hoped she hadn't accidentally buried it.

When she saw the waiting horses, she knew the bounty hunter was still working for Las Anclas. The horses had antlers like deer, and a large gray rat perched on a saddle.

Her enemies mounted up, guided their horses in to circle Kerry's, and rode due west. When Dumpling started to speak, she was quickly hushed.

Kerry waited until the direction they were taking was clear, then checked as best she could to make sure no one was looking. Wedging her ear into a bit of tack, she jerked her head and tore out her other earring. No one noticed.

That was her last triumph. Otherwise she endured a nightmare of discomfort, while she alternately wondered what they thought they'd gain by kidnapping her, and whether Father would still go ahead with his plan and risk Santiago's life.

They stopped a few times to pour water into her mouth, but they didn't make camp until nightfall. Kerry was dismayed to see how far they'd come. If Father didn't find her earring until now, any search party would be a full day behind.

"Father's search parties are right behind us," Kerry said. "If you let me go now, I'll walk back and intercept them, and you can escape."

Nobody replied. Jug Ears began making a fire.

Kerry couldn't believe they were ignoring her. "I'll have all your heads on pikes. After I'm done playing with you."

They ignored that, too. Kerry recalled Father's lessons on how to intimidate people. For people who didn't fear their own death, threatening the ones they loved worked nicely. It was too bad she didn't know who they loved, but Father had taught her how to deal with that, too.

"Father will come to Las Anclas with an army." Kerry watched them carefully. "He won't spare anyone. Not even your little sisters." That got a good flinch from Jug Ears, Beanpole, and Ox. Ah-ha.

Kerry went on, "If your little sister is lucky, she'll be beheaded without being tortured first. But since her big siblings kidnapped me, she won't be lucky. Father has very skilled torturers. They can make an execution last all day. Usually, they begin by placing hot coals—"

"Shut up!" Ox snapped. "One more word about torture or executions, and I'll gag you."

Kerry sat back and enjoyed the unsettled silence that descended on the camp.

It was broken by Dumpling. "You know what would be great right now? A nice, juicy, roast rabbit."

"You want it, Brisa, you shoot it and cook it," Ox said.

"Got it, Jennie. Jerky and tortillas it is." Dumpling—Brisa—began passing out stiff tortillas and unappetizing strips of jerky.

When she came to Kerry, she paused, head to one side. "I guess I could feed you."

"I don't want your filthy hands on me," Kerry said.

"Aren't you hungry, Princess?"

"Not enough to eat food *you've* touched."

Brisa's forehead puckered with hurt. Then, to Kerry's surprise, Brisa gave her a sympathetic look. "I'd be in a bad mood, too, if I'd been kidnapped. You'll feel better if you eat."

Was it some ploy? Kerry decided to play along. "I can't eat unless you untie my hands."

Brisa turned to Ox—Jennie—who seemed to be the leader. "Can I?"

"No," Jennie said.

There was the distinctive clatch-and-click of a rifle chambering a round. The bounty hunter sat opposite Kerry, the firelight beating on his face. "I'll guard her."

Kerry didn't flinch. "Go ahead and kill me. I'll be so useful to you then."

The bounty hunter smiled. "You'll be plenty useful with a smashed kneecap."

There's the stick. She hoped there'd be a better carrot coming along than jerky and stale tortillas. Keeping her dignity, Kerry said, "Untie me. I won't hurt you."

"Brisa, you can untie her," Jennie said. "But stay out of the line of fire."

So much for the idea of shoving Brisa at the bounty hunter.

Brisa untied Kerry's hands, her silly ribbons drifting down. "Your hair's all tangled. Would you like me to brush it out for you? I'm very gentle. My girlfriend Becky loves it when I brush her hair."

Without asking permission, Brisa picked up one of Kerry's braids.

Kerry wanted to jerk her hair free of Brisa's paws. But she held herself back. Her threats had upset them, but not intimidated them. She glanced at the bounty hunter with the rifle on his knee, and had to admit that his threat was far more effective. All Kerry had accomplished was to make them hate her.

Wait, not all of them.

Since the stick failed, let's go back to carrots.

Kerry forced herself to sound grateful. "Yes, please."

Her reward was a completely genuine-looking smile. Kerry realized that Brisa wasn't engaged in any ploy: she felt sincerely sorry for Kerry. What a fool! And what a stroke of luck for Kerry.

Kerry made herself sit still as Brisa undid her braids, then brushed out the tangles. The light tug was soothing on her scalp. She had to admit that Brisa did have a gentle touch.

Kerry liked it enough to make the next step easier. "I'm sorry I made those threats. I'd never hurt a child."

"I knew you were bluffing," Brisa said. Jennie snorted with disbelief as Brisa went on, "We won't hurt you, either. We just want to get Ross back."

Kerry clenched her jaw to keep a laugh from escaping. She dangled another carrot. "You *are* gentle. Does your girlfriend have long hair like mine?"

"No, it's shoulder-length, but very fine, so it tangles easily. It's yellow as corn—no, yellow as sunlight!" Brisa gave a dreamy sigh.

"Oh, that does sound pretty," Kerry said sweetly. "What's she like?"

Brisa looked even dreamier. Love could turn otherwise intelligent people into babbling nitwits, but Brisa had obviously been one to begin with. What sensible person would sympathize with an enemy?

"Becky is the sweetest, kindest, nicest person in Las Anclas." Brisa's voice dripped with mindless adoration. "And smart, too! She's our doctor's apprentice…"

Kerry listened carefully for useful information. Becky sounded even more sentimental than Brisa. A wounded animal or insect couldn't limp into Las Anclas without Becky trying to fix it. A girl like that might be talked into releasing a harmless, homesick princess.

"Oh, your ear is bleeding," Brisa exclaimed. "Does it hurt?"

"She's bleeding?" Jennie roughly grabbed Kerry's shoulder and held her hair out of the way. "Did you tear your earrings out?"

Kerry longed to retort, *No, they grew wings and flapped away.* She forced herself to say, "They got ripped out in the fight." She sensed Jennie's disbelief, and added, "You did all dog-pile on top of me."

Jug Ears stood up. "Whether she left them deliberately or accidentally, the result is the same. A search party is sure to find them. It could be right on top of us. We should ride tonight."

Jennie dropped Kerry's hair. To Kerry's annoyance, she carefully wiped her filthy fingers on her equally filthy clothes, her mouth curled in disgust. Then she turned to Jug Ears, her muscles tense. The way their gazes met then averted sharpened Kerry's interest. Hatred? No, not the way Jug Ears looked back at Jennie.

"None of us have slept since the night before yesterday," Jennie said. "If we ride out now, we'll be so tired, we might as well be drunk. It's safer to stay here. We'll set an extra guard at a wide perimeter."

Something had happened between those two, Kerry thought. How could she use it? She schooled her face as her captors began eating their revolting rations and tending one other's wounds. While Kerry choked down the jerky, she surreptitiously studied her captors.

Brisa was clearly the weakest link. Unfortunately, she was also the youngest in the party, and unlikely to be put in sole charge of Kerry. The bounty hunter didn't seem to have any weaknesses in the literal sense, but anyone who switched sides once might do it again. Maybe she could bribe him, if she got him alone. From their body language, Jennie and Jug Ears definitely had history. But they were both so wary and tough that Kerry didn't see how to translate that into weakness.

The gray rat, which Kerry couldn't help finding cute, seemed to belong to Beanpole. Other than that, she didn't have a sense of Beanpole at all. In fact, she couldn't recall him saying a single word.

Then he spoke. "Jennie, you knew—"

Kerry gnawed on her jerky, pretending she wasn't listening. He had a different accent from the others, one she didn't recognize.

"Knew what, Yuki?" Jennie asked in a weary voice.

Yuki glanced at Kerry.

Jennie moved as if she was getting up, then sank down with a sigh, obviously too tired to walk out of earshot. Good.

Jennie offered a bit of tortilla to the rat. "Yes, I knew. But I was sure *he* didn't know, so I didn't say anything. He doesn't know, right?"

Kerry listened, fascinated. What in the world were they talking about?

Yuki shook his head. "He would have told me. What should we say?"

"Maybe the best thing would be for you to find him as soon as we get back, and tell him yourself," Jennie said.

Yuki stroked the rat. "He's been having such a hard time. I hate to do that to him."

Brisa looked from one to the other, then said brightly, "You're talking about Paco, right?"

Paco! Kerry forced herself not to react. After Deirdre had been killed, and Father had told Kerry that he'd give Las Anclas to her, he'd said, *Then you'll have to decide what to do about your brother, the one they call Paco. Do you have any ideas?*

Uncertain of the correct answer—Give him an important position? Execute him? Test his loyalty, and decide based on that?—she'd said she was still thinking it over.

Instead of answering Brisa, Yuki gazed at Jennie. "Is that why they wouldn't let him on this mission? They were hoping he'd never find out?"

Jug Ears spoke from across the campfire. "Sera never said a word about it."

Of course his traitor of a mother didn't tell anyone, Kerry thought scornfully. Then they'd kill Paco before he could go ally with his father. She hoped they wouldn't kill him now, or there went her best bet for an ally. But Kerry had nothing to lose by pointing out that she already knew, so long as she wasn't hostile about it. The reactions might be illuminating.

Kerry cleared her throat, noting how their attention snapped her way.

"I'm looking forward to meeting my half-brother."

She enjoyed their reactions. Brisa was the best: a piece of jerky actually fell out of her mouth. Jennie and Jug Ears started, then glared at Kerry. Even the bounty hunter blinked. Only Yuki didn't react at all.

The rat broke the silence. With a happy squeak, it scurried up to grab Brisa's fallen jerky.

Brisa took another piece. "Would you like some water, Princess?"

"Yes, please." Kerry responded with the politeness that Min Soo had drilled into her. *Let's see if it actually works.*

Brisa handed a cup to Kerry. "You live in a palace, right? Is it beautiful?"

Kerry eyed Brisa's ridiculous pink ribbons. "My mother's rooms are especially beautiful. The carpets are the color of pink roses and soft as petals."

Jennie made a disgusted noise, and got up to collect the dishes. Jug Ears drew her aside, saying, "Do you have a moment?"

They walked out of earshot, leaving Yuki sitting there. He hadn't moved, not even a muscle in his face, since Kerry had mentioned her half-brother.

He was obviously concerned about Paco. Were they close friends? Boyfriends? Kerry would have to find out. But for now, she'd focus on the easiest target.

In her best Encouragement Tone, Kerry said, "So, Brisa. Tell me more about Becky."

CHAPTER TWENTY-TWO
GOLD POINT
ROSS

The gates of Gold Point loomed ahead, lit by the setting sun. Ross bent his gaze to Sally's silver mane so he wouldn't have to see the gleaming skulls. The guards joked back and forth, clearly happy to be home.

Santiago had never stopped chattering, though his voice was wearing out. "Kerry and I will have been dating for two years next month. The fifteenth is our anniversary." He took a drink of water. "I don't know what I can get a princess on a soldier's salary."

Kerry will like anything you give her, Ross thought. *I'd like a rusty bolt if Mia gave it to me.*

"Though they say it's the thought that counts." Santiago's voice was so hoarse that Ross could barely understand him. Ross listened absently, in case Santiago let any useful information slip, but so far it had all been about his home and family. Ross knew everyone's names and ages, even down to the pets.

Conversations died abruptly when a commotion around Voske resolved into individual voices.

"Kerry didn't come back," someone said.

"The princess is missing!"

Voske's voice rose above the hubbub. "Assemble all scout teams, duty and liberty. North Companies One and Two as well. Comb every path and arroyo between here and the ruined city. And around Gold Point, in case she decided to loop around town and ran into trouble. Send a medic with each team. Move!"

Santiago pressed forward, trying to catch Voske's attention. "I'll go! Sire, I'll go!" No one heard his raspy croak.

And no one seemed to be paying any mind to Ross. This could be his chance. He quietly slipped off his horse and took a step to the side, trying to blend in with the milling soldiers.

A huge hand gripped his shoulder. "I've got the prisoner," a man shouted.

"Santiago, take our guest home," Voske said.

The sinking rays of the sun sharpened the grim angles of his face. His voice was soft and even, but the way the tired soldiers snapped to unnerved alertness made Ross's neck tighten.

Santiago hustled Ross into his room, then ran off, looking frantic. Ross wondered what could have happened to Kerry. The guards had said she was an excellent rider. He hoped she hadn't been killed, and was surprised at his own thought. She'd threatened him, but she'd also noticed when he had a headache and gotten him medicine. She'd been fun to spar with. He hoped she'd turn up—for her own sake, and for Santiago.

It had been a strange end to a strange trip. Ross had been ready to make a show of refusing to prospect, then let himself be threatened or bribed into walking in—assuming the singing trees would let him in—evading the guards Voske was sure to post, and making his way back to Las Anclas. Instead, Voske had told him it was only a scouting trip, and they'd returned to Gold Point.

Now Ross was again trapped behind iron bars. He sat beneath a window to feel the night air and picked up one of Deirdre's books, to practice his reading and put off falling asleep. Most nights he woke up time and again, muscles rigid, drenched in sweat, from a dream of cave-ins or singing trees or Luis's bloody hands. But worse than the nightmares was awakening to the knowledge that he was a prisoner, locked up in his enemy's house, alone.

He read the same paragraph three times without taking in any of its meaning, but he couldn't bear to lie down on a mattress so soft that it oozed around his body like quicksand, beneath the looming ceiling. He turned off the lights and curled up on the floor, his face toward the open window.

*

The sound of his door opening made him leap to his feet, scrabbling for weapons that he didn't have.

The blue light of dawn illuminated Voske, his face in shadow, his hair glittering. "Is the bed not to your satisfaction?"

Ross pressed his back against the wall, his heart pounding. Voske had never come into his room before.

Voske closed the door. "I believe that Tom Preston is behind my daughter's disappearance. I expect the next step will be to propose a hostage exchange."

The light shifted on Voske's face as he glanced out the window. "How much are you worth to Las Anclas?"

Nothing, Ross thought, but kept silent.

"Well?" Voske said, studying Ross's face.

Jennie would want to rescue him. And Mia. Ross could imagine them trying, but he couldn't imagine them kidnapping Kerry. And Mr. Preston certainly wouldn't stir himself for Ross's sake.

As if Voske had read his mind, he said, "So you think this wasn't about you?"

"I don't know what it's about."

"Maybe Las Anclas didn't value you, but I know what you're worth. Santiago will meet you after breakfast. Dress in your best clothes. You're attending his cousin's quinceañera." Voske left, closing the door softly behind him.

The Santiago who collected Ross seemed like a different person. There was no smile, no chatter about the Brat Patrol, no talk at all as he escorted Ross toward the garrison. He looked so miserable that Ross gave up on his resolve to keep silent.

"Did you go looking for Kerry?" Ross asked.

Santiago shook his head. "The king ordered me to stay back. But I heard it was freezing in the desert last night. Kerry didn't even take a coat."

"She won't freeze. She had a horse. I used to lean up against Rusty— my burro—on cold nights." *Before Voske's soldiers stole him,* Ross thought bitterly.

Santiago frowned. "The king thinks she was kidnapped."

"If she was, they'll keep her alive. Like you guys did with me."

"That's true." Santiago looked a little less gloomy, but he didn't continue the conversation.

They walked in silence past the royal stables, then a corral where work horses and burros grazed. A familiar bray startled Ross. *Rusty?* Disbelief made him turn his head to scan the herds. It *was* Rusty!

Rusty clearly recognized Ross, too. The little donkey's long ears pricked forward, and he headed straight for Ross. Ross's heart lifted. He was about to whistle to Rusty to come and get his ears scratched. Then he dropped his hand.

If Voske found out about Rusty, he'd have another threat to hold over Ross. It would probably end in Rusty getting killed. Ross turned his back. Santiago, lost in his own thoughts, hadn't noticed a thing.

Rusty kept on braying, getting louder and more desperate with every step Ross took. The poor animal must think Ross hadn't noticed him, or, worse, was deliberately ignoring him. Ross steeled himself to not look back.

Behind him, there was a rattle and crash.

"What's got into that burro?" Santiago asked, glancing back. "It's trying to kick down the fence."

Ross shrugged. He didn't want to talk within Rusty's hearing. The little donkey knew his voice so well, it would only encourage Rusty to keep trying to get to him. Rusty might even hurt himself trying to jump the fence.

For once, Ross wished Santiago would keep talking. But that was all he said. Ross clenched his teeth and stepped up his pace, until Rusty's frantic braying faded in the distance.

He was relieved when that annoying lightning girl, Bankar, came charging out of a building and almost ran them down.

"Hello-o-o-o, Santiago," she cooed. "Didn't see you in the search party. Does your widdle collarbone hurt too much?"

"I had other orders." He took a breath that Ross could hear. "Where did you search?"

"Past the power plant, all the way up to the dam." She flapped a dismissive hand. "Was *that* a waste of time! As if East Company Two wouldn't have spotted her."

"Did anyone find anything?" Santiago asked.

"Nah. But some things found some of us. Not *my* team. Six bought it, and more than twenty were injured."

Santiago froze. "Who died?"

"No idea. Want to know what got them?" Before Santiago could answer, she smirked. "Three of them walked right into a jelly trap, a pit mouth got two, and one got bitten by some poisonous… thing. Oh, and your buddy Max got clawed by a Gila monster."

"How bad?"

"He's already out of the infirmary. There's a list posted at garrison HQ." She jerked her thumb at the building she'd emerged from.

"Thanks, *Shanti*. Would you stay with Ross while I take a look?" Santiago hurried inside.

Bankar studied Ross. "I hear *he's* been talking to you a lot." She flicked two fingers at the hair by her temples, as if not saying Voske's name would keep him from overhearing. "Has he told you about Prince Sean?"

Ross shrugged, though he couldn't help being curious.

Bankar lowered her voice. "He was the king's oldest son. The crown prince. He was Changed from birth." She slowly turned her head, as if something was going to pop out from behind the feed sheds. "He was invisible all the time, unless he chose to appear. So nobody noticed when he left. *If* he left."

Though Ross could tell she was trying to scare him, his neck tightened.

Bankar continued, "They say he died on patrol, but no one ever found as much as a bone or a tooth. Not even an invisible bone or tooth! We all think he's still here...watching. He could be in your bedroom, with a knife. The knife would be invisible, too."

Santiago came out of the office, looking relieved. He must not have known anyone who'd died. In Las Anclas, everyone knew everyone. It once again brought home to Ross how huge Gold Point was, and how easily Voske could muster a bigger army to set on Las Anclas.

"Sweet dreams," Bankar sang. She flipped back her blue-black hair and sauntered away.

"What was Bankar going on about?" Santiago asked.

"Telling me ghost stories about invisible Prince Sean lurking in my room with an invisible knife."

Santiago looked around, then spoke quietly. "Sean was a friend of mine. He didn't lurk with knives."

"Was he really invisible?"

"Not exactly. His Change was active all the time, so you tended to not notice him unless he concentrated on making himself noticeable. But if you remembered to look for him, you'd see him."

Dr. Lee had told Ross the same thing, before the battle at Las Anclas. "Is that why everyone keeps glancing around? They're looking for Sean?"

Santiago nodded. "People were scared of him, because..."

Because he reported back to Voske, Ross thought.

"Well, they shouldn't have been. He was a good guy. But he disappeared. Really disappeared." Santiago leaned in to whisper, "The king was furious. That's why we don't talk about him. But yeah, people look around because...the king knows things."

Maybe not as much as you think, Ross thought. Though Voske had known what Ross had said to the gophers, he didn't know about Mia's weapon. That confirmed Ross's theory that the spy thing couldn't see in the dark.

Santiago sighed. "I keep looking for Sean because I hope I'll see him. I like to think he's still alive somewhere."

A deep boom echoed back from the distant mountains. Ross jumped.

"It's just blasting at the construction site. We're building another dam." Santiago waved his hand in an easterly direction, then smiled brightly. Too brightly. "Let's go. I promised Maria-Luz I'd help bake the cake for her quinceañera. Did I ever tell you how I learned to bake, Ross? It all began..."

*

It was evening when they headed back to the palace. Ross couldn't wait to be alone, even though it meant being locked up. It wasn't that he disliked Santiago. If he had, the desperation behind Santiago's smile wouldn't have bothered him so much.

Except for the little kids, Santiago's entire family had been like that, watching Ross anxiously while they asked him if he liked the food, if he wanted anything more, if he was comfortable, if he wanted to dance. Whenever he spoke, everyone fell silent to listen. A quinceañera was supposed to celebrate the girl's fifteenth birthday, but the party guests had been more focused on Ross than on pretty Maria-Luz in her tiara and sparkling pink dress. It was unnerving.

As he and Santiago started up the garden path, soldiers began running toward the palace.

"There's news of the princess!" one shouted.

Voske appeared at the palace door, and the crowd of soldiers immediately quieted. He held up a small object that sparkled red under the electric light.

"Princess Kerry's earring has been found." The king paused as the crowd gave a loud cheer. "I believe she left it as a message for us. The search is continuing. Once we find her other earring, we'll have a vector. You may return to your duties."

The crowd dispersed. Santiago dashed up to salute the king.

"You think she's been captured?" Santiago asked.

"I am certain now, yes. I expect when we find her other earring, it'll point us straight to Las Anclas." Voske smiled.

Ross felt that smile aimed at him like a crossbow bolt.

"Are you going to attack?" Santiago asked eagerly. "I volunteer."

Voske shook his head. "We'll wait for their messenger. I'm sure one will be along soon. If we rush to the attack, I'm afraid the first casualty would be Kerry."

"I volunteer to intercept the messenger," Santiago offered.

Voske clapped him on the shoulder. "I appreciate your enthusiasm. But you have your orders."

CHAPTER TWENTY-THREE
LAS ANCLAS
KERRY

Kerry's first sight of the walls of Las Anclas revealed at least three breaches of discipline that should have earned the slackers twenty lashes. Instead of standing in proper formation, the sentries—a large number of them teens — clumped together, leaning recklessly over the shields and presenting themselves as easy targets. They chattered loudly and excitedly when they should have kept silent. Most disgraceful of all, several held their crossbows dangling carelessly and their longbows loose.

She'd been captured by a town of incompetents. How humiliating.

Several sentries squealed like pigs as they came closer. Kerry tipped her head back to get a better look at the shameful commotion. Sunlight fell on her face, making her squint.

All noises stopped.

A voice broke the silence. "Who's that girl?"

"Haven't I see her before?" another voice inquired.

"Where's Ross?" a third person called.

Every sentry began shouting at once. Discipline was totally unknown here, obviously. A guy yelled into a bullhorn, but was ignored.

"Quiet!" It was a woman's voice. Now everyone shut up. "Open the gates."

As the party rode through the gates, a woman with two black braids descended the steps from the sentry walk. Maybe that was the mayor.

Kerry's captors dismounted. She toyed with the idea of making a break for it, but the reins whipped away from her hand as if they had a life of their own and smacked into Jennie's outstretched palm. Kerry dismounted, pretending not to notice.

As a kid led her horse away, Kerry turned. A skull stared at her. She jumped, then realized that it was only a Changed face. The woman with the braids watched Kerry from one brown eye in half of an elegant face, and one yellow snake eye from a deep socket in thin skin stretched over bone.

Kerry was impressed. That face had to be great for intimidating people. And if you weren't intimidated—Kerry was not, of course—it was amazingly cool. She couldn't stop looking at it.

Kerry wondered who the woman was. She couldn't be the mayor. The renegade Tom Preston hated Changed people, and he was the mayor's husband.

"Jennie, who is this?" the skull-faced woman asked.

Kerry summoned all the dignity Min Soo had taught her. "I am Princess Kerry Ji Sun Voske."

The woman clapped. "Lockdown!"

The crowd broke up almost as fast as they would have in Gold Point, scrambling up the stairs to the wall or dispersing in an orderly fashion across the square.

Interesting, Kerry thought. Maybe this woman was the *real* power in town.

She was startled by a bell ringing out the same pattern used in Gold Point. Preston had even stolen the bell patterns from Father!

"Julio! All patrols to the outer perimeter!" A big, scowling man strode up, scattering the last of the gawkers.

He wore silver-rimmed glasses, and his pale blue eyes were startling against his dark skin. That had to be the traitor Preston. Father had described him in detail.

"Is there any pursuit?" Preston asked.

"We haven't seen any signs of it," Jennie replied.

But they're coming, Kerry thought. She hoped Santiago would lead them.

Preston addressed the skull-faced woman. "Sheriff Crow, we'll take this discussion to my house."

"No," Sheriff Crow said. "We'll take it to the jail."

She talked to Preston like they were equals. Even more interesting. Maybe Preston had been demoted for poor performance in the battle. Father had taught her to detect rivalries between people and use that to her advantage, and these two certainly seemed to have a rivalry.

Sheriff Crow started down a path between paltry vegetable plots, flanked by Jennie and Preston. Mr. Vilas and Yuki closed in on either side of Kerry, preventing her from following on Jennie's heels. Brisa and Indra were so close behind Kerry they were practically breathing down her neck. The four of them herded her like an old cow. She couldn't hear a word of the report Jennie must be giving.

They were taking her to the jail. That meant she'd be interrogated. And, most likely, tortured.

Kerry forced herself not to flinch, but her heart tried to burst through her chest. She reminded herself that she was a valuable prisoner. They'd hurt her, but they wouldn't do any permanent damage.

Remember your training, Kerry thought. *They'll want to know about Father's 'spy device.' I have to come up with enough plausible lies that if I break and tell the truth, they'll never be able to tell the difference.*

She couldn't help wondering what sort of torture they'd use, though Father had said she shouldn't obsess about that. He'd warned her that if she was ever captured, her jailers would give her plenty of time to sit by herself, getting more and more scared. Exactly like they'd done to Ross.

Well, *she* wasn't going to curl up in a miserable little ball in the corner of the room. She'd show them how a princess behaved. Kerry raised her head high.

"Jennie!" a hysterical shriek rose up. "Where's Ross?"

A short, slovenly girl erupted from behind a hedge, clutching a screwdriver. She was splattered with grease from her glasses to the knees of her overalls.

"Is Ross dead?" she wailed.

"He's alive," Jennie said. "We just couldn't get to him."

Brisa bounced up to Grease Girl, and patted her kindly. "We saw him. He really was alive."

"Did he see *you?*" howled Grease Girl. "Does he know he's not alone? It's been nineteen days! Nineteen days and seven hours! Nineteen days, seven hours, and twenty—"

To Kerry's surprise, the tough, emotionless Jennie didn't annihilate Grease Girl and her stupid questions. "I *will* get him back to you, Mia. I promised you I would, and I will."

Kerry examined the disheveled girl with new interest. *That* was Ross's girlfriend?

Mia wormed between Mr. Vilas and Yuki to snatch at Kerry's sleeve. Her eyes were startlingly like Kerry's own, behind those filthy glasses.

"What did you do to him?" Mia demanded.

Kerry offered her a sympathetic look. "He's perfectly fine—"

"Mia," Preston said warningly. "Your father will tell you what the council hears. Your Lockdown position is in the surgery."

Mia opened her mouth as if she was longing to talk more, then fled.

Good, Kerry thought. *One more tool for me to use.*

They reached a low adobe building. The windows on the left-hand side had iron bars in them. Kerry's insides tightened.

Don't borrow trouble, she reminded herself. *Remember your stories. You were taught by the best. You're prepared for anything.*

Everyone crowded inside the jailhouse. Kerry didn't see any torture devices, only racks of weapons and a table with wooden chairs. The jails in Gold Point were much better equipped.

"Good work," said Preston to the team. "I wish I could give you some liberty, but you'll have it after Lockdown. Go take your positions."

As everyone but Preston and the sheriff filed out, Kerry took a better look around the room. The weapons were locked up, but she spotted the back wall through a window. It wasn't all that far away...

The front door was five steps behind her. The sheriff, who undoubtedly had a Change power, was heading for an iron door. Preston had gone around the table to grab some chairs. He looked as tough as his reputation, but she knew he wasn't Changed, and there was gray in his hair.

It took five of them to capture me, Kerry thought. *I can handle two.*

She bolted for the door.

Before she made her second step, a powerful force slammed her to the floor. A knee like iron dug into the small of her back, and hands like steel claws pinned hers to the ground. Kerry tried to wrench free, but all she could move was her head.

The hand pinning her wrists shifted. Kerry gasped as fingers closed around the scruff of her shirt, and she was slung like a sack of grain through the cell door onto a hard dirt floor. That sheriff was incredibly strong and fast. Why hadn't Kerry been briefed on her?

"You can sit there and think about being more cooperative," said Preston.

"Deputy," Sheriff Crow called.

A woman walked in, rifle tucked under her armpit.

"She can create invisible weapons," said the sheriff. "Don't get within six feet of her."

The sheriff and Preston left Kerry alone with the deputy.

Kerry tried not to be too disappointed at her failed escape. She'd gained valuable knowledge, so it hadn't been a waste. She'd use the time she was supposed to spend worrying about being tortured to review her stories.

CHAPTER TWENTY-FOUR
LAS ANCLAS
YUKI

Yuki's Lockdown station was at the front gate. But his mother waved him off, saying, "I have enough coverage. Go get some rest."

Yuki couldn't rest until he'd seen Paco. He paced impatiently around the front gate. Paco and his patrol should have been back by now. Yuki had to be the person to tell Paco about Kerry—about Voske.

Paco had thought his father had been a traveler, maybe a musician like himself, someone carefree and light-hearted. Not a tyrant. Not the man who had killed his mother.

His sister Meredith pounded up, panting. "Yuki! Paco's patrol is coming in through the back gate."

"Damn!" Yuki ran, leaping over the low fences dividing people's vegetable patches. The way news traveled in Las Anclas, he might already be too late.

He skidded up to the back gate just as Julio said, "No, I didn't know. I'm as surprised as you are."

"Poor kid," Frances replied, scratching her head. "No wonder Sera never talked about his father."

Paco stood beside his horse, the reins trailing in the dust where he must have dropped them. His face was as blank and tense as when he'd gotten the news that his mother had been killed.

Yuki felt like he'd been kicked in the stomach. He put his hand on Paco's shoulder, then snatched it away when Paco stiffened. "I only found out in Gold Point, Paco. I ran here to tell you—"

"No, really, it's perfect." Henry Callahan smirked at them. "It all makes sense now. Of course a prince would only want to date another prince."

It was like someone else took over Yuki's body. Without ever making a decision, there was a flash of pain in his fist, and then he was looking down at Henry sprawled in the dust, nose bleeding.

"What was that for? Can't you take a joke?" Henry said thickly, hand pressed to his nose.

Sheriff Crow grabbed Henry's collar and yanked him to his feet. "Aren't you supposed to be on the front wall?"

"We just rode in," Henry began protesting, but the sheriff gave him a hard shove. He ran off, muttering plaintively, "What's got into everyone?"

"Paco, I wanted to tell you first," Yuki said.

Paco's stricken gaze lifted to Sheriff Crow's face. "But they all knew," he whispered. He sounded utterly betrayed. "The adults."

"Not everyone," Frances said. "I'd just joined the Rangers when she came here. She never told any of us who your father was."

The Sheriff looked away, and Paco said flatly, "*You* knew, Sheriff Crow. Mr. Preston sure knew. That's why he wouldn't let me go to Gold Point. He didn't trust me."

Sheriff Crow shook her head. "Paco, no. He was trying to protect you. Your mother only told her best friends. We hoped you would never find out. That's what she wanted."

At the word 'mother' Paco's eyes shuttered.

Mr. Preston pushed through the crowd. "Everyone without a Lockdown station, go back to work. Everyone else, go home. Show's over."

That broke up the crowd.

"We can talk at the harvest barn," Mr. Preston said. "Yuki? Why aren't you at Lockdown?"

"My mother dismissed—"

"Don't go." Paco grabbed Yuki's arm, then said to Mr. Preston, "Anything you have to say, he can hear."

Yuki would gladly have gone if Paco hadn't wanted him there. Dread tightened his neck as they walked into the barn. Mr. Preston left the door open, but Paco slammed it. The hot air suffocated Yuki, thick with the smells of dust and hay.

Paco faced Mr. Preston. "You don't trust me. You thought if I found out, I'd betray this town."

Mr. Preston raised a hand, palm out. "Stop. Stop right there, Paco. None of us ever thought that. Keeping the secret was your mother's wish."

Paco muttered, "That's easy for you to say. She's dead."

Yuki had seen Mr. Preston lose his temper when people gave him backtalk, but not this time. "You can ask Dr. Lee. He delivered you. It was almost the first thing Sera said after you were born."

Paco made a noise almost like a sob. Then he shut his teeth with a click.

Mr. Preston took a step away, like he was trying to figure out what to say next. Then he came back. "We hoped you would never find out."

"Was she *married* to him?" Paco asked.

"No, no." Mr. Preston waved like he was pushing the words away, "We were teenagers. Your age." As if he was trying to make a joke, he said, "I know that must seem hard for you boys to believe."

Neither Yuki nor Paco smiled.

"Back then, Gold Point was ruled by Voske's mother." Mr. Preston shuddered, something Yuki had never seen him do before. "The queen had the most horrific Change I've ever seen. She wore a black leather glove over her right hand—just the right one, to make sure nobody ever forgot what was underneath. It was a skeleton hand, nothing but rattling white bones. If she touched you with it, you died."

Yuki's skin crept. Was that the origin of Mr. Preston's prejudice against the Changed?

Mr. Preston went on, "The princes and princesses had hand-picked bodyguards their own age. They liked to start them young, to make sure they grew up loyal. Orphans were preferred, so they'd be as close to their charge as if they were family. Omar and Sera and I were Voske's bodyguards—he was Prince Ian, then. The queen specifically picked Norms for him, so he wouldn't be jealous."

Paco clenched his fists. "If you're working up to telling me that he raped her, just go ahead and say it."

"Nothing like that." Mr. Preston shook his head. "Ian was good-looking and popular, even apart from being a prince. We were all friends."

Paco made a noise of disgust.

Mr. Preston ignored that. "I was about to go to Las Anclas as a spy, to learn its weaknesses before Ian led his first attack against a major town. We all knew my mission was dangerous, and even if it went fine, I wouldn't be back for months. The four of us went camping, and we took a jug of hard cider. When I woke up the next morning, Sera and Ian were in the same sleeping bag. It was the first time for them both. We all thought it was funny."

Paco dropped his head, hiding his face. Yuki wanted to hide too, but with embarrassment. He couldn't imagine what Paco was feeling.

Mr. Preston cleared his throat. "You both know how I fell in love with Valeria, and decided I wanted to have a new life in Las Anclas. But I wasn't sure what I should do, or who I should tell. When I headed back to Gold Point, Sera met me outside the walls and told me she was pregnant. I thought she should know that there was another town where no one could order your head chopped off on a whim."

Paco's shoulders tensed as he crossed his arms. Yuki wiped his damp hands down his pants.

Mr. Preston had paused, as if waiting for Paco to respond, but when the pause turned into a silence, he continued in the tone adults used when they reminisced. "My first thought was to tell Ian I wanted to move to Las Anclas, and ask him to leave it alone. Back then, civilians were allowed to leave Gold Point if they wanted. Soldiers had to get permission, but it was usually granted. Ian was my friend. I thought he'd let me go."

Paco was still. Yuki could feel him listening intently.

Mr. Preston sighed. "Luckily, I talked to Sera first. She and Ian had gotten close while I was gone. He'd confided in her that he'd killed the crown prince the year before—his own brother! It was while Sera, Omar, and I were on a training mission. Ian had made it look like an accident. His brother had argued with him about his plan to make Gold Point into an empire. Sera convinced me that if I told Ian how I felt, he wouldn't hesitate to put my head on a pike."

Paco said bitterly, "And that's my father."

"It takes more than blood to make a father, Paco," Mr. Preston replied. "Ian Voske is nothing to you, no more than that girl sitting in jail right now. You are your mother's son."

CHAPTER TWENTY-FIVE
LAS ANCLAS
KERRY

Kerry estimated that an hour had passed before Preston and Sheriff Crow returned, and wondered why they'd given her so little time to terrify herself. In Gold Point, prisoners were usually left alone overnight. She remembered Ross huddled in the corner of the cube, trembling, his hair and shirt soaked with sweat. He must have sat like that all night...

Kerry shook her head, driving out that image and the unpleasant feelings that accompanied it. It was time for the Prisoner Game—and she meant to win.

Sheriff Crow dismissed the deputy, and she and Preston sat in chairs just out of Kerry's range.

"How does Voske get his information?" Preston asked.

Excellent. Other than the time frame, everything was going exactly as expected. Kerry could definitely handle these people.

She hastily reviewed the order of her lies. Start with the one everyone in Gold Point believed. "He found an artifact. It shows anything you want to see and hear. He always keeps it with him."

Preston and Sheriff Crow didn't look surprised. Like Kerry had thought, they'd heard those rumors in Las Anclas. Good. Maybe they'd believe it.

"How is it powered?" Preston asked.

Kerry considered possible answers, then remembered what her father had said: *'I don't know' is always safe.*

"I don't know." She tugged at her collar. Time to test them. Would they give her a carrot right away? "Can I get a drink of water?"

Preston said, "No."

Simultaneously, the sheriff said, "Earn it."

"I did earn it," Kerry protested.

Sheriff Crow dangled a carrot. "Tell us something everyone in Gold Point doesn't already know."

Kerry pretended to think. "Um…it only works about ten minutes every day." By the way Preston's eyes narrowed and the sheriff's chin lifted, they found that plausible. Gold Point citizens also found it a plausible explanation for why her father knew some things, but not others.

"Who found it?" demanded Sheriff Crow.

"A prospector," Kerry replied.

"What prospector?" That was Preston.

"Her name is Pru."

"When did she find it?"

"Three years ago."

"Where?" The questions were coming faster, almost interrupting her answers.

"Somewhere out east. In the mountains."

Sheriff Crow asked, "Is your father watching Catalina?"

Kerry hadn't thought of an answer for that one. Who cared about Catalina? They didn't even have a military, just traders and winemakers and goat-breeders and entertainers. "Um…"

Preston snapped, "Making up lies?"

"No!" She gulped in a deep breath. Did that sound upset that they disbelieved her, or rattled because she'd been caught in a lie? "I don't know."

Now she sounded weak. She had to do better. She'd been trained to resist interrogation by the king of Gold Point!

"How many soldiers in your father's army?"

"Enough." It would be plausible for her to refuse to answer that. She waited for the threat of violence.

It didn't come.

"When is your father planning to attack Las Anclas?"

Today, I hope. She tried not to think of Santiago. Surely Kerry getting captured would be a bigger priority for Father than exploring the ruined city.

"Well?"

"I don't know!"

Sheriff Crow leaned in. "Where did that prospector find the device?"

"I don't *know*," Kerry repeated. "Father never told me."

She saw the trap a second after the sheriff closed it.

"The truth now," Sheriff Crow said warningly. "How does your father get his information?"

Time for the second lie. It would sound better if she let them threaten her first. She folded her arms and kept quiet. Would threats be enough, though? Maybe she should let them hit her.

But they just sat there, watching her. Were they trying to outwait her? It was strange—they'd followed the script she'd been taught, except that they hadn't gotten to the threats yet.

Kerry decided to prompt them. "Can I have some water? I'm so thirsty."

Preston said, "Answer the question."

Sheriff Crow said, "If you're honest with us, we'll give you some water."

Ah-ha! Preston was playing the tough captor, and the sheriff was the nice one. Kerry knew that game. She addressed the sheriff. "Promise?"

The sheriff nodded.

"Well," Kerry said, dragging it out like she hated telling the real truth. "It's not a device. It's my brother Sean. He's Changed. He can turn invisible. We tell everyone that he ran away, but really he's out spying. He's been all over your town."

"Liar," Preston said so sharply that Kerry jumped. "I look for Sean every day. He's never been inside our walls."

"I need water," Kerry said. "It's hot in here. I could get heat stroke."

Preston retorted, "You think I care? Did you think you were taken as a hostage? Your father doesn't do trades. You're only valuable as a source of information. So you had better start producing, or you can sit there and die of thirst."

Jennie and Indra had argued over whether it had been right to take her as a hostage to exchange her for Ross. Preston must be lying. Or had Jennie and Indra staged that argument so she'd cooperate all the way here?

Preston's chair creaked as he shifted his weight. "Start talking, or I walk out of here and don't come back until it's time for your execution."

The sheriff stood up. Kerry stared at her back as she walked out the door. Preston stood, too.

"Wait!" Kerry said. "Give me some water and I'll tell you everything."

Preston put his hands on his hips. "No lies, now. No clever little pauses while you think up your next answer."

"I promise."

The sheriff returned with a glass of water and set it on the hard-packed dirt of the floor, out of Kerry's reach.

Kerry licked her dry lips. "There's a spy in your town. I don't know who it is, and I swear I'm not lying about that. Father didn't tell me because he was afraid something like this might happen."

Preston's eyes widened—he was going for it! "How long has this person been here?"

She'd thought that one out. Everything she said had to fit with the actual time that Pru had Changed three years ago. "I think—I'm not sure, but I think it's someone who's been here for a long time, but only started talking to us a few years ago."

"How many years?"

"About three."

The questions started coming faster and faster. "How are they passing the information on to your father?"

"He has someone meet them."

"Where?"

"Outside of town somewhere."

"Where exactly?"

"I don't know. Not very far."

"When was the last time they met?"

"I'm not sure. I don't know every time it happens."

"When was the last time that you know about?"

"After the battle."

Preston leaned forward. "Is the person Changed?"

He obviously wanted her to say yes. Kerry had been trained to take advantage of exactly this moment, when you realize what your captor already wants to believe. But if she agreed, she might get some random Changed person in town killed. Not that she cared about anyone in Las Anclas. Then again, this would be her town someday. Her people.

"I don't know," Kerry said.

"You're lying. You made up the entire story." Sheriff Crow kicked over the water glass.

Kerry barely kept herself from lunging after it. She forced herself to look away from the puddle darkening the floor, and it was a good thing she did, because she caught the quick glare that Preston sent at Sheriff Crow. The sheriff thought Kerry was lying, but Preston believed the story. Perfect. Now to drive a wedge between them.

Kerry turned to Preston. "You were hoping I'd say the spy was Changed, whether it's true or not. You hate Changed people." Now she deliberately moved her head to gaze at the sheriff. "What's it like to work with someone who can't stand to look at your face? In Gold Point, someone like you would never have to put up with that."

She sneaked a peek at Preston, whose lips were pressed in a line. Excellent! "My father values our Changed citizens. He's Changed himself. It's not too late to go where you'll be appreciated."

Sheriff Crow gave a short laugh. "Nice try."

Preston started to stomp out. Before he reached the door, a man popped in. "Mr. Preston, the patrols have searched all the way to Sepulveda Arroyo. There's no sign of pursuit."

"Thank you," Preston said. "Tell the bell ringer to signal the end of Lockdown. There is no danger from Gold Point."

With that, the sheriff and Preston walked out, without even a backward glance.

Kerry flopped onto the narrow cot. The cell really was hot, and she really was thirsty. Her head ached. She wasn't sure if she'd actually tricked Preston, or if he'd been playing her. Being interrogated was much harder in real life than it had been at prisoner-of-war camp, even though nobody had hit her here.

But now that she thought about it, nobody had hit her very hard in training. Maybe they hadn't pushed her as much as they should have. Father had said they wouldn't go easy on her, but maybe they had out of fear. She'd never been afraid of the trainers.

Even her night in the hell cell hadn't been that bad. It had been cold and uncomfortable, but she wasn't afraid of small places. She'd even gotten some sleep, knowing that her breakfast would be waiting in the palace when the training was over. Kerry wished she was back in the hell cell right now.

As soon as the lights were out, she'd create a trowel and see how hard the wall was.

*

Finally. *Finally*, it was quiet. Kerry waited until she was sure it was about three in the morning. Nobody would expect her to make a move at that hour.

In the coal-black darkness, Kerry held out her hand and created a pickaxe. She began to quietly dig into the adobe of the north wall of her cell. If she could make a hole big enough to fit through, she'd dash to the wall, evade or kill the sentries, and flee into the desert.

One scrape at a time, careful, slow, steady. After an hour or so had crawled by, she'd dug a hole about the size of her fist. But she resisted the urge to hurry. She had time—so long as nobody heard her.

Light glared on. She instinctively threw up her hands, blinded. There was a scrape of metal against metal. A fist slammed across her cheek and jaw, knocking her down.

She sprawled onto her stomach. Before she could summon a weapon, a knee thumped painfully into her back, knocking her breath out, and her hands were pinioned to the floor.

Preston's voice roared, "Sheriff!"

Kerry lifted her head, one eye blurry and throbbing. The sheriff appeared in rumpled practice gear, her long black hair loose and messy.

"Look at the wall," Preston snarled. "Your prisoner needs watching twenty-four-seven."

Preston's knee lifted, and his hard fingers closed on Kerry's collar and slung her against the back wall.

Before she could recover, he was out of the cell. The door slammed shut.

"You had no call to hit her." The sheriff turned to Kerry. "A half-inch more and you would have hit stone. Feel free to keep tunneling if you don't believe me."

Preston stomped away, as the sheriff called, "Deputy!"

A young man walked in.

"Watch her." The sheriff pointed to a chair out of Kerry's reach, and walked out with Preston.

Kerry turned her back on the deputy. Her face hurt, but Preston hadn't knocked out any teeth or broken any bones. She'd been hit that hard during sparring. She could take it. What's more, it made Preston predictable. Maybe later she could make use of his temper. As Father said, true power lay in understanding other people and using their weaknesses against them.

She lay down on the cot. Sleep would make time pass faster. But she'd scarcely closed her eyes when roaring voices broke into her doze.

The sheriff and several deputies hustled four yelling, staggering drunks into the jailhouse.

"Ooooh my darrrling, ooooh my darling…" a man bawled at the top of his lungs—off-key.

"You won't get away with this," a woman slurred. "My uncle, I mean my cousin—my uncle's cousin is on the council!"

Iron rattled as other cells opened and slammed shut.

It couldn't be as late as Kerry had thought. She had totally miscalculated. She covered her ears in disgust, but her hands were no match for four loud drunks.

"Hey! You can't put me in here! This is a supply closet!"

"Shut up, Pham. You're always complaining."

"*You* shut up. It's your fault."

"You shut up! Why did you have to throw your beer in Jack's face?"

"It was flat! Jack's an idiot. You're an idiot. Let me out of here, you idiot!" Iron bars rattled.

Through it all the fourth drunk caterwauled his way through three verses of "My Darling Clementine," Kerry's least favorite song of all time. Bankar liked to sing it to annoy her.

At least it only had ten verses.

The singing drunk got to verse four, paused … then started over at the beginning.

"Shut up!" all three of the other drunks bellowed.

The singer sang louder.

I'd rather be in a hell cell, facing torture, she thought. *No, this IS torture. I bet Preston got them drunk on purpose!*

Drunk Two threw up.

CHAPTER TWENTY-SIX
LAS ANCLAS
JENNIE

"Jennie. Time to wake up, honey."

Jennie groggily opened her eyes, wondering how she'd gotten into bed. She remembered leaving the princess at the jail, coming home, and Ma and Pa making her eat a bowl of stew. She must have fallen asleep at the table.

Ma was leaning over her bed. "I've got your breakfast waiting."

Jennie never slept this late. It was strange to see sunlight coming in at that angle. She found both her parents in the kitchen, which rarely happened during the day. No one else was around, which was also rare.

"We kept some corn muffins warm for you," Ma said, as Pa cracked a couple of eggs into the frying pan.

"What's going on?" Jennie asked.

Pa turned away from the stove so Ma could read his lips. "There's going to be a town meeting to discuss and vote on the situation with the princess."

"The town is voting?" Jennie asked, alarmed. "You mean they might not even do the hostage exchange?"

Ma said gently, "It's hard to say how the town will vote. To me, the princess is just a girl. But to others, she's the mutant daughter of our worst enemy. And Ross is also Changed. I wish it was a simple situation, but it's not."

"It seemed simple enough to me." The anger Jennie had felt when the bounty hunter had tried to kill Ross rose up again. Her voice rose to a shout. "I know kidnapping is wrong! But I had to do *something* to save Ross."

Pa slid the eggs on to Jennie's plate. "We're not second-guessing a choice you made in the heart of enemy territory. It's just a fact that quick decisions can have very long-lasting consequences."

"I had to do *something*," Jennie repeated. Staring down at her eggs, she muttered, "I don't even know if I want to be a Ranger anymore."

The moment she said it, she hoped that Pa hadn't heard and Ma hadn't seen her lips.

"Maybe that's for the best," said Ma. "I don't think it's right for someone your age to have to make those sorts of decisions."

Jennie had thought she'd had her fill of horrible moral dilemmas. But once Ma implied that she wasn't mature enough to handle them, her temper boiled over. "Well, someone has to."

She left her breakfast uneaten and flung herself out. She hated fighting with her parents—she hadn't slammed the door on them since she was thirteen.

She started for the town hall, then realized that she didn't know when the meeting would be. Then she turned toward the Ranger practice yard. But what if Mr. Preston was there?

Jennie couldn't avoid the defense chief forever. But she was afraid that if he asked her for a report—if he questioned her *at all* about her decision —she wouldn't be able to stop herself from shouting, *You told that bounty hunter to kill Ross!*

Let the bounty hunter deliver the report. He probably had already.

Jennie wondered who else she could ask about the town meeting. It was noon. The students would be outside for lunch. She ran to the school, where she spotted Brisa, Becky, Meredith, and Sujata, eating under an ironwood tree.

That was new. Sujata was friends with Becky, but not with Brisa. Meredith was friends with Brisa, but not with Becky. And Jennie had always been under the impression that Sujata and Meredith disliked each other. But they all seemed friendly now. Maybe Sujata and Meredith being in Ranger training together had changed things.

"Have some dead bread!" Brisa offered Jennie a bun frosted with an unnervingly realistic skull. "I made it early."

Jennie's empty stomach lurched. "I'm stuffed, thanks."

Jennie had forgotten that Day of the Dead was coming soon. All over town, people would be building altars, decorating graves, leaving offerings of food and flowers, parading around in skull masks, and praying for and remembering loved ones who died.

Not a day goes by that I don't remember Sera, Jennie thought. *I wish there was a special day to forget.*

Meredith cheerfully bit into a skeleton-frosted bun. "What was it like, hauling that princess over the mountains?"

Before Jennie could answer, Brisa said happily, "It was fun! Well, not at first. But we won her over. She's dying to meet you all, especially you, Becky. I told her all about you."

It certainly looked as if Kerry had won over Brisa. But Jennie had caught Kerry shooting a contemptuous glance at Brisa's back. "She was play-acting, Brisa. She hates us."

Brisa looked hurt. "Imagine if you were her. She was riding along peacefully when she got kidnapped, dragged away from her home, and then thrown in jail. She had every reason to be mean to me, but she wasn't."

"Will you take me to meet her?" Becky asked.

Sujata added, "I used to love stories about princesses."

"I never cared about princesses," remarked Meredith. "But her power sounds cool. The challenge you'd get, fighting with someone who can create invisible weapons!"

Jennie couldn't believe that Kerry had managed to not only win over Brisa, but to get Brisa to sway others to her side. All it convinced Jennie of was that Kerry was dangerous. "Brisa, don't get so friendly with her that she talks you into some ridiculous scheme to let her go."

Brisa's eyes rounded in shock. "I would never! It's treason!"

Jennie wished she'd been more tactful. "Sorry. I know that. Hey, when's the town meeting?"

"Half an hour," said Meredith. "School's been closed. Everybody's going."

Teenagers who still attended school seldom went to town meetings, since they didn't have a vote. Despite Brisa's assurances, Jennie couldn't help being suspicious.

"You all want to know what will happen to Voske's daughter?" Jennie asked.

Brisa nodded guiltily.

"And Ross," Becky said softly.

*

Jennie had never been at such a long, unendurable meeting. She was appalled to see people stand up and argue that Ross was too dangerous to have in town, and therefore no hostage exchange should be attempted. Nor did she like the arguments for letting Kerry Voske wander around town under armed guard. Jennie respected Kerry's power, but her most lethal weapon was her tongue.

Mr. Horst was *still* going on about Changed monsters. Jennie's rage rose up in a blinding red fog.

Sheriff Crow interrupted him. "I think the 'Changed monster' side has had its say."

The mayor nodded. "I agree that all sides have spoken. I will sum them up, and then we will hold a vote."

Felicité wrote fast as Mayor Wolfe counted on her fingers. "One: we send a messenger to Gold Point, to request an exchange of hostages." When people started muttering, she held up her hand, silencing them. "Two: we execute the prisoner. Three: we keep her indefinitely as a hostage against the safety of Las Anclas. Four: we let her go."

Jennie blinked. That was the first time she'd heard that suggestion. It would make her entire mission pointless.

Mr. Preston spoke loudly. "My vote is to attempt the exchange. The girl has clearly been trained to resist interrogation, so we're unlikely to get any useful information from her. Ross, however, has proved his value to the town. But if Voske doesn't agree to the exchange, we should cut our losses and kill the girl. If nothing else, it will prove that we don't make empty threats."

The way Mr. Preston raised his voice, Jennie wondered if he was addressing Voske's mysterious spy device.

Judge Vardam spoke up, her voice thin but steady. "We do not kill people who have not committed a crime." Next to her, Dr. Lee nodded.

Someone shouted from the back, "No matter what, we have to treat her better."

Someone else chimed in, "Yeah! What if Voske does conquer Las Anclas? If we've kept his daughter in a cell for years, he'll kill us all."

"That kind of thinking is a surrender before the first arrow flies," Mr. Preston retorted.

The mayor held up her hand. "We are repeating ourselves. Let us vote now on the question of a hostage exchange. Hold up your fan, green side toward me for yes, red side for no."

Jennie immediately put up her fan green side out, as did the rest of her family. To her enormous relief, most fans were green.

Mayor Wolfe announced, "The majority favors the hostage exchange. Now, it will be at least two weeks before we get Voske's response. The next question is, what do we do with Kerry Voske in the meantime? Our options are keeping her in jail, or allowing her limited freedom of the town, escorted by an armed guard."

"Prison!" Mr. Horst bellowed. "What if some soft-hearted traitor feels sorry for her and lets her go?"

The mayor's annoyance showed in her voice. "We have discussed this, Mr. Horst. Las Anclas is not easy to leave unnoticed. *If* the vote is to let the girl out, she will be guarded during the day and returned to her cell at night. Should those precautions prove insufficient, she would still need to get over the walls unseen, obtain a horse and provisions—also unseen—and make her way through the desert, alone and while evading pursuit."

Mr. Horst opened his mouth, but Mayor Wolfe spoke first. "Citizens!

Raise your green fans if you want the girl allowed outside under guard. Red if you want her to stay in jail."

Ma and Pa put up green fans. Jennie bit her lip. Kerry probably couldn't escape, but what if she somehow did? Then they'd never get Ross back. And it bothered Jennie deep down to think of the girl walking around town, pulling the wool over people's eyes, like she'd done to Brisa. Voske had killed Sera. His daughter could rot in jail, as far as Jennie was concerned.

Gritting her teeth in anticipation of her parents' disapproval, Jennie jerked up her fan—red side out.

Not only did her entire family stare in surprise and disappointment, so, from across the room, did Mia. Jennie dropped her gaze.

But the vote, by 23 fans, was to let Kerry be released under an armed guard.

Sheriff Crow addressed the voters. "If any of you ever see Kerry Voske alone, raise the alarm."

"Final vote," said the mayor. "If any further decisions need to be made regarding Kerry Voske, will they be by the vote of the town, or by the decision of the council? I will give you a few minutes to think about it."

"What's this vote about?" Jennie whispered. "Why does it matter?"

Pa looked grim, and Ma looked sad.

"It's in case Voske refuses the exchange," Ma explained softly.

"He won't refuse," Jennie said, too loudly. Someone shushed her.

"But if he does," Pa replied. "The next vote will be whether or not to execute the girl. If the town votes to let the council decide, they're saying that they don't want her blood on their hands."

Ma articulated her words carefully. "They'll want the council to vote for her execution, and afterwards they can blame them for killing a teenage girl in cold blood."

It was the most cynical thing Jennie had ever heard from Ma. Jennie was sickened. Of course it wouldn't come to that…but if there was one thing Jennie believed in, it was not shirking responsibility. If she had blood on her hands, she'd own it.

"Final vote," called the mayor. "Green for town. Red for council."

Jennie raised her fan green side out. But across the hall, fan after fan went up, until all she saw was a sea of red.

CHAPTER TWENTY-SEVEN
LAS ANCLAS
MIA

Mia ran to Jennie's house. Six months ago she would have plunged headlong into her idea, but this time she'd do the smart, careful thing and talk to Jennie first.

Actually, six months ago, she wouldn't have had the nerve to do it at all.

She nearly ran Jennie down at the kitchen door. To Mia's surprise, Jennie was loading buckets of smelly garbage onto a cart.

"Isn't that a twelve-and-under job?" Mia asked.

"I took it over," Jennie replied. "I had a fight with my parents, and I wanted to make up for it."

"*You* had a fight with your parents? Over what?"

Jennie looked embarrassed. "It was stupid. I was in a bad mood."

"I'll help you feed the earthworms," Mia offered as they pulled the cart toward the compost heaps. "I wanted to talk to you about an idea I had. You know Mr. Preston—you can tell me what I should say to convince him."

"Convince him of what?"

"I want to guard Princess Kerry."

Jennie stopped in the middle of the path. "What?"

She spoke so loudly that people weeding their kitchen garden nearby looked up. Then she began walking so fast that the garbage slopped all over the cart. Mia trotted alongside, glad that she'd been doing extra exercise. At the rate Jennie was going, two weeks ago Mia wouldn't have had enough breath to talk.

Mia held up her diagram. "I designed manacles to prevent her from escaping or using her powers to attack anyone."

Jennie said over her shoulder, "Great. Make the manacles. Someone else can be her guard."

"No, the reason for the manacles is to give *me* an excuse to be the guard," Mia explained. "See, obviously the princess knows what they're doing to Ross, but Dad said she lied all the way through the interrogation. But they didn't give her any reason not to. Mr. Preston punched her in the face! No wonder she wouldn't tell the truth."

Mia stopped to catch her breath as Jennie stopped at the pungent black compost heap. The pink, ringed backs of the giant earthworms writhed in and out of the rich soil, like the dolphins Mia sometimes saw playing in the sea.

"Look! That one's a six-footer." Mia pointed, hoping to get Jennie to smile. When they were kids, they'd loved watching the worms turn the town sewage into mulch.

Jennie didn't answer. She picked up a bucket and flung the contents far out in the heap. Mia gave her a nervous glance. Jennie was obviously angry about something. The "stupid" fight she'd had with her parents?

"Jennie, are you okay? Is something wrong?" Mia tried to match Jennie's garbage throw, but hers splattered a disappointing twenty feet away.

Jennie's bucket clanged as she dropped it into the cart. "Mia, this is a terrible idea. I don't think you should have anything to do with that girl."

She picked up the last bucket. This time, the contents cleared the entire compost heap to splatter against the city wall, right above where the pipes emptied sewage into the compost. Potato peelings and something orange and slimy oozed down.

A teenage sentry, hurrying past to avoid the worst of the smell, hooted, "Nice throw!"

Mia wondered what he'd done to get stuck with the punishment duty of guarding the stinky stretch of the wall. Jennie ignored him.

"The princess knows about Ross," Mia protested. "Don't you want to find out what's going on with him?"

"I captured that girl *for* Ross." Jennie directed her angry gaze straight at Mia, who shrank back. Jennie had never looked at her like that before. "Once we do the hostage exchange, Ross can tell us himself what happened to him at Gold Point. But you have to stay away from that girl. She's dangerous. She has Brisa twisted around her little finger."

Mia snatched off her glasses and polished them, as if a clearer view would restore the world to normal. But when she jammed them back on, Jennie's angry glare was still directed at her. "You think I don't know that? What do you think I'm going to do? Let her go? Don't you trust me?"

"It's not a matter of trust," Jennie started.

"Okay, then. Back to my plan. I thought it all out, beginning with asking you how to approach Mr. Preston. How do I convince him?"

"You can't." Jennie shook a bucket hard over the compost, dislodging a long curl of carrot peel. A gaping pink mouth surfaced and sucked it in.

Jennie watched the worm like her life depended on it.

"You *don't* trust me." Mia couldn't believe she was saying that to Jennie — she couldn't believe that she believed it. "Nobody in town takes me seriously. None of you think I can handle anything important that isn't mechanical. I thought you were different. You saw me save Ross's life in the battle!"

The memory rekindled the fierce joy that had overwhelmed Mia when she saw Ross begin to breathe again. But the joy vanished when Jennie's profile stayed frozen, as if that didn't matter at all.

Anger made Mia hot and prickly. "And also, who used her flamethrower to startle Voske so he missed when he tried to shoot Mr. Preston dead?"

Jennie stood still as a statue.

"Ah-ha!" Mia exclaimed, clapping her hands and rubbing them. "I bet *Mr. Preston* remembers who *saved his life*. I'll go make my manacles now, and then I'll remind him of that. That'll make him listen."

She left Jennie alone with the empty buckets.

*

Mia rattled the manacles nervously as she stepped onto the mayor's sun porch. She forced herself not to wipe her sweaty palms down Dad's second-best shirt. She'd tried to dress up for this interview, but she'd grown out of her blue linen dress—not a surprise, as Dad had bought it for her when she was twelve. Her only other fancy outfit was her mother's ruffled pink dancing dress, and she didn't think that would make the right impression.

Dad's silk shirt and linen trousers were big on her, but at least they weren't stained with oil or rust. She shoved her glasses up and patted her pockets and tool belt for the fiftieth time. She had everything she needed.

Mr. Preston himself answered the door. He looked larger and loomier than ever, scowling down at her. "Mia? Did the mill house water pipe burst again?"

"Pipe? No." Her voice sounded squeaky. "I wanted to talk to you. About an idea I had."

"If it's about weaponry, you can have any supplies you need," Mr. Preston said.

"Yes. I mean, no. Well, it *involves* weaponry."

"Come on in."

Mia froze in the doorway. She hadn't been in that house since Felicité's tenth birthday, when the mayor had invited the entire schoolhouse to Felicité's party. Mia had spent the whole time worried that she would accidentally break something.

She wished she hadn't remembered that. The place was full of delicate relics of china and glass. She looked up, trying to avoid the sight of things she might collide with. A huge crystal chandelier hung threateningly overhead.

A cold gust of wind blew past her, making the crystal drops chime. Mia jumped. At least they weren't red.

She slid off her shoes, followed him into the parlor, and sat on the satin chair that Mr. Preston indicated. She was glad she'd put on Dad's clean clothes.

"Would you like something to drink?" Mr. Preston offered.

A skittering sound distracted Mia. Wu Zetian appeared, her little pink nose twitching. Then the rat scampered off.

Mia nodded, then decided not to risk having anything slop over Dad's shirt and the pale pink satin. "No, thank you."

The mayor walked in, bringing a scent of verbena. Now there were two of them staring at Mia. She had no idea where to put her hands. Mia stuck them in her armpits, yanked them out, then clutched them together.

"Hello, Mia," the mayor said. At least she wasn't wearing the Button Dress, which made her look as tall as Mr. Preston, who looked as tall as the bell tower.

Mia gulped in a huge breath. Now for her neatly organized, memorized explanation. "I had a—"

Felicité walked in, with Wu Zetian trotting at her heels. "Town business, Mia?"

"Yes. I think." To the mayor and defense chief, Mia said, "I'd like to be Kerry's guard."

"What brought this about, Mia?" Mr. Preston asked.

Mia sucked in another breath, forgetting her memorized phrasing. "Well, she hasn't talked to anyone, but she must have lots and lots of useful information, but no one can get at it, because she's guarded by an adult, and why would she trust another adult? They're the ones that locked her in that miserable little cell, and punched— So I made something!"

Mia pulled out her manacles, and demonstrated as she spoke. "See, as long as you move slowly, you can walk and use your hands, but if you move fast, like to run or to attack someone, they snap tight and lock your wrists or ankles together. And then you need a key to unlock them. See?"

Mr. Preston and the Wolfes looked sincerely impressed.

"Very clever," remarked the mayor.

"And even if she did attack me very slowly, I do know how to fight, even though it's not the main thing I do, but I've been training very hard recently. And also I have this."

Mia brandished her cudgel.

Mayor Wolfe sat back, looking surprised. Mr. Preston said, "What use is that little thing, Mia?"

Mia smiled triumphantly. "Ah-ha! It's bigger than it looks."

She swung hard, forcing the magnets that held it together to snap apart. The segments sprang out, and the tip smashed into a bronze bowl filled with multi-colored candies. The bowl flew across the room, smashed into the opposite wall, and scattered candies everywhere. Mia gasped in horror.

"I'll pick them up." Felicité seemed to be stifling a giggle.

The mayor was trying not to laugh, too.

So was Mr. Preston, clearly. His voice shook slightly as he said, "That's an interesting implement, Mia."

"I made one for Ross, for inside the ruined city. In case there was something in there totally different, you know, that regular weapons might not handle, or if he was too busy to get his weapons out, on account of prospecting, and then there's his left hand, which, you know, he's still getting used to the gauntlet…"

Mr. Preston and Mayor Wolfe looked at Mia with identical expressions of doubt.

Mia forced herself to stop babbling. "I thought he might need it."

Mr. Preston exchanged a long look with the mayor, who gave a tiny nod.

Felicité glanced up from the floor. "Should I get my scribe implements?"

Mr. Preston began to say, "That's not necessary," but the mayor laid her fingers on his wrist. "An excellent idea, Felicité. Let's put this on the official record."

Felicité ran to fetch her tools. Mia hastily scooped up the candies while Mr. Preston examined her cudgel, snapping it in and out. Then he returned it. "I have never forgotten that you saved my life, Mia."

Mia swallowed. She'd completely forgotten to remind him!

"Let's give your idea a try," Mr. Preston said.

The mayor took the bowl of ruined candies. Mia caught herself before she could wipe her sticky fingers on Dad's good pants.

"I concur," the mayor said, setting down the bowl. "Perhaps Kerry will open up more to another teenager."

Mr. Preston put his fists on his knees. "Let's set down some rules, shall we? Mia, never let her out of your sight. She goes back to jail every night, or if you have a job outside the walls. Never tell her anything important about the town. And every night, write down everything she said that you didn't already know, even if it seems insignificant."

"I promise," said Mia.

CHAPTER TWENTY-EIGHT
LAS ANCLAS
KERRY

As Kerry waited for her new guard, she reviewed everything Min Soo had taught her about ingratiating herself with people. If it got her out of Las Anclas alive, she'd apologize to her mother and admit that she had been right. This much was surely true: you couldn't rely on techniques that only worked if you were already in power. You also had to know how to create power—the power of influence—from a powerless position.

Preston would surely find a guard who was even bigger and meaner than him. How should she handle it? Brave and stoic? Sorrowful? Weak and non-threatening? She loathed the idea of pretending to be weak, but if made the guard careless...

In came Brisa, hand in hand with a freckled blonde girl, pale as an overwashed sock. *That* was the girlfriend Kerry had heard so much about? Kerry had expected her to be prettier.

"Hi, Princess Kerry!" Brisa chirped. "Dr. Lee said Becky could examine your face. How's it feeling today?"

Kerry put fake brightness into her voice. "Oh, it's fine."

Both girls looked gratifyingly indignant. Kerry was certain they were picturing Preston and his ham hands. Kerry had felt how swollen her face was, and she'd caught a flash of pity, then anger on Dr. Lee's face when he'd examined her injuries the night before. Much as it hurt—she hadn't been able to sleep on that side—it had to look even worse.

Becky spoke in such a soft voice Kerry barely heard her. "If you could come to the cell door, I'd like to apply some witch hazel." She held up a bottle and a piece of linen.

Kerry stood still under Becky's careful ministrations, as Brisa said, "Can we get you anything? Is the food all right?"

"The food is fine. I'm just bored. Well, to be honest, lonely." Kerry watched in satisfaction as Becky looked sympathetic and Brisa gazed down guiltily. "Could you two stay and keep me company?"

Brisa said reluctantly, "We have to go to school. But we can come back in the evening."

"Thank you," Kerry said, trying to sound sad but brave.

"But you'll be out soon," Becky consoled her.

"Hey, that gives me an idea," exclaimed Brisa. "Everybody wants to meet you. We could throw you a party!"

The deputy spoke up, startling all three. "Nobody is throwing the prisoner a party."

Brisa scowled. Becky hung her head. Kerry said wistfully, "Thank you anyway. It was a sweet idea."

The girls said a subdued goodbye and walked out. Before they reached the jail door, they were whispering.

Kerry turned away to hide her grin. Those girls had to be planning a secret party. Perfect. Assuming she could somehow get to it, Kerry would have all her potential allies gathered conveniently together for her inspection.

She lay on her cot, preparing for her second challenge of the day, the guard. But when the door opened again, the last person Kerry expected walked in: Ross's grubby girlfriend, Mia.

The girl unclipped a pair of manacles from her belt. Her hands shook nervously, making them clank together. "I made these myself. I tried them on. They should be comfortable. I mean, for walking around in."

Kerry revised her tactics. *Be nice, but not so nice you seem fake. The more sincere you are, the more believable you'll be.* She did have something sincerely grateful to say. This girl did not have to go out of her way to provide the prisoner with comfort.

Kerry offered her wrists. "That's very considerate."

The deputy cut in. "You try anything, just remember, most people in this town would love to be the one to take you down."

Kerry gave him a shocked, reproachful glance. "I would never hurt her. She hasn't done anything to me."

The deputy said with obvious disbelief, "The keys are on my belt, Mia." And he leveled his rifle at Kerry.

"Thanks, Mia," Kerry said.

Mia unlocked the door and cautiously approached Kerry. "If you move slowly, the chain stays as it is. If you move fast, it snaps together and locks."

Clever, Kerry thought. Still, if Mia stopped watching Kerry for fifteen minutes or so, she could create a file and saw through the chain. Slowly.

Kerry went out, relieved that the manacles were light enough to allow her to walk easily, and surveyed the town from the jailhouse porch. There were long buildings behind the jail, and behind those rose the wall, with sentries every fifty paces. A huge square with buildings all around lay in front of her.

Every person in sight stopped whatever they were doing to stare at Kerry. Some teens seemed curious, and one fluttered her fingers in a half wave. But the adults either gave her a hostile glower, or walked away as if Kerry were invisible. But they knew she was there. Even without the manacles, if she made a break for it, she'd be jumped within seconds. As it was, she could take comfortable but small steps, but even without the snap effect, running would be impossible.

It had rained in the night. To test the limits of the manacles, Kerry raised her hand with medium speed and made an umbrella. As she stepped under the dripping eaves, water bounced off the air above her head and sluiced down at either side.

She was surprised by an excited squeak from Mia.

"That is so cool!" Mia exclaimed. "They told me about your power, but I hadn't realized how versatile it is. I thought you could only make weapons."

Mia's obvious delight in Kerry's power called Ross to mind. "Go ahead. Touch it, if you want."

Mia grinned. "Can I?" She stretched out a finger. "This part feels like wood. I can even feel the grain." She stood on her tiptoes and spread her fingers, patting gently. "And this is silk, right? Is it based on a real umbrella you have?"

Kerry was startled. No one had ever figured that out so quickly before, not that she often got quizzed about her power. There didn't seem to be any reason to conceal the truth. "Yes, it is."

"How old were you when you got your power?" Mia asked. "You were born with it, right? It seems like it would take that much practice to get that much control."

"Yes. When I was a little girl, I could only do simple things, like sticks." Since her power intrigued Mia, Kerry ran with it. She made a stick, bent, and—she only knew how to design clothing—sketched Mia's overalls in the mud.

Mia laughed. "Perfect!"

"You really stupid enough to make fun of your guard, *Princess?*"

A bunch of teenage boys came up, with a tall hulking one in the lead.

"Who're they?" Kerry asked under her breath.

Mia whispered, "Tommy Horst and his Norm friends."

Tommy kicked away the drawing. "Your mighty Change power didn't give you any more talent than it did smarts." The way he said 'Change' made it sound like 'cockroach.'

A blond boy laughed and drew his finger in the air as if he was chalking something on a slate. "Horst: two points. Princess: zero. Come on, Princess. Show us what you've got."

"Henry, leave us alone, okay?" Mia asked.

The boys ignored Mia, whose shoulders hunched in intimidation. Because of the boys' size? Because of their social status?

If Mia was assigned to guard Kerry, she couldn't be that low in the town hierarchy. But maybe it was like Santiago being set to guard Ross: Mia wasn't important in herself, but was close to someone important.

The thought of Santiago hurt, like bumping a bruise.

"You want to be aloooone with the princess, Mia?" asked one of the boys. "Have you forgotten all about your mutant boyfriend?"

Tommy chimed in, "And found a mutant girlfriend!"

Henry began making kissing noises, which were promptly picked up by the rest of the boys.

Kerry considered possible reactions. Being hostile to anti-Changed bigots wouldn't make Kerry look bad to Mia, who obviously cared about Ross. And since Mia seemed too timid to stand up for herself, she might appreciate being defended.

Kerry faced Henry and Tommy. "I notice *you* two weren't on the mission to capture me. What were you doing here while the competent people were at Gold Point? Hiding?"

Mia laughed in surprise, but turned it into a cough.

Oh, yes. This felt good. "You boys think you're so tough?" Kerry gave them Father's smile, exulting inside when two boys actually stepped back. "The reason my father has an empire is that he rewards success. But the reward for failure is death. You two, with your stupid prejudice against Change powers, are walking, talking failures. Remember that when he arrives with his army."

Henry's head turned sharply. Kerry automatically shifted to a defensive stance. Then she relaxed at the sight of a pretty girl with her hair dyed bright red, but still glossy and soft-looking. That took expensive dye. Her clothes looked even more costly—a matching hat, frilly parasol, gloves, scarf, *and* a veil in eggshell blue.

The girl cradled a golden rat in her arms as she minced along in high-heeled boots, avoiding puddles as if they were acid.

The boys shut up and looked at the newcomer as if waiting for cues on how to behave.

"Who's that?" Kerry whispered.

"Felicité Wolfe," Mia whispered back.

Preston's daughter!

"Tommy. Henry. Is this any way to treat our visitor?" Felicité's voice was sweet as mesquite syrup.

Imagining that she was swallowing down a candied rose petal, Kerry said, "Hello, Felicité. I've heard all about you, but I didn't know you had such beautiful red hair."

Felicité's cheeks dimpled as she smiled. "It was golden until recently. I hope your night wasn't too bad, Princess?"

"Not at all," Kerry said in Min Soo's sweetest voice.

Felicité came right back, even sweeter. "I'm sorry we had to meet under these circumstances." She held out her golden rat. "This is Wu Zetian. Say hello to the princess, Wu Zetian."

Kerry stroked the rat's adorable, twitching pink nose. At least Wu Zetian didn't give her a fake smile. The rat's fur was as soft as Kogatana's had looked, but Yuki had never let his rat within six feet of Kerry. She'd truthfully assured him that she would never dream of harming a sweet little creature like his rat, but he clearly hadn't believed her.

Out of the corner of her eye, Kerry caught a row of boggling faces, including Mia's.

"This way, Kerry," Mia said. "Unless you want to visit the granary."

Kerry followed Mia, who walked as if she wanted to get away from that crowd as quickly as she could.

Tommy's blustering voice rose up behind them. "Henry, do you want to be on the firing squad?"

"I'm a great shot," Henry said, laughing like it was a joke. "I dropped nearly thirty of 'em in the battle. I like target practice."

"You should volunteer," Tommy said.

"Me and half the town!" Henry laughed louder.

"Tommy," reproved Felicité. "Don't you all have wall duty?"

From behind came the sound of scampering feet.

"I'm sorry you had to hear that, Kerry." Mia seemed to struggle inwardly, then said firmly, "It won't happen. I can't imagine anyone looking someone in the eyes—someone who can't fight back—and pulling the trigger."

Kerry could imagine it. She'd been attending executions since she was five.

As they skirted a patchwork of pocket gardens and entered a wide street, a string of children ran by, turning to stare at Kerry.

"There's the monster," one squeaked.

"*You're* a monster," another snapped.

"Ma says to be proud of your Change," a third put in.

"Come on, we're gonna be late for school," the biggest said.

As they ran off again, one of the kids shrilled, "Everybody knows Voske is the *real* monster!"

Half the citizens in Gold Point didn't even dare say Father's name.

Those kids would learn fast enough when he took the town.

Kerry glanced over the low tiled roofs, hoping to spot the wall. But she couldn't see past a stand of timber.

"Here we are." Mia stopped at a cottage with a yard full of metal scraps and machines, many of them clearly artifacts. Kerry had seen such things before, of course, but not so many at once.

Mia shifted uneasily. Kerry understood. This was Mia's private space. Some fools—maybe even Tom Preston's dainty daughter—must look at those disassembled artifacts and see a junk heap. Mia was probably bracing for some similar comment.

"This is a treasure trove," Kerry said, letting her admiration show. She nearly added that Father paid well for such useful items, then decided that mentioning him would ruin the moment.

Mia blushed, then led her inside. A dismantled crossbow lay on a work table, and a disassembled engine rested on the bed. The second table had several projects in various states of progress.

There were two chairs. Hanging over the back of one was a worn shirt that was too big for Mia, but just right for Ross. The way it sagged, it had been there for weeks. Kerry wondered how to make use of such obvious sentimentalism. But she couldn't prevent the uncomfortable realization that if Santiago had been captured, she too would secretly cherish something of his.

Mia began tidying a table full of tools and papers. Kerry joined her.

"*You* designed this?" Kerry touched the design for Ross's gauntlet. "And built it? It was beautifully made."

Mia burst out, "What's happening to Ross? Is he okay? Jennie said she'd seen him, and she said he looked okay, but that was a week ago. Is your father planning to do anything to him? He's just planning to make Ross prospect for him, right? Right?"

"Yes, exactly," Kerry said soothingly. "He wants Ross to prospect inside our ruined city. Ross has an incredibly valuable talent. My father would never hurt him."

Mia carefully set down the gauntlet design. "Even if Ross won't work for him?"

Both her parents had warned Kerry that many people notice outright lies, but far fewer could detect lies of omission and shadings of the truth. "My father intends to persuade Ross to do it voluntarily."

Kerry turned away to examine the crossbows. Mia was watching her so closely that Kerry was afraid that her worry about Santiago might show and be misinterpreted. *Ross* was in no danger. He could easily let those crystal trees kill Santiago, then walk away free.

Mia's voice rose. "Is there something wrong? Did something bad happen to Ross? *Please* tell me."

"He's fine. Really."

"What was he doing the last time you saw him?"

Kerry had to lie. If she said anything related to Father's plans for Santiago, she might lose control of her voice. "Father loaned him one of the royal horses, Sally. Ross loves riding her."

Mia gave her a very strange look. "Ross loves riding, huh?"

Kerry immediately knew her lie had been caught. She had to be more careful about what she said about Ross to Mia, who knew him much better than Kerry did.

Mia said shortly, "I have to get to work."

"Can I watch?" Kerry asked—as if she had a choice. It was that, or back to the cell.

Mia looked up warily. "Sure."

Kerry prepared to be bored as Mia started arranging an incomprehensible pile of mechanical parts. But she needed to repair the damage she'd done.

"What are you making?" Kerry asked in her best Encouragement Tone.

It worked. And to Kerry's surprise, she found Mia's explanations about energy and efficiency interesting. You could translate that to military efficiency, Kerry thought as she watched Mia's sure hands dart among the gears and pulleys and bolts.

"Want some lunch?" Mia's voice was decidedly more friendly.

Kerry was startled to see Mia's clock read noon. She'd listened to Mia talk about machines for three hours! "I'd love some."

Mia lifted a pile of papers off a cooler. "Dad made enough for both of us."

She took out a jug of barley tea, and two covered dishes. Mia lifted the lids with a flourish, revealing prettily arranged lunches, consisting of three types of kimchi and a main dish of shredded meats and vegetables.

Kerry didn't need to feign her enthusiasm. "That looks great. My mother sometimes has the palace cooks make Korean food, but it's the fancy banquet stuff. I like what the cooks make for themselves better."

Mia peered at Kerry's face as if she hadn't seen it before. "Oh, is your mother Korean?"

Kerry nodded. "Is your father?"

"Both sides, actually. Well, some of Dad's ancient ancestors were Italian. But he loves Korean food. Grandma taught him. Are your banquet foods family recipes?"

"My mother was an orphan. I think she collected them from antique recipe books. But she isn't that interested in food, except for sickly-sweet desserts. What she really likes is clothing. I must have a hundred hanbok, but I never wear them. I don't like big poofy skirts."

"Is that a kind of dress?"

"It's a traditional Korean outfit. It's got a full skirt and a tight blouse." Kerry eyed Mia. "You'd look good in one."

Mia looked gloomily at the front of her overalls. "In a tight blouse? I don't think so."

Kerry laughed. "No, they look better if you *don't* have huge breasts. Let me show you."

She reached for a slate. Mia watched intently as Kerry sketched the bell-shaped skirt and long-sleeved top. "I'd do a floral block print for you. Ice-blue flowers against forest green. With gold embroidery. I design my own clothing. I could do a full sketch, if you like. Someone in town could probably make it for you."

Mia made a face. "Mrs. Callahan. She'd probably stick me with a pin while she was doing the measuring."

Kerry examined Mia's face again. It was strange to think that hundreds of years ago, their ancestors had come from the same place. Otherwise, of course, they had nothing in common. "Do you have a Korean name?"

Mia gave Kerry a nervous look, as if she thought Kerry was mocking her. "Lee."

"I meant a given name."

Mia shook her head. "Do you?"

"Ji Sun."

"That's pretty," Mia said. "Who calls you that?"

"No one. I've always gone by Kerry."

Father allowed his wives to give their children whatever names they liked, but the names they used were the names *he* gave them. It wouldn't surprise Kerry if, say, Fiona's mother called her Busisiwe in private. But Min Soo never called her anything but Kerry. She'd explained that Kerry was the name that marked her as a princess and her father's daughter. She should use Ji Sun when she announced herself by her full name, Min Soo had said, but never by itself.

"I use it as a middle name," Kerry finished belatedly.

Mia didn't seem to notice the long silence. "More kimchi?"

Kerry realized that she'd cleaned her plate. While they'd been eating, she'd actually forgotten that she was a prisoner. She couldn't remember ever casually chatting with another girl, other than relatives.

Mia was running her forefinger around the plate, searching for stray crumbs. She'd clearly also forgotten that she was a guard, though Kerry was certain that she'd remember fast enough if Kerry tried anything.

Don't lose sight of the goal, she told herself. She'd never get a better moment than this to get a truthful answer to the question Kerry had been sitting on all day.

Keeping her voice casual, she asked, "Has the town decided what they're going to do with me?" Her heart pounded.

"Oh, I'm sorry, Kerry. I didn't realize no one had told you. They're going to do the hostage exchange." Mia gave Kerry a big smile. "You've got nothing to worry about. It'll take about two weeks for the messages to go back and forth, but you should be back in Gold Point before the month is out." With an even bigger smile, Mia added, "And Ross will be back here. So enjoy your stay. I'll show you the town later, when I go to fix Jack's backup generator."

Kerry returned Mia's smile, but it took an effort. Father would never agree to a hostage exchange. Maybe they didn't know that in Las Anclas, but he had a policy of never negotiating with the enemy.

Even if he did, he would never believe that Preston would return Kerry alive. Kerry didn't believe it, either. Preston probably intended to use her as bait to get Ross back, then double-cross Father and kill her anyway.

Father would undoubtedly mount a rescue mission, but Kerry didn't dare wait for that. In two weeks, Las Anclas would learn that there would be no exchange.

If she didn't escape first, they would kill her.

CHAPTER TWENTY-NINE
LAS ANCLAS
JENNIE

It was early afternoon when Mr. Vilas finally arrived at the stable. Jennie sighed with relief. She'd traded stable duty with Carlos so she could catch the bounty hunter alone, and her shift was almost up.

She'd planned out what she had to say. She was still a Ranger—and she loved the challenge, the workouts, the camaraderie. Making hard decisions was part of the package.

Mr. Vilas saddled Sidewinder before he spoke. "Got something to say?"

"I do." They were alone, but she lowered her voice, just in case. "I know you were ordered to kill Ross if we couldn't free him. I just want to tell you that if you hurt him, don't bother coming back to Las Anclas. I'll be waiting."

She looked straight at him, hoping that he could see how serious she was.

"What makes you think I want to come back?" he retorted, but with a half-smile. Then the smile vanished. "This is why I don't like towns. Things get complicated. Look. My orders are just to pass on the message, and bring Ross back if Voske gives him back. That's all. And that's all I'm going to do."

"Thank you." She didn't try to hide her relief. But she thought, *If he's lying, I know what I'll do.*

She was still in an unsettled mood when she got home. Would she really be willing to kill someone in cold blood, for revenge? An image flashed into her mind for about the tenth time that day, for the thousandth time since the battle: Ross lying dead at her feet. The bounty hunter had meant to shoot him in the back outside of Gold Point. That was cold blood.

Yeah, I could do it.

She walked into the kitchen, and discovered her parents sitting at the table. Waiting for her—like she'd waited for the bounty hunter. The kitchen, always so crowded, was otherwise empty.

"Where is everybody?" Jennie asked, uneasy.

"We sent them off," Pa said. "So we could talk."

That was ominous. Her hunger vanished.

Reluctantly, Jennie sat down. Plates of steaming cornbread, stewed turnip greens, and baked beans waited for her. Ma had saved her the curl of salt pork on the top of the beans. She started to scoop beans onto her plate, but her hand shook. She dropped her hands into her lap and gripped her fingers together.

Ma touched Jennie's shoulder. "Jennie, what gave you the idea of taking Kerry hostage? Was it really your decision? If Tom Preston ordered you to do it, you can tell us."

"It was my idea, Ma," Jennie said. "Mr. Vilas was about to shoot Ross. *That* was on Mr. Preston's orders. It was his secret backup plan to keep Ross out of Voske's hands if we couldn't rescue him."

Pa sat back, frowning. Ma looked upset.

Jennie went on. "I was trying to stop him when I saw Kerry riding by. It came into my head, and I made it an order. She *is* the enemy. I was with her for a week coming back. She's Voske's daughter, through and through. She told us she'd inherit Las Anclas once her father conquered us."

Pa pushed back his dreadlocks with a sigh. "Like we said before, we won't second-guess a decision made in the enemy's territory. But now that she's here, you have a responsibility toward her. Can you imagine sitting in a cell, alone except for the weekend drunks and hot-heads, not knowing if you'll be executed?"

"That's what she'd have done to me if she'd captured me," retorted Jennie. "No, she'd have had my head cut off without even bothering to put me in a cell. She told us that, she even described it, and I promise you she enjoyed every word."

Ma looked away, and Pa grimaced. Jennie realized her voice had gotten loud. She forced herself to talk calmly. "You can ask anyone in my team." Now she sounded sulky and defensive.

Ma said in a low voice, "So you're taking Voske as an example to follow?"

"Of course not," Jennie exclaimed. "How can you think that of me?" But her ears burned. She heard her voice when she'd faced Mr. Vilas: *Don't bother coming back.*

Her thoughts circled around and around. Had she done the right thing? What *was* the right thing? Sera's voice came back to her: *You never abandon your team.* Wouldn't it have been abandoning Ross if she hadn't done anything to save him?

She became aware of her mother's hand, still on her shoulder. Jennie's nails cut into her palms. The pause had become a long silence.

"We're worried about you, Jennie," Ma said.

Jennie closed her eyes. She'd never kept back important things from her parents, but she didn't know where to start. Images flashed into her mind. Flickering firelight, and Sera falling. Dawn light, and Ross falling. Her throat tightened. She couldn't talk about that. She couldn't bear thinking about it.

"I'm fine," Jennie said. "Really."

Pa said gently, "Jennie, if you don't feel you can talk to us, maybe you should talk to Pastor Carlotta. Or to Dr. Lee."

Jennie drew in a deep breath. "I'll talk to Pastor Carlotta. Tomorrow. I have to train with the Rangers tonight."

"That's a good idea," Pa said, and Ma kissed Jennie's cheek.

As Jennie bent over her meal, she thought about what she could tell Pastor Carlotta. She'd already told her parents why she kidnapped Kerry, and though she hadn't enjoyed discussing that, nothing terrible had happened.

She could talk about that. She didn't need to mention anything else.

*

By afternoon, when Jennie reached the practice field, a layer of dark gray clouds hung so low that she felt like she could reach up and touch them. She hoped Ranger practice wouldn't get cancelled on account of a storm. But the air was still hot and oppressive as they did the preliminary stretches. The rainy season had come, but summer still tried to hang on.

They broke ranks to divide up into pairs for the deeper stretches. Jennie turned toward Meredith, to find her already partnered with Brisa. Jennie's nerves flared hot and cold when Indra stepped up expectantly.

She let her breath out, trying to be casual. Until the mission to Gold Point she had tried to avoid him. While traveling, she'd gotten used to being around Indra again, but she still got that punch in the heart when she saw him. Why? Feelings were supposed to go away after a breakup.

She sat down and held out her hands. His long fingers closed around hers, just like the old days. They seesawed back and forth in silence.

Jennie lay back until her head touched the ground, enjoying the stretch and the heat of his hands. His natural temperature was fever-hot. Even several feet apart, he warmed her like a fire.

"Ready?" Indra asked.

"Sure," Jennie replied.

He slowly pulled her up as he fell backward. Jennie tried not to think about how different Ross's hands were from Indra's, bony but strong. Since he couldn't grip with his left, she held his wrist, and felt his pulse beating under her fingers…

She raised her eyes past Indra to the handful of onlookers. Kerry was there, with Mia. As Jennie leaned forward, the last thing she saw was Kerry's sharp-featured face watching her.

"All right!" Julio called through his bullhorn. "On your feet—"

His words were drowned as a bluish flicker was followed by a boom of thunder.

A shock of cold rain instantly drenched Jennie. Henry, Tommy, and Brisa looked around, clearly expecting to be dismissed. Most of the onlookers took off. Mia gestured toward the path, but Kerry shook her head.

Julio let out a howl of laughter. "Great weather for the obstacle course," he roared through the horn. "It'll be good and slippery!"

Lightning flared, and the thunder drowned out his voice. The Rangers trotted over with practiced ease, followed more slowly by unhappy candidates. Mud squished under Jennie's feet. The air smelled like rain and mud and the burned electrical smell that came with lightning.

Indra nudged Jennie. "Relax. You're so tense. You could do this blindfolded."

He was right. Her muscles had all locked up. She made them relax, but she could feel her heart pounding. Strange. They hadn't even started moving yet.

Julio made swooping gestures as thunder rolled above. Too late, Jennie saw that he was pairing them up. They began counting off, and Jennie was stuck: she was one and Indra was two.

Julio shouted, "We'll warm up with a carry! Twos lie down! Ones, carry your partner."

Indra dropped obediently at Jennie's feet. She froze. The rain, the lightning, the mud, Indra lying at her feet—it was just like the battle. She couldn't possibly do this drill with him. She might…cry, or scream, or something.

Jennie's jaw clenched. She'd never asked to switch partners for any reason…and she couldn't possibly explain why…but she couldn't do this exercise with Indra.

The rain turned to hail. It struck the mud with a clatter. All around her, people were lifting their partners.

Without giving herself a chance to think twice, she grabbed at Julio's sleeve. "I want to switch partners."

"What? Why?" Lightning flared again, revealing his black hair hanging in his eyes, emphasizing his amazement.

"I might hurt Indra. He's still recovering from the battle." Jennie hated the lie. She hated herself for lying. But she couldn't even look at Indra, still lying there on the ground. She didn't want to imagine what he might be thinking.

Julio shrugged and motioned to the pair beside her. "Okay. Switch. Tommy, don't drop him." She grimaced at his sarcasm, but mostly she was relieved.

For one heartbeat.

As Tommy Horst bent to pick up Indra, Jennie turned to Paco, who lay on the ground, waiting. Lightning flashed, exaggerating the sharp lines of his face. *Sera's* face, when she lay dead on the ground.

Voske's face, when he stood there surrounded by torches, grinning. Jennie knelt beside Paco. She was being ridiculous. This was just an exercise. Paco was Paco.

She gripped his wrist and yanked. He cooperatively leaned up so she could sling him over her shoulders. She started to stand. He was heavy across her shoulders. Too heavy. She'd never be able to lift him. The fire from the burning trees illuminated the battlefield. The arrows and spent bullets clattered around her. Indra's blood ran down the back of her shirt. His skin was cold as ice. He'd die if she left him there, but she couldn't lift him. She couldn't lift him. She couldn't lift him…

"Jennie!" Someone was shaking her.

Jennie looked around wildly. She was on the Ranger practice field. Everyone was standing in a circle around her, including Paco. They were all staring. Julio had his hands on her shoulders. He was shaking her. What had happened? What had she done?

Indra pulled Julio away and took his place. "Jennie? What's wrong?" He cupped his hands around her face.

His hands were hot. Alive.

A huge sob burst from her chest. Burning tears ran down her face. She broke away from Indra and ran.

CHAPTER THIRTY
RUINED CITY OUTSIDE GOLD POINT
ROSS

Ross knew where he was the instant he woke up: outside the ruined city. He heard the sounds of the rousing camp, but he kept his eyes shut, reviewing his plan.

Voske was bound to send him in with a guard, probably Santiago. Ross would refuse to go until Voske leveled a gun at his head, then reluctantly agree to take Santiago into the ruined city. Inside, he'd offer Santiago a choice: he could accompany Ross to Las Anclas, to be with Kerry and even live there if he wanted, or Ross would walk him through to the other side and let him run back to Voske the long way. Ross was sure he could get well away before Santiago could reach Voske to report.

Ross had fought Santiago before, and knew he was better. If he had to, he'd knock Santiago out and drag him through the crystal trees. Voske probably had guards stationed in the rough country on the other side of the ruined city, but Ross could evade them.

"Rise and shine, boys." Voske's voice was nearby.

Sure enough, Santiago was fitted out with a leather jacket and a rifle. Ross could have told him that a pistol was better for prospecting, given the narrow spaces you had to worm through. He didn't comment.

Santiago caught Ross's gaze. Before Ross could look away, Santiago gave him a nervous smile and offered him three buns wrapped in a checkered bandana.

"Do you celebrate Day of the Dead in Las Anclas?" Before Ross could reply, Santiago went on, "I have sugar skulls, too, but we can save those for later. My siblings baked these. Maria-Delia loves molding little corpses with their arms crossed."

Santiago pushed the bread at him. The buns smelled like anise and orange peel. Ross took one and bit off the head. Santiago's fixed grin reminded Ross suddenly of a death's head. The wad of bread stuck in his throat.

"Time for breakfast."

Ross and Santiago jumped. Voske gestured at the cook tent, where pancakes and fresh eggs were being dished out. Ross stuffed the rest of the bun into his mouth. He was determined to eat as much as he could, no matter what Voske did or said. He'd need the energy.

He let the cook heap his plate, then sat on a rock. Santiago sat beside him, while Voske leaned against a boulder nearby. Ross ignored them both and dug in. The food was delicious. Maybe it tasted better because he knew he'd be free soon.

He was halfway through his pancakes when a crash startled him. Santiago had dropped his coffee mug into his plate of uneaten food. He stared at the spilled coffee as though he'd lost something.

"Nervous? You'll be safe. Have some more." Voske snapped his fingers, and a young soldier hurried to refill his cup.

Santiago started to raise it to his lips, but coffee spilled down the front of his shirt. His hands were shaking. He put it down. "I've had enough."

Ross had been right. Santiago had been assigned to guard him, and naturally he was afraid of the singing trees. Ross wished he could tell Santiago that he would be safe, but he couldn't say anything in front of Voske. He silently finished his meal.

"Come along, boys," Voske said.

His guards closed in, rifles at the ready. Ross had expected that, too. He scowled at them, and followed with lagging steps. Santiago was breathing heavily as he walked, obsessively fingering his belt knives.

The last time Ross had visited the city, he'd only seen the forest from a distance. Now he could see that while these singing trees were also the dull colors of the desert animals they'd killed and grown from, their shapes were subtly different from the trees by Las Anclas. Rather than sharp thorns and spikes, the branches ended in complex patterns like the frost he occasionally saw on winter mornings. The seed-pods, too, were different: not round, but shaped like teardrops.

Ross halted. He'd been keeping the walls in his mind built up, so he hadn't sensed anything. He'd let Voske force him to agree to go in, and then explain that he needed a little time to make his power work.

"Go ahead, Ross," Voske said. "Find me some good artifacts. Especially, look for weapons."

"No," Ross said, as sulkily as he could. He folded his arms across his chest. "I won't do it."

He waited for Voske to threaten him, but the king just laughed. "Ross, when are you going to learn that it's easier to follow orders? Santiago, it's time. Go."

His face blanched to gray, Santiago started toward the crystal trees. One hopeless glance from his dark eyes, then he was past Ross, walking stiffly up the ancient road that led into the forest. Shocked, Ross waited for him to stop, but he kept going.

The trees began to chime.

Ross shuddered. "Wait!"

"Keep going, Santiago," Voske said, still chuckling. "Over to you, Ross."

Ross bolted, sick with fury. He didn't have time to contact the trees in the careful way he'd planned. Ross grabbed Santiago's bare hand, shut his eyes, and tore down the walls in his mind.

One brutal stab of pain, and Ross managed to shove the death memories aside.

The singing trees had been born from the deaths of animals. There were fewer memories to contend with, and they were less vivid than those of human-born trees. It was much easier to avoid them, and communicate directly with the trees themselves.

He saw himself as the trees perceived him: a blood-hot, moving source of food or reproduction. He forced a new image of himself and Santiago on the trees: a cold, crystalline self. *We're part of you. We're part of the forest.*

Ross sank into the perceptions of the trees, trying to believe that he was one of them until they believed it, too. He willed his branches to be still— sensed the cool water deep under his roots—listened to the distant murmurs and chimes. In the walled-off corner of his mind that was still human, he felt himself moving forward. He fiercely told the trees, *The wind is moving in my branches.*

The nearest tree was trying to communicate in the language of words that Ross was trying not to think in. He ignored the distraction. Instead, he let his awareness spread throughout the forest. He could perceive slow-eddies of heat, and above those the cooler, moister current rolling toward them from over the hills.

He was falling. There was nothing beneath his roots—his feet. He sucked in a gulp of cold, moist air, and choked on it. Ross thrashed frantically. He could see nothing but murky green. He couldn't breathe. A weight on his back pulled him down, but he fought his way upward.

His face broke into hot air and greenish light. Water! They'd fallen into a pond. He treaded water. Someone thrashed desperately a few feet away. Santiago obviously couldn't swim, and his pack was weighing him down.

Ross swam over and grabbed him. Santiago clutched at him in a panic, pinning his arms.

"Let go!" Ross shouted. "I've got you."

Santiago released his grip.

"Hold on to my shoulders," Ross told him.

Santiago's fingers dug into muscle as Ross towed him across the water. The whole pond was at the bottom of a high-walled green funnel.

Ross scrabbled at the walls, but his hands slipped off. The funnel was smooth and resilient as the leaves of a succulent plant. He dug his nails into the wall, and they broke through. Sticky juice oozed out, sending out a pungent odor.

He lifted his left hand, straightened his fingers, and locked them into place in the gauntlet. Ross drove his fingertips into the wall. They punched through, leaving him a handhold.

"Climb out," said Santiago. "I'll follow you."

Ross punched his way up the succulent wall, until he hauled himself over the edge and lay panting on a mossy bank. He scrubbed his sticky hands off on his shirt, then wiped green slime from his face.

Santiago flopped down beside him. He, too, was covered in bright green sap from the wall and darker green algae from the pond. He sat up and looked back at the crystal trees on the other side of the pond. Their chiming had stopped.

Greenish light filtered through a leafy canopy that blocked out the entire sky. Vines threaded through the canopy, and furry animals darted and bounced through it, high above. Leaves drifted down in the animals' wake. Here and there Ross glimpsed little bridges and catwalks woven from the vines, similar to the raccoon-built structures infesting the Vardams' fruit orchards. Creatures with long furry tails bounded in and out of their woven homes.

Huge smooth boles of the supporting trees grew everywhere, but through them he made out the remains of the ancient road. Once he'd dealt with Santiago, he should be able to walk straight through.

His head ached, but it wasn't as bad as it had been the last time he'd contacted the crystal trees. It must be easier when the trees hadn't grown from humans.

Santiago was shaking out his rifle and grimacing. Good. His gunpowder was ruined.

"Thanks for fishing me out," Santiago said. "I guess you learned in the ocean, huh?"

Ross ignored that. "Listen, Santiago. I'm leaving. Come with me. Kerry's in Las Anclas. If you want to go back there with me, I'll speak up for you. Trust me, life is much better there. People don't look over their shoulders—"

"Don't say stuff like that!" Santiago looked over his shoulder, then up at the thick foliage overhead.

"Voske can't hear us here."

"You don't know that."

"Anyway, it doesn't matter if he can. If we get moving now, we'll be out the other side before he can do anything." Ross stood up.

Santiago leaped to his feet, one hand on his knife. "I can't let you escape."

Ross stepped out of striking distance. "If you'd rather, I'll make it look like I dragged you out through the trees, then knocked you out and ran. But I'm not prospecting for Voske. And I don't see why you should be loyal to him. He nearly got you killed."

"Come closer," Santiago muttered, still clutching his knife. He looked fearfully around again. "I won't hurt you."

Ross took a step nearer, ready for anything.

Santiago spoke barely above a whisper. "If I don't bring you back, Voske will kill someone in my family. Sometimes people do run away from Gold Point. When they do, Voske makes an example of whoever he thinks they loved most. Maria-Elena is only six. But the king wouldn't hesitate."

Ross stared at Santiago in horror. He wanted to believe that Santiago was lying, but he remembered how desperately his family had tried to please Ross— how his littlest sister, Maria-Elena, had showed Ross her pet walking stick and its "tricks." He remembered the quinceañera where he had been the center of attention, not the girl supposedly being feted. Now it all made sense.

"I know you can beat me," Santiago added. "But please don't. The king knows Maria-Elena is my favorite. He teases me about it. She's only—"

"I get it!" Ross could easily see Voske killing a six-year-old. He'd never even stop smiling. His hatred for Voske nearly choked him, but there was nothing he could do about it now. "Let's check out the city."

As they walked up the cracked concrete road, Ross tried to figure out how to escape without endangering Santiago's baby sister. He couldn't ditch Santiago in the city, or even outside of it. He'd have to wait to make his escape until Santiago wasn't around at all. In the meantime, he had to stall Voske.

They emerged from the forest. Uneven mounds of moss and lichen lined both sides of the road, which wound up into the hills. Based on his experience with ruins and on the pictures he'd seen of ancient cities, he guessed that the smaller mounds were cars, and the larger ones were the overgrown ruins of buildings. Ross kept walking, not paying them any special notice, hoping Santiago would take them for natural formations.

Santiago looked around eagerly, still clutching his ruined rifle. "What's that over there? It looks like a door!"

Santiago ran toward what was, unfortunately, clearly a building turned on its side. The rectangles on the fallen roof, covered with a subtly different type of plant life, were probably valuable solar panels. Ross didn't feel inclined to give Voske any.

"Don't run in," Ross called. "These structures can collapse on you if you step wrong."

"I know," Santiago called back. "Pru's told us gory stories. I'll just stick my nose in that opening there."

Reluctantly, Ross joined him at the door. If it looked like anything valuable might be inside, Ross would swear that the whole place would fall down around their ears if they so much as set foot inside the doorway. The structure looked stable, but nothing was visible inside but a few moldering shovels and rakes.

"I have to inspect the structure," Ross said. "It'll take a while."

Santiago turned away impatiently. "Why? This one is worthless, even I can see that." He looked up the street, his impatience vanishing. "Hey," he exclaimed. "All these mounds? I think they're *all* buildings! Little ones and big ones!"

Ross hid a sigh. So much for claiming nothing was here.

Santiago pointed to what had to be a moss-covered car. "How about that one there?"

Ross surveyed the untouched street, frustrated. It was the best prospecting site he'd ever seen—and he couldn't do any real prospecting. In fact, he had to do the opposite of prospecting, and try *not* to find any treasures.

If he could figure out which buildings were most likely to have finds, he could direct Santiago away from those. But he could only stall so long. If there was anything valuable lying out in the open, eventually Santiago would find it. And since they were the first people to set foot here in hundreds of years, every building might contain some priceless artifact.

Santiago trotted up to the nearest mound, grabbed a mass of greenery with his bare hands, and pulled it out of his way so he could peer into a window.

"Don't do that!" Ross exclaimed.

Santiago gave him an exasperated look. "Nothing can fall on me from here. I checked."

"You didn't check those plants. They might be toxic."

Santiago stepped back, and Ross scanned the plant life. Much of it was unfamiliar, but he recognized enough. He saw plenty that would make you sick, but only if you ate it. Santiago was undoubtedly familiar with poison oak. Then he spotted a doorway overgrown with the delicate fronds of itching nettle, weaving in and out of a net of harmless passion vine.

Hoping that Santiago either wouldn't recognize or wouldn't notice the itching nettle, Ross pretended to survey the buildings. "Nothing much here." He indicated them one by one: "No way in there... That one looks unstable… Definitely don't go in that one, it'll collapse like a house of cards if you cough on it."

"You're a terrible liar," remarked Santiago, but he sounded amused, not angry. "So the house of cards looks good, huh? Let's check it out. You first."

Ross pulled some of the vines aside, making sure to get a good grip on the nettles. The interior was full of moldering lumps that might have once been furniture, and the structure looked stable. Ross pushed through, letting the nettles brush against his cheeks, then dropped them so they fell against Santiago as he followed Ross in.

Before Ross could warn him not to touch anything, Santiago curiously poked at a large lump on the floor. It collapsed in an explosion of yellow dust that reminded Ross of fungus spores. Holding his breath, he gestured to Santiago and hurried out.

The nettles were already beginning to have an effect. His face and right hand itched fiercely, burning as a rash spread over them. Santiago scratched his hands without seeming to notice the red bumps puffing up into welts with every scratch.

"We have to get out of here," said Ross.

"What do you mean? We haven't found anything yet."

"Look at your hands," Ross held his own up for inspection. "And my face. We have to get out of here before our eyes swell shut."

Santiago frantically brushed at his eyes—ensuring that he spread the nettle hairs all over his eyelids. "Was it that dust?"

Ross shrugged. "It looked like fungus spores. Some kinds of spores can give you rashes."

It was true. And some kinds could germinate in your lungs and grow until they choked you to death, but Ross decided not to scare Santiago pointlessly. If there was a next time, he'd warn Santiago about holding his breath.

"Never touch anything unless I say it's okay," Ross added.

"How long do you think we have?" Santiago looked madly in all directions. "We can't leave empty-handed. The king will think you did it on purpose."

Ross pretended to survey the area before zeroing in on the fallen solar panel he'd spotted fifteen minutes ago, half-hidden in the undergrowth. "There's a solar panel. Quick, let's strap it to your back."

Santiago ran to unearth it, looking satisfied.

Ross hated to give Voske anything, but Santiago was undoubtedly right that leaving empty-handed would raise suspicion. At least solar panels, while rare and valuable, couldn't be used to kill anyone.

But though Ross had managed to cut this trip short without giving

Voske any weapons, he didn't feel as if he'd won. He'd been so sure he'd be heading back to Las Anclas today, but now escape felt further away than ever.

CHAPTER THIRTY-ONE
LAS ANCLAS
KERRY

Kerry walked into her secret party, manacle chains clinking musically. Though the location left something to be desired—it was held in a barn to hide it from the adults who would undoubtedly have forbidden it—she hadn't been so pleased since she'd come to Las Anclas. Mia had instantly agreed to go to the party with her. Nearly everyone here was a potential ally, or they wouldn't have come. That blowhard Tommy Horst and his annoying followers were noticeably absent.

She smiled at everybody, greeting the ones she knew and introducing herself to the ones she didn't, ending with, "How are you, Jennie?"

"Hey, Mia. Kerry. I have to get going." Jennie set down the last of the cupcakes she'd been arranging, slipped through the crowd without meeting anyone's eyes, and headed for the door. Mia stared wistfully after her.

"When the party's barely even started?" Sujata asked. But the door had already shut behind her, and clearly no one wanted to talk about the strange breakdown Jennie had had on the Ranger training ground.

The people who appear strongest are often concealing a secret weakness, Kerry thought. Father's advice was sound, as always. Though it would be hard to exploit Jennie's secret weakness when the girl vanished every time she saw Kerry.

"I'm so glad you got a chance to meet everybody, Kerry." Becky gave her a sweet smile—a real one, too. "It's too bad that as soon as we get to know you, you'll be going home again."

Kerry smiled back, but it took an effort. Becky's innocent words were an inescapable reminder that she was living on borrowed time. *And no one knows it but me.*

"I know this will sound weird." Kerry lifted her arms and rattled her chains. "But I like Las Anclas."

Everybody laughed.

"Yes, I'm sure you'll be quite sad to leave." Felicité's smile was also sweet, but as fake as her hair color.

Kerry couldn't resist saying, "Maybe someday I'll be back."

Felicité's smile didn't change, but Kerry was certain that the girl had caught the double meaning. She turned to talk to Henry, whom Kerry had been surprised to see at the party. She'd thought he was part of Tommy's Norm crowd. Then she saw him take Felicité's hand. Ah-ha. Felicité had come to spy on Kerry, and Henry, her boyfriend, had accompanied her.

Those two were useless.

Kerry poured out fruit punch and counted to herself. She now knew the names of everybody at the party, and she was sure she'd charmed at least two-thirds of them. But were they the right two-thirds?

Her walks around town with Mia had taught her that she'd need the cooperation of more people than just Mia to escape Las Anclas. After all the time she'd spent working on Brisa and Becky, she'd regretfully realized that they couldn't help her even if they were willing. She needed to befriend people with power in the community.

It was too bad that Felicité was clearly armored against her. She'd had more luck with Felicité's pretty golden rat, who wandered as freely as the gophers in Gold Point. Wu Zetian was always willing to come up and be petted if Kerry chirped to her. Unfortunately, though Kerry had tried the same commands she'd heard Felicité use, Wu Zetian was clearly trained to only obey Felicité.

"It's too bad we don't have any music," Carlos remarked.

Kerry hadn't yet learned what he did. But maybe it was something useful. She smiled at him, created a pair of hand cymbals, and clinked them together. A soft chime rang out.

Meredith began a complicated dance, her feet kicking up dust. More people joined, dancing in a group. Carlos snapped his fingers, and Kerry tapped out a syncopated beat.

Kerry couldn't talk to anyone while they danced. But providing music for it would make people see her as harmless, helpful, and fun, so she kept the chimes going. Then Henry leaped on to the rickety table. It collapsed, sending apples bounding.

"You idiot, Henry!"

"Shush!"

The dancing stopped as everyone looked nervously at the door. But no one barged in.

"At least we already ate the tacos." Becky began picking up the apples.

"It's too hot, anyway. We can dance at Luc's." Yolanda Riley wiped her forehead on her sleeve. "I love your power, Kerry. It's the coolest I've ever heard of."

"Are you Changed?" Kerry asked.

Yolanda's smile vanished. She brought up her hand. A wind whipped through the barn, bathing Kerry's face.

"That's a great power," Kerry said sincerely.

"Yeah, I like it, too." Yolanda sighed. "But when I Changed, my parents kicked me out of the house. None of my blood relatives talk to me any more."

Kerry had seen how prejudiced Norms could be here, but that shocked her. "That's horrible."

Yolanda gave Kerry a wistful smile. "I bet when you Changed, people congratulated you."

"They did, and that's how it should be," Kerry replied. "I was born Changed, but my power was weak until I got older. When I was five, I created a tiny sword and cut down one of my mother's rose bushes. I thought she'd be angry, but she hugged me instead. My father put the best rose in a golden vase, and said, 'Someday you'll be the pride of Gold Point.' Yolanda, your parents should have told you that you'd be the pride of Las Anclas."

Yolanda's chin came up. "My new parents do."

Alfonso Medina, a boy with gecko-like fingers and toes, appeared at Yolanda's shoulder. "Does everyone in Gold Point feel that way?"

If anyone didn't, they didn't dare say so.

"Yes," said Kerry firmly. If Alfonso wanted to flee Las Anclas, she'd be happy to help him. He could probably carry her over the wall. "In fact, in Gold Point, people compete for the chance to Change."

"The chance to Change?" echoed Mia. "The Change is inherited. You can't just decide that you want it."

"If you inherited the potential, my mother has the power to activate it." Kerry spoke carefully, aware of her enthralled audience. "We have a monthly festival called Opportunity Day, when we offer citizens that chance. Though there's no guarantee what you'll get. One guy couldn't even figure out what his power was, until he passed a pond on the way back home. It turned out that he had the ability to summon turtles. "

Everybody laughed, and Kerry laughed with them. But she couldn't help thinking of Luis, and of the girl Sean had picked, who died right there on the dais. Even some powers that seemed good at first hadn't turned out to be so wonderful in the end. Deirdre had been ecstatic when she became a stormbringer, but when she gained the ability to control the weather, she'd lost the ability to control her emotions. Six months later, her power killed her.

"I'd try it," Sujata said. "I'd love to have a power."

Kerry brought out the Encouragement Tone. "I'm sure you'd get a wonderful power, Sujata. Much better than turtles! Which one would you like?"

As Kerry had hoped, everyone immediately began talking about the powers they'd like to have. She was uneasily aware that she'd also left out the fact that nowadays, there were hardly any volunteers. Santiago had been the only one in that entire year. Again, she saw Sean's horror as his friend fell dead on the dais. What had her name been? Guilt pulsed through Kerry when she couldn't remember.

It was a relief when the door opened. The slanting late-afternoon sunlight outlined Father's distinctive profile. Kerry gasped. Then the barn door closed, and she recognized her half-brother, Paco.

Here was her ally. Preston had obviously been keeping him from her. But her brother had finally managed to slip his leash.

"Paco," she called out. "I'm so glad to finally meet you."

Everybody had gone silent. Kerry turned to the bug-eyed crowd. "Do you mind? I'd like to have a little private time with my brother."

Paco stood absolutely still, watching as first Yuki, and then everyone else walked to the other side of the barn. Mia backed up too, but not very far.

As Kerry passed her, Mia said, "I won't eavesdrop." Her round face was solemn behind those winking glasses.

Kerry forced a smile. "I know. You're just doing your job."

She walked up to Paco. He took a step back, staring unnervingly at her face. Kerry stayed where she was, trying not to crowd him. She didn't want to stare back, but she couldn't help it. Out of all her half-siblings, Paco looked the most like Father. And the most like her.

Kerry dropped her voice as low as she could. "You know we can't talk here."

She waited for a response, but he just stood there. She couldn't tell what he was thinking. Though he had Father's face, his expressions were totally different. But she knew what she had to offer. As Min Soo had said, what boy wouldn't want to wake up and find himself a crown prince?

When the bounty hunter returned from Gold Point, Preston would kill her. She had to seize this chance.

"Meet me at Mia's cottage after the party," she whispered. "Mia won't interfere. Then we can talk."

She searched his face on each word, her nerves chilling when his eyes narrowed and his mouth twisted with hatred. Of course. He thought she had stolen his rightful place.

She leaned closer. "I promise, I won't try to usurp your position. I know you're the crown prince."

"Shut up!" Paco yelled. He flung himself away from her, his back banging into the door. "I am not a traitor! Mia's not a traitor! And you—

you're just like your father!"

The barn door slammed behind him. Yuki ran after Paco, and the door slammed again.

Kerry turned around to a sea of open mouths. Mia looked like she'd been punched in the gut. Kerry raised her hands so fast the chain jerked tight, locking her wrists together.

Brisa's voice cut through the ringing silence, "What did you say to him?"

Kerry hastily recalled her words. Whatever she told them now had to match with whatever Paco said later. Letting her surprise and dismay show in her voice, she said, "He must have totally misunderstood me. I asked him if we could talk privately, but I only wanted to get to know my brother without so many people around. I said Mia wouldn't mind if he came to her cottage to talk to me." She turned to Mia. "You wouldn't, right?"

Looking bewildered, Mia shook her head.

Kerry said quickly, "Oh, I realize now what he must have thought. I said that I'd heard so much about Paco, the crown prince. My father always wished he could meet his son. I mean, if things were different." Her voice wobbled. She swallowed past the thickness in her throat. "I know it's never going to happen. I wish I could take it all back."

For once, Becky's soft voice was easily heard. "Let's all pretend this entire party never happened."

"Excellent idea." Felicité Wolfe stepped forward with the ease of one used to giving orders. "Let's get things cleaned up, shall we?"

CHAPTER THIRTY-TWO
LAS ANCLAS
YUKI

Yuki swam empty-handed out of the sea cave, and glanced back at the crack in the cliffs that led to it. With Ross gone, he'd limited himself to exploration and mapping, not daring to try to move anything. But the ocean creatures weren't so cautious. Fish swam in and out, and barnacles and sea anemones had begun to attach themselves to the walls and wrecked furniture.

Paco tapped Yuki's shoulder and made a throat-cutting sign: he was running out of air. Yuki gestured to him to surface, and started to follow.

A sea magpie swam out of the cave, with something shiny grasped in its tentacles. The eyes on the tips of its stalks swiveled as it spotted Yuki, and it darted toward the open sea.

Yuki arrowed after it, intent on its prize. The sea magpie dove deeper. Yuki followed, slipping past a strand of grasping kelp, down to the base of the cliff. Here the light was dim and blue-green, and the weight of the water pressed on his eardrums. Tightness banded his chest, and his pulse galloped loud in his ears.

But he was closing in on the creature. He grabbed a trailing tentacle. It slipped out of his hand, but the startled sea magpie dropped the shiny thing. Both it and Yuki dove for it. Yuki was faster. He grabbed the chunk of metal, then swam for the surface, his lungs burning.

Beneath the cliffs, he took a long breath of air and pushed up his goggles. Treading water, he held out his find. "Look!"

Paco barely gave it a glance. "A metal…lump."

"It's an artifact," Yuki said. "See? It's got plastic attached to it."

The boys swam back to the beach. Yuki sat on the sand and examined his find, a corroded metal thing with a yellow plastic switch. He flipped the switch, but nothing happened. Then he tugged on a metal tab. A yellow tape with writing on it spooled out.

Excited, Yuki held it up to read. Then he saw what it was, and laughed.

Paco sat back, looking disappointed. "A tape measure."

"An ancient artifact tape measure. Think about it, Paco. Hundreds of years ago, some person used this to build their home. And we're holding it now."

The idea of all those years awed Yuki, but Paco only shrugged. Yuki couldn't remember him smiling once since he'd found out who his father was— certainly not since his confrontation with Kerry.

Yuki fished for something that might catch his enthusiasm. "I wonder if I could train a sea magpie to help me prospect?"

That caught Paco's attention, but not in a good way. "Train a *sea magpie*? They're fish! You can't train a fish!"

Yuki decided not to point out that technically, they were mollusks. "You never know until you try."

Paco stood up. "I have to get back. See you."

Yuki scrambled to his feet. "Ranger training isn't for hours. We only did one dive."

"What's the point?" Paco nudged the ancient tape measure with his toe. "How's that going to defend us against Voske?"

Yuki felt as disoriented as when he'd gotten trapped in the sea cave, drowning in ink-black waters. Usually Paco was the one person in town who would choose flowers over dumplings, as they said on the *Taka*: someone who looked beyond the practical and everyday. Paco's contemptuous gaze at the artifact made Yuki feel betrayed.

"There's more to life than fighting," Yuki retorted. "How's music going to defend us?"

Paco straightened up. "It isn't. That's why I quit the Old Town Band."

"What?" Yuki exclaimed.

Paco shrugged, as if what he'd said had no significance. As if he hadn't practiced for years to get good enough to be invited into that band. "I have more important things to do."

Yuki was too surprised to think before he spoke. "What could be more important to you than music?"

"What do you think?" Paco shouted. "Getting stronger. Protecting this town. Voske's coming back. We all know it. And I mean to be the one to take him down."

He stalked off.

Yuki watched him, hurt and frustrated. Unable to think of anything else to do, he dove into the ocean, swimming down.

Usually, underwater, he felt free—free of gravity, free of worries. His entire being was focused on perceiving his surroundings and where he was in space. He had no attention to spare for anything else.

But not even diving could distract him now. Paco was right that the town was in danger, but was giving up everything else that he loved really going to help? At best, it was driving a wedge between them, as Paco systematically rejected everything that had attracted Yuki to him to begin with. Or was Yuki being selfish and shallow, to expect Paco to remain unchanged after all he'd been through?

Yuki dove deeper, trying to force himself to concentrate, but his thoughts pursued him. He'd abandoned Ross. Paco had changed until Yuki barely recognized him. And Yuki was still trapped in Las Anclas, since there was no way he'd leave while the town was in danger. Even if he was willing to go, Paco wouldn't come with him. After everything Yuki had done, he'd gotten absolutely nowhere.

His lungs screamed for oxygen, forcing him to surface. Maybe Paco was right, in a way. Wasn't the tape measure—wasn't everything in the sea cave —wasn't prospecting itself—nothing more than a distraction from what Yuki had lost? He'd been born to rule a city that no longer existed. Anything else he did with his life would always, inevitably, be nothing more than a consolation prize.

Yuki floated beneath the cliffs, feeling as lost as he had when he'd first come to Las Anclas, watching the empty horizon line for the rescue that never came.

CHAPTER THIRTY-THREE
GOLD POINT
ROSS

Ross paced around the palace garden, with two guards following close on his heels. Santiago was still at home with his eyes swollen shut, no doubt bored out of his mind.

Voske had looked puzzled when they'd emerged from the crystal forest so soon after they'd entered. But when they'd come close enough for him to see their swollen faces, he'd ordered everyone to keep their distance. Ross had scrubbed off in the stream while Santiago reported to the king. When Santiago was done, Voske ordered them all back to Gold Point.

"Santiago knows not to touch anything without your permission now," Voske said to Ross as they mounted up, then added, "As soon as the swelling goes down, you can return."

Ross prowled the garden, trying to come up with an escape plan. He'd hoped being outside would make him feel less trapped, but it didn't. There were so many electric lights in Gold Point, shining from windows and atop the poles that lined the streets, that the night sky glowed an eerie purple-gray. He couldn't see a single star.

He was so used to navigating by the stars that the lack of them made him feel disoriented, almost dizzy. The sky seemed low and looming, as if he could destabilize it with a touch, and send it toppling down...

Ross yanked his gaze downward, his heart pounding. He couldn't start getting afraid of the *sky*. He'd lose his mind. He lifted his head deliberately, scanning the jagged black line of the mountains against that dim sky. High mountains. Plenty of air. Lights winked at the distant dam that supplied all that electricity.

He walked on, the guards' footsteps a steady beat behind him, until he came to Luis's guest house. The windows were dark. Ross hoped that meant he'd learned to control his powers and has been returned to his garrison.

But the front door stood wide open. The moonlight from the window outlined a silhouette sitting alone at a table, like a scene from one of Bankar's ghost stories.

"Luis?" Ross asked.

The silhouette jerked upright. "Ross?"

Even at his lowest, Ross had never in his life felt as utterly miserable as Luis sounded.

"I'm sorry, Luis." He'd already ruined Luis's life. He didn't need to pester him as well.

Ross backed away.

"Wait. You can come in. Just don't get too close." To Ross's guards, Luis said, "I just want to talk."

The guards saluted, then took up positions, one outside each door. Ross came in, and Luis closed the door behind him.

Ross said, "I guess the experiments aren't working?"

"I stopped," Luis said.

Ross grimaced, trying not to imagine what had happened. But the memories of five crystal trees gave him a vivid picture of Voske's smiling face presiding as Luis touched prisoners and burned them to the bone.

"That is, the king let me stop while he was gone. I'm sure he'll have more for me to do now that he's back. But they're not experiments any more. It's obvious that I'll never be able to control my power. If it wasn't for Sophie—" Luis looked around furtively.

Ross knew Luis was about to say something fake-cheerful, rather than whatever honest thing he'd been about to disclose. He couldn't stand hearing one more sentence spoken for the benefit of Voske's eavesdropping. Besides, Ross owed him.

He touched his finger to his lips. Luis glanced curiously at him, but stayed silent. Ross pulled down the shades. Once his eyes adjusted to the darkness enough to see shapes, he returned to his seat.

Ross lowered his voice. "The king's eavesdropping thing doesn't work inside a dark room."

Luis's breath hitched. "Are you sure? How do you know?"

Ross hesitated. "I can't tell you exactly. But if I could... Well, I wouldn't still be in the palace. You'd have seen me in the hell cells when Voske sent you to 'experiment' on prisoners."

Even in the dim light, Ross saw Luis flinch.

Luis spoke softly. "The king doesn't allow anyone to escape from Gold Point. He specifically told me that he considers suicide to be a form of escape. If I kill myself, he'll execute Sophie. I want to die, but I can't."

Ross could imagine how terrible it must be to be unable to touch anyone without hurting them, but he couldn't fathom that depth of despair. He'd risked his life plenty of times, but always with the hope that he'd survive and succeed. He couldn't imagine deciding that he'd *prefer* death.

He had to convince Luis that there was some other way. "What sort of experiments have you tried? Real experiments, I mean."

"The king wants me to be able to kill with a single touch. But I've been trying to make myself not hurt anyone—to make it so I only burn people when I'm trying to. But it happens no matter how hard I try."

"Maybe it's too hard to concentrate with Voske standing over you."

Luis shook his head. "I tried with Sophie. She insisted."

"That was right after you got your power, wasn't it? Listen, Luis, my own power was hard to control, too. At first it was like it was controlling me. And then I tried to concentrate as hard as I could. But that isn't how it works. I don't force my will on those crystal trees." Ross frowned, trying to put it into words. "I open my mind to them. I let them come to me. Like you'd tame a wild animal."

"I don't know how I'd do that."

The image of Min Soo's hands dripping blood flashed into Ross's mind. But Luis was so desperate, and Ross had chosen him. He had to make it right.

Ross slipped off his gauntlet. Then he put his left arm on the table before Luis, scarred side turned down.

"Oh, no," Luis said. "I'm not going to do that."

"That arm's no good anyway. You can't make it worse." Ross tried to remember what it had felt like when he'd first successfully spoken with his crystal tree. "Don't force yourself to do anything. Just imagine yourself touching me and nothing happening. Imagine the last time you touched someone, before you Changed."

Luis sat still for a long time. Ross waited. Finally he heard the creak of a chair. He heard a slow intake of breath. The vague shape of Luis's hand hovered over his arm. Then he brought his fingers down.

Five burning coals pressed into his arm. Ross gasped, forcing himself not to cry out in pain. Luis jerked his hand back. Blood welled up and dripped down Ross's arm.

Ross hastily flexed his fingers. They closed as far as they ever had. The damage was only skin-deep. "It's okay."

"It's not okay!" Luis yelled.

The door banged open. A guard said, "Are you all right?"

Ross's voice collided with Luis's. "We're fine."

"We were experimenting," said Luis.

"The king will not like his guest experimented on." The guard sounded horrified. To Ross, he said, "Come along, sir."

"I volunteered." Ross followed the guard out, then turned back at the door. "Don't give up."

Luis was silent.

CHAPTER THIRTY-FOUR
LAS ANCLAS
MIA

When Mia and Kerry went into the surgery to check the chalkboard, both stopped as if they'd hit an invisible wall. Mia happily inhaled the delicious aromas.

"What *is* that?" Kerry whispered.

"That," Mia intoned reverently, "is Great-Grandma Lee's white radish kimchi. And broiled mackerel."

A calico cat glided down from atop a cupboard, its wing-flaps outstretched, and landed at Mia's feet with a thud. It was quickly followed by the tabby cat who had been perched beside it, and a fluffy white cat that scampered in from another room. All three sat at Mia's feet and meowed hopefully.

Mia laughed. "Mention fish, summon cats. I smell flower biscuits, too —they're shaped like flowers, not made of flowers. Thank goodness. It's all very traditional. Dad is definitely trying to impress you."

Kerry looked suitably impressed as she bent to tousle cat heads. "That sounds more promising than the turnip-and-goat-cheese pancakes."

"Those were revolting, but believe me, there have been worse experiments. Much worse."

Dad poked his head out of the kitchen. "I thought I heard your voices, girls. Lunch is at noon. Don't be late."

Mia tapped the chalkboard. "Then we only have time for the south forge generator. That'll be the twenty-third repair this year on that thing."

"Why don't you build a new one?" Kerry asked.

"Grandma Johanssen insists it's still got plenty of use in it, and Mr. Horst's north forge gets priority because..." *Because he's making the new weapons the Defense Chief wants.* Should Mia be talking about that? "...Mr. Preston likes him." That was true enough.

Kerry slung a tool belt over her shoulder. "Let's go. I don't want to be late for that lunch."

As they walked down the road, Mia tallied how the people they passed responded. Five dirty looks, eleven ignores, and two hellos, which were both from teenagers.

It was an improvement over the first few days, which had averaged sixty percent dirty looks. But it made Mia nervous. She'd never had to face that many glares before. And they weren't even directed at her! She couldn't imagine what Kerry must feel like.

Mia loved numbers, but so much of what she couldn't help counting recently were things she didn't want to think about. It had been two days and twenty-one hours since that disaster of a party (which meant two days and twenty hours since Mia had last said 'hi' to Jennie), and six days since Jennie had broken down at Ranger training and had been put on temporary medical leave.

Since that night, Mia had exchanged fifty-three words with Jennie, most of which were variations on 'Hi, how are you?' and 'Fine, how are you?'

Jennie was obviously very, very far from fine. At least she was talking to Dad, but that was only because she'd been ordered to. She went in and out of Dad's house every day, without once approaching Mia's cottage. Jennie wouldn't talk in front of Kerry, even if she wanted to. But if she wanted to talk to Mia alone, she could come over at night, when Kerry was in her cell.

Mia couldn't help wondering if the distance between them was her fault. Dad had told her that some experiences left wounds on the inside that took a very long time to heal. She'd known how much Jennie loved Sera. Why hadn't Mia tried harder to ask Jennie what was wrong? Did Jennie feel like Mia had abandoned her? Or was Jennie still angry that Mia was guarding Kerry?

The picket fence beside Kerry clattered as she walked, her hand outstretched, and Mia realized that she had created an invisible stick to run along it. Mia couldn't help laughing.

With a quick grin, Kerry opened her other hand to Mia. "Guess."

Mia loved this game. She put her hand over Kerry's palm, feeling something round and fuzzy, a little squishy, with a cleft in one side... "A peach!"

"You got it!" Kerry replied.

Mia wondered if Jennie was right that Kerry was cold-bloodedly manipulating her. It didn't feel like she was, but Mia knew she was no good at figuring out people. But Dad was, and he thought Kerry's friendliness was genuine. At least part of the time.

I've never seen Ian Voske, but I believe I know exactly how he smiles, Dad had said privately to Mia on the second day, before Mia went to fetch Kerry. *When Kerry smiles that certain smile before she asks a question, I suspect she's hiding her real intent.*

Yesterday, Dad had commented that he'd seen the Voske smile less often. Mia liked Kerry's scientific curiosity, the fun she had with her Change power, and her way with animals. The cats loved her. To Mia's intense fascination, they seemed able to *see* her invisible objects. She and Mia were still trying to design an experiment to determine if they really could, or if they were extrapolating from the movements of Kerry's hands.

I wish Jennie could see her like I do, Mia thought as they splashed under the dripping pines to enter Main Street. *They have so much in common.*

The rapid tattoo of horses' hooves brought them to a stop. Four Rangers galloped by, kicking up mud. Indra caught Mia's eye and lifted his hand, his gaze sliding right past Kerry.

"Is he as good as he looks at practice?" Kerry watched the Rangers gallop through the gate and vanish along the east road. "I'd love to spar with him."

"They're all good." Mia grimaced down at the mud. How much did it hurt Jennie to see the Rangers going on missions without her? As much as it hurt Mia that Jennie wouldn't talk to her?

"Santiago and I used to spar every day that he wasn't on a scouting mission," Kerry said wistfully. Then she brightened. "He loves to say that on our first date, I knocked him out cold. He thinks that's hilarious. He always leaves me to explain that it wasn't actually during the date, it was at the tournament we were in before the date. And also, it was a complete accident. You see..."

Mia memorized the tournament details, in case Mr. Preston thought they were important. But she was more interested in how Kerry talked about Santiago. She didn't get all swoony, the way some girls (and boys) did—all that stuff about lips and eyes and meaningful glances and fiery passions. She talked about him the way she'd talk about a best friend— how they sparred together, how they rode together, how much they had in common. She never spoke like that about anyone else, making Mia wonder if she even had any other friends.

Mia didn't mind hearing about Santiago. He sounded nice. The problem was, the way Kerry talked about Santiago was the way Mia thought about Ross. And every time Mia thought about Ross, she felt like a screwdriver had stabbed her right between the ribs. She was desperate to ask Kerry about him, but the one time she had, Kerry had lied. And if there was one thing worse than not knowing anything, it was knowing stuff when she didn't know if it was even true.

By the time they finished with the generator, Mia decided that there was one thing that she *had* to know. And it wasn't about Ross. After the delicious lunch, she told Kerry that her next project was outside the gates, so she had to take Kerry back to jail. Then Mia sped back across the town square, and reached the surgery just as Jennie was leaving.

They spoke simultaneously. "I'm sorry."

Jennie breathed a laugh. "Mia, *you* don't have anything to be sorry about."

"Yes, I do. I knew how you felt about Sera—"

"Don't." Jennie winced, holding up her palm. Then she dropped her hand. "No, I'm sorry. Again. You can mention her. You saw what happened when I didn't talk to anyone about what I was feeling. About the battle. About Sera. Ross. Everything. I know your dad is right that I can't keep it all bottled up inside of me. But every time I think about the past few months, I feel worse, not better."

Before Mia could think of anything to say, Jennie added, "Speaking of the last few months. Where's the princess?"

"Jail. I told her I had to fix the water line by the mill. I do, eventually. Slimegrass got in it again, like it does every year when the rains start."

"Let's make it true. I'll help." As they went to get Mia's tools, Jennie said, "I wish I hadn't closed you out. I closed Ross out, and…" Jennie shook her head. "I should have been there with you at the ruined city."

"Ross and Yuki were there," Mia pointed out. "And you know how well they fight! If you'd been there, all that would have been different would have been that it wouldn't have *seemed* quite as hopeless. Then Yuki wouldn't have dragged me away, and then all of us but Ross probably would have been killed."

"That's what my parents say, too." Jennie looked down at her strong hands. "But I can't believe it."

Twenty-six days, twelve hours, and forty-two minutes since Ross got taken, Mia thought.

She wished she had a countdown until he arrived safely home.

CHAPTER THIRTY-FIVE
LAS ANCLAS
KERRY

"How do you feel about bees?" Mia asked.

"I'm not crazy about them," Kerry admitted, wondering where that was going. "My brother Sean got stung once and his arm swelled up to twice its size. But I do love honey."

"There might be honey involved." Mia had arrived late, which meant, Kerry knew by now, that she'd been up half the night working on something. "The pump at the apiary jammed."

As they left the jail, Mia pulled two napkin-wrapped objects from her bag and offered one to Kerry. "Chicken tamale? Dad just made them. Still warm."

Kerry bit in with enthusiasm. As she munched, she glanced up at the sky, hoping Pru was watching her. But she saw no hawks. Was Father disappointed that she hadn't escaped by now, or was he expecting her to gather intelligence first?

She hadn't been to the apiary yet, so that might be useful knowledge. If it was near a lightly guarded part of the wall, she could knock Mia out, go over, and file off the manacles once she was well out of town.

When she'd first planned her escape over the wall, she'd meant to kill her guard. But she'd gotten…maybe not fond, exactly, but at least tolerant of Mia. Enough that she didn't want to kill her.

The apiary was in sight of the wall, but there were almost as many sentries as at the gates. Kerry saw a mill wheel looming beyond the wall. Of course a mill would be well guarded. Furry bees buzzed around, most the usual scarlet striped with black, but some a brilliant blue.

"What kind of honey do those blue ones make?" Kerry asked.

Mia glanced up as she unloading her bag beside an ancient well pump. "Same as the red ones. The blue ones are a mutation. The only thing that's different is that they're meaner. The beekeepers are trying to breed them out."

Each hive hummed a different note. Kerry wondered if the bees in Gold Point hummed the same notes. She'd never seen where the honey for her toast came from, or how the beekeepers got it out of the hive. She hoped she'd get to see it now, but the beekeeper was nowhere in sight.

Kerry sat back, content to watch Mia work. She enjoyed how clever and fearless Mia was in dealing with complicated machinery, and it amused Kerry when Mia started absently talking to the machines.

"There's your problem," Mia informed the pump.

With a pair of pliers, she tugged at something stuck in the mechanism. With a loud snap, a metal nut flew out in a high arc and slammed into the nearest beehive. The hum rose angrily as a swarm of blue bees arrowed toward them.

"Kerry, look out!" Mia yelled, dropping her pliers and flinging her arms over her head.

Kerry grabbed Mia's wrist with one hand and held her other out, palm flat, surrounding the two of them with a bowl-shaped shield. Bees ricocheted off the invisible wall.

Mia slowly raised her head, her eyes enormous behind her glasses. "Thanks. I don't want to think how many times I'd have gotten stung if you hadn't done that. How long can you keep this up?"

"It's no strain," Kerry replied. "But we only have as much air as the shield holds: about ten minutes' worth. Let's yell for the beekeeper."

But he was already there. The man hummed softly, waving his arms in intricate gestures. The bees swarmed around him until he became a silhouette inside a dark, constantly shifting cloud. He moved sedately to the hive, still humming, then whistled a low note. The bees all flew back inside their hive.

Mia was eyeing her pliers, lying near the hive. Kerry darted away and retrieved them for her.

"Thanks." Mia made a face. "Want to know the truth? I hate bees."

Kerry replaced the shield over them as Mia finished her job. Just in case.

The beekeeper walked up when she was done. "Here's a jar of fireweed honey for you and avocado honey for Dr. Lee."

Kerry released the shield.

"Thanks, Mr. Hassan." Mia nestled the jars into her bag.

To Kerry's surprise, Mr. Hassan turned to her. "And for you, a honeycomb."

"Thanks, Mr. Hassan," Kerry said. "Honey is the one sweet thing I actually like."

She began eating the honeycomb as she took a last glance at the wall. It was still heavily patrolled. No go here. On the positive side, she wouldn't have to get past the bees when she made her escape.

On their way back, they passed the north forge. Kerry's attention was caught by a shower of sparks. Inside, the huge ironmonger, Mr. Horst, was hammering a glowing piece of metal. As he plunged it into a vat of water, he turned his head to avoid the billowing steam. His eyes met hers. Mr. Horst slammed the object down on a tray, and came storming out of the forge.

"How dare you spy on my forge, monster girl?" Mr. Horst roared.

"She's helping me, Mr. Horst." Mia held up her tool bag. "She's not spying."

Mr. Horst ignored Mia and advanced on Kerry, snarling, "I'm counting the days until you're as dead as my brother. They're going to shoot you anyway. Maybe I should save them the ammunition."

He pulled a hammer from a loop in his leather apron. Kerry regretfully dropped the last bite of honeycomb and snapped up a shield.

Mia jumped in front of Kerry. "I'm guarding her. She's my responsibility."

Kerry couldn't believe that Mia was standing up to that huge man to protect *her*. "Mia, I have a shield."

Mia raised her voice. "Mr. Horst, leave her be. She hasn't done anything!"

People came out of the pottery and brewery nearby to enjoy the scene.

"Kill the mutant, Horst," someone yelled.

A woman called out, "There he goes again, King Horst! Gonna put her head on a pike?"

"Sheriff!" a third person bellowed.

The crowd shifted as Preston shoved through, his light blue eyes glaring. Behind him came a patrol of armed people on horseback.

"Break it up," Preston ordered. "Get back to work."

"Your work is to get rid of this spying monster," Mr. Horst shouted at Preston. "Are you afraid of her, or are you afraid of her father?"

Before Preston could reply, a woman shook her broom at him.

"Kidnapping Voske's get was *your* stupid idea," she yelled. "It's brought nothing but trouble."

A man holding a lump of clay added, "We voted you in, Preston. We can vote you out."

"You'll have your chance at the election," Preston said calmly. "Mia, get her out of here."

He stalked away, followed by the patrollers, who walked their horses through the crowd to break it up.

"Come on, Kerry," Mia said. "I'm sorry. I shouldn't have taken that shortcut."

Kerry followed Mia to her cottage, her emotions in a spin. All those people had yelled at Preston, contradicted him, challenged him, insulted him, even, in a way, threatened him. But he'd done nothing. Or was he biding his time?

"What'll happen to all those people?" Kerry asked, once they were inside.

Mia set the honey jars on her table. "What do you mean?"

"The ones who talked back to Preston. What's he going to do to them?"

"Nothing."

"I mean, the ones who called him stupid? The ones who threatened to vote him out?"

"Nothing," Mia repeated. "They can say whatever they like. If you want to hear more, go over to Jack's saloon. Don't they blabber on about politics in Gold Point?"

Kerry was amazed that the townspeople could get away with that. It was so ... so *reckless!* How could you control people who felt free to blurt out anything they thought? But she was also aware of her jealousy at the freedom that these idiot Las Anclas citizens took for granted.

That jealousy was dangerously disloyal.

"No, they don't." As if Father stood in the next room, Kerry said loudly, "Father can hear everything. If anyone were to speak like that of him, even if they were hiding in a basement in the middle of the night, he would hear. And he'd have their head on a pole. Loyalty is very important to him."

"That's horrible." Mia spoke with a sober sincerity that Kerry didn't know how to answer. "I hate to say this about somebody else's home, but I'm so glad I don't live there."

Kerry wanted to defend Gold Point, but she knew it would turn into an ugly argument. She had to charm Mia, not alienate her. She kept silent.

That night, when Mia escorted Kerry to her cell, she stopped at the door with the air of someone determined to say something.

Here it is, Kerry thought. The lecture on how horrible Gold Point is.

But Mia's words were unexpected. "I'm sorry, Kerry. About what Mr. Horst and those other people said. Not everybody thinks it."

"I know."

"The battle was terrible. But it wasn't your fault. You weren't even there, were you?"

"I wasn't. My sister was. She died at your wall."

"I'm sorry about that, too." Mia sounded like she meant it.

Kerry grimaced as Mia left. Why did she say that about Deirdre? She hadn't meant to. She had to get a better grip on herself. Father would be disappointed at how she'd let her emotions rule her tongue. She shouldn't say a single word that wasn't to a pre-planned purpose.

*

Kerry jolted awake at the clang of the bell, staring into the darkness of the jail; a cage of bright moths silhouetted the deputy who had been snoozing in his chair. He shot to his feet, rifle in hand, and hit the lights.

Sheriff Crow burst out of her door barefoot, her loose hair swinging as she buckled on her pistol.

The deputy sniffed, then yelled, "Fire!"

"Might be a diversion," Sheriff Crow said to the deputy. "Stay here."

Kerry grabbed the bars of her cell, hoping the sheriff was right. This could be her rescue!

She heard the sound of running feet outside her cell. Someone shouted, "Behind the schoolhouse! The woods are on fire."

The sheriff ran out. Kerry heard her shout, "I want guards all around the jail! You. Cover this door. You, too. Anyone with a weapon, follow me!"

More running feet. Then, close by, the night erupted into an uproar of yells, clashing weapons, gunshots, and crackles of lightning. Bankar's shrill, gloating laugh rose above the commotion.

Kerry pressed her face against the bars, gripping a sword. She never thought she'd be so delighted to hear Bankar's voice. If Bankar was here, Santiago must be, too! It was his team.

Someone wailed, "I can't see!"

That's Charles's touch, Kerry thought, grinning fiercely.

Bankar's laugh rose up again, then cut off abruptly.

More gunshots and shouts crescendoed in a clash of metal. Then silence, except for the ringing of the bell. Sharp voices rose, but Kerry couldn't distinguish individual words.

"Everybody, quiet!" That was the sheriff.

Kerry listened frantically, hoping it was just a pause in the fighting, but the only voice was the sheriff's. "You, fetch Dr. Lee. You, go report to the Defense Chief. This might not be the only attack team. You three, stay here and keep guarding the jail."

"I can't see," a woman exclaimed.

"I can't either," said a man, an edge of panic in his voice. "I'm blind!"

The sheriff spoke. "Calm down. Dr. Lee is on his way. Let me take a look."

Kerry flexed her hands and her swords vanished. The attack had failed. The only question was, was the team dead, or had they escaped? Where was Santiago?

The jail door opened. Sheriff Crow came to Kerry's cell, stopping out of weapons range. Her pajamas were spattered with blood. Santiago's? Kerry held her breath, fighting for control of her heartbeat.

The sheriff didn't speak. Waiting for Kerry to let something slip? Kerry ought to wait, too, but she had to know. Anyway, the rescue attempt was hardly a secret.

"Are they all dead?" Kerry demanded.

"I don't know," Sheriff Crow replied. "How many are on a team?"

"Depends," Kerry said, trying to match the woman's cool tone. "How many were here?"

"Eight."

Without meaning to, Kerry's voice rose in a shout. "Are they all dead?"

It was never easy to read Sheriff Crow's expressions, but Kerry felt a shift in the atmosphere. Kerry's emotions had given her away. And the sheriff knew it.

"Let's make a deal." Sheriff Crow held out her hand in the 'deal' sign. "I'll tell you whatever you need to know about what happened to that team, if you'll tell me something about their Change powers."

Kerry knew she shouldn't make any deals, or at least any deals that she intended to fulfill. But she couldn't help herself. She held out her hand, palm up. "Deal."

She was surprised when Sheriff Crow laid her warm palm across Kerry's. For all the sheriff knew, Kerry could have held a handful of invisible razor blades. But before Kerry could debate the merits of taking the opportunity to hurt her, the sheriff took her hand away.

"Two people got blinded," Sheriff Crow said. "Is it permanent?"

Kerry shook her head. "It wears off in five or six days. There's a guy my age with short black hair, probably using a staff. What happened to him?"

Sheriff Crow's brown eye widened in what looked like genuine surprise. "He wasn't there. There was a girl about your age with lightning powers. Everyone else was my age or older."

Kerry turned away, relief flooding through her.

The sheriff looked down at her blood-stained hands, and spoke as if to herself. "They wouldn't surrender. I gave them the chance. They *chose* to fight to the death. Why did they do that?"

Kerry hesitated. The deal had only covered the team's Change powers. But the sheriff had been honest with her. "They were afraid to go back and tell Father that they'd failed."

"I see." Sheriff Crow walked out.

Kerry sank down on the cot. Santiago's team had been killed, but he was alive. Somebody else had taken his place.

Then it hit her: that could be because he was already dead.

CHAPTER THIRTY-SIX
LAS ANCLAS
MIA

Mr. Preston gave Mia a dismissive look. "Is that it?"

Mia nodded. "You've got all my reports, right there. I wrote everything down, just as you ordered."

"None of it has furnished us anything of the least importance." Mr. Preston dropped Mia's reports and faced the other members of the council. "Those of you who were in favor of keeping the prisoner alive to extract information from her can see that was pointless. Not only does holding her make us look weak, it makes Las Anclas a magnet for attacks. We lost two people and had five wounded. Unless a miracle occurs and Voske decides to make the hostage exchange, we should kill the prisoner sooner rather than later."

Judge Lopez interlaced her bony brown fingers. "Let's take the long view on this. The Gold Point empire isn't going to go away. But neither is Voske going to live forever. Kerry is his heir. By Mia's account, if she's treated with respect, she responds with respect."

Dad spoke up. "I agree. The girl has been eating at my home. She talks readily, though we can't expect her to reveal her father's secrets. Still, I believe we could win her over, given time."

Judge Lopez went on. "If we were to let her go, she will someday be the ruler of Gold Point. And she will remember that Las Anclas extended a gesture of good faith."

Mr. Appel shook his head and scowled. "Voske will have taken over Las Anclas long before the girl can inherit anything."

"Voske's going to come after us anyway," Dad replied. "But *Kerry* didn't attack us. She's neither a combatant nor a criminal. Killing her would be murder."

"This is war," Mr. Preston retorted. "Civilian rules don't apply."

"We do have rules of war," said Judge Lopez. "For instance, unlike Voske, we don't hold people's families hostage. Until now."

Mr. Preston waved a dismissive hand. "The only way to answer Voske is in terms he understands."

Sheriff Crow turned her yellow snake eye on Mr. Preston. "I think this is personal. I think you're so angry with Voske that you'd kill his teenage daughter just to get back at him."

Mr. Preston banged his fist on the table. But before he could start yelling, the mayor stood up. "Council members, we are taking a break. We will hold the vote in fifteen minutes."

Mia waited until the mayor followed Mr. Preston to the far end of the room, then whispered to Dad, "Should I leave?"

Dad looked tired and unhappy. "Better not, Mia. The council might have further questions for you."

Once the council was done voting, Mia would ask if she could take Kerry out of her cell again. There was no reason why she needed to be locked up all day. *She* hadn't tried to escape.

Mia had been worried at the start of the meeting, but now that she'd heard all the arguments, she relaxed. Dad, Judge Lopez, Sheriff Crow, and the mayor would vote against killing Kerry, and that made a majority. At worst, she'd be stuck as a prisoner in Las Anclas.

One thing was for sure, Mia liked Kerry a whole lot better than she liked Tommy Horst or Henry Callahan. Or even Felicité.

The mayor returned with Mr. Preston. He looked pleased. She looked upset. Had he been yelling at her? Quietly yelling.

"Council members, let us hold a vote," said Mayor Wolfe. "All in favor of executing Kerry Voske in the event that her father refuses to hold a hostage exchange, raise your hands."

Mia glared at Mr. Preston as he held up his hand, followed by Judge Vardam and Mr. Appel. Then, to Mia's shock, the mayor slowly raised her hand. So that was what Mr. Preston had been doing—he'd pressured her into changing her vote.

Felicité calmly bent over her scribe book to record the vote. How could she not care about her parents voting to kill a girl her own age?

Mia's stomach knotted. "This is wrong. I've been spending all day with Kerry, for *ten days*. She's not a bad person. She saved me from getting stung by bees!"

"She saved you from getting stung by bees," Felicité repeated. Once Felicité said it, Mia realized how ridiculous she had sounded.

"A swarm!" Mia added hastily. "It really was dangerous. People end up in the infirmary for that. Anyway, my point is, she protected me, and she didn't have to. You can't just *kill* her."

"The vote's been held," Mr. Preston said. "There's nothing more to say. Thank you for your service, Mia. You're released from guard duty."

Mia shook her head so fast that her glasses nearly flew off. "I don't want to be released. Kerry talks to me. She might still give me enough valuable information that you wouldn't want to kill her. Anyway, Mr. Vilas isn't back yet. You won't kill—um, do anything to her before then, so can I at least get her back out of her cell and keep her talking?"

Sheriff Crow gave Mia an approving look. "Yes, you may. But Mia, don't let even a hint slip of our decision. If she knows she has nothing to lose, she could turn on you."

Mia wouldn't have told Kerry for the world. How horrible, to know that you were going to be killed and there was nothing you could do about it. "I promise."

CHAPTER THIRTY-SEVEN
GOLD POINT
ROSS

Voske smiled when the guards brought in the new solar panel. Ross and Santiago had uncovered two more of them, and carried out the best of the pair.

"Excellent," Voske said. "Success is always rewarded. If you find me weapons, I'll give you each one of the royal horses."

"Thank you, sir!" Santiago said with what sounded like genuine delight. With a chuckle, he added, "Whatever color I get, I've got a name ready. I've dreamed of those horses since I was a little boy."

But Ross was sickened at the thought of owning a living creature that could be used against him. He still avoided the corral where Rusty was kept.

Voske gave Santiago an indulgent, fatherly look. "For now, Santiago, go to the garrison smith. Have her forge you a dagger of her very best work. Tell her I said it should be fit for a prince."

Santiago beamed. "Thank you, sir!"

Voske turned to Ross. "And what reward would you like?"

A dagger to kill you with, Ross thought. "I don't want anything."

"I could give you the book you admired when you visited the shops on Opportunity Day."

Ross's stomach clenched at the memory of how he'd been forced to participate in ruining Luis's life.

Voske went on, apparently oblivious to his reaction. "Or if you'd prefer something more active, you could participate in the war game the day after tomorrow."

A war game would have people running in all directions. He might get a chance to escape. He might see more of Voske's territory, and maybe spot a weakness he could exploit later. At the very least, he'd delay his next expedition for a few days.

"The war game," said Ross.

*

The game was held on a hot, windy morning with thunderheads crowning the distant line of mountains. Ross had been given army fatigues like Santiago's, loose and comfortable. But he wore his own old boots rather than the new ones that had appeared in his closet, cut exactly to his size.

Santiago looked grim as they walked out, and Ross wondered if he was missing Kerry. Would a princess ever participate in war games with common soldiers? From what he'd seen of her, Kerry might.

Ross's thoughts of escape evaporated when he saw several hundred soldiers lined up at the north gate.

"Companies rotate into this kind of training every month," said Santiago. "This is North Company One against East Four. The palace guard has their own training."

Ross did some hasty calculations. Four companies per compass point equalled eight hundred times four, plus the palace guard. Voske had an army of nearly four thousand soldiers.

He remembered Mia proudly telling him the total population of Las Anclas—barely a thousand people, including newborn babies. Voske could return to Las Anclas with an army three times the size of his first one and crush the town's defenses like Ross could step on a bug, while still leaving plenty of soldiers behind to guard the rest of his empire.

Ross felt crushed himself. He would never escape Gold Point. Even if he did, Voske could follow him to Las Anclas with an army, and kill him along with everyone he cared about.

Santiago beckoned Ross toward the soldiers. They all wore red or green sashes. "Red defends. Green attacks."

Ross forced himself to concentrate on the task at hand. If he allowed himself to believe that everything was hopeless, he'd never notice if a chance came up to escape. And then Voske would have won. Ross wasn't going to help Voske by sliding into despair.

"We're with the scouts," said Santiago.

"Oh, your squad." That cheered Ross up. Under other circumstances, he'd have liked Charles and Greta. And he could ignore the annoying Bankar.

Santiago didn't reply, which wasn't like him. Finally, he said, "They're on a mission. We'll be with Scout Team Five, West. My cousin Jorge is on it."

The scouts welcomed Ross with the forced enthusiasm that he'd come to expect, though it never got any less uncomfortable to experience.

A horn signal sounded. Everyone marched out the gates, continuing for half a mile until they came to a sturdy wall. The gates were open, allowing Ross to catch a glimpse of an entire fake wooden town inside. In Las Anclas, only the wealthiest families had wooden houses. It even had a practice field big enough to make the Ranger training grounds look like a schoolyard.

The scouts were motioned together by their leader, a blonde woman whose cat eyes reminded Ross of Ms. Lowenstein.

"Today's objective is a covert infiltration." She squatted down to draw with a stick in the dirt. "Our squad will skirt the hill to take out the perimeter guards, then sneak down when squads six and up attack the gate, to draw the enemy off. We'll come around the other side. Get over the wall here." She made an X on the wall she'd sketched. "At that time, Scout Team Two goes over there. Once we breach, it's a race to see who secures the three targets first." She tapped three little squares inside the big circle. "Got it? Let's go!"

Ross ran with the rest. He'd expected tension, and dreaded questions about Las Anclas. What he hadn't expected was to have fun.

Alternating belly-crawling and leap-frog runs, the scouts penetrated the red army's outer perimeter almost as soon as it was established. Then they had to take the hill, from which they could spy inside the walls.

Ross wriggled through the golden grasses and weeds, blowing away tiny glowing insects that kept trying to fly up his nose. A yellow blob vaguely resembling a tumbleweed dissolved at his approach, and the rabbit that had cast the illusion stamped and bolted.

He popped up to sight Santiago and the rest of the scouts. There were enough shrubs and scrubby trees to mask the ascent of the scouts until they could hear the crunch of the sentries as they made their rounds. The leader held up two fingers, pointed at Ross and Santiago, then aimed them at a pair of guards coming around a boulder.

Santiago indicated for Ross to take the one on the right, and tackled the left-hand guard.

Ross ran up, determined not to let down Las Anclas. But within one block and a feint he sensed his opponent holding back. Of course. Nobody would risk hurting Voske's "guest." Ross eased up, barely tapping the guy as he swept him and pretended to club him behind the ear. As the guy hit the dirt, Ross was sure he saw relief.

He turned to help Santiago, who was wrestling with a wiry redhead. Ross was about to join in when voices rose from behind the scrub oaks on the hilltop.

"You're dead!"

"No, I'm not! You only got me on the shoulder, but I got you in the side."

"Dead! I hit you first!"

It could have been one of Mr. Preston's drills. Ross smothered a snicker as he cleared the oaks. But his amusement died when the scout and the sentry looked up fearfully. Ross, too, looked around. The oaks were barren except for a few withered leaves. Beyond them was nothing but sky, and a couple of hawks riding the currents lazily as clouds moved in.

The scout and patrol leaders ran up to settle the argument.

"You're both unconscious," the scout leader suggested.

The patrol leader added, "For three hours. Both of you."

The two sighed and sat down.

The hill had been taken, so the dead trooped down to be put to work. The scouts began patrolling so from a distance they would look like the enemy. They had one pair of field glasses, which they passed from hand to hand.

Ross was surprised to get a turn. He obediently peered down into the camp, though he'd already decided he wasn't going to offer any ideas; he was more interested in looking beyond the camp—beyond Gold Point—to the mountains behind the city, and the dam that everyone was so proud of. But he knew better than to linger on it, and the glints of sun on steel indicated—as usual—that it was bristling with armed guards.

He passed the glasses on.

Two rounds later, Santiago's cousin Jorge gave a quiet exclamation. He pointed toward the west road, barely visible against the dark line of the distant Joshua Tree forest.

Ross made out a tiny figure on horseback. When Santiago got the field glasses, he stiffened into a tense silhouette. Ross held out his hand for the field glasses. Santiago gave him a strange look as he wordlessly handed them over. Ross saw the bounty hunter, Mr. Vilas, riding under a white cloth tied on a stick.

"All right, you've all seen him," the scout leader said. "Get back on patrol."

Hostage exchange, Ross thought. His chest hurt with the strength of hope, then he tried to dismiss it. So far, he'd been wrong about everything he'd predicted of Voske. He couldn't let himself believe that he'd be freed.

Santiago was clenching his jaw so hard his compressed lips had gone white. Ross wasn't the only one who was trying not to hope too hard.

"There's the signal from Five," said the scout leader. "We'll—"

"There he goes again," Jorge whispered.

Ross didn't need the field glasses to spot the bounty hunter riding through the gates.

"Pay attention," the scout leader snapped.

Jorge straightened, flushing to the ears.

Santiago's breath hissed as the scout leader began outlining the plan of approach to the fort. But before she finished, a new figure on horseback galloped through the gate, leading two saddled horses and carrying a signal flag with a red circle on it.

"Message from the king," someone said.

Everyone watched as one of the green team ran out to meet the runner, then made a series of hand signals to the scout leader.

She turned to Ross and Santiago. "You're wanted. On the double."

Running downhill would probably give away their position. But as far as Ross was concerned, the game was over. Maybe his stay in Gold Point was over. He and Santiago raced side by side until they reached their horses.

When they arrived at the palace, Ross's heart was pounding as if he'd run all the way instead of his horse. They were led to the throne room, where the king waited. Ross wondered if the formality was a good or bad sign.

One look at Voske's face, and Ross knew it was bad.

"Mount up, boys." Voske's teeth gleamed white in the smile Ross hated. "Your guides are readying the horses for your next expedition to the ruined city. You know what I want."

Ross's nerves chilled.

"Sir!" Santiago saluted.

Ross followed him out. With every step they took away from Voske, hot anger replaced the chill. Voske must have refused the hostage exchange. What other possible reason would the bounty hunter have in coming, when everyone knew Las Anclas had Kerry?

Voske was keeping Ross. Would Las Anclas let Kerry go?

Ross wanted badly to ask questions, but one look at Santiago's distraught profile kept him silent.

CHAPTER THIRTY-EIGHT
LAS ANCLAS
KERRY

Kerry should despise the Lees. But she didn't. And not despising them—worse, looking forward to another meal with them—made her feel guilty, as if she was betraying Father. Min Soo would despise them, too. The Lees were exactly the sort of people who deserved conquering: sentimental, weak, trusting.

As he always did, Dr. Lee named each dish he set on the table. This time it was noodles in black bean sauce, startlingly purple kimchi, and crab dumplings.

"I love crab." Mia piled a huge helping on her plate, with no thought to dainty manners. Then she looked up suspiciously, the serving spoon suspended mid-air. "Dad, you didn't do anything weird to it, did you?"

Dr. Lee shook his head. "Not unless you count 'added crunch' as weird."

"Depends on what's crunching." Mia used her chopsticks to dissect a dumpling.

It was so different from dinners in the royal palace. Different and... better, though Kerry would never admit it out loud. There were no gold utensils or beautiful porcelain plates, or silent servants expertly making sure everything was perfectly prepared and steaming hot.

There was just Dr. Lee, who couldn't resist experiments, some of which were revolting, and his daughter, who treated everyone according to how much she liked them, not their degree of power and influence. Dr. Lee didn't mind hearing that he'd ruined a dish, and Mia laughed with him instead of laughing at him. It was nothing like the palace meals, with the mothers watching their own children's manners and watching the other children to compare. And Min Soo watching them all.

And Father always testing.

There's nothing wrong with that, Kerry scolded herself as she bit into the dumpling. It was the responsibility of a king to test his heirs. Physical strength and skill wasn't enough. You had to be strong in mind to keep your empire together, and that meant constantly thinking ahead of everyone else.

I should think about things I could take back when Las Anclas is just one town in my empire. Gold Point was too far inland for her to have ever tasted crab. This dish was definitely successful. Bits of crisp noodle had been folded into a delicate, savory filling. *But there's no way to get it to Gold Point fresh.*

Kerry turned her attention firmly to the other dishes. The thick black sauce over the wheat noodles was rich with bits of meat, the kimchi sharp and pungent. For all Min Soo's bragging about the wonders of her Korean heritage, she'd never had the cooks make food like this.

"Isn't it delicious?" asked Mia.

"Do you like the black bean noodles?" Dr. Lee added, with a man's version of Mia's hopeful expression. "They're my grandmother's specialty."

"She used to run the saloon before Jack took over," Mia said. "Her cooking was famous all over town."

Kerry's eyes burned. What was *wrong* with her? Why would a good meal make her tearful? Or was the problem not the food, but the company?

"It's okay," she said flatly. Though the others didn't say anything, she saw the hurt in their eyes that were shaped so much like her own.

Weakness!

Nobody spoke. The only sounds were the tap of chopsticks on plates, and from outside, the excited voices of children playing some stupid game.

Kerry finished her meal. It was easy when the food was that good. But her mind kept drifting. Father's testing. Min Soo's royal tastes. Bankar, dead at seventeen.

Dr. Lee scooped another helping of each dish onto her plate. She dug in, determined to crush those sentimental thoughts. Bankar was—had been —a soldier, and she'd failed in her mission. *The price of failure is death.*

Santiago...

"The crab dumplings are great, Dad," Mia said.

"I thought they turned out well," Dr. Lee turned to Kerry. "Have you had a chance to see the ocean?"

Kerry shook her head.

"I could take you," Mia offered.

Kerry had a brief fantasy of materializing a boat for herself and escaping. But no doubt if Mia did take her, Preston would provide an escort of rifle-toting guards.

"I don't care." Kerry knew she sounded even more sullen than when she spoke to Min Soo.

But did either of the Lees call her on it?

No.

Dr. Lee said to Mia, "Just before you girls showed up, Mr. Chen scribbled something on your board. I couldn't read it. My guess is the water pump by the senior village."

Mia's glass banged down on the table. "Ross did *that* a month ago. Did a beautiful job of it, too." She sniffed loudly, then grabbed the last crab dumpling and stuffed it in her mouth.

Mia said thickly around the dumpling, "Mr. Chen caught me before the —before breakfast. The back wall generator's been making weird noises ever since Henry and Tommy decided they'd enjoy sentry duty more if they had popcorn."

Dr. Lee laughed. "They didn't."

"They weren't stupid enough to pour it into the machinery. They put it into a frying pan and set it on top. But corn kernels jump when they pop, and a few probably got into the gears."

Kerry had learned to loathe Henry almost as much as that loud Tommy Horst. They both taunted Kerry every time they saw her.

"Too bad I missed the whipping," she said.

The Lees looked at her as if she'd grown an extra arm.

"The what?" Dr. Lee said.

Kerry put down her chopsticks. "Don't tell me you've never heard of punishment in Las Anclas?"

"Of course there's punishment," Mia said. "Henry's been assigned to feed smelly garbage to the eater-roses on the walls, and his sentry station for a month will be Mulch Row, since it was his idea. And Tommy Horst is probably shoveling out the stables right now. They'll be nice and soupy after that rain."

"How bad does a crime have to be to get a whipping?" Kerry asked.

"We don't do that here." Dr. Lee began picking up the plates.

Kerry jeered, "So murder gets a whole month in the stables?"

Dr. Lee answered her seriously. "For very serious crimes, like arson or murder in the heat of passion, we have exile. And for the most serious crimes, like premeditated murder or serial rape, the punishment is death."

Exile was the one punishment they didn't have in Gold Point. You could be whipped or jailed or executed, but you were never allowed to leave. Did people really love Las Anclas so much that being kicked out was the worst thing they could think of?

Dr. Lee brought a covered dish to the table. "Dessert will be a family favorite, apple crumble from Jack's saloon."

Dr. Lee set a big helping before Kerry. The scent of apples and cinnamon rose up. It was Santiago's favorite dessert. He could be dead, and here she was, with the dessert they should have been sharing on the roof of the palace…

Kerry threw down her spoon, ran to the bathroom, and locked the door. She wadded up her shirt and stuffed it into her mouth as sobs came ripping up from deep inside her.

Santiago had to be dead. Why *wouldn't* Ross run away and save himself? Kerry would have. The death of an enemy was a cheap price for success. Only a weak person would refuse to pay.

Ross was strong. She'd known it when she'd heard of his blind journey, she'd experienced it when he sparred, and she'd become certain of it from Mia's stories about him. He'd killed thirty of Father's elite guards!

Father was wrong. Ross wasn't weak. Therefore, Santiago was dead.

She wanted to kick and rip and tear the world apart, but that wouldn't bring Santiago back. And it had been so *pointless*. Just so Father could test her loyalty.

Somebody tapped at the door.

"Go away," Kerry snarled.

"I need to use the bathroom." Mia's tone was apologetic.

Kerry scrubbed her face on her sleeve, but wiping away her tears wouldn't conceal her reddened eyes.

To hell with it. It wasn't like they didn't know what she'd been doing. She yanked the door open. "All yours."

"It can wait," Mia said surprisingly. "If you want to be alone, we can go back to my cottage, and I'll sit outside for a while."

Kerry walked out. The sky was clear, the cloudy sweep of the Milky Way bright overhead. She remembered the meaning of its other name, El Camino De Santiago: The Road To Santiago. The space behind her ribs ached with emptiness. That was a road she'd never walk again.

Mia paced along quietly beside her till they were inside her cottage, then said," Apple crumble is Ross's favorite. I couldn't eat it, either."

Kerry scowled at her. "It *was* Santiago's favorite."

"Was?" Mia gasped. "So he was at the attack after all?"

"No. *Your* boyfriend killed him."

"Really?" Mia looked startled. "I'm sorry. In the battle for Las Anclas? Why didn't you tell me?"

"No, no, *no*. In Gold Point."

"I'm sorry," Mia repeated. "Was Ross trying to escape?"

"No," Kerry snapped impatiently. "I mean, who knows. It would have happened after I was kidnapped."

"Kerry, if it would have happened after you were gone, how can you possibly know Ross killed him?"

"He must have," Kerry said bitterly. Why not? It wasn't like anything she said would change the facts. "It was a test. Of loyalty. For me."

"I don't get it," Mia said.

"Father set it up. He wants Ross to prospect the ruined city outside of Gold Point. But he can't send Ross in by himself because he'd escape. So Father ordered Santiago to befriend Ross. The plan was to send them in together. Father said Ross wouldn't let Santiago die, and Santiago could guard him. But of course Ross would let him die. What would he care?"

"Did you see this happen?" Mia asked.

"No. Your kidnap squad got me first. But it was planned for two weeks ago. And Father never changes his plans."

Mia was slowly shaking her head.

"What?" Kerry asked, as irritated and angry as she'd been sad a few minutes ago.

"Ross wouldn't do that. Your father was right. I'm sure Santiago is fine."

Angrily, Kerry burst out, "Who would give up their own chance of escape to save an enemy?"

"Ross," Mia said simply. "When I first saw him, Sheriff Crow was carrying him to the surgery. He'd lost a lot of blood, cutting that crystal shard out of his arm, and he'd been shot, too. Dad said another hour in the desert, and he would have died. But when Sheriff Crow found him, he warned her that he was being chased. He told her to leave him and come back with help."

Kerry found that hard to believe. But she couldn't think of a reason for Mia to make up such a story.

Mia went on, "Ross didn't know a thing about her, except that she didn't mean him any harm. But that's how he is. He won't kill anyone, except in self-defense or to defend someone else. And he won't let anyone die in his place."

If two people as different as Father and Mia agreed on something, it had to be true. Father had certainly been convinced of Ross's weakness and sentimentality.

Relief flooded through her. "Maybe you're right." Relief and...guilt? Kerry squelched that feeling. Guilt was a weakness.

"Anyway, where is he?" Mia asked. "If he killed Santiago and escaped two weeks ago, why isn't he here?"

Kerry searched for some other explanation, but she couldn't find one. "Yeah, he'd have come here. He got away from the capture squad the first night they got him, even though he was blind. When they finally caught up with him, he was halfway back to Las Anclas."

Mia let out a piercing yell, making Kerry jump. "I knew it! I *told* them! But they wouldn't believe me. I should have gone after him myself."

If Mia is telling the truth, Santiago is alive. Kerry tested the idea carefully. Hope was as bad as guilt. Powerful people didn't *hope*. They conceived plans, studied the enemy, executed the plans, and got what they wanted.

"You would have been captured. And Father would have used you as leverage over Ross." Kerry was unsettled at how bitter her voice sounded. Why? It was smart tactics.

"Two weeks," Mia said slowly. "How long will your dad wait?"

"Wait for what?" Kerry asked, disconcerted.

Mia's shoulders tightened. "He wants Ross prospecting for weapons, right? It doesn't sound like he's interested in archaeology, biology, or art. Or does he want Ross to use those crystal trees *as* a weapon?"

Both, Kerry thought.

"Probably both," Mia said, her gaze unnervingly steady. "But Ross won't do it. He'll stall as long as he can, but he won't help your father find weapons, and he'll never use his power as a weapon again."

Kerry remembered Ross's horror when Father had asked him to pluck a crystal seedpod, and Ross shouting that Father had experimented on his own soldiers.

A spurt of anger made Kerry think, *You got me into this, Father. You got Santiago into this. Why am I protecting you when you didn't protect me?*

Deliberately, Kerry opened her mouth, drew a deep breath, and said, "Yeah, I believe you." *Take that, Father.*

"So how long will your father let him stall?"

Kerry had spent her entire life learning to school her face, but Mia must have seen something in her expression, because she shot to her feet.

"He's going to kill Ross." Her voice thinned with horror. "I've got to rescue him. I should have gone the first time!" She kicked a bag of bolts, sending them spilling across the floor. "I have to talk to…Or I could go myself…I have maps…but I've never been out in the desert. I can talk to Dad—"

Mia stopped short, and her gaze slid away. "No, I can't. He has to abide by the council's…"

Kerry watched, unable to think of a thing to say. Mia picked up a screwdriver, apparently at random, and set it down carefully on the edge of the table. It rolled off and clattered to the floor.

Mia's intent gaze turned on Kerry. "Dad won't be able to talk them into letting you go. Not even if I came with you. You'll have to tell me the way."

"You're serious?" Kerry couldn't believe it. "You're really going to head out into the desert by yourself?"

"I hope not by myself. But if I have to, I will."

"You're crazy. Your best team couldn't get Ross out. And if they had, Father would have had half the army after them in seconds."

Mia crossed her arms. "Okay, fine. But I have to try. Even if Ross and I get killed out in the desert, that's better than our heads ending up on your walls."

Kerry rubbed her aching eyes. Nothing seemed real anymore. "You'll get yourself killed before you even see Ross."

Mia's pacing took on a new purposefulness. "Compass...crossbow... Did Ross have anything with him when he was captured?"

"Just ordinary prospecting stuff. They confiscated his weapons."

Mia beamed. "Did they? Did they confiscate a little piece of solid pipe?" She pulled a chunk of metal from a holster on her belt. "Like this?"

"You have one, too? We thought that was scrap metal."

One side of Mia's mouth curled up. With a snap of her wrist, she flicked the bar. It snicked out into a club.

"Wow," Kerry said before she could stop herself.

"Designed and made it myself," Mia said. "If he's got that, he's got a weapon. He can't take on an army with it, but it's better than nothing."

Can't take on an army... The reward for failure is death.

Kerry's stomach churned. Santiago—Ross—even Bankar, ordered to the rescue of someone she loathed. People would keep dying until Father got what he wanted.

And Kerry knew how to fix that.

After all her worries, her solution was right here. Right now. And it would fix everyone's problems.

"You don't have to go." Kerry's heart thumped so hard that she crossed her arms over her chest as if to hold it in. Now she knew exactly what to do. "I'll get him back for you."

Mia let the bar drop with a clank, then her face reddened. "Don't joke. I'm serious."

"So am I."

Mia sat down on the floor, and beckoned Kerry to sit across from her. "So, what you're saying is, if I let you escape, you'll let Ross go."

Kerry looked straight into Mia's eyes, willing her sincerity to show. "I will. I swear it."

Mia rubbed her forehead, then spoke as if to herself. "I know what Jennie would say about this: 'She's manipulating you. Once she's gone, she has no reason to let Ross go.'"

Kerry held her breath. One wrong word, and this moment would evaporate like water in the sun. One right word, and she could be free.

Father's voice came to her mind: *What motivates her?* And then Min Soo's sweet tones: *You can do much more with people's loved ones than merely hold them hostage.*

"I do have a reason," said Kerry. "Ross is stubborn. You're right—he'll keep resisting until Father gives up and kills him. Nobody crosses Father.

Nobody. The first person he executed was his older brother. But he trusts me, and he respects intelligence. I'll tell him I made a deal with you. He'd have to respect that, if I give you my word as crown princess of Gold Point. And I do."

Mia's eyes shone bright; she was on the verge of tears. Yes, this was the right tack to take.

Kerry let her genuine belief in her words infuse her voice. "Even if Father could convince him to cooperate—and I don't think he can—Ross would never be happy in Gold Point. He hates being locked up. It's like keeping a hawk in a cage. Just looking at him made *me* feel trapped. I wish we'd never taken him. Mia, I will let him go because *I* want to."

Mia chewed on her lower lip, her gaze darting wildly from Kerry to her club to Ross's shirt, still hanging off the back of the chair. "I can't believe I'm even considering this. It's treason. Though maybe it wouldn't be if I went with you, so I was still guarding you. Technically."

Kerry was nearly overwhelmed with the temptation to agree. Mia had already sold herself on that idea. But if Pru spotted them, Mia would be captured immediately. And killing or torturing her would be just another stick for Father to use on Ross.

"You can't come." Kerry had to say it, though she dreaded ruining her own chances. "Father would see you, and you'd be captured. You don't want to end up a hostage yourself. If I go, it has to be alone."

Mia sucked in a deep breath, then held out a shaking hand in the "deal" sign. "I let you go, and you let Ross go. Deal?"

Kerry covered Mia's hand with her own. "Deal. You won't regret it."

If I get back home, and Santiago's alive, the deal's on. But if he's dead, I don't owe Ross anything but death.

CHAPTER THIRTY-NINE
LAS ANCLAS
JENNIE

Jennie sloshed the dishes into the tub of soapy water. A couple of tiny bubbles floated up, catching light from the window. She used to love those when she was little. Remembering that made her sad.

Everything made her sad. Dr. Lee insisted it was a good thing to acknowledge her feelings—it was the beginning of healing—but she hated feeling sad, and then thinking about how sad she felt.

Slosh! Impatiently she scrubbed chili sauce off a plate, then plunked it into the clear water pan. Where were Tonio and Yolanda, who also had kitchen patrol this week? She was completely alone.

Yeah, wasn't *that* the truth.

"Want a hand?"

Jennie spun around, dropping a plate.

Pastor Carlotta stood in the doorway. "The door was open."

Jennie recognized a parental conspiracy. Well, she couldn't blame them.

"Sure," Jennie said. "Except, can you stand that long?"

Pastor Carlotta limped into the kitchen, then leaned her cane against the kitchen table. "Gets stronger every day." During the battle she'd been on the firefighting team, where she'd taken an arrow in the knee.

She leaned her hip against the sink and began drying dishes, as if she walked into people's houses and helped them wash up every day. She probably did, Jennie reflected, and wondered if she was training Benjy Plum, her pastoral student, in Dishwashing While Ministering.

"Your parents asked me to talk to you," Pastor Carlotta said as she began to stack the dry plates. "But if you would rather work in silence, that's up to you."

"Being silent hasn't done me much good," Jennie admitted, and braced herself. She'd always liked Pastor Carlotta, who was a tall, comfortable sort of person, her fly-away gray hair catching the morning light at services, reminding Jennie of a halo. She hated the thought that Pastor Carlotta was going to make her feel guilty for skipping church for the past few weeks.

Slosh, clink, rub, rub. Pastor Carlotta stacked a couple more plates, then said, "This is not going to be a conversation about church attendance, unless you want to talk about it."

"I don't, really."

Pastor Carlotta nodded, and began hanging cups on their hooks. "I will say I missed you at the Blessing of the Animals last month. I remember when it used to be one of your favorite holidays."

"I wanted to come," Jennie said. She took a deep breath, then said, "But I couldn't. It seems hypocritical to treat animals like kings that one day, when some of those pigs and sheep and cows will be slaughtered a week later so their meat can be put up for winter." She gave an extra hard scrub at a pot with beans stuck at the bottom, sending a splash of sudsy water into her shirt. "I couldn't look at them, and remember that."

Pastor Carlotta nodded soberly. "You'd be surprised how many people have had similar conversations with me, especially since the battle. Or maybe you wouldn't. That day made us all face death in a way most of us had never had to, before."

"So why do we bless animals, then turn around and kill them? Does that really mark their souls for special treatment? Do they even have souls?"

Pastor Carlotta hung up the last cup. "Blessings are our way of respecting other forms of life. Life in the world requires us to eat, and what we eat are things that used to live. That's nature. Everything, us included, has to die. That, too, is nature. What we can do is limit suffering. The butchers take pride in making it quick. Blessing the animals is supposed to remind us to respect them all year long, not just before we eat them, until the time comes for our souls to join the others beyond the boundaries of life."

"But we don't have proof that anybody's souls do anything," Jennie said, handing her the pot to rinse and dry. "I know, this is where faith comes in."

"Like I said, others are also wrestling with these questions. There's an informal group—interfaith, actually—that began meeting at Jack's on Monday nights, to talk about these issues. You'd be welcome to drop in."

"Thanks. I'll think about it." Quickly, Jennie added, "So what do *you* think about Voske's daughter?"

Pastor Carlotta set the last pan on the stove, then hung the dish cloth on the rack before she spoke. "I feel some sympathy for that girl, raised as she's been. I'd like to think that while she's among us, she might be exposed to a different kind of life." She smiled a little. "Though some of our fellow townspeople might disagree about the definition of 'different.'"

"Thanks."

Pastor Carlotta picked up her cane, asked Jennie to give her greetings to her parents, and left.

Jennie's kitchen chores were done—and so were Tonio's and Yolanda's—but time still seemed to press on her. She changed into the workout clothes she'd been avoiding for a week, and went out for a run, hoping to clear her head.

Twenty steps past her house, Mia came charging round a corner, nearly smacking into her. "Mia! What's going on?"

Mia looked around in an amazingly shifty way. As Jennie stared in surprise, she muttered, "Came to find you. Let's go to my place."

"Princess Voske isn't there, is she?" Jennie didn't feel ready to face Kerry.

"No. Back in her cell for the night." Mia tugged Jennie's arm. "Come on."

Mia didn't speak until she'd shut the door to her cottage. The windows were already closed, and the stuffy air stank of machine oil and cleaning solvent. "There's something you should know. The council is going to execute Kerry if Voske refuses to do a hostage exchange."

"Good riddance," Jennie said, but immediately felt guilty. "I don't mean that. Anyway, he'll do the hostage exchange. She's his daughter. Of course he'll want her back."

Mia shook her head. "Voske doesn't negotiate. It's his policy. The council already knew that the day you brought Kerry here. They're making the offer, just in case, but they know he won't take it."

Jennie's stomach lurched. She hadn't rescued Ross, she'd just brought that girl to her death.

"Did you think I could talk Mr. Preston into letting her go?" Jennie asked doubtfully.

Mia shook her head. "Dad already tried. Mr. Preston was the one who talked a majority of the council into voting to kill her. It was four to three. I was there."

Jennie had never felt so helpless in her life. This was worse than thinking about the battle. Execution was nothing more than deliberate, legal murder. Jennie hadn't chosen it, but she was responsible for it. And there was nothing she could do to stop it.

"I have a plan," Mia said. "But I need help."

"What kind of plan?" What sort of machine could Mia build that would fix this mess?

Jennie noticed what Mia was fingering on her table: a backpack. "Mia?" she said warningly.

"Not for me," Mia said, her eyes wide behind her glasses. "For Kerry.

She's promised that if I can get her out, she'll let Ross go. She's the only person who can do it."

Hope twisted Jennie's heart, followed by a rush of anger. "Kerry is a liar and a manipulator. Yuki told me about the offer she started to make to Paco. You can't believe a word she says."

"I believe what she told me about Voske's plans for Ross. Jennie, Ross is going to be as dead as Kerry will be if we don't do anything. I *totally* believe that."

Jennie wasn't inclined to believe anything Kerry said, but as Mia described their conversation, she couldn't help finding it plausible. Much more plausible, Jennie had to admit, than the conviction that Jennie had clung to so hard, that a hostage exchange would bring Ross back, because she'd failed to.

Jennie felt as if the words were dragged out of her. "What do you want me to do?"

Mia let out a long sigh of relief. "Just two things. One, unless you have a better idea, help me talk Yuki into loaning Kogatana to Kerry."

"He'll never do it," Jennie said immediately. "He protects that rat like his own life."

"Second thing. I need you to come up with a plan for actually getting Kerry and Kogatana, and also she'll need a horse, out of Las Anclas. Without anyone figuring out that we're the ones who did it."

Jennie laughed bitterly. "Oh. Just that. Why don't we build her wings and fly her home?"

Mia answered Jennie's sarcasm with fervent seriousness. "This is exactly the sort of thing you're good at. I know you can do it."

Jennie felt even more bitter. "If I was good, we all wouldn't be in this situation."

"But you can fix it. I know you can." Mia was looking at Jennie the way she'd looked ever since they were little, hopeful and expectant.

Jennie pushed aside some engine parts and sat on Mia's bed. "Maybe. Possibly. But I don't believe Kerry would lift a finger for Ross. She'll run home, then come back with an army, like the council says. She changed her tune pretty quick, but right after we captured her, she threatened to kill us all and torture little kids to death. That's the real Kerry."

Mia unscrewed a metal plate from an engine, then screwed it back on, her forehead creased. "I believe you, Jennie. But I've seen something different. Maybe there's more than one real Kerry."

"You seriously think she'll let Ross go." Jennie couldn't keep the sarcasm from her voice.

"I know you think I'm gullible." Mia's face reddened. "Stupid little Mia, everyone knows she's great with numbers, but she doesn't understand a thing about real life!"

Jennie was taken aback. "That's not what I meant."

Mia slumped down, her angry blush fading. "Everyone treats me like I'm a kid. You're only six months older than me, but people do whatever you ask them to. Everybody trusts you."

"I wish they didn't," Jennie blurted out.

Mia let out a watery giggle. "Too late! I still do. I told you all my treasonous plotting. You could go to the council right now and have me arrested."

"You know I'd never do such a thing."

"Yeah. I know. So, will you at least talk to Kerry?" Mia's expression was completely guileless.

That expression was trust. Faith. The last time someone had looked at her that way, it had been the kids she'd taken on the mission to blow up Voske's ammunition. And Jennie had sent them away by themselves so she could stay to help Sera. And hadn't saved her.

She might have to start all over again in trying to figure out what faith meant, but at least she could choose not to abandon Mia. "I'll talk to her. Set it up."

*

Jennie found Mia, Yuki, Kogatana, and Kerry waiting in Ross's room. Kerry sat in Ross's single chair, rigid with tension, but Jennie had no sympathy for her. If she tried to manipulate anyone by pretending to care about him, Jennie was going to punch her out, powers or no powers.

"Go on, Kerry," Mia said. "Convince her!"

Kerry clenched her fists, setting her manacles jingling. "Father doesn't negotiate. The only way to save Ross's life is for me to return home before Father gets tired of waiting for Ross to cooperate. He'll be so glad to see me that he'll give me anything I want, and I'll ask him to let Ross go."

She has to be playing us.

Jennie let her disbelief show, "And then what? After you free Ross, I mean. Come back here leading an army?"

"You're going to get the army if you *don't* let me go," Kerry retorted. Finally, the arrogant princess was showing. "Father already sent a rescue team. Next time he'll come himself. He's just waiting for the perfect moment to strike. "

Jennie could believe *that*. "Fine. But why should I believe you'll let Ross go?"

"Eight citizens of Gold Point died because of me." Kerry's steady gaze reminded Jennie for a brief, disturbing moment of Mia's. "If Ross doesn't give Father what he wants, he'll lose patience, and that will be Ross's death warrant. I won't pretend that he and I are friends. But I don't want him to die, too, when I could have saved him."

Maybe the princess was lying. Probably she was. But lying didn't warrant being killed in cold blood.

Capturing Kerry had been wrong in Ma and Pa's eyes. While Jennie still thought it had saved Ross's life, standing by to let Mr. Preston execute Kerry would be wrong in her own eyes. She already had Sera's death on her conscience. Kerry's death would double the burden.

Jennie's gaze went to Mia, who smiled hopefully. When Mia made a friend, it meant she was in it forever—and that she had come to trust the person. Jennie didn't know what had happened to allow that trust to grow between Mia and Kerry, but she did know this: Mia trusted Jennie, and trust had to go two ways.

"All right," she said. "I'm in."

CHAPTER FORTY
LAS ANCLAS
YUKI

While Jennie and Kerry were having their face-off, Yuki glanced up at the stars shining through the glass ceiling. If he ever managed to set out as a prospector, they would be the last thing he saw every night. He wondered if, after years and years of sleeping under the stars, he'd get to hate sleeping under a solid roof, too.

A clink of Kerry's manacles brought Yuki's attention back to Kerry, whose face was sharp with anger and pain—the same expression Yuki had been seeing in Paco. The resemblance was unnerving. Except for Kerry's eyes, which were like Mia's, and the feminine cast to her features, she and Paco could almost be twins. Though he knew it wasn't rational, it made Yuki want to help her.

But he was certain that if he gave Kerry his rat, he'd never see Kogatana again. He'd had her since he was thirteen, and she was an orphaned pup he'd fed with a dropper.

When he'd washed ashore, he couldn't understand any of the languages spoken in Las Anclas. But he hadn't needed speech to communicate with Kogatana. He'd lost his entire world, but at least he had her. He'd clung to her, and she to him.

Five years later, she never left his side unless he ordered her to. The thought of never seeing her again made him feel desperate and lost, like he was drowning in dark waters.

Kogatana nuzzled him, sensing his tension. Her pink tongue flicked out to comfortingly lick his hand.

"I'm in," Jennie said.

Yuki let out his breath. "I want to talk to her alone."

Mia and Jennie glanced at each other, then went out.

"I swear I won't hurt Kogatana," Kerry said, as the door closed. "I love animals."

"I know," Yuki replied. "I watched you with the horses. I'm not worried that you'd hurt her. I'm worried that you won't give her back."

"I would never steal someone else's pet." Kerry sounded horrified at the very idea.

Honesty? Or good acting? Yuki had no idea. He'd never been particularly good at sifting truth from lies, and he suspected that Kerry was very, very good at lying.

She went on, "I don't know what I can say to convince you I'm sincere…"

Yuki held up his hand. "Don't bother. Either you are, or you aren't. I wanted to ask you something else. Assuming you do mean to keep your word… *Could* you let Ross go?"

Kerry seemed surprised by the question. "I'm the crown princess. I can do anything I want. You know how that works—Mia told me you were a prince yourself."

"That's why I asked. *I* couldn't do anything I wanted. My first mother used to say, 'Being a ruler means having less freedom and more responsibility than you give to your people.'"

"*Less* freedom?" Kerry echoed incredulously.

Yuki couldn't believe that Kerry, a princess herself, was unfamiliar with the most basic tenet of rule. "The welfare of every single one of your people is your responsibility. If anything goes wrong, the fault can always be traced back to you. You have much less free time than your subjects, because you have so many more duties. And, of course, you can't do what *you* want to do—you have to do what's best for your kingdom."

Kerry stared at him in disbelief. "Wow. Well, that explains something I've been wondering about."

"What's that?"

"Why you don't have a position of power in Las Anclas. I'd assumed you were deliberately kept down. But that's not it, is it? You think having power means being trapped."

Yuki felt off-balance. "It was my duty. It was what I was born for. That's not a trap!"

Kerry raised her eyebrows. "Would a king have been allowed to prospect?"

"We prospected all the time!"

Kogatana squeaked in protest. He hastily loosened his fingers that had unconsciously tightened around her.

Memories of the *Taka* drifted back into his mind, tugging at his emotions like strands of seaweed wrapping around a swimmer's limbs. It was true that the *Taka* had often stopped to send divers into caves and reefs, hunting for artifacts. But his mother had rarely gone diving with him. She'd been too busy in her throne room, reading reports and giving orders.

And every year that had passed had given him less and less time to dive and explore, and more and more spent in the throne room, learning to rule.

"Sorry," Kerry said. "It's none of my business. Anyway, things are different in Gold Point. If I want to free Ross, I can."

Yuki believed that much, at least: that in Gold Point, power meant freedom, and royal heirs were taught to be selfish, not selfless. If he had been raised in Gold Point and then come to Las Anclas, would he have immediately sought out power? Was Kerry right that he saw it as a trap?

What would Paco have been like, if he'd grown up as the crown prince of Gold Point? What would Kerry have been like, if she'd been Sera's daughter?

He studied that half-familiar, half-alien countenance. Yuki didn't believe that Paco had inherited anything from Voske but the bones of his face. How could he be so certain, then, that Kerry was as ruthless as her father?

"What's your mother like?" Yuki asked.

"My mother?" Kerry echoed blankly. "She has a unique Change power…"

"I know about that. I meant, as a person."

"She likes roses and art and history and proper manners and old traditions. We don't get along very well, to be honest. Someone like Felicité or Sujata would have suited her better." Kerry scratched her head, her manacles clinking. "Did that answer your question?"

That was no help. Knowing that Kerry didn't take after her mother didn't prove that she took after her father. None of the conversation had been helpful. Yuki had intended to get answers, but he'd been left with more questions than ever—not only about Kerry, but about himself.

All he knew for sure was that Paco had intended to kill King Voske before he'd learned the man was his father. If anything, finding out the truth had intensified his resolve. He'd been furious when Kerry had tried to bribe him with a crown. He was far too angry to speak up for his sister's life, but Yuki knew Paco was not a ruthless person. If Paco stood by while Kerry was executed, one day he'd get over his anger, and then he'd never forgive himself.

Yuki had to get Kerry out of Las Anclas before Paco did something he could never take back.

He opened the door. "You can come back in now."

He sat back down across from Kerry. Everyone was watching him, Jennie curious, Mia and Kerry anxious. Yuki took Kerry's hand, and brought their linked fingers up to Kogatana's twitching pink nose.

He had to unclench his jaw to speak. He could hardly bring himself to do it. "Kogatana. Obey Kerry. Obey Kerry. Obey Kerry."

He released his own hand, and left Kerry's there. Kogatana glanced at

Yuki, her nose wrinkling with what he couldn't help seeing as hurt and betrayal. Doing the right thing felt exactly like making a horrible, irrevocable mistake.

"Thank you," Kerry breathed. She patted her shoulder. "Kogatana, sit."

Kogatana swarmed to her shoulder. Kerry's elated grin was so like Paco's that Yuki had to look away. Paco hadn't smiled like that for months.

He gave her what he hoped was an intimidating glare. "I hope you're going to send Kogatana back with Ross. But if you decide to go back on freeing him, at least order her to go home. She can make her own way back if she has to. If you try to keep her for yourself, I swear I will come fetch her."

Kerry sighed. "I told you I wouldn't do that."

"Hang on," Jennie said. "Yuki, if you don't think she'll let Ross go, why are you helping her?"

"I *hope* she will," Yuki replied. "But I'm mostly doing it because of Paco."

Jennie's lips parted. "Oh. All right."

Kerry's sharp gaze flicked between them. "Is anyone going to explain what this has to do with my half-brother?"

Nobody replied.

Yuki was thinking rapidly. "I can arrange for horses. But not getting her outside."

"Leave that to me," Jennie said.

"We need to make it look like she escaped on her own," Mia said. "If we get caught, we could be exiled."

"Exiled, at best," said Jennie. "We could end up in front of a firing squad."

Yuki thought, *If we get caught, Paco will never forgive me.*

CHAPTER FORTY-ONE
LAS ANCLAS
KERRY

Kerry couldn't quite believe that Mia would go through with the plan.

Even after Mia let her out of her cell the next morning, Kerry waited for a trap to spring. Tense and wary, she followed Mia to her cottage.

The first sign that maybe the plan was real—that this wasn't an elaborate test, like Father might devise—was the huge breakfast waiting in the cottage.

"Eat up," Mia said. "You've got a long trip ahead of you. Oh, and make sure you can cut the manacles. If you can't, I'll loan you this." She rummaged among her tools, then brandished a saw.

Kerry created her own saw, set the edge against her manacle, and pulled. There was a loud grating noise. Mia jumped.

"Keep yours." Kerry's heart lifted with hope. Her whole body felt light. In less than a week, she'd be sleeping in her own bed, with Santiago pillowed on her shoulder...

If he was still alive.

If he was dead, she'd kill Ross herself.

Kerry dug into the breakfast. "Thanks for thinking of this."

Mia fidgeted with every tool within reach, barely touching her own eggs and burrito. She didn't look like she was expecting to be sleeping with *her* boyfriend in two weeks.

A wave of bitterness corroded Kerry, killing her appetite. "You don't trust me."

"I don't trust..." Mia flapped her hands. "Myself? That we won't get caught? Yesterday Felicité Wolfe dropped by my cottage right after our meeting, and I was sure she'd somehow figured out what we were doing. But her dad puts her in charge of stuff for our—" She stopped, her eyes wild.

"Your military drills, one of which is today. They aren't exactly covert."

Mia flapped her hands again. "You see? I don't trust myself, because everything and everyone looks suspicious." She sighed. "I just don't want anybody killed." She straightened up, jammed her glasses firmly on her nose, and said, "You remember what to do, right?"

Kerry nodded. "We carry the raccoon traps to the Vardams' orchard. I cut off the manacles, and I tie you up and lock you in a fruit shed. Do you want me to hit you over the head? It'd be more realistic."

Mia shook her head. "Dad would notice if it wasn't hard enough to knock me out. I won't make him lie for me. Anyway, everyone knows I'm no good at fighting."

"I count how long it takes the sentries to reach the far point before they turn around. I get over the wall in that time, and sneak through the seed corn to the corral where Yuki's waiting with the horses he's supposed to be training. Then I tie him up, take the horses, and go."

Mia's face contorted with a flurry of expressions, too fast for Kerry to read. "You really will let Ross go, right?"

"How many times do I have to tell you that I keep my promises?" Kerry struggled not to show her annoyance.

"In case something goes wrong." Mia's voice was high with strain. "In case you have to break Ross out—"

"I won't have to break him out," Kerry said, relenting. "We went over this. I'm the crown princess. If I say a prisoner should be released, he'll be released."

If Mia was caught, she wouldn't get a flogging or a day-long date on the execution platform. But for someone like her, exile would be almost as bad. *Maybe worse, because it lasts longer.* Where would she go? Kerry couldn't imagine her surviving long in Gold Point, the way she blurted out... *The truth.*

Kerry shied away from examining that.

"We went over this," Kerry said. "I'll tell Father, and *only* Father, that I made a deal and Ross is to be set free. As far as anyone else knows, I escaped all by myself. Father can say he threw Ross out for being useless, or because I requested it, or whatever he likes. Father saves face, you get Ross back, no one ever learns that anyone helped me escape, and I get home."

"Yeah, I know. But in case something goes wrong. I want to make sure Ross knows to trust you."

As Mia started babbling about the first time she met Ross and how exciting that had been, Kerry ran her fingers over the saw she had created. Of course Father would allow her to set Ross free. She was his daughter. Ross was only a prisoner—a valuable prisoner, but not the crown princess of Gold Point. Kerry smiled to herself.

Mia clutched at her sleeve. "Kerry, you have to listen. The first time I met Ross, I asked him to use his left hand to pick up a wrench. His left hand! The one he can't use. Remind him of that. It's something only the two of us know about, so if you tell him, he'll at least know that I trusted you."

A now-familiar sense of vague guilt seized Kerry by the throat. There was no reason for it. Kerry had only agreed to let Ross go *if* Santiago was safe, and she'd keep that promise. It was the way that Mia looked at her… and the way Mia talked about Ross. The two of them seemed to trust each other so deeply. Like Kerry and Santiago trusted each other. That must be it. It brought back Kerry's worries about Santiago.

"Wrench in the left hand," she repeated. "Got it."

Mia grabbed the raccoon traps. "Let's go."

All the way across the town square, Kerry's heart thumped against her ribs, her mind racing with a thrilling mix of happiness and anticipation. But she'd had too many tests to let any hint of her elation escape.

The Vardams weren't even at home. Everybody was somewhere else, getting ready for their big drill. Even the sentries seemed preoccupied, Kerry noticed, talking and pointing to the west. It was the perfect time for a solitary figure to get over the wall.

Kerry silently saluted Jennie for being a master planner as she and Mia put down the traps in the empty orchard. Mia wrapped a cloth around Kerry's manacles to muffle the sound. Kerry sawed.

Mia picked up the manacles. "The fruit shed is—"

She froze, and the manacles clattered to the ground. Jennie and Yuki came charging into the orchard, waving frantically. They'd changed their minds!

No time to look for the sentries. Kerry bolted for the wall.

Mia exclaimed in horror, "Felicité?"

Kerry skidded to a stop and spun around.

Felicité Wolfe stood facing Mia, arms crossed in righteous indignation.

"I knew it!" Felicité exclaimed. "You're all traitors!" And she drew in a breath for a scream.

Jennie took Felicité down in two lightning-fast moves, clamping her hand over Felicité's mouth. Yuki dove in the other direction, thrust his hands under a bush, and yanked out a struggling golden rat.

Jennie said in a low voice, "Mia, get the rope."

Mia reached into her satchel. Kerry stared. What she'd taken as sweat were tears running silently down Mia's face.

Yuki looked up at Kerry, pale and grim. "Run."

Kerry didn't stop until she reached the last of the trees before the wall. Using it as shelter, she waited for the sentries to stroll away, still watching whatever was going on at the armory. She vaulted over the wall in two heartbeats, and dropped down on the other side. As Mia had promised, the backpack was waiting for her in by a water spigot, hidden, like Kerry, by the tall stalks of corn.

No alarm was raised. She couldn't believe it. Felicité had somehow discovered the plan, but rather than covering for themselves by turning on Kerry, Yuki, Jennie, and Mia had covered for her. They'd let her go even though their careful plans to hide their actions were all for nothing. The only way they could get away with it now would be to kill Felicité and blame her death on Kerry.

I'd kill her, Kerry thought as she ran. But Mia would never kill anyone in cold blood. That thought nearly ruined her sense of triumph.

But it didn't stop her from running. At the corral, she found two horses already saddled, and Kogatana perched on her little riding seat. Everything had gone as planned—except that Las Anclas would know that Mia, Jennie, and Yuki had betrayed their own town to rescue an enemy.

Kerry mounted behind Kogatana, hoping that her lessons in desert survival had been more realistic than her prisoner-of-war training had been.

Time to find out. She took the reins of the remount and rode up the arroyo toward the desert, thinking of Mia's silent tears.

If Santiago is alive, I'll give you Ross back, she vowed.

She hoped he'd follow Mia into exile.

CHAPTER FORTY-TWO
LAS ANCLAS
YUKI

They decided to surrender to the sheriff at sundown. Yuki was the first one there. Jennie was still with the Ranger candidates, and Mia had returned to the fruit shed to free Felicité, who'd been tied up there all day.

When Yuki confessed to Sheriff Crow, all she said was, "Take the cell at the end. Leave the door open for the other two."

The bench in the cell wasn't big enough for three. Yuki sat on the cot and left the bench to the girls. Mia drooped, but Jennie sat with her arms crossed. She looked as angry as Yuki felt.

Jennie unwrapped a dusty bandage from her left hand, and examined a set of bloody bite wounds.

"Was that from Wu Zetian?" Mia asked, eyes wide.

"Felicité."

Mia said earnestly, "Better have Dad look at that. Human bites are more dangerous than animal bites."

"You're right," said Jennie dryly. "She could be rabid."

Mia smothered a chuckle, but Yuki found nothing amusing.

"I've been wondering all day," said Mia. "How did you two know Felicité was following me?"

"I didn't," Yuki said.

"I saw her rat." Jennie rewrapped the bandage. "Felicité was hanging around all three times you and me and Kerry were together. This morning, when I was with the Ranger candidates, I saw Wu Zetian watching me, and I knew it couldn't be coincidence. I told Yuki, we gave Julio an excuse, and as soon as we left the Ranger field, we saw Wu Zetian streaking off, like she was going to report. And there was Felicité."

Wu Zetian must have been better trained than Felicité had ever let on. Yuki wondered what his own rat was doing now. Once Kerry realized how useful Kogatana was, how sweet and affectionate, she would never let her go.

Voices outside indicated that the crowd was growing larger. Great. This day was getting better by the second.

The jail door creaked. Mia leaped up, throwing her arms out in a wild, useless gesture. Then she collapsed back onto the bench as if she'd been shot.

"It's okay, Mia," Jennie whispered. "Mr. Preston can't attack us with these iron bars between us and him."

Mia giggled weakly, but her shoulders were up by her ears. Yuki's heart hammered against his ribs—but the man who walked in wasn't the defense chief. It was Mr. Vilas.

Sheriff Crow glanced up from her chair. "Nice timing, Furio."

"Want my report in private?" he asked.

The sheriff gave her head a shake. "Jennie and her friends have a right to know."

Mr. Vilas set his rifle in the rack and hitched a chair beside the sheriff. "Voske said no."

"No surprise there."

"Specifically, he said…" Mr. Vilas looked upward and quoted, "'I don't make deals. I'm not releasing the prisoner. Tell Las Anclas to give my daughter back. If they don't, I'll kill everyone when I take the town. As for you, Vilas, I'm only letting you live long enough to deliver that message. Once it's delivered, I'm coming after you.'"

Mr. Vilas dropped his head. "So, up to you. I'm happy to stay and fight when Voske shows up with his army, but if you're worried that he'll send assassins, I'll leave now. Try to draw 'em off."

"He already sent assassins," Sheriff Crow said. "We took care of them."

"But we did give Kerry back," Mia piped up. "She'll get back there before he can send an army."

"Let's hope that's how it works out." Sheriff Crow didn't sound as if she thought it was likely.

The door slammed open, and Mr. Preston strode in. He paused just long enough to see Mr. Vilas shake his head.

"I knew he'd refuse." Mr. Preston glared at Yuki and the girls through the bars. "Give me one good reason not to have the three of you shot. What you did was treason. Whether it was out of cowardice, greed, or stupidity…"

He paused between breaths, giving Mia a chance to squeak, "You were going to kill her. That's wrong."

Mr. Preston stepped closer, sending Mia skittering backward. "What do you know about right and wrong? You don't understand anything unless it's made out of metal. You may officially be an adult, but you've never grown up and as far as I can tell, you never will. I was a fool to have trusted you."

Tears were running down Mia's face by the end of Mr. Preston's speech.

Anger flared in Yuki, stronger than the sick feeling of guilt. "Mia's right. Killing Kerry would have been cold-blooded murder."

The rage in Mr. Preston's face struck Yuki like a blow. "And you! How dare you endanger the town that saved your life, took you in, and treated you like one of its own? The only thing you've ever cared about is your precious lost ship. Will it bother you, I wonder, when Voske comes back, and the citizens who named you their brother and son lie dead at your feet?"

Yuki forced himself to stand his ground, but he couldn't manage a reply. It was all too easy to imagine Mom and Meredith killed in battle. He told himself that Voske had always meant to return to Las Anclas and that what Yuki had done didn't change that. But the words stuck in his throat.

Mr. Preston turned away from Yuki in disgust, then glared straight at Jennie. "I sent you on a straightforward mission, a mission *you* demanded to lead. Not only did you fail, you brought ruin upon Las Anclas. I trusted you, and you betrayed me. You sold out the entire town to protect a mutant enemy. I expect you all to be exiled or shot, but on the off chance that the council decides to go soft on you, I want you to know one thing, Jennie Riley. No matter what else happens, you are banned from the Rangers for the rest of your life."

Jennie got to her feet and grabbed the bars. The rage written in every line of her body was so powerful that Yuki half-expected the iron bars to tear out of the floor. Her voice, trained to project across an exercise field, rose until the entire jail seem to vibrate.

"You want to know why I kidnapped Kerry?" Jennie pointed an accusing finger at Mr. Preston. "It was because of *your* order. *You* told that bounty hunter if we couldn't get Ross back, he should kill Ross so Voske couldn't use him. I had to do something to stop that. Taking Kerry was a distraction. Yes, it was the wrong thing to do! But I did it to stop *you* from murdering a citizen of Las Anclas."

Sheriff Crow's head turned sharply. "Furio. Is this true?"

Mr. Vilas glanced at the defense chief, then back at the sheriff. He nodded.

Sheriff Crow faced Mr. Preston. "Did I miss the ceremony where we crowned you king?" She pointed at the door. "Out. We'll be discussing this further, *with* the council."

Mr. Preston's heels rang on the cement floor. The door slammed.

"You too, Vilas." She jerked her thumb at the door.

Mr. Vilas gave her a slight nod—in anyone else Yuki would have said it was apologetic—and followed Mr. Preston with his usual noiseless tread.

The door opened again. This time it was Paco. Yuki saw and heard nothing else.

Paco walked to him in silence. The floodlights outside cast the shadows of the bars across his face, revealing a fury Yuki hadn't even seen during the battle.

Yuki wasn't aware of getting up. He grabbed the bars, wanting to reach through them to Paco, but Paco stood still, arms tightly folded, out of reach.

"How dare you." His voice so low Yuki almost couldn't hear it. "I can't believe that you would betray everyone in the town—betray your own family—betray me—for the sake of an enemy."

Yuki thought his heart would stop. "She's just a girl. They were going to kill her."

"I would have volunteered for the firing squad," Paco retorted.

Yuki couldn't hold back any longer. "Paco, that's why I did it. She's your sister. I couldn't let you be responsible for killing her."

"I have no sister." Paco made a violent gesture of repudiation. "I have no family. My mother is dead because Voske killed her. And you think it matters that there's some girl out there who I never knew, who shares some of my blood? If that's what you believe, then you think of me as Voske's son."

Yuki started to stammer a denial, but Paco turned his back on Yuki and walked out.

Yuki gripped the cell bars, aware of the silence from Jennie, Mia, Sheriff Crow, the deputy over by the arms rack. Of voices outside, and somewhere, a laugh that reminded him of Henry, *haw haw haw!* Closer by, some guy saying cheerfully, "I can't wait to get home. My brother will love this—he's had a crush on Paco for years."

Yuki walked to the corner of the cell, sat down on the floor, and buried his face in his hands. It was the closest to privacy he could get.

Mia said in a small voice, "I'm so sorry, Yuki. *We* know you meant well."

Jennie began talking to Mia, which kept Yuki from having to answer. He couldn't have answered. He felt like he'd swallowed dynamite, and it had blasted out his brains and heart. It even hurt to breathe.

But he had to breathe, in and out. Slowly he became aware of the girls talking, wondering how far Kerry might have gotten. The jail door opened again, bringing the scents of bread, braised fish, and cinnamon.

"Oh, wow, what's that?" Mia interrupted herself to say.

Jack Lowell said, "Dinner time! Deputy, can you open the door for us?"

Yuki looked up. The sheriff was gone. Jack was followed by a crowd, filling the jail—Meredith, Ma, and Pa Riley at the head of half the Riley clan, and Grandma Lee with three more Lees.

Meredith called, "Hey, Yuki! Mom said she'll be along as soon as she gets off watch."

The deputy let Jack into the cell, to set the dinner tray on the table. "I want you all to know that this isn't just me being nice. You have lots of supporters in town, more than just your families. I was tempted to post a note outside my kitchen saying 'Yes, I am making the prisoners' dinner.'"

The family members gathered outside the cell.

Meredith grabbed the bars. "Hey, Yuki, you should have told me! I would have helped you."

Yuki indicated the cell. "And look what it would have gotten you."

"Yes, free crumble." Meredith rubbed her hands. "And the chance to knock down Felicité Wolfe and lock her in a fruit shed."

"Look what *that* would have gotten you." Jennie indicated the bite marks on her hand.

"And an excuse to bite her back," Meredith said cheerfully.

Grandma Lee said, "Mia, your father is at the emergency council meeting, but he'll come by afterward. Is there anything you'd like us to bring you?"

Mia brightened immediately. "My tool kit. And everything on my bed."

"Including the engine?" Dee Riley asked.

"Both the engines." Mia held up two fingers.

"We'll put 'em in a wheelbarrow," Aunt Sofia Lee said.

Mr. Riley beckoned Jennie to come close. She sat cross-legged on the floor, and Mrs. Riley reached through the bars to take her hand.

Jennie said, "I can tell you now why I did it. Why I did everything."

"We know why," Mrs. Riley said.

Mr. Riley smiled. "If you mean why you took Kerry in the first place, you were shouting loud enough for half the town to hear. They're all outside, in case you didn't notice."

Yuki winced. That *had* been Henry laughing.

Mr. Riley went on, "You did the right thing. Not everything is about laws. There is a higher authority than Mr. Preston and the town council."

Mrs. Riley added, "And we're glad to see you answering to it."

To Yuki's surprise, Jennie's face lit up in the most genuine smile he'd seen from her since…he didn't even know when. Since before Ross was kidnapped. Since before the battle, the night Jennie and Mia and Ross walked together to the dance.

A physical pain stabbed through his chest at the memory of Paco leaning against him the night of the dance, while they watched the rain fall. He could almost feel Paco's warm body against his side.

He'd never touch Paco again.

"Come on, Yuki," Mia said. "There's plenty for all of us."

Mrs. Riley let go of Jennie's hand. "Get something into you, dear."

Mr. Riley said, "Don't let Jack's excellent food get cold."

Jennie picked up her fork. But she glanced at Yuki, her expression concerned. "Come on, Yuki. You'll feel better if you eat something."

He shook his head. Nothing could make him feel better. He'd abandoned Ross and then failed to rescue him. Voske was about to show up with an army, which they could never fight off. Yuki would rather stay and fight to the death than leave everyone to their fate, but Mr. Preston wouldn't even let him do that.

He felt more lost than he had since the day he'd woken up in the infirmary bed, surrounded by people he couldn't communicate with, and they'd managed to convey to him that the last three people he'd known were dead. He'd realized then that his entire world was gone forever.

Now he'd once again lost everyone he loved. Kogatana was gone for good. He'd never be allowed to return to Las Anclas, so he'd never see Mom or Meredith again. And just as he'd feared, Paco would never forgive him.

Jennie seemed to be happy just knowing that she'd done the right thing, but for Yuki, that was no comfort at all.

CHAPTER FORTY-THREE
RUINED CITY OUTSIDE GOLD POINT
ROSS

"You think everything's too dangerous," Santiago said. "'The ceiling will fall down on your head. The floor will collapse. Those are *venomous* mice.' There's no such thing as venomous mice!"

"That's what I thought," Ross retorted. "Until I got bitten by one. Look, you'd better trust me, or you'll end up squashed under fifty tons of ancient concrete."

Ross glanced around the moss-covered structures that lined the steep road. He had to throw Santiago a bone, or he'd ignore everything Ross said, charge into the first building he saw, and fall through the floor for real.

He surveyed the nearest buildings, trying to figure out which was least likely to contain anything Voske would find valuable. One reminded him of a collapsed house he'd explored a couple years ago, where he'd found a few pages of an ancient children's book with bright cartoon illustrations. Now he wished he'd kept them rather than trading them for coffee and flour. He could have given them to Jennie. Ross swallowed, pushing away the memory of Jennie holding him, teaching him to dance.

He'd let Santiago explore the ancient home. Voske could enjoy his kids' books.

Ross pointed. "That one. The upper story looks too unstable, but we can try the lower one."

"No tricks. You know the king is watching everything we're doing." Santiago glanced upward, at the dense foliage that blocked out most of the sun.

Voske couldn't see in the dark; could he see into the dimly lit interior of a ruin? To be safe, Ross had to assume that he could.

He approached the tilted entrance of the building he'd chosen. It had slid over a foot from its foundations. With the upper story still mostly intact, the whole thing could be balanced like a house of cards. He was careful not to touch anything as he peered past the vines that curtained the entrance. Santiago joined him, holding up a lantern.

"What do you think it was?" Santiago asked.

"Probably a store." To Ross's relief, there were no giant insects, and it didn't smell like any carnivores nested there.

What he could see from the doorway was a huge empty space, without even the remains of furniture. At the rear were what had probably been a number of rooms, but several had collapsed and all the doorways were at least partially blocked. There was a staircase leading to the second floor, but the bottom had been crushed when a pillar had fallen across it. The rest of the staircase had no supports, and would fall in the moment you set foot on it.

He raised his lantern until the golden glow illuminated the ceiling. An army of beetles skittered into its crevices and cracks. A long shadow resolved into a gaping hole, through which mossy pipes were visible. From the slimy thickness of the moss and the dampness on the floor below, the pipes were full of water. If one broke, it wouldn't just produce a trickle of water, but a flood.

"There's nothing in this room," Santiago said, sounding disappointed. "Let's check out those rooms in the back."

"No, I see something," Ross said, bending down.

He picked up a plastic ball and socket. Holding it up, he spun the tiny ball. After all those years, it moved as smoothly as if it had been made yesterday. Mia loved those things. Sometimes she made toys for the little kids out of them. He automatically stashed it into his pack to give her, then wondered if he would ever see her again.

"There's nothing *valuable* in this room." Santiago headed for the nearest door.

Ross grabbed his arm. "Stay behind me." He cautiously stepped forward.

A low wall divided the room. As he skirted it, something chittered from the deep tangle of vines. Santiago started, hand on his machete, and Ross brandished the sledgehammer, but nothing jumped out at them.

While Santiago held his lantern over the wall, Ross lifted his and studied the ceiling. One of the two support pillars was intact, but another listed to the side. Its top was less than a foot away from the biggest water pipe.

"See that pillar, Santiago?" Ross warned him. "If that comes down, it'll break the pipe and flood the whole building. Don't even go near it."

Santiago gave the pillar a wide berth as he headed toward a door. A rustle was the only warning, then a huge shape hurtled out. Santiago nearly dropped his lantern as the thing flew overhead, shrieking.

"Bat," Ross said.

"Not many that size in Gold Point," Santiago said.

Ross could hear how he was trying to be casual, and grinned to himself.

Santiago let Ross go first. Ross poked his head through the door to the bat cave. His eye was caught by the gleam of light on metal.

The entire room was lined with racks of guns.

Ross stared incredulously. There were pistols, rifles, and weapons he couldn't even identify except that they were obviously firearms of some kind. All were far more complex than any weapon he'd seen, but he recognized some from books in the Las Anclas library. These were the weapons of ancient times that could kill hundreds of people in an instant.

Voske would use those guns to kill every last person in Las Anclas.

Ross lowered the lantern, backed up, and tried to sound as casual as he could. "Nothing in that one. Let's try the next one."

His voice betrayed him, the way Santiago's had before.

Santiago pushed past Ross. "Let me see." He held up his lantern, then gasped.

Ross grabbed Santiago's arm. "Pretend you didn't see that. You know what Voske will do with these. He'll kill hundreds of people with them. Thousands."

Santiago held up his lantern. His eyes were huge. "But these weapons are exactly what he wants. I can't try to hide them from him. He'd kill my whole family. We have to take these guns to him."

"Listen, Santiago, Voske's spy thing doesn't work in the dark. I've tested it. If you don't say anything, he never needs to know."

Santiago blinked at him. "What? How did you test it?"

Ross couldn't tell Santiago about Mia's weapon. He tried to think of something plausible, then gave up. "I can't tell you that. But it's true."

"Why should I believe that? Anyway, it's not dark." Santiago indicated the lantern he still held. "Let's get as many of these guns as we can carry. Think of it this way, Ross. Isn't this what every prospector dreams of? The king is generous with prospectors who bring him valuable finds. You'll be set up for the rest of your life."

Ross's right hand clenched around his sledgehammer. He didn't want to hurt Santiago, but he'd kill him to protect Las Anclas. If that was the only way ... But it wasn't.

"Run!" Ross smashed his sledgehammer into the weakest part of the pillar.

The pillar started to topple toward the water pipes. Santiago bolted, and Ross dashed after him.

Metal screeched as the pillar ripped through the pipes. A wall of water slammed into Ross's back, knocking him off his feet. He lost his grip on the sledgehammer as he came down hard. The world roared around him, slimy cold water filling his eyes and nose. He thrashed around, trying to find air. A foothold. Anything.

Ross was thrown hard into something solid. He gasped, and found that he could breathe again.

Before he could move, a thunderous crash sent the stink of rotting drywall rising up a second before he was knocked flat again by a shower of debris. A mob of tiny insects flew into his hair and clothes, trying to escape the ruin of their colonies.

He curled into a ball to protect his head and neck. When the debris stopped hitting him, he tried to get up. He was pinned down.

He could breathe—just—but he was trapped under the remains of the ceiling. He couldn't see, he couldn't move. He was going to die there, buried alive.

A ray of greenish light pierced the darkness.

"Ross! Ross!" It was Santiago's voice.

"Here," Ross managed to gasp. "Get me out of here."

Dust and debris showered on to his face, and then the weight lifted from his back. Santiago's fingers closed around Ross's arm and jerked him upright. Ross stumbled into the green jungle light, then collapsed onto the mossy street.

Gradually he became aware of a hoarse voice shouting at him. Even more gradually, he began to follow the words.

"…I can't believe you did that! You nearly got me killed! You nearly got yourself killed! I should have left you there!"

Ross tried to sit up. The world tilted, and he lay back down.

Santiago stopped yelling. He crouched down beside Ross. "Are you hurt?"

Ross muttered, "I don't know."

He felt Santiago checking him over for broken bones. All Ross could do was lie there and shiver. His chest ached as though the debris still pressed down on him, crushing the air out of his lungs.

He was so cold… But gradually the shivering faded as his wet clothes began to dry. His desperate gulps for air slowed, and he lay there, appreciating the warmth…feeling the soft moss of the road beneath his back. All around him, forest creatures howled and chittered and chirped.

Ross opened his eyes and sat up.

"Careful." Santiago stuck out his arm between Ross and a glowing red chunk of rock.

Ross remembered Santiago's power. He leaned into the warmth, his breathing getting easier. "Thanks."

"You're out of your mind," Santiago said. "You could have died."

"I couldn't let Voske get his hands on those guns."

The building had collapsed into a hollow half-filled with filthy water. Wet debris ringed the new pond. The ruined building creaked as the water shifted the last of the support pillars, and the roof came apart, landing in pieces on the top of the pond.

Ross should have been triumphant at depriving Voske of the weapons, but he only felt shaky and exhausted. His entire body ached. And he still had to go back through the singing trees. "I can't prospect any more today."

Santiago settled back, his wrists resting on his bent knees. Ross recognized that as his storytelling pose. Sure enough, he said, "Let me tell you a story, Ross. When my aunt Maria-Luisa was a teenager, she captured a wild stallion. He was the most beautiful horse she'd ever seen—perfect conformation, and pure black except for a white blaze down his face and two white socks. My aunt put him in a corral and started trying to tame him. She came in every day for months, but he never let her get near him."

Ross was familiar with Santiago's metaphorical stories. "I get it. I'm the stallion, and Voske's your aunt, and eventually I'll get used to the corral."

"She tried sugar, she tried carrots, she tried sitting there with him for hours and hours. After she'd had him for six months, she came to the corral one morning…"

Ross sighed. "*I get it.* He'd finally been tamed, and he was much happier in Gold Point than he'd been in the wild."

Santiago shook his head. "She found him dead. He'd broken his neck trying to jump a twelve-foot fence."

He glanced over his shoulder, then spoke softly. "Come on, Ross. You've had so many chances to kill me, and you didn't take any of them. Let me save your life this time. You know the king has to have seen what happened. Tell him you're sorry and you'll never do it again. And mean it. He's invested a lot of time and effort in you, so I think he'll give you one more chance. But you can't keep defying him. Don't kill yourself for nothing, out of pride."

Ross could try doing as Santiago said, to buy more time, but Voske would know he was lying. There wouldn't be any 'one more chance.'

Ross had to kill Voske before Voske killed him.

CHAPTER FORTY-FOUR
LAS ANCLAS
JENNIE

Jennie edged around Jack's mechanical butter churn, which took up most of the cell. Only the lower half of Mia's body was visible as she worked deep in the guts of the thing.

Jennie circled the moat of tools surrounding Mia's feet, and glanced through the bars at Yuki in the next cell. He sat in the corner, knees drawn up, his forearms resting on them, hands loose, face blank. Like he'd sat for the past five days.

Guilt squeezed Jennie's chest. She dropped down and began a set of pushups, as clanks and thuds emanated from deep inside the butter churn.

The jailhouse door opened, and Jennie heard a familiar laugh. She gritted her teeth and kept going.

Henry called out, "Hey, your highness. Missing your prince? And your royal rat?"

Yuki didn't move.

Two sets of footsteps approached, and a skittering sound. Jennie peeked past her swinging braids. Wu Zetian? Felicité had to be with Henry. Came to gloat? Jennie counted under her breath, ignoring them.

"Watch this," Henry whispered, raising his hands.

A loud clap resounded through the jail. Mia's lower body jerked. The bong of a head hitting metal was followed by a muffled yelp from inside the churn.

Henry let out a guffaw.

"Henry, stop being a jerk," Jennie said, sitting up. "Are you okay, Mia?"

"What was that?" Mia's head popped out. She rubbed her scalp, wincing. "Oh. Henry, that was mean."

"Just kidding!" Henry said. As usual.

Mia went back to work. Jennie reached up to the iron bar that Jose and Mia had rigged under the ceiling for her, and began doing pull-ups.

Felicité spoke in her candied-sugar voice. "Henry, would you give us a

253

moment? This is council business."

"I'll hold a table for us at Jack's. Bye, your majesty," Henry added as he passed Yuki's cell. He might as well have been talking to the wall.

Jennie kept right on with her pull-ups.

"The council sent me to inform you that a vote has been taken." Felicité paused until Jennie stopped exercising and hung from the bar, anxiety twisting in her gut. Felicité went on, "You three have until New Year's. If Ross isn't back by then, it's exile for the three of you."

No firing squad. Relief made Jennie giddy. It was followed by gratitude, which vanished when she looked down into Felicité's brown eyes.

Once Jennie had wondered what Felicité's true voice sounded like under all that sugar. She'd heard it after the battle, when Felicité had called Ross a monster. And she heard it again now, in the word 'exile.'

Jennie shut her eyes and resumed her pull-ups, counting under her breath. She heard the rustle of Felicité's skirt, and the scratching of her rat's claws. She smelled the fresh floral scent that Felicité used to rinse her hair. She had to be right up against the bars.

Irritated, Jennie spoke. "What do you want, Felicité?"

Muted clanks echoed from the butter churn.

"Why did you do it?" Felicité's voice wasn't sugary any more. It was angry, accusing.

Jennie opened her eyes and dropped down. She wanted this over. "I could give you three reasons. I don't think you'd understand one."

"Try me."

Jennie flexed her hands. "Because it was right. Because it was the only way to save Ross. Because one more death is one death too many."

"Who says it was right?"

"I said you wouldn't understand."

"How is betraying the entire town right? She'll come back with her father's army."

"The army is coming anyway." A trickle of sweat tickled Jennie's brow. She wiped her forehead on her sleeve. "We all know that. Go away, Felicité. If you really wanted to understand, you could have asked us instead of spying."

"Do you seriously believe that girl will free Ross when your team and the council's negotiating couldn't?"

"Mia thinks she will. I give it a fifty-fifty chance. Which is better than the zero chance we would have had if we'd let your father bully the council into *murdering* a girl who never did anything but talk."

"Mia took her all over the town," Felicité said sharply. "Kerry saw our defenses. She has to be describing them to her father this minute. What you three did was treason."

"Every trader who comes here sees our defenses. And Voske has spies, remember? How else would he have known exactly when to attack a few months ago?"

"You were under orders," Felicité's voice rose. "Mia was *trusted*—"

"What Felicité isn't telling you," Sheriff Crow said, coming up from behind, "is that if it comes to exile, there are several families who are going with you. The Rileys, the Lees, and the Lowensteins for certain. And there are others talking about—"

A confusion of noises rose from outside. Jennie recognized Henry's whoop, then a sharp cacophony of men's voices. Sheriff Crow took off in a blur of speed.

Mia pulled her head out of the churn, pushed her glasses back up her nose, leaving a smear of grease on them, and looked around. When she saw Felicité, she put her head back in the churn.

"I'd better go," Felicité said, the sugary voice back.

Don't let the door hit you in the ass, Jennie wanted to say.

Exile, really? Ma and Pa were ready to give up their home for Jennie? Guilt squeezed her heart once again.

The distant voices shut up abruptly, like an electric light turning off. In the ominous silence that followed, the only sound was the deputy checking the chamber on her rifle.

Then Meredith appeared at the open door. "I want to see my brother."

The deputy said, "Sheriff said no entry."

Sheriff Crow returned and spoke quietly. "Sorry, Meredith. I had to call curfew. You'll hear the bell in a minute or so. Run along home."

Meredith stuck her head inside and yelled, "Mom says hi, and if you want anything, Yuki, I'll be back in the morning!"

Mia emerged again, her eyes huge behind her glasses.

"There was a fight at Jack's." Sheriff Crow grimaced. "Some you'd expect, and some you wouldn't."

"Tommy Horst?" Jennie asked.

The sheriff nodded. "Mixing it up with Indra. Paco decked one of the Willet brothers for knocking out Jack."

"Jack?" Mia and Jennie exclaimed. Even Yuki looked up. Or maybe it was hearing Paco's name.

"He's in the infirmary, but he'll be all right." The sheriff sighed. "What Felicité didn't tell you is that the entire town has been arguing these past few days. Including Preston and Mayor Wolfe. That's why the council took so long to decide. Up until five days ago, when you all took action, everybody was going to look the other way while we executed a girl for being born with the wrong name."

"Dad called it the first step down an evil road." Mia's voice quavered.

Again, a nod from the sheriff. "Some townspeople would never forgive themselves. And some—co-workers, neighbors, even family—would have liked nothing better than to line up and watch the firing squad."

"It's my fault." Jennie's throat was so tight she could barely speak. Her hands wrapped around the bars. "I'm the one who brought her." The daughter of the bloodthirsty King Voske who had killed Sera Diaz.

Another betrayal.

"Stop that." The sheriff smacked her hand over Jennie's. "What you did, all of you, was wake up this town, and just in time. I wasn't going to bring her up, but one thing Sera always used to say, *It's easy to make people dead, but nobody can make them alive again. Life is precious*. If she were here, she would be marching out the gates with you and your family. That's why she came here in the first place, because we were the town that didn't do that kind of thing."

CHAPTER FORTY-FIVE
GOLD POINT
ROSS

The setting sun burned red over the hills when Ross and Santiago reached the palace garden.

Santiago pulled Ross to a halt at the orange arch. "You're going to do what we talked about, right?"

Ross nodded, trying to keep his face expressionless. Nobody ever seemed to have any trouble figuring out what he was feeling, so he'd try not to let anything show at all.

Sure enough, Santiago said, "Ross? You're listening, aren't you?" He grabbed Ross by the shoulders. "You'll confess to the king, and you'll beg his forgiveness." He shook Ross. "Right?"

"Sure." Ross's voice came out flat. He tried harder. "I said I would."

Santiago let go. "Good. But when you say you'll work for the king, you have to mean it! You want to live, right?"

Ross heard the truth in his own voice when he said, "I want to live."

As they walked on, he tried to forget that he was almost certain to be dead within the hour. He had to make himself believe that he would beg Voske's forgiveness, and live. That man could take one look at your face and know exactly what you were thinking. The only way Ross could fool Voske for long enough to get within range was to not even think about his intent until he was ready.

And keep his head down. Ross casually brushed his hair back, then let it fall forward, hiding his face as much as he could.

Once they passed the door guards, he reached into his pack. He pulled out his canteen and had a drink, then put it back in. When he took his hand out again, Mia's club was concealed in his palm.

He made himself loosen his grip and let his arm swing naturally. He couldn't help thinking about how happy Mia must have been as she'd made it for him. He remembered how she'd measured his hand for the gauntlet. He could almost feel the softness of her skin as she held his hand in hers.

She had been the last person to touch this weapon.

He wished he could tell her how much it meant to him. How much *she* meant to him. At least, if he killed Voske, he'd be keeping her safe.

A guard opened the door of the throne room. Ross lowered his head even further. He couldn't see Voske, but he heard that hated voice say, "Another trip come up empty? I'm losing my patience."

Santiago said, "Ross has something to tell you, sir."

Ross shuffled forward a pace or two, then stopped. If Voske did what he usually did, he'd think Ross was scared, come forward to intimidate him, and stop just out of striking range. The footsteps came closer. Ross's stomach clenched. He only had one chance.

A pair of polished boots stepped into view, then swiftly retreated a step. Voske had somehow sensed Ross's intent.

Ross snapped out the cudgel as he slid forward, desperately trying to close the distance. Santiago lunged at him, but not quickly enough. Fierce triumph burned in Ross as he struck.

Voske's arm flashed up in the fastest block Ross had ever seen. The cudgel slammed into Voske's forearm with a crack. Ross leaped forward, his gauntleted hand lashing out. One hard blow to the throat was all it would take.

Santiago threw himself in front of Voske, deflecting Ross's blow. The gauntlet skidded off Santiago's upraised arm and smashed into the side of his face, knocking him down.

Then all the guards piled into Ross. One grabbed his gauntlet. Another slammed into him from the side. A third struck his right arm, trying to knock the cudgel from his hand. Ross swung out with it, connecting solidly with a guard's shoulder, and kicked another guard in the knee, taking him down. Then a ridge-hand strike hit him in the throat.

Choking for breath, Ross went down under a mass of bodies. Someone kicked him in the side, and he felt something snap. There were more hard blows, but he hardly felt the pain past the suffocating agony in his throat. Faintly he heard Voske's voice, "Don't kill him."

Some air was getting through, but Ross felt as if he was breathing fire through a hollow straw. Someone yanked off his gauntlet, rubbing the lining painfully against the fingerprint burns Luis had left on his arm. At least five guards had him pinned to the floor. One of them even clutched a handful of Ross's hair. All he could see was the guards and the carved wood ceiling.

Then Voske stepped into view. His left arm hung limp at his side, but that seemed to be his only injury. For once, he wasn't smiling. If Ross could have moved, he would have flinched back from the white-lipped fury in Voske's face.

It seemed forever that Voske stood over him, silent, staring down into Ross's eyes. Then the smile returned. "Break his arm."

Determined to make one last effort, Ross forced a deep breath past the tearing pain in his throat. As his chest expanded, agony knifed deep into his side, leaving him dizzy. A cold sweat broke out all over his body. He couldn't fight with broken ribs. He could barely even breathe.

The guards jerked him to his feet. Voske gestured to the corner, where Mia's weapon had rolled. "Use that."

Ross fought for breath as footsteps clomped away, then back. Hard hands yanked his right arm out and forced it straight with a hand under his elbow. Ross heard a whistle of air. Then blazing agony exploded in his arm, searing a path all the way up to his jaw.

Everything went white, then broke up into darkening fragments. The ground dissolved under his feet.

A stinging slap against the side of his face, hard enough to make his neck snap back, returned him to consciousness. The guards were holding him up by the shoulders, putting excruciating pressure on his broken arm. He tried to stand on his own, but his legs wouldn't support him. He couldn't even get his eyes to focus.

But though everything else was hazy, he could hear every word that Voske said.

"It didn't have to end this way, Ross. You could have gone back to your room in the palace, fallen asleep on your soft bed, and dreamed of the rewards I'd give you. But you chose stupidity and rebellion. Your execution will begin at dawn. I'll make sure it lasts all day."

Fingers snapped. "Take him to the hell cells."

CHAPTER FORTY-SIX
GOLD POINT
KERRY

Kerry resisted the urge to nudge her tired horse into a gallop. She'd known she was close to home when she encountered the outer perimeter riders. Her first question after their delighted exclamations was, "Where's Santiago?"

To her immense relief, the patrol captain said, "He and the guest returned from the royal city—" He glanced upward. "They returned," he finished awkwardly.

So Mia had been right. Ross was still a prisoner, and he hadn't taken the opportunity to kill Santiago. In that case, Kerry would keep her word and send Ross back. She sent a mental message to Mia, *Hang on. He's on his way home.*

Giddy with relief, with anticipation, even happiness, she settled back to enjoy the rest of the ride. She recognized every bend in the trail, every rock formation. She was nearly home.

Soon she'd be relaxing in her own room, after a hot bath and with Santiago by her side. Her father would be so proud of her for arranging her own escape, and for surviving the desert alone. She'd give the horses from Las Anclas to Ross when he left the next morning, along with Kogatana.

She scratched the gray rat behind her ears. It was too bad Kerry couldn't keep her. She'd gotten quite fond of the furry little creature, who had curled up so warm and soft in Kerry's arms during the miserable cold nights, and warned her when predators were near.

But there wouldn't be any more cold nights! And no more predators. Soon she'd be in her own bed, sleeping under down covers, on clean sheets, with a pillow, in perfect safety. In all those uncomfortable desert nights, Kerry had missed pillows the most.

She was grinning as the tired horse plodded around the tangled wall of spines of the Joshua tree forest. There was the familiar glow of floodlights outlining the crenellations of the city wall, and there were the familiar heads on spikes.

For the first time in her life, Kerry saw those heads as more than objects and warnings. Even the oldest skulls, the ones so worn down by weather that you could hardly even see what they were, had once belonged to real people.

They were traitors and criminals, she reminded herself.

Mia and Yuki and Jennie were traitors and criminals.

The features weren't clear on the freshest head, but Kerry thought it was male. As she came close enough to distinguish color, she saw that its hair was gray. Some old traitor or criminal. She wondered what they'd said or did.

Kerry hadn't believed Mia's claim that no one would be punished for defying Tom Preston, but days after the commotion outside of the forge, Kerry had seen the same people who'd argued with Preston freely going about their business. Kerry grimaced up at that silent skull. In Gold Point, townspeople who'd argued with Father would have added their heads to the wall.

She averted her gaze from the heads. Why spoil her homecoming? Better to think about how proud Father would be at her escape. Of course he'd let Ross go—as long as Santiago was still safe. *I keep my word.*

The gates screeched open, and people began shouting. "The princess! Welcome back, Princess Kerry!" Everyone was saluting and cheering.

Kerry waved and smiled at her people. She turned right and left, the way Min Soo had taught her, including everyone. But the second she was past, they stopped looking at her and began talking urgently to each other. It hardly seemed possible, but they were acting as if there was something more important going on than the return of the kidnapped crown princess.

Someone said, "What's that furry thing?"

"It's a giant rat!"

"That's got to be one of the trained rats from Las Anclas," a third person said, and added loudly, "The princess captured one of their rats!"

As a cheer went up, Kerry thought, *That's more like it.* She chirruped to Kogatana, who leaped down obediently. Kerry was about to explain that the rats were way too smart to get captured, when everyone backed away.

Min Soo came running gracefully along the garden path.

Kerry dismounted, bracing herself for a scolding about how careless she'd been to ride off without an escort and get herself kidnapped, probably crowned with a lecture about how untidy and dirty she was.

She imagined Min Soo's too-sweet tones saying, "Even without bathing water, a princess always finds a way to keep herself clean and lovely."

Min Soo reached her, beautiful in fluttering silks. There was no way she'd even touch Kerry, who hadn't bathed in six days and wore filthy, sweaty riding clothes.

Without hesitating, Min Soo embraced her. "My darling daughter," she whispered into Kerry's dirty hair. "You're safe."

Surprised, Kerry patted her mother awkwardly on the back, afraid of wrecking her beautiful clothes. Her mother's back seemed so small under the silk, so fragile. The floodlights gleaming on tear tracks marring her smooth face.

Kerry remembered her promise to herself.

"Mom," she said hesitantly. "I wanted to tell you. You were right. I needed everything you taught me to escape from Las Anclas. Your lessons saved my life, and…um…I'm sorry I was so horrible to you."

Mom blinked fiercely, then gave Kerry a quivering smile. "I confess, sometimes I wondered if you were paying any attention. I'm so glad you were. So, even the rose petal sweets were worthwhile?"

Kerry laughed. "They were. I never have to eat them again, do I?"

"Never. They served their purpose." Mom bent to offer a hand to Kogatana. "What a lovely rat. Now, let's get you inside. Your father's waiting. We want to hear everything!"

As Kerry accompanied Mom into the palace, with her mother talking sweetly about ordering Kerry's favorite foods for dinner, Kerry realized that her mother's voice didn't bother her. It was almost…soothing.

Mom paused outside the king's rooms. "Your father has had a difficult day. Nothing could please him more than your appearance. Why don't I leave you to your reunion? I'll order you a scented bath."

Automatically Kerry said, "I hate scent. No scent."

Mom's smile was quick, but a little strained. What was going on? "I should have remembered. No scent."

For the first time in ages, Kerry said, "Thanks, Mom."

Her mother fluttered off. Kerry passed the guards, who stood stiffly, hands to their weapons. That was odd. They couldn't be expecting a Las Anclas army to magically appear at the gates.

Kerry barged into her father's private study, expecting an even better welcome than Mom's. The room was full of guards. Her steps faltered when she saw her father's arm in a sling. She'd never seen him hurt before.

Her gaze reached his face, and she froze. She'd never seen him this angry before, either, not even after the failed attack on Las Anclas where her sister Deirdre had died.

"Father?" she said hesitantly. "What happened?"

Santiago stepped out from the crowd, his face bruised and bloody. Kerry had pictured herself flying into his arms when they finally saw each other again. But neither of them moved. There was a strange, oppressive atmosphere in the room. Kerry fell back on her training and kept her face blank.

Father smiled, but not the warm smile she'd expected. It was too thin, angry at the corners. "Welcome home, Kerry."

Kerry found herself babbling about how happy she was to be back. "... and they had me locked up in this horrible little cell. With drunks!"

Father held up his hand. Kerry instantly fell silent. "Guards, you're dismissed. Santiago, you can stay." He glanced at Kerry. "If you like."

Kerry looked at Santiago, whom she'd thought about, worried about, for weeks. The happiness she'd expected to see was there in his quick smile, but his shoulders were tense, and the way he kept flicking sideways peeks at Father made her neck prickle. Something was terribly wrong.

Kerry returned her attention to her father. "What happened to your arm?"

"Tell her, Santiago."

Santiago rubbed his elbow. "Ross Juarez tried to assassinate the king. This little chunk of metal he'd been carrying around this whole time turned out to be a weapon." Santiago pointed at the metal thing on a table next to Ross's gauntlet, which Kerry had never seen off his hand. Her heartbeat accelerated as she recognized a twin to the weapon that Mia had been so proud of.

Why couldn't Ross have waited *one* more day to make a break for it? Kerry had counted on being able to make a quick report, ending with her promise. Father would set Ross free, and Kerry could drag Santiago to her room to catch up on weeks of missed kisses.

"Was that how you hurt your face?" Kerry asked Santiago.

He touched his cheek, and seemed mildly surprised when his fingers came away bloody. "It's nothing."

"He protected me with his own body. I won't forget that, Santiago." Father was still smiling strangely, making her neck stiffen. "Let's have your report, Kerry, then I suggest you get some rest. You'll want to be fresh for the execution at dawn."

Santiago looked like he was about to throw up.

Kerry clamped down on herself, showing no reaction. She had to keep her promise. But how could she possibly get Father to agree to release someone who'd tried to kill him?

Father said softly, "Kerry?"

Her nerves chilled. He whispered only when he was angry, and when he was angry, somebody always died.

She began with her capture, in words she'd already thought out. Her heart thumped painfully, but she controlled her voice, her face. It was like her lessons about enemy interrogation, but the person she had to resist getting inside her head was her own father.

The thought made her falter.

Father's eyes narrowed. Alarm spiked through her. "Sorry." She flung back her hair, hoping there was still a trace of bruising around her eye. "When I think of that brute Tom Preston punching me..." She talked wildly about how much she hated him, and saw Father smile again.

Always tell as much of the truth as is harmless—that was Father's first rule of resistance. You could always remember the truth. Lies were hard to keep track of.

Her heartbeat thundered in her ears as she said, "...and so I promised Mia Lee that I would release Ross as soon as I got back. Then she and her friends helped me escape."

Father tipped his head back and laughed. "Excellent work, Kerry. I couldn't have handled them better myself."

'Handled them.' Kerry saw it then. Even if Ross hadn't broken Father's arm, Father would never have permitted her to keep her promise. To him, it was a clever ruse.

Was this what happened to you, Sean? She was almost dizzy, the image was so vivid: her brother standing where she was now, and thinking the same thing: *I have to get away.*

"When word reaches them of Ross's execution, they'll know what's coming," Father said, his teeth showing in that strange, angry smile. "I was going to ride to Las Anclas with an army to fetch you back, but I think you've earned the privilege. When you're rested and ready, you can ride at the head of that army yourself, and take your own town." He paused, clearly expecting her to be thrilled.

Kerry presented him with a thrilled expression. "Father, I'm... Wow, I don't even know what to say."

"I wasn't much older than you are when I took my first town, but it was half the size of Las Anclas. You noted all its current defenses from the inside, right?"

"Yes."

"It should take you a day at most. You can start your rule by mounting the heads of the team that captured you."

Kerry forced herself to grin. Her teeth felt cold. "I know exactly where to put them."

Father laughed again. It was the same laugh she'd grown up hearing. Even admiring. But it made her head hurt. Everything was wrong. The things she'd wanted her entire life sounded horrifying.

I took my first town. For the first time in her life, she understood what that meant: killing people like old Mr. Hassan the beekeeper, Dr. Lee, Mia, and Becky Callahan. She imagined Brisa's beribboned head on a pike. That was supposed to be something Kerry would enjoy?

Her own father was the most dangerous enemy she'd ever faced.

"You did like Las Anclas, didn't you?"

"Oh, yes." *Stay close to the truth*, she told herself. "I liked it fine."

"Did you get inside any of the big houses? I imagine Preston's would make a good palace."

Kerry shook her head, trying to look regretful. She hoped Father couldn't hear her heart clattering against her ribs. At least she had her breath under enough control that her voice had whatever inflection she chose to give it. "No, but I saw it from a distance. I liked the looks of it."

"Do what you want with his family, but save Preston for me," Father said, still in that soft voice.

"Absolutely." And because his gaze was still narrow and watchful above that smile, she remembered another lesson: *When they begin to doubt, ask questions. Act eager to learn.* "How did you make them accept you as king, when you conquered your first town?"

Father liked that question. His expression relaxed a bit. Kerry held her breath, alert to every change. "First, kill the leaders of the resistance. Show them the price of rebellion. In your situation, you should begin with this Jennie Riley, who disobeyed a direct order in bargaining with you. That kind of person can never be trusted not to turn right around and betray you, if the price is right. And any of her followers you think might be a danger…"

Jennie? 'And 'her followers', like Mia? Kerry caught a gasp in her throat before it could escape. If Jennie and Mia had helped *him*, he'd be making pets of them this very minute. But in helping Kerry, they were weak and untrustworthy.

Kerry's indignant reaction turned to sick anger. Father was furious right now, so he might be saying things he wouldn't if his mood had been better, but Ross would be just as dead the next day.

It was always going to be like this. Always.

She had to get away.

If she left, she'd never be a queen. But she didn't want the kind of power you could only get and hold by killing people.

She wanted to live where she could keep her promises, and not be afraid. She wanted to live where people didn't have to worry about who might be listening. She wanted to live where you didn't have to evaluate people only for their political usefulness. She wanted to live where commoners could yell at the ruler and get away with it. Much as she detested Tom Preston, at least he hadn't ordered the deaths of any of those argumentative townspeople.

I won't do it, Kerry thought.

In the time it took for her father to deliver his familiar lecture on the effect of executions, she had made her decision. She would not only run away, she would take Ross with her. And Santiago, once she figured out how to keep his family safe.

Father's lecture came to a close. Aware of his silent expectation, Kerry smiled at him. "You've given me so much to think about!"

Now she had control of herself, from her smile, which she knew looked exactly like his, to her fingertips. Father was the enemy, and she was a prisoner about to make a break.

I know what to do. You trained me yourself.

"Thank you so much, Father. That was so helpful. You must be tired. I should let you go rest that arm." Before he could reply, she exclaimed as if she'd just thought of it, "Oh. Would you mind if I saw the prisoner? I'd love to tell him my plans for his town."

Father laughed, then winced. The painkillers must be wearing off. "Certainly. He's in the hell cells." Father turned to Santiago. "You two run along. Santiago, I won't forget how you protected me."

Kerry turned to go, then picked up Ross's gauntlet as if she'd only just noticed it. He'd hate to lose it, she was sure. "I never got a chance to get a good look at this before. Look how beautiful the workmanship is. And so sturdy, too." She tried it on, then shrugged and laid it back down. She must not give herself away!

"Keep it. Maybe you can have it resized to fit you." Father's free hand touched his splinted forearm, and Kerry knew he wanted them gone.

Santiago followed Kerry out. The moment the door was shut, she took his hand. He walked beside her quietly. He was obviously too upset for the reunion kisses she had hardly dared to imagine until she'd heard that he was safe.

Safe. Nobody in Gold Point was safe. She squeezed his fingers as she sorted out her goals. She had to get Ross out immediately, so they could get a head start before Father noticed they were missing. She had to protect Santiago, and Santiago's family.

By the time they reached her bedroom, she had a plan. She set Kogatana and the gauntlet on the bed, beckoned Santiago inside, closed the door, and pulled the curtains. Pru's hawks didn't fly at night, but there was no point in taking chances.

They locked their arms around each other and lost themselves in kisses, every bit as sweet and wild as she'd hoped. More. But his body was tense, and his breathing stuttered from more than passion.

She forced herself to break away and set her hands on his shoulders. He instantly dropped his arms.

"My team's dead, aren't they?" He spoke flatly, clearly already knowing the answer.

Kerry nodded, feeling guilty for not breaking it to him gently, as she'd planned.

A tear overflowed and ran down his cheek. He didn't wipe it away, or even seem to notice. "I knew they'd rather fight to the death than come back and report that they failed to rescue you. I wanted to go with them, but the king wouldn't let me. And now..." His voice trailed off.

"Santiago, what happened with Ross? Why did he try to kill Father? Was he trying to escape?"

He shook his head. Kerry listened in amazement as he explained how Ross had nearly killed himself to prevent her father from getting weapons.

"I knew the king had seen everything. I told Ross to confess and beg for mercy." Santiago sounded as if he was confessing himself.

No hawk could see inside the ruined city, with its impenetrable canopy of green. From the sound of it, if Santiago had known that, he would have covered up the entire thing.

But what the king could and couldn't see was a royal secret. It had never occurred to Kerry to tell Santiago, no matter how much it annoyed her to see him nervously glancing over his shoulder.

Santiago was rushing on, somewhat incoherently. "Ross pulled me out of the lake! He offered to take me to Las Anclas! He saved my life three times—four times—I don't even know how many times! I tried my best to save him, but there was nothing I could do. I couldn't save him, I couldn't save my team, I couldn't save you! I wish—"

He looked around wildly, then said, louder, "But of course your father is doing the right thing."

"What Father's doing is terrible," Kerry said bluntly. "You don't need to pretend it's all right. Everything here is wrong. I have to leave Gold Point."

"What are you saying? Don't talk about things like that!" He made a wide gesture, as if spies were hidden all over the room.

"Father can't hear us at night or indoors." She meant to tell him the details, but the habit of secrecy stopped her. "You know that if you ever ran away, Father would kill someone in your family. You can't tell me you agree with that."

Santiago looked around again. "Are you sure no one's listening?" When she nodded, he whispered, "Of course I know that's not right. What happened to you?"

"I got away from this." She gestured widely, like he had. "I got away from people being afraid for their families. Afraid to speak up, afraid of the truth. I got away from heads on pikes. And sending armies to kill people in towns that didn't do anything to us. I don't want to live that way anymore, Santiago. And I want you to go with me."

He jumped up, then sank back down again, whispering, "I can't."

"You can," she whispered back. "I have a plan. All those lessons Father gave me about strategy and tactics were really useful. Here's what we'll do. First, I'll get travel supplies. Then I'll take Ross out of the hell cell."

"You can't do that."

"I'm the crown princess. I can do anything I want."

"That's not what I meant," Santiago said. "The guards beat the hell out of him, and the king had them break his arm. They had to drag him out. He couldn't even stand up. He's not going anywhere."

"I'm getting him out if I have to carry him."

"Forget it, Kerry. It's impossible."

"You don't tell me what to do." She didn't speak in anger, but she heard the icy threat in her own voice.

Santiago froze, then cautiously stood up backed away. Suddenly they were no longer boyfriend and girlfriend, but princess and subject. Had that always been what they were, and she'd just never noticed?

She caught his hands, drawing him back. "I promised, Santiago. I gave my word, and I mean to keep it. I can't let him die. Especially after he saved *you*." With him sitting beside her again, she went on. "I have a plan to protect you and your family. You can't come with us right away. It'll look suspicious. I'll leave a note saying that I fell in love with Ross and I'm running away with him."

Santiago exclaimed, "You think the king will believe that?"

"I think he'll find it easier to believe than the truth. I have to convince him that I don't love you any more, and he won't have any trouble believing that I fell for someone new. Think how many stepmothers I've got!"

Santiago grimaced.

"It'll work," Kerry insisted. "Father is pleased with you, and if he thinks I don't love you any more, then he won't need to make an example out of you. Wait a couple months, then disappear while you're on patrol. People will think some animal got you. If it seems like an accident, Father won't blame your family."

Santiago was shaking his head slowly.

"You want us to be together, don't you?" Kerry asked, doubtful and uneasy. Everything seemed unreal. Santiago had never argued with her before.

"More than anything," he replied, and she knew he meant it. "But you're not the first person to think of staging an accident. A patroller disappeared last year. The king thought she'd run away, and he put her husband's head on a pike. A couple months later, we found her body in a crevasse. She'd died in an accident. But we were ordered not to tell anyone.

I can't risk it."

Santiago squeezed her hands so hard it hurt, but she didn't care. "Kerry, let's pretend this conversation never happened. You're the princess. Some day you'll be the queen, and you can change things. You could allow people to leave. You could make it the sort of place no one would *want* to leave."

Kerry looked away from his pleading gaze. Here was her room, with her bed turned down. Here was her bathroom, with steam curling up from her bathtub, the only scent fresh water. Here were her shelves of ancient books and wardrobe of clothes that she'd designed herself.

If she left, she'd be giving it all up. Even if she and Ross made it to Las Anclas, she'd never be a princess again. Worst of all, she'd never see Santiago again.

Her eyes burned. "I made a promise."

Santiago leaned closer, his breath warm on her cheek. "You didn't see what they did to Ross. I did. If you try to escape with him, you'll both end up dead. I hate to say it, Kerry, but the kindest thing you could do for him would be to go to his cell and kill him yourself."

Santiago's hands gripped hers. Kogatana cuddled trustingly against her hip. Images blew through her mind like leaves in the wind. Yuki's grim face as he shouted at her to run. Ross curled up in a corner, shivering in a hot room. Mia reaching out to touch Ross's old shirt hanging over a chair. Becky dabbing witch hazel on her bruised face. Townspeople yelling at each other without a single one looking up at the sky or making the silver hair gesture, because none of them feared being executed for their opinions.

Father gesturing at the headman to let the axe fall, with all of Gold Point gathered to watch.

"I have to go."

Santiago flinched as if she'd hit him. She held him tight, pressing kisses to his eyes, his forehead, his soft, warm lips.

"I broke up with you, Santiago." For the first time, her voice was not under her control, but she didn't care. "And that's all you know. Go home. Stay in your room. When someone comes to find you, tell them you loved me and I broke your heart. Be mad at me, call me names, do whatever you have to do to stay safe. Got it?"

"Got it." He wiped his eyes. "I loved you. You broke my heart."

"Go," she said fiercely, pushing him toward the door.

He hesitated in the doorway. "But if I'm ordered out and we find you..."

Kerry clenched her fists. "Shoot me first."

CHAPTER FORTY-SEVEN
GOLD POINT
ROSS

Ross squeezed his eyes shut. An electric bulb glared bright from behind a mesh in the ceiling of the hell cell. Even with his eyes closed, he saw a dull red glow. The walls were so close that he couldn't lie flat, and the ceiling so low that he couldn't sit up straight. He sat hunched in the corner, trying to support his broken arm and ribs with his knees. Every breath was agony.

The only thing worse than the pain was the regret. He should have waited for a better opportunity to get at Voske. What he'd done had only made things worse, like smashing a wasp's nest. Voske would once again attack Las Anclas, and Ross had completely failed to protect it. He'd have no chance at fighting back when they took him from the cell at dawn to...

He tried not to think of what might last all day. Voske had to have said it so Ross would imagine the worst, but he couldn't stop imagining it. Hot coals. Electric shock. Scorpions. Fire ants. Acid. Drowning. Buried alive. Tortured with all those tools in the room the guards had made sure to show him on his way to the hell cell.

He had to stop thinking about that. He should imagine himself somewhere else. He had the power to actually put himself somewhere else, if he could reach the crystal trees outside of Gold Point.

Ross reached out with his mind, feeling for the bright sparks in the darkness. He could barely sense the five singing trees outside the walls. Desperately, he tried to push his mind into them, to leave his own body behind. But he was too far away, and his link with them wasn't strong enough. All he could get from them was a sense of their presence.

There was no escape inside his mind. He was trapped here, in this box of stone.

The air whistled in his throat. Every breath was a fight. If the swelling got any worse, he could choke to death. Panic gripped him at the thought. But why should he fight it? It would be a better way to die than whatever Voske had planned.

Voices. The clink of keys, and the creak of iron. Footsteps. The wooden door to his cell opened, but there was no rattle of metal. The iron grid between Ross and the door was in place, allowing whoever was in the adjoining room to reach into Ross's cell.

Already dawn? Fine. Get it over with.

"No, leave me alone with him. I'll knock when I'm done."

Ross recognized that voice. It was Luis.

The door closed. Luis said in a low voice, "I'm sorry, Ross. The king ordered me to…" He sighed. "Don't worry. I won't hurt you. There's so much blood already, he won't notice if I don't. I'll just sit here for a while."

Maybe Ross was already in so much pain that Luis burning him wouldn't make that much of a difference. But even as he thought it, Ross knew it wasn't true. Pain could always get worse. Still, nothing Luis could do to him now could be as bad as what Voske had planned for him tomorrow.

A breath of air tore its way down his throat. Ross wished he could simply stop breathing. He could bear any amount of pain if he had some hope of making it through to the other side. But he was hurt far too badly to fight or run. He'd given everything he had in his attempt to kill Voske, and he had nothing left. If anyone from Las Anclas had ever tried to rescue him, they'd failed, just as he had failed them. There was no hope, and Ross had come to the end of his endurance.

Ross forced the words out. "Kill me."

"What?" Luis said.

Ross made himself peel an eye open. He flinched away from the sight of the hell cell's close walls, and tried to focus through the iron grid. Luis's silhouette loomed within arm's reach, surrounded by glaring light. Then Ross caught a glimpse of the stone ceiling, so close overhead, and shut his eyes again.

"Kill me." With his left hand, he tapped the artery at the side of his throat. "Burn. Here."

"I can't do that," Luis protested. "I have strict orders."

"Say. Accident. I fought." Talking hurt even more than breathing. Ross didn't recognize his own voice. "Please."

Ross heard Luis draw in an unsteady breath. "You know I don't want to hurt you." There was a silence. Ross hoped Luis was thinking of what would be done to him at dawn. "All right."

Ross tipped his head back, giving Luis easy access to his throat. He was afraid, but the fear felt distant and small, smothered under a crushing, numb exhaustion. If there was anything else he could have done, he was too tired to think of it.

He did regret that he couldn't at least die outside, under the sky. He tried to imagine himself into a desert night, but his mind went straight to the image he'd called up so many times since his capture: sitting on his bed with Mia and Jennie holding his hands, looking up through the skylight at the stars blazing white in a perfect night sky.

Cloth rustled. He braced himself, but the burn of Luis's fingers across his throat made him flinch. Luis jerked his hand back.

"Do it," Ross whispered.

The cell was silent except for Luis's long sigh. Then he pressed his hand into the side of Ross's neck. It burned like it was made of flame.

In Ross's mind, Jennie and Mia held his hands tight. He clenched his teeth, forcing himself not to move as he dragged in a long, harsh breath. It would be over soon. Another breath. That one didn't hurt quite as much. The third breath didn't hurt at all. His skin burned where Luis's hand rested, but the inside of his throat felt as if he'd taken a gulp of cool water. His breathing no longer struggled.

Luis took his hand away.

Ross tried a deep breath, and winced. His broken ribs were still excruciatingly painful. He could only take shallow breaths. But he could breathe.

He opened his eyes. Luis's eyes were wide, his forehead dappled with sweat. He rubbed the fingers of his bare hand together. "That felt different. It felt... Did you get hit in the throat?"

"Yeah." Ross was still short of breath, but his voice sounded like himself again. "It's better."

"It was like I could feel inside your body. I knew when I had to take my hand away." Luis leaned forward. "Where else are you hurt?"

Ross indicated his swollen forearm. His hand was mottled purple, each finger like an overstuffed sausage.

Luis rubbed his forehead. "I don't know about this. I've only ever been able to hurt people. Maybe we're both imagining things."

Ross wasn't imagining the air that moved so easily in and out of his throat, though the skin still burned where Luis had touched it. "Try. Can't get worse."

Luis reached through the bars, and set his fingers lightly on the black bruise over the break. It was like having five hot coals held to his arm, but the sensation that spread from there was like cool water flowing under his skin.

"The bone's in the wrong place," Luis muttered. He reached out with his gloved hand and twisted Ross's forearm. To Ross's surprise, it didn't hurt. Luis continued moving Ross's arm until he said, with satisfaction, "There."

Luis let go, leaving five stinging, bloody fingerprints. But the terrible pain had faded to a dull ache, and the swelling was visibly going down.

"You didn't..." Ross took a shallow breath. "...know?"

Luis shook his head. "This must be what my power is supposed to do. I can feel it, now. But the king always had me practice on healthy criminals. He said they'd be best able to appreciate it."

Ross pushed up his shirt, his left hand clumsy. "Got kicked. Here. Broke my ribs."

Luis reached in more confidently, then stopped with his hand an inch away from Ross's side. "I think... No, I know it. Your skin is a barrier. I have to get through it to reach inside. If there's no injury, my power keeps burning, searching for something that isn't there. But I don't think I have to touch quite so much."

He laid one fingertip on Ross's side. Ross gritted his teeth as the burning pain slowly intensified.

"A little more." Luis let his other fingertips touch.

Ross was thankful when Luis did no more, though if it would ease that stabbing pain in his side, Ross would have invited him to lay down his entire hand. Once again, coolness flowed out from beneath the surface burn of his touch. Ross took a cautious, shallow breath, and then a deeper one. It didn't hurt. The relief of pain was as intense as the pain itself. Ross felt dizzy with it.

But Luis didn't move his hand. His forehead was creased in concentration. "It's not just the ribs. You're bleeding inside."

He pressed the first joints of his fingers into Ross's side. Ross forced himself not to pull away. Sweat beaded on Luis's forehead, then began to drip down. The cool sensation flowed outward from Ross's side, filling his chest, as if he'd taken a deep breath on a cold night.

"Got it." Luis sat back, panting, and wiped the sweat from his eyes with a shaking hand.

Ross felt better, stronger, clear-headed. He hadn't even realized how sick and faint he'd been until Luis had finished healing him.

He sat upright, forgetting the low ceiling. His head thunked into stone. "Ow." He reached up with his right hand and rubbed his scalp. His fingers ached as if someone had stamped on his hand, but he could use them. "That was amazing. Thanks."

For the first time, Ross saw Luis smile. Then it fell away. "I know that wasn't what you wanted me to do."

"I don't want that any more." Though the situation was almost as hopeless as it had been before, Ross's numbing misery had vanished. Almost hopeless wasn't completely hopeless. At least now he could go down fighting.

"Hey!" Ross exclaimed. "Can you heal my other arm?"

Luis put his fingers to the long scar inside Ross's forearm, and Ross gritted his teeth as blood began to well up. Then Luis snatched his hand away and shook his head.

"It doesn't seem to work on old injuries." Luis sounded disappointed. He peered down at Ross's side. His fingerprints stung and bled above the pale track of the bounty hunter's bullet. "Yeah, that scar didn't get fixed either."

Ross sat back with a sigh. He'd have had a better chance if he could use both hands, but at least he had the use of his right back. "Don't worry about it. What you did was plenty."

Luis brightened at that, but only for a moment. "I'd get you out if I could."

"I know." Ross hastily planned his next move. Just being able to think again, without being overwhelmed by pain and despair, was cheering. He indicated the throbbing burn on his throat. "It looks like you did your job. Tell the guards I passed out. When they come for me, I'll pretend I'm still hurt. But whatever happens, I won't let them take me alive. They'll never find out what you did for me."

And maybe I'll get another chance at Voske.

"All right. When you make your break for it, I'll act as surprised as everyone. I hope you escape! Later on, I can 'find out' that my real power is healing. And then I can 'figure out' that I accidentally healed you, but you didn't let on." Luis straightened up, looking less glum. "There's no one with healing powers in Gold Point. Maybe if I fix his arm, the king will find better things for me to do."

"I'm glad." Ross meant it. It made him feel better to think that he'd helped Luis, even if he couldn't help himself.

Luis started toward the door, then turned back. "Ross, I'm really sorry."

Ross heard an echo of his own voice after Opportunity Day, and his answer was the same as Luis's. "It's okay."

Ross curled up on the floor, pulling his arms and legs in tight so he wouldn't touch the walls. He heard Luis knock and get let out. With nothing to distract him, Ross could once again sense the walls and ceiling of the hell cell pressing in on him. Terror set his heart racing and his body trembling. His chest tightened painfully. He was encased in stone, already buried alive. He couldn't breathe.

No. He could breathe. Luis had healed him. There was the same amount of air in the cell that there had always been. Ross couldn't stop his heart from pounding, but he could remind himself that he wasn't suffocating. He was just afraid.

He lay still, fighting off the panic, hanging on to the hope he now had. When they came for him at dawn, he had to be ready to fight.

CHAPTER FORTY-EIGHT
GOLD POINT
KERRY

Kerry hid the backpacks in the garden tool shed, beneath an empty feed sack. "Kogatana, stay."

The rat obediently curled up behind a barrel.

Kerry eyed the wall a few hundred paces away. Could she really haul Ross over it before the sentries spotted them? It looked as high as the palace roof.

Well, she'd have to.

She dashed through the trees to the royal path. *Have to*, she thought. She didn't *have* to do anything. She could go back, eat the dinner Mom had ordered for her, get a good night's sleep, and tell Santiago in the morning that it was all a joke, ha ha... and then she'd head to the royal pavilion to watch the execution.

She'd just see how Ross was doing. Nothing would be irrevocable until she got him out of the cell. If he was half-dead, she could finish him off. Problem solved.

Promise broken.

At the hell cells, she waved to the night guards. "I'm here to talk to the prisoner."

"You might have to poke him awake," a guard said, laughing. "Luis just left."

"Didn't let us in to watch the fun, either," said another.

Kerry forced herself to laugh with them, cursing herself for not coming earlier. Whatever terrible shape Ross had been in before, it had to be twice as bad now.

She gave the guard a cheery smile, and held up her hand. "I've got poking equipment right here. If he can talk, I'll take him back to the palace so Father can observe my interrogation techniques. If not, I'll leave him here."

The guard unlocked the door. "Have fun, Princess."

Kerry stifled a shudder. Neither the guards nor Father had any trouble believing that she would enjoy tormenting a wounded, helpless prisoner. A month ago, she wouldn't have questioned it, either.

She walked into the silent cell. Beyond the grating, Ross was curled up in a ball, utterly still, his face hidden. His black hair fanned out on the stone floor. She could hear him breathing, shallow and fast, or she'd have thought he was already dead.

The words she'd spoken to Mia came back to her: *a hawk in a cage.*

"It's Kerry, Ross."

He didn't move. She crouched down and reached through the grate to grip his shoulder. His bones stood out stark and hard. Had Father starved him? He was shivering, reminding her of when she'd first met him, locked in another room without windows.

Kerry shook him lightly. "Look at me, Ross. I'm not going to hurt you."

He shifted a little, so she could see his face. At first he didn't look too bad: bruises and cuts, but no worse than if he'd been in a fight. Then he turned his head, blinking up at her with his long lashes stuck together with dried blood, and his hair fell away from a huge seeping wound on his throat. His shirt was more red than white, and his scarred left arm cradled his right arm against his chest. Both his forearms bore bloody fingerprint burns. And those were only the injuries she could see. What she couldn't see was probably even worse.

Nausea clawed at Kerry's throat. She stared hopelessly inside the cage. There was no way Ross could walk. She'd have to carry him over the wall, get him on a horse, tie him on... They'd never travel fast enough to escape pursuit, not even with an entire night's head start.

Santiago was right. Killing him would be a mercy. She couldn't imagine the Ross that Mia had described, who had danced and fought and mended engines. It had been Kerry's father who had taken him away from that life, tried to break his spirit and, when that failed, broken his body. And Kerry had come too late to save him.

She materialized a dagger in her hand. One blow to the heart. If Ross knew her intention, he'd probably thank her for it. But she couldn't bring herself to hurt him more than he'd been hurt already, unless she made absolutely sure that death would be welcome.

Kerry let the dagger vanish and laid her palm back down on his shoulder. He flinched, and she jerked her hand away.

"Listen to me, Ross. I came to get you out of here. I'll tell the guards I'm taking you to my father for interrogation. Don't believe it. I'll take you to the wall and carry you over." By the time she was done, her mouth had gone dry and her hands trembled. Every word carried her down this new road, into an unknown future.

Ross's eyelids flickered in surprise.

This is it. "Ross? Do you understand?"

"How did you get here?" His voice was pitched low, but stronger than she'd expected.

"Mia, Jennie Riley, and Yuki Nakamura helped me escape, in exchange for letting you go."

"Letting me go," he repeated flatly, clearly not believing it. "Why?"

Kerry didn't know where to start. Because she didn't want to be her father? Because Ross had saved Santiago? "Because I promised Mia."

"You promised Mia?"

Kerry was frustrated at the doubt in his voice. What did he have to lose? "Yeah. Actually, Mia said you might not trust me. She told me to tell you something that only you and she knew about, so you'd at least know that *she* trusted me. She said that the first time you met, she asked you to pick up a wrench. She specifically said in your left hand. Do you remember that?"

Kerry hoped she'd remembered it right. It didn't sound at all memorable.

Ross met her gaze straight on. To Kerry's amazement, he flashed a brief smile. "Yeah, I remember. Okay. Let's go."

Kerry unlocked the grill. Ross didn't move. She got her hands under his armpits and dragged him out, then braced her feet, bent her knees in the proper form, and hoisted him up onto her shoulders. He was lighter than she'd expected, but still a dead weight. This was going to be murder.

Ross lay limp as she banged on the door. It popped open, revealing three guards with identically surprised expressions.

"He's awake enough for questioning," she said.

"You don't have to carry him," a guard said hastily. "I'll take him."

Kerry gave her an icy glare. "Do I look weak?"

Three heads shook violently.

"You three stay at your post," Kerry commanded, tossing one the grill key. "The prisoner will be returned when Father and I are done with him."

The guards leaped back to attention. She tried to look casual as she headed for the garrison gate, but any watching soldiers had to be wondering why the princess was lugging a body. She hoped no one would dare send a messenger to the palace to inquire.

The gate guards saluted, and the gate clanged shut behind her. Kerry's back hurt already. Ross stopped shivering, and his breathing slowed. He'd just been afraid, not dying of shock. Kerry tried to be glad, but it was hard to appreciate anything with her back and knees on fire. The path to the garden, usually a brief, pleasant walk, seemed a hundred miles.

If she could barely carry him across level ground, how could she ever get him over a twenty-foot wall?

Once she was hidden within the trees, she headed straight for the garden shed. She knelt down, grateful to get the strain off her knees, and tried not to dump Ross on top of Kogatana, who had scurried up to greet her.

She laid him down as gently as she could, then dug into the medical supplies in her pack. "Where are you hurt?"

"It's not that bad." Ross stood up and stretched, wincing as he tilted his neck from side to side.

Kerry dropped a pressure bandage. "I carried you all the way here!"

"Sorry." He didn't sound at all regretful. "I had to make sure this wasn't one of your father's tricks."

"Santiago made it sound like you were half-dead."

"It looked worse than it was. I do have some burns, though." He indicated his neck. In the unlit shed, the bloody wound looked black.

Kerry breathed a sigh of relief. She wouldn't have to carry him over the wall! Not only that, but if Ross could walk under his own power, the entire plan had a far better chance of success.

Kogatana squeaked, as if she agreed, and trotted up to nibble on Ross's boots. "Yuki loaned you his rat?" he asked incredulously, petting her.

Kerry pulled out a bottle of disinfecting alcohol. "Yes. Hold still."

He knelt down and held his hair out of the way, so Kerry could clean the burn. His fist clenched around a handful of black hair as she pressed an alcohol-soaked pad into his neck, then relaxed when she took it away. She started to wind a bandage around his neck, but Ross put up a hand to stop her.

"Tape it on. I don't want anything wrapped around my throat."

As Kerry taped on a pad, she realized that he'd been using both hands. "Santiago said they broke your arm."

"Just bruised." Ross flexed his fingers for her inspection.

Maybe it was the dim light, but his hand didn't look half as swollen as it had in the hell cell. So much for the splint and sling she'd packed, not to mention the bottles and packets of witch hazel, goldenseal, comfrey, and willow bark. If Santiago hadn't exaggerated so much, she'd only have taken an emergency medical kit, and she'd have had room for four or five books, and maybe her second favorite gown.

Too late now.

"You were using your left hand, too," she said belatedly. "Do you really need the gauntlet?"

He held up his left hand, fingers curled inward. "I can use my hand more than I let on. But I can't grip with it. I only got the gauntlet recently, though. I can get to Las Anclas without it."

"You don't have to. I got it for you." Kerry slid his backpack toward him. "Your pack, too."

"Thanks." Ross strapped on the gauntlet. "So what's the plan?"

"I was going to carry you over the wall, then bring the horses to you. But we can save time if you crawl through the Joshua Tree forest. I'll meet you on the other side. Our only chance is to get as far as we can before Father realizes we're gone."

"How are you getting out?" Ross asked.

"I'm the crown princess. Nobody questions me."

Ross spoke softly, as if to himself. "That's right. They don't." He rummaged in his pack. "Oh, good. You got this." He brandished a slide rule. "I have a better idea."

Kerry gave him a skeptical look. "You have a better idea? And it involves your slide rule. You're going to *math* us out of here?"

"No." Ross tapped the slide rule against his palm. "I've been planning this for a while. I thought I'd need an army, though. But we have something better than an army."

"What's that?"

"You," Ross replied.

"What are you talking about?" asked Kerry.

"We're going to blow up the dam."

Kerry gasped. "You're out of your mind. It's got an entire company guarding it. Plus the maintenance workers."

"You can order them all to leave."

"It's four hours in the wrong direction."

Ross spoke with more confidence than she'd ever heard from him before. "If the dam goes, the river will flood the power station. The power goes out for the entire city. The armory is on higher ground, but the gunpowder is stored in the basement, and it'll all be ruined. If we blow up the dam, there won't be any pursuit. And Voske won't be making war on anyone for a long time."

It was the longest speech Kerry had ever heard from Ross. He'd obviously thought it through, but she couldn't imagine blowing up the dam. It had taken ten years to build. The power plant fed by the water from the dam had taken another ten years. And Ross was proposing destroying them both in a single night.

"How would you even do that?"

"Santiago said there's a road under construction between this dam and the one they're building in those mountains over there." He pointed to the east. "I've been hearing explosions the whole time I've been here. If there's explosions, there's explosives. I'm a prospector. I know how to blow things up."

Kerry glanced at the slide rule again. Now it made sense. "If you flood the town, innocent people will drown."

"No one will drown," Ross replied. "You'll order everyone out of the power plant. Except for the garrison, your entire southern end is raised farmland. By the time the water hits the town itself, it'll have spread out so much that it won't be more than a few inches deep."

"You really have planned this," she said, amazed.

"It was a way…" He stopped, then said shortly, "It was a way to keep from going crazy. But I never figured out how to deal with the guards."

Kerry opened her mouth to make another objection, but she couldn't think of one. It was disconcerting to have her helpless prisoner taking over her plan, and proposing a much bigger and more dangerous one. But she was also reluctant to damage Gold Point.

I'm no longer the princess of Gold Point, she thought. *If the dam breaks, the army will be too busy for pursuit. And Santiago won't be ordered to come after me…*

"All right," Kerry said. "You take the packs. I'll get the horses."

Ross didn't move. "If you're bringing horses, I want you to get my burro, too."

"*Your* burro?"

He nodded. "He got taken from me when…when I first came near Gold Point. He's in the corral for the palace work horses, with the other burros. You won't have any trouble picking him out. He's the smallest one."

It would be hard enough getting the horses out. Why would a princess have any need of a burro, let alone any particular one?

"We don't have time for that," Kerry said impatiently. "Leave him. He'll be fine. Work animals are treated well here."

"I know. But I want him back. I've had him my whole life."

The desperation in his tone reminded Kerry of Yuki's half-threat, half-plea to her to send back Kogatana.

Ross saved Santiago, she reminded herself. *Several times over. I owe him.*

"Okay, fine," said Kerry. "I'll get your burro, and I'll get rid of the guards by the dam and everyone at the power plant. Meet me there."

"Got it." Ross slung both the packs over his back, checked for sentries, ran low to the wall, and swarmed up and over in the space of two breaths, leaving Kerry alone with Kogatana.

What had Santiago been thinking, claiming Ross couldn't walk? Then she remembered that Ross had escaped from the scouts while he was blind. He was clearly a whole lot tougher than he looked. *Yeah, real weak, Father.*

But here was another nasty thought. Ross could decide to run for Las Anclas alone, leaving her with no head start, no supplies, and all her bridges burned behind her.

Mia had trusted her to free Ross. Now she had to trust him.

At the royal stable, everyone was asleep except the night guard and the head groom. Kerry gulped in a breath and marched into the office. They both leaped to attention.

"I need horses saddled for a night ride," she said imperiously. "Owen, Bridget, Fiona, and I are taking a moonlight ride to…" What would be scenic at night? "Saffron Hill, to see the bright-moths dance."

"I'll saddle the princesses' and prince's horses," said the groom.

Kerry bit her lip. She did not want three fat, elderly horses suitable for little kids. "They want to ride like grownups. I want…"

She was going to have to make a whole new life for herself. If she chose a good breeding herd, she'd have valuable stock wherever she went. She'd need three mares and a stallion who had proven their fertility, but were young enough to have plenty of breeding years left.

In a burst of rebellion, Kerry opened her mouth to name Coronet, her father's silver stallion, then snapped it shut again. She couldn't bring herself to dare. But her own horse, Nugget, was a stallion, and he'd sired two foals already. If she wanted to breed him, she should choose mares who got along well with him and weren't closely related to him. Sean's horse, silver Sally, would do. She'd had three fine foals, and she was gentle. Ross could ride her.

"I want Sally and Nugget. And…" Better take an alpha mare. She'd always admired the beautiful bronze Tigereye. And for the last mare… Kerry grinned to herself. She'd get five horses for the price of four. "Tigereye and Penny."

The head groom didn't snap to do her bidding. "Penny is pregnant. You know how touchy these mares get late in their term. I wouldn't put the little princesses on her. How about Topaz?"

Kerry glared at him. "Bridget is thirteen, and she specifically asked for Penny. Do you doubt her ability to handle that horse for a short ride?"

"No! I only… I'll go saddle her."

Reluctantly, he moved to obey. Kerry followed, chatting about how nice it would be to shake off the dust of Las Anclas with a good ride. She pointed out the prettiest saddles, with handsome saddlebags attached. And while she sent the poor groom back three times for different bridles, she slipped trail rations into the saddlebags, then smoothed the caparisons over them to hide the bulges. Water, they could find, now that the rains had come, but fodder would be scarce in the desert.

Kerry clicked her tongue, as if she'd suddenly remembered something. "I almost forgot! Fiona wanted me to bring one of the burros. The littlest one."

"A burro?" a groom echoed incredulously.

Kerry gave him a murderous glare. "Yes. The littlest one. Fiona thinks he's cute." She snapped her fingers. "What are you waiting for? Get him!"

The groom hurriedly fetched a small, scruffy-looking burro. "This one, Princess?"

"Yes." She certainly hoped it was the right one. If it wasn't, Ross could go back to the corral himself, as far as she was concerned.

To her relief, Nugget wasn't in a touchy mood. She mounted him and led the mares and the burro, certain that the grooms would start discussing her high-handed ways once she was out of earshot. Well, by tomorrow she wouldn't be a princess any more—she'd either be riding for the west, or dead. She might as well enjoy handing out orders while she still could.

The palace lights shone peacefully through the garden trees, and the street lights cast a pretty purple glow on the starless sky. It would be terrible when the entire city went dark.

But at least everybody will be safe, she thought as she peered up at the nursery windows. Safe…without her. She would never see Fiona again, or Owen or Bridget. Would they miss her the way she missed Sean? Nobody had missed Deirdre much, because she'd gotten so bossy and moody and mean after she'd Changed.

Is that how they think of me?

At least her half-siblings would be safe from Father's anger, because they were his children. Mom, too, would be safe, protected by her unique power. Father would never give that up.

Except for Santiago, there was no one else Kerry was close to. No friends, no favorite sparring partners, not even a tutor of whom she was particularly fond. Certainly none who was particularly fond of her. She'd had more personal conversations with Mia than she'd had with any girls in Gold Point.

Nobody knew her as anything but *the princess*. And she'd never tried to be anything else.

The gate guards saluted. She was already there—she must be way more tired than she'd thought! Startled, Kerry tried to remember the excuse she'd made up for the gate guards, but her mind went blank. She scrambled for a new one. Moonlight ride with her siblings? But where were they? Taking the horses and one little burro to stretch their legs? That made *no* sense.

She lifted her chin and rode through the gate, her heartbeat thundering in her ears. Nobody spoke. If they wondered, they kept it to themselves.

Kogatana scampered ahead, vanishing then returning, her little nose twitching as if to say all was well. Now that it was quiet, exhaustion began to press on Kerry. The slow rhythm of the ride acted on her like chamomile tea, and she kept catching herself dozing off. Her entire body ached, the day's tiredness made worse by carrying Ross out of the garrison. She wished she'd soaked longer in the bath…Ross had better not run off with the pack containing her pillow…

The power plant's lights forced her to wakefulness again, though her eyes burned. She wished she'd brought a flask of hot coffee with her—and some of that lovely dinner Mom had left in her room. But her choice had been to bathe or eat—she hadn't had time for both. And she couldn't stand the thought of not bathing for twelve days. Her clothes would probably rot off.

She tied up the horses, then rode to the power plant, her story ready.

A sentry called, "Halt!"

"It's all right," Kerry replied, forcing her voice to cheerfulness. "It's Princess Kerry."

"Princess! You're back!"

"I am. My father has decided to step up the construction of Dam Two. He wants everybody out of the plant and at Dam Two by morning, so we can get an early start."

"But, Princess—"

"Now. The sentries, too. They need to guard the technicians. The second shift is right behind me. They'll take over as soon as you all leave."

"But—"

Kerry strove to sound like her father. "Brief the head technicians, now."

"That's why I'm trying to tell you, Princess. They're all up at the dam, on the king's own orders." His earnest expression changed to puzzlement. "You did know that, right?"

In a heartbeat that confusion would change to suspicion. "Of course I knew that. I meant the junior technicians left in charge." Kerry snapped her fingers. "If you hurry, you'll get some decent rest before morning."

The guard's face cleared, and he saluted. He ran to the power plant, and soon emerged with a handful of technicians and two guard squads. They streamed up the road toward Dam Two.

As soon as they were out of sight, Kerry retrieved the mares, then turned up the steep mountain road toward the dam.

I can do this. It's going to work.

Her exultant mood lasted until she glimpsed the dam between ridges and hills, looming impossibly large in the moonlight. The moon was dangerously low in the sky; it was mere hours before dawn.

Where was Ross? There was no sign of him.

She kept one sword at the ready as the horses plodded up the steep road. At the dam, she again left the animals out of sight, and rode up to the floodlit sentry station.

The guard quickly ran to do her bidding. But time stretched on, and instead of a neat line of guards herding their technicians, the guard returned alone, looking annoyed and frustrated. "I'm so sorry, Princess, but the technicians are refusing to leave without orders directly from the king."

"My orders *are* directly from the king." Kerry fought to keep control of her voice. She couldn't get shrill. She was the princess. The heir to Gold Point.

The guard looked apologetic. "Can you tell them that, Princess? I think it's just me they don't believe."

Kerry made a move to dismount, then sat back. She needed the height, and anyway, she was afraid her legs would give out. Already her head swam unpleasantly.

"Send them out," she commanded.

A mob of frowzy-headed, red-eyed technicians marched out, grumbling and shuffling mutinously. Kerry snapped her spine straight, squared her shoulders, and repeated the speech she'd given to the sentry.

The technicians looked at each other, then a tall woman spoke. "Princess, the king himself ordered us up here. He said we don't leave till we've finished repairing the intake."

Kerry had no idea what an intake was. "He sent me with a new order. Never mind the intake. You all need to leave now."

They didn't budge. The tall woman obstinately repeated, "The king said we don't leave. Princess."

"He's riding right behind me."

Another technician spoke up. "Then we'll wait."

Kerry ground her teeth. The moon was beginning to set. It was far too late to abandon the idea of blowing up the dam and flee across the desert. Ross's escape would be discovered the moment the sky blued. The entire army would come after them.

"I just escaped from Las Anclas. You did hear that I got captured?" she added sarcastically.

"Very glad to see you safe," a technician said hastily.

"I'm glad to be back," she replied, trying to stay regal. Calm. In control. "But the news I brought my father was not good. There is an army on the march toward Gold Point. Father wants you out of here, and reporting to Dam Two now. South Company Two is on the way here, with your replacements."

"But he didn't send a message," the woman said.

"And we're not done with the intake," a man in the back said. "He won't like us leaving it unfinished."

The first woman repeated stubbornly, "The king *always* sends a message."

"*I* am the message." Kerry took a deep breath. "I didn't want to have to say this, but he gave me strict orders. If anyone is here when he arrives, their heads will be on pikes by dawn." She forced herself to raise a hand toward the guard. "Ready weapons!"

"Never mind, Princess," the woman exclaimed. "Forgive me! It's just… highly irregular…"

They were all muttering by now, but they were moving. They were moving!

Kerry watched them vanish down the path, guards going first with torches, the techs straggling. If anyone in the city looked up at the mountains, they would see those torches. If anyone decided to send a messenger to confirm Kerry's orders, everything would fall apart. It was all so precarious, and she was so tired.

Where was Ross?

CHAPTER FORTY-NINE
GOLD POINT DAM
ROSS

Ross leaned against a boulder and looked up at the stars. They weren't as bright as they should be, because of the lights around the dam, but at least they were visible. Maybe if he watched them a little longer, he'd stop feeling so lightheaded and strange, as if his feet weren't touching the ground. Even the pain of his burns felt distant and unreal.

He couldn't believe Kerry had let him go.

He couldn't believe he was really free.

He couldn't believe he had tried to kill himself.

Pull yourself together, he ordered himself. *You still have work to do. You can think about that other stuff later.*

Maybe he'd feel better if he ate something. He spotted a prickly pear cactus, plucked a fruit, stripped off the spiny peel, and popped the fruit in his mouth. He made himself focus on its juicy texture and sweet flavor, and the hard smoothness of its inedible seeds.

He hadn't had a prickly pear since he'd walked blind toward Las Anclas. He remembered fumbling with the peel, and dropping a pear and having to feel around for it. He'd been so clumsy back then. After wearing it constantly for more than a month, the gauntlet almost felt like part of his hand.

Ross felt steadier after he'd eaten. He ached with exhaustion all the way down to his bones, but he'd be able to fight if he had to. He had a hard task ahead of him, but he could do it—as long as Kerry did her part.

Straightening his spine, he continued through the scrub toward the dam. A voice startled him. He ducked behind a bushy mesquite.

A whole lot of feet were tramping down the nearby road. Kerry had kept her promise.

"...I don't agree. We should send a messenger to the king."

"Do *you* want to run down the mountain at night?" another jeered.

"I'd rather do that than get my head piked," the first person retorted.

"Do you seriously think the princess would go against the king's orders?" a third person asked incredulously.

"Prince Sean did."

A chorus of hisses broke out, shushing the speaker.

Once they were gone, Ross bolted up through the scrub. He found Kerry pacing beside her golden stallion, clutching Kogatana.

"There you are," she exclaimed sharply. "What took you?"

"Sorry." Ross still didn't understand why she was helping him, but he knew she was risking her life to do it. "The people you sent away walked past where I was hiding. We'll have to hurry. One of them wants to send a messenger to Voske."

Kerry lashed out with her hand, sending dirt flying up in a spray as if she'd hit the ground with a whip. "This was a terrible idea! We could have had a head start by now. If they send that messenger, the entire garrison will be here in two hours. We have to run *now*."

"If we blow up the dam, no one will come after us."

Kerry grabbed the stallion's reins. "The horses and your burro are this way."

Ross didn't budge. He wasn't giving up the chance to keep Voske away from Las Anclas. "I'm blowing up the dam. It'll go faster if you stay and help. If you don't, please leave Rusty here for me."

He hurried to the supply shed, which was still lit. The air inside was rich with the smell of fertilizer. There were more than enough barrels of explosive to crack the dam.

Mia would love this. He wished there was some way he could show her what was sure to be a bigger explosion than any she'd ever seen. He'd just have to describe it as best he could.

Grinning to himself, he loaded the final barrel on to a push cart and hauled it outside. He almost bowled over Kerry, with Kogatana trotting at her heels.

"What can I do?" Kerry asked.

"Load another cart and follow me."

As he set up the explosives at the base of the dam, Ross wondered again how this had all come about. He hardly even knew where to start with his questions.

"Kerry, Santiago told me what happens when people run away from Gold Point. Is he going to be all right? What about your family?"

"The royal family has different rules. When Sean disappeared, Father questioned his mother, but that was it. He didn't even exile her from the palace. Mom and my half-sibs will be fine. And I made sure that Father thinks I don't care about Santiago anymore."

"How did you do that?"

"I left a note saying I'd fallen in love with you."

Ross almost dropped a coil of wire. "What? Seriously?" Then an even more alarming thought occurred to him. "You haven't, right?"

Kerry shot him an appalled look, then snorted. "When I had Santiago? Not a chance!"

"Good," Ross muttered. "Here, hold this." He shoved the wire at her, hoping that would end the entire subject.

The moon had set by the time Ross had finished setting the last charge. He stepped back to survey his work. He felt dizzy with elation.

"We did it," he started to say.

He was interrupted by a chorus of bells, clanging up into the silent night from the city below.

Kerry's eyes were huge and black in the glaring electric lights. "They sent that messenger. Father is raising the garrison."

"Come on!" Ross was already running uphill.

Kerry bolted after him, clutching Kogatana. She had hidden the horses away from the blast radius, sheltered from any possible rock falls.

He only had time for a quick ruffle of Rusty's fur before he dove down to complete his final task. Rusty's bray sounded much happier than the last time Ross had heard it. He grinned, but didn't stop working.

His fingers trembled as he finished connecting the wires. The bells were still ringing in Gold Point. When Ross looked down, more and more lights were blinking on in the city.

Ross set his hands to the plunger and pushed. He threw himself flat as the ground jolted like an earthquake. A deafening crack split the air. He jammed his thumbs in his ears, covered his eyes with his fingers, and buried his face in his backpack. Gravel and dirt rained around. The shockwave followed a heartbeat later, blowing back his hair in a hot wind.

He glanced at Kerry, who lay with her arms outstretched. Debris bounced off the invisible shield she'd raised. Kogatana had burrowed into her shirt.

A jagged black line appeared in the dam. Massive slabs of concrete ground against each other as the crack in the dam widened. Water began to seep through. Ross watched, biting his lip. Then, with an enormous crash, a huge chunk of concrete peeled off from one side of the crack. Water smashed through, a furious cataract racing toward the power plant below. More cracks spiderwebbed out.

Before the wave could reach the plant, the rest of the dam collapsed with another jolting quake. Boulders the size of houses spun and smashed their way down the mountain, water spilling over the banks of the river. The power plant was drowned in the flood.

Ross turned to look down at Gold Point. In an instant, every light went out. The city vanished into darkness.

He lay listening to the new river smashing its way down, barely audible over the ringing in his ears. He wished he could see Voske's face when the power went out. Better yet, when Voske realized who had done it. Ross bet he wouldn't be smiling then.

CHAPTER FIFTY
DESERT
KERRY

Santiago marched out between guards toward the execution platform, his hands empty, his face bleak.

"Santiago!" Kerry yelled, but he couldn't hear. She tried to run to him, but she couldn't move.

"Kill her," Father ordered. He stood on the dais, with the royal family lined up behind him. "Kill them both."

"Kerry!"

She sat bolt upright, her heart thundering. Where was she?

"Kerry!" Ross shouted. "Roll!"

Kerry threw herself to the side. A cougar thudded down on her blanket. It loomed before her, pale in the starlight, tensed to pounce. She could have touched its yellowed fangs.

Still lying in the sand, Kerry created a whip and cracked it across the face. The great cat screamed in pain, jerking its head aside, and lashed out with a huge clawed paw. Its paw bounced and scraped against the shield she'd created in her left hand, slamming her elbow painfully into the ground.

Kerry struck out with her whip again, opening a line of red in the tawny fur of the cougar's neck. With a final scream and a flick of its tail, it bounded away up the arroyo, sending rocks skittering down.

Ross stood panting, a bloodied knife in one hand and his gauntlet still raised to block. A second cougar raced after the first, then both vanished into the shadows.

Kerry dissolved the weapons, aware of a raw sting in her throat as she ran to the plunging horses.

Ross had already reached his frantically braying donkey and threw his arms around its neck. "Shh, Rusty, it's okay."

Kerry hurried to Nugget, whose tail was snapping nervously. Soothing words and a firm hand got Nugget and Tigereye calmed down. Penny and

Silver followed the dominant horses' lead and also quieted, only their ears flicking. Soon the horses stood still, their coats shimmering in the starlight.

Kerry's breath condensed in plumes of mist. She returned to the campsite and warmed her icy hands over the coals. Kogatana stuck her cold nose into Kerry's side.

"Some lookout you are," Kerry told the rat, her voice ragged. Her heart was still thumping against her ribs.

Ross sat beside her. "She was asleep. I'm the one who missed them."

The sky was brilliant with stars everywhere but the east, which was clouded by the departing storm. It was a few hours before dawn. "Why didn't you wake me up for the second watch?"

"I couldn't sleep." His hand brushed the bandage on his neck.

Kerry had gotten badly sunburned once. She'd tossed and turned all night, unable to bear even the weight of a sheet on her blistered skin. She could imagine how much pain Ross must be in, with the raw patches on his throat and arms and side that she helped him clean every night. "Because of your burns?"

"Yeah..." Ross started to lower his head, then pushed his hair back and looked straight at her. She still wasn't used to him making eye contact; it was startling every time. "No. I have nightmares, too."

"Nightmares are for children," Kerry retorted angrily.

His gaze fell away. They sat in silence, except for the distant shriek of a night bird, and closer by, the gulping of frogs in rain puddles.

"I dreamed that Father was going to execute Santiago and me," she admitted. "It felt so real. I wish I could know he was safe."

"He protected your father when...um...when I went for him," Ross said. "I don't think the king will hurt him."

His reassurance did nothing to satisfy her. Every muscle was tense, and no matter where she turned, she always felt like there was something creeping up behind her. At any moment, Father might crest the hill behind them, or show up around a bend.

"When was the last time you went to scout?" Kerry demanded.

"Maybe half an hour ago. There's still no sign of pursuit. Listen, we're wide awake and so are the horses. We might as well get an early start."

If it wasn't for the horses, Kerry was certain that Ross would have tried to make the entire journey without resting at all. He wasn't afraid of Father; he was worried about Mia and Jennie and Yuki. The blood had drained from his face when she'd told him they'd been caught letting her go.

That was the only reason Kerry was even considering stopping by Las Anclas. She too wanted to make sure Mia was all right. On the other hand...

"Are you *sure* Preston won't throw me back in jail?" Kerry asked. It was about the tenth time they'd had that conversation, but she couldn't stop herself.

"You set me free. You helped blow up the dam. You saved Las Anclas. You'll be a hero." Ross sounded as tired of the topic as Kerry felt. "But if you're scared—"

"I'm not scared!" Kerry snapped.

Ross didn't answer. The words echoed in Kerry's mind until she realized what a fool she was making of herself.

"You can go anywhere you want," Ross said at last. "But if you do come to Las Anclas, I promise to protect you."

"*You* can protect *me* from Tom Preston and an entire town that thinks I'm the enemy?"

The question came out in a jeer, but Ross answered her seriously. "Yes. I'll tell them what you did."

"*If* I stopped by Las Anclas," Kerry began, ignoring Ross's frustrated sigh. "Would you and Mia consider coming with me, when I go?"

Ross's dark, startled eyes met hers. "What? Why?"

"Because Father's coming to kill you!" Her voice rose in a shout. "If you're all going to die anyway, then everything I did was for nothing!"

"I honestly don't think he'll attack Las Anclas any time soon," Ross said.

Kerry couldn't suppress a gulp of hysterical laughter when she recognized his soothing tone as the one he used to talk to his donkey. She'd lost all her self-control once she'd left Gold Point, as if it had been drowned in the flood. She was a disgrace.

Ross went on, in that same gentle voice, "Thanks for asking. I know how much you gave up to let me go. But if you're right, and the town needs defending, I have to stay and defend it."

"Fine," Kerry said ungraciously. "Then let's get going."

After they fed and watered the horses, they mounted in silence and set out for the west.

When her tears started again, at least it was still dark.

CHAPTER FIFTY-ONE
LAS ANCLAS
ROSS

Ross had been hearing chimes since noon. He'd felt the rage of the obsidian trees, too, undimmed by the passage of time, and had to quickly build up the wall in his mind. But nothing had prepared him for the elation like a sunburst behind his ribs at the first sight of Las Anclas.

"It's Ross!" Henry Callahan shouted from the wall.

Brisa squealed, "With the princess! Kerry came back!"

The 'stranger at the gate' bell toll stopped.

The gates swung open, revealing a huge crowd. Some glared at Kerry, and others grinned. Ross heard the roar of voices as he scanned the town. It seemed like years had passed. The jacaranda trees lining the town square, that had been completely bare when he'd left, were covered in lavender blossoms. Gardens and window boxes overflowed with the flowers that grew after rain.

Mr. Preston dashed up, panting as if he'd run all the way across town. Before he could speak, Sheriff Crow came tearing up in a rush of wind, her braids flying behind her. "Is Voske on your tail?"

"No. There wasn't any pursuit." Ross had to stop himself from snatching at the sheriff's sleeve. "What happened to Mia and Jennie and Yuki?"

"They're fine," Sheriff Crow replied. "They're in jail, but the deal was that they'd be released if you came back."

Ross's head swam with relief. He felt as if he'd been holding his breath for the entire journey, and could finally relax.

"What's Voske's girl doing here?" Mr. Preston asked suspiciously.

Kerry sat very straight, her profile tense and wary.

"She's with me," Ross said. "She's not the enemy."

The onlookers broke into a confused uproar. Ross's heart thudded as he looked at the crowd, which was getting bigger by the second. But he'd promised to protect Kerry. "Everyone! Listen to me!"

The crowd fell absolutely silent. Hundreds of people stared at him. His mouth went dry, but he forced the words out. "Kerry broke me out of jail, against Voske's orders. She helped me blow up the dam and flood the power plant. We saw the lights go out in Gold Point."

As 'broke him out of jail' and 'blew up the dam' echoed back and forth through the crowd, scowls turned to amazement, then to joy and relief.

Ross added, as loudly as he could, "Gold Point has no electricity, and if the water went as far as I think it did, they won't have much gunpowder, either. Las Anclas is safe now. Because of Kerry."

To Ross's relief, the crowd's focus shifted from him to her.

Brisa cheered. "Yeah, Kerry! I *knew* you were awesome!"

Scattered cheers broke out. A little smile brightened Kerry's face. *She* clearly didn't mind hundreds of people staring at her.

Sheriff Crow beckoned to Ross. "Let's go to the jail."

Ross nudged Sally, who lashed her silver tail, forcing people back. Then she swung it up to smack him across the back of the head. Scattered giggles echoed through the crowd.

"Sally," Kerry said warningly. She caught the reins as Ross slid off.

They started up Main Street. Ross left Sheriff Crow, Mr. Preston, and Kerry to a question-and-answer about the dam, and fell back to walk with his hand on Rusty's soft neck. The burro brayed happily and nuzzled him, causing more laughter. Ross didn't care. Kerry could keep her showy, bad-tempered horses. He was glad to have his own Rusty back.

At the jail, they handed off the animals to delighted volunteers. Ross leaped up onto the jail's porch, then froze in the doorway, his heart juddering at the darkness and the close air. He could smell the granite of the floor, like the granite of the hell cell.

"What's going on?" Jennie called out.

Mia's voice chimed in, "It must be Ross. Ross! Is that you?"

Their voices pulled him inside. Mia and Jennie stood in an amazing clutter of engines and machines and tools. It looked like Mia's entire cottage had been moved into the cell.

Mia hurled herself against the bars, laughing. "You're here! I knew you'd come back." She caught Ross's hand, then let go as the cell door swung open.

She leaped out and grabbed him in a hug. Her glasses banged into his cheek as she kissed him fervently. He kissed her back even more fervently. It was the moment he'd been imagining the entire time he'd been trapped in Gold Point. He never wanted to let her go.

Ross didn't know how much time passed before she loosened her grip, and there was Jennie. Without even thinking, he reached up, grabbed Jennie's shoulders, and pulled her in for a kiss. Her lips were warm against his, and her braids fell down and brushed his cheeks. His entire body caught fire.

It was only when they broke apart that Ross realized that it had been their first kiss. Jennie looked as light-headed as he felt. Mia was laughing.

When Kerry spoke behind him, he jumped. He'd forgotten that anyone else was there. "You…and *Jennie?*"

The three of them nodded. Mia said, "Oh yeah. I guess I never mentioned that." Beaming at Kerry, she added, "I knew I could trust you. Thank you."

Kerry gave her a little smile. "Thank *you*. I'm glad you're all right. Then she turned to Yuki. "Here's Kogatana. I'll miss her."

The rat gave a happy squeak and leaped at him. Yuki caught her in midair and held her close so she could lick his face. He looked relieved, but not as happy as Ross would have expected.

"Thanks, Yuki," Ross said. "Thanks for everything. Especially the night I was kidnapped. Thanks for listening when I told you to run."

"Thanks for *running away and abandoning you?*" Yuki said incredulously. "I've regretted that every single day since I did it. Mia never would have left you."

"Yeah, I know," Ross replied. "Thanks for saving her life."

Yuki looked surprised, then thoughtful. "I'm glad you're back." He walked out, holding his rat tight.

Ross could feel the pressure of the jail's heavy ceiling and thick walls. "Let's get out of here."

Mr. Preston was waiting outside, along with the mayor, Felicité, and what looked like half the population of Las Anclas.

"Welcome back, Ross." The mayor added, more to the crowd than to Kerry, "Welcome back, Princess."

"Dad!" Mia shouted, and let go of Ross to launch herself at her father.

Dr. Lee squeezed through the crowd to hug his daughter. "We'll have to get your equipment back out of your cell. And after we finally got it all in there, too!" Then his smile vanished into the professional scrutiny of a doctor. "Ross? What happened to your throat?"

Ross flinched, tilting his head forward so his hair covered the bandage. "Someone's Change power. It's like a burn."

Dr. Lee beckoned. "Come to the surgery, please."

The mayor broke in. "We will need you, doctor. I'm about to call an emergency council meeting."

"I'll be along," Dr. Lee said. "Ross comes first."

"Wait." Ross looked for Kerry, whom he had promised to protect. She was in a fighting stance, lightly balanced on the balls of her feet, with her hands open, ready to create weapons. His stomach clenched at the thought of again addressing a crowd.

Remembering how Mia had stood up for him when he'd first come to Las Anclas, he turned to the defense chief and the mayor. "Kerry's a guest. My guest. And I'm a citizen, so that means she has guest privilege."

The mayor inclined her head. "That's very gracious of you, Ross. But not necessary. You have vouched for her deeds, and here you are, as proof of her sincerity." She addressed Kerry, but in a voice which carried to the intently listening crowd. "I consider you a guest of the entire town. Kerry Voske, welcome to Las Anclas."

Kerry lifted her head proudly, but Ross saw her throat bob as she swallowed. Her voice rose high and clear above the murmuring crowd. "That's not my name any more. You all know who my father is, but I have a mother, too. Her name is Min Soo Cho. And from now on, my name is Kerry Ji Sun Cho."

As a chorus of voices rose up again, Mr. Preston stepped forward. "Let's continue this conversation somewhere more private."

"Please wait at my house," the mayor suggested. "I am sure you're in need of rest and refreshment."

Mr. Preston nodded. "We want to thank you, Kerry. That's all."

Kerry followed them, accompanied by Sheriff Crow.

Mia and Jennie closed protectively on either side of Ross, Mia fiercely rubbing tears from her eyes, and Jennie smiling in a way that Ross hadn't seen since the night of the dance.

He was unable to utter a word. In all the time he'd been held prisoner, he'd always believed they'd remembered him, and that they would rescue him if they could. But he'd never imagined they would risk everything in their lives, just for him.

Jennie's strong, callused fingers squeezed his right hand gently then shifted to rest on his waist. Mia's small palm slid over his left hand, patting the gauntlet before she tucked her arm under Jennie's and grabbed his other side.

Mia tugged, Jennie shifted, and Ross wavered, almost off-balance, but only for a moment. One step, two, and the three of them found their rhythm.

CHAPTER FIFTY-TWO
LAS ANCLAS
KERRY

It was strange to get invited to the house that could have become Kerry's palace. It had a rose garden like Mom's, though smaller, full of thorny flowers taking up more than their fair share of precious water. Kerry wondered if the mayor candied the petals.

Here, like at Dr. Lee's, everyone took off their shoes at the door. The mayor invited them into a room with fussy carved furniture and an even fussier crystal chandelier. Kerry gingerly sat down in a chair cushioned in pink satin. Mom would have loved it. She set her pack at her feet and folded her hands in her lap the way Mom had taught her.

She'd claimed her mother's name, but she'd never see her mom again. Kerry's eyes prickled. Then she took a deep breath. She had to keep that thought for later. Crying in front of Tom Preston and Felicité would be the ultimate in humiliation.

"Would you care for lemonade?" the mayor asked.

Kerry hated lemonade. She was about to shake her head when the mayor went on, "Felicité? Remember, Clara is off duty."

Kerry thought of Mia crammed in that cell for two weeks, and said with her most polite smile, "I would love a glass. Thank you so much."

The sheriff also assented. Felicité gave them a perfect fake smile before heading for the kitchen.

Mr. Preston sat beside Kerry. "I didn't expect to see you back, but I confess I'm glad I was wrong."

I bet you are, Kerry thought. She hadn't forgotten how he'd hit her across the face, or threatened her with a firing squad.

He continued, "I know what it feels like to realize that everything you always thought was true was wrong. And what it feels like to want to make amends."

Kerry was used to thinking of him as the enemy interrogator, but she realized that he was being honest. And not only that, he was right.

Cautiously, she nodded.

"It must have been difficult and dangerous to free Ross. I appreciate that you took that risk for a citizen of Las Anclas. And helping him blow up the dam protects the entire town." Mr. Preston leaned forward, his brow furrowed, his gaze searching.

"There's something else you could do to protect this town, since you clearly want to," the mayor said with her lovely smile.

Kerry found herself smiling back. She hadn't thought past making sure Mia was all right, but now that the mayor had mentioned it, Kerry realized that she did want to protect the town. Maybe not everyone in it, but enough of them. And she knew what Mayor Wolfe was getting at.

"There's an old prospector, Prudence, in Gold Point," Kerry said. "She Changed a few years ago, at menopause. She got the power to see and hear through hawks. That's Father's secret."

The defense chief drew in a deep breath, and he and the mayor exchanged glances. The sheriff leaned back, her one normal eyebrow lifting.

"Pru can only use her Change power for a little while every day," Kerry explained. "And hawks only fly in the day. She has to be within a couple miles of them, so Father has to send Pru any time he wants to check on other towns. When she comes here to spy, she hides in the hills."

"Why didn't he know about our singing tree?" asked Sheriff Crow.

"They turn transparent sometimes," Kerry said. "It must have been invisible when her hawk flew over it. After the battle, Father commanded her to stay hidden above Las Anclas until Pru figured out how Ross had managed to defeat his elite attack squad. And Father knew when Ross was going to the ruined city because the hawks flew close enough for her to hear people talking about it."

Mr. Preston's heavy brows pushed together. "And that's how he spies on his own citizens?"

Kerry nodded. "Father encouraged my little siblings to make pets of the town gophers. It's become a fashion—everybody feeds them, and nobody dares trap or poison them. With all those fat, slow gophers to eat, there's hawks all over Gold Point."

Felicité appeared with a tray of glasses. She passed them out, setting Kerry's down last and with a little bang.

"Is anyone hungry?" asked the mayor. "We have some tea cakes, and there might be some smoked fish left."

The Sheriff declined, but Kerry said, with a bright smile to Felicité, "I would love some fish."

Felicité had just sat down. Her obliging expression didn't change as she rose and went out, but Kerry hoped she was boiling inside. *That's for Jennie,* she thought.

"Thank you, Kerry," Preston said. "That explains a number of things that have been puzzling us. So. You said you had to break Ross out of jail. I'd like to hear more about that."

Sheriff Crow held up her hand. "Let's hold it for the council."

Felicité reappeared with her tray of smoked fish. Kerry waited until Felicité had offered it around, again bringing Kerry's last. As Felicité sat down, Kerry said in her politest voice, "I would love a tea cake after all, if it's not too much trouble."

Felicité got up and headed out, with a tiny sigh. Mom was completely right. Courtesy was a weapon.

Kerry chatted politely until Felicité returned with a plate of tea cakes. *This is for Yuki,* she thought.

She said brightly, "One regret I have is that I couldn't bring back the horses I took. They were too tired to take on another journey. I'd like to pay for them instead. With this."

Kerry reached into her pack, and brandished her golden crown.

CHAPTER FIFTY-THREE
LAS ANCLAS
JENNIE

Jennie looked around the cell where she and Mia had lived for two miserable weeks. Finally, it was almost as bare as when they'd first been locked inside. She squatted to gather up the last tools.

The jail door opened, sending in a warm breeze. Mr. Vilas knocked on Sheriff Crow's door. The sheriff came out, then stood there without speaking.

"Got something to tell you." Mr. Vilas caught Jennie's eyes and gave his head a jerk toward the front door.

Jennie grabbed the half-empty box. She'd seen enough of Sheriff Crow and Mr. Vilas to know there was *something* going on between them, and she had no intention of being a witness to whatever romantic quarrel or making up—or worse, making out—was about to happen.

Sheriff Crow folded her arms across her chest, like a shield. "There's nothing private between us, Vilas. Finish packing your tools, Jennie."

Jennie began cramming tools into the kit as fast as she could.

Mr. Vilas leaned his rifle and backpack against the wall. "It'll take Voske years to rebuild. I don't think he'll be bothering you any, so I'm off."

"Thanks for staying till now," Sheriff Crow said.

"Listen, Elizabeth. I'm sorry I took that order from Preston. I'm sorry I didn't tell you about it. I don't want to get between Voske and Preston anymore."

"All right."

"I'm done with this town," Mr. Vilas went on. "I'm done with taking orders. From anyone. I'm going up north, to the mountains. Why don't you come with me?"

Jennie froze, praying that they would forget she was there. As the silence stretched, she wondered what Sheriff Crow was thinking. She couldn't possibly be tempted to go off with that man. Could she?

Sheriff Crow finally spoke. "Thanks. But no. My home is here."

Cloth rustled. "Take this."

Jennie had to look. The bounty hunter's weathered hand was outstretched, cupping a little beaded pouch. "If you ever need to find me, go north and show this around. I'll be wearing the other one."

The sheriff took the pouch. Jennie hastily looked away, feeling more like an intruder than ever.

The sound of footsteps prompted her to look up. Mr. Vilas was heading out the door. "Goodbye, Elizabeth."

"Goodbye, Furio." Sheriff Crow shut herself into her office.

Jennie couldn't get out of there fast enough. She felt bad for Sheriff Crow, but mostly she was relieved to have the bounty hunter gone for good.

She dropped off the tools at Mia's empty cottage. The windows were open, letting in rays of late afternoon sunlight. The Ranger candidates would be running the obstacle course right now. Her entire body knew it was practice time, but she had nowhere to be and nothing to do. The space behind her ribs hollowed out.

For lack of a better place to go, she headed home, wishing she could think about anything else besides the Rangers. But as she passed the surgery, she recalled her talks with Dr. Lee. If there was one thing he'd taught her, it was that denying the truth didn't work. She'd been banned from the Rangers for life. She couldn't pretend that hadn't happened.

Some things hurt, and you had to let them hurt.

She began to run, enjoying the rhythm of her feet hitting the ground. Not everything hurt. Ross was back. Jennie had saved Kerry's life, and in turn Kerry had saved Ross. Mia was happy again. Jennie's family was proud of her. Even more importantly, she could respect herself again.

Though she'd been banned from the Rangers, she hadn't been banned from teaching. In all the free time that used to belong to Ranger practice and patrol, she could contribute to the newspaper again—it had been months since her last article had been printed.

She considered headlines as she ran. *Heroes Hailed! Villain Voske Vanquished!* Maybe less alliteration. Ross would rather have his teeth pulled out than have the town read about him. But maybe Kerry would do an interview.

And there was the former princess herself, riding her magnificent golden stallion. Jennie raced up, wondering how much of a grudge Kerry still held for kidnapping her.

Kerry gracefully dismounted. "Jennie, I wanted to thank you for letting me go. I'm sorry you were locked up all that time on account of me. If there's anything I can do to repay you, just say the word."

It was the last thing Jennie had expected. "You brought Ross back.

That makes us even."

It came out sounding flatter than she meant. What would Voske do to Kerry if he ever caught up with her? Now she was in as much danger from Gold Point as anyone in Las Anclas.

Jennie tried again. "My parents are fixing dinner. Want to join us?"

Kerry gave Jennie a slightly forced smile. It was strange to see Kerry's pointed nose and prominent cheekbones, so like Paco's, but with such a different set of expressions. Jennie wondered if she would ever get used to the half-siblings' resemblance to Voske.

"Thanks," Kerry said. "But I already accepted an invitation from Brisa and Becky."

Jennie could tell Kerry was dying to get back on her horse and away, but she couldn't resist offering her hand to the stallion. He held back, then, after a click from Kerry, condescended to let Jennie stroke his velvety nose. "He's beautiful."

Kerry smiled, more sincerely this time. "His name is Nebraska Gold. But I call him Nugget. I raised him from a foal."

Like the other royal horses, Nugget was exquisite, with long legs, a slim body, and a coat like polished metal gleaming in the sun. Yuki would love him. Poor Yuki. Miserable as Jennie had found the last two weeks, it had been even worse for him. And he hadn't even gotten a reunion at the end, except with Kogatana.

Jennie eyed Kerry. Had the princess meant it when she said she'd do anything? What if it required a real sacrifice?

"There is a way for you to repay me," Jennie said. "It might be too much, though."

Kerry glanced up from nuzzling her stallion. "What is it?"

"You could give one of your horses to Yuki Nakamura."

Kerry's hand froze on the stallion's shimmering neck. "Seriously?"

Jennie was tempted to snap, *You asked.* But Kerry clearly didn't think of her horses only as valuable possessions, but as animals that she loved.

"I can't tell you the details," Jennie said. "But take my word for it, he gave up a lot to save your life. And he loves horses."

Kerry gave Jennie a sharp look. "Gave up a lot? Oh, you mean Paco."

"Who told you Paco broke up with him?" Jennie demanded. Then she remembered Kerry's trick of mentioning something that *might* be relevant, and letting other people's reactions tell her what she wanted to know. "Right. I guess I just did. Don't pry into Yuki's life, okay? He hates that."

But Kerry didn't look smug. She drew in a deep breath, then another, as if she was controlling some emotion. When she spoke, her voice was calm. "He loves horses, huh? He does ride beautifully."

"We all think he's never more princely than on horseback."

"I do owe him. And you." Kerry twined Nugget's mane around her fingers. "But these horses are all I have. Let me think about it, okay?"

Naturally, the princess wouldn't give up one of her royal horses. Or would she? Eyeing Kerry's troubled face, Jennie wondered if she might feel guilty enough over Yuki to reconsider.

But Jennie didn't want her to feel guilty. Kerry had given up her entire life to save Ross. To protect Las Anclas. No wonder she was hanging on to her horses. To Jennie's own surprise, she wanted to cheer Kerry up.

"Now that we're not on opposite sides of a jail cell, you should train with me," Jennie suggested. "You're a good fighter. It would be fun."

"I'm not staying in Las Anclas. But while I'm here, sure. It *would* be fun." Kerry rode away.

At home, Jennie's entire family had gathered in the kitchen. The warm air was scented with turnip greens, fried fish, and corn bread.

"Jennie," Pa said. "Have a glass of barley water?"

"Let me," Dee exclaimed. "Let me!"

Pa laughed as he passed Jennie an empty glass. On the surface, everything seemed back to normal.

But Jennie would never again be a Ranger. And Sera was still gone.

Dee took the pitcher in both hands, and scowled at it. The tea began to swirl into a whirlpool. A water spout lifted from the center of the whirlpool and made a graceful arc into Jennie's glass. Barley water filled the glass nearly to the brim, then the spout withdrew into the pitcher. Not a single drop was spilled.

Life goes on, and things can change for good, as well as for bad. I have to remember that. Jennie clapped. "Your control is fantastic, Dee."

Someone knocked at the door, and Tonio sprang to open it. Ross stood in the doorway, his hair wet. He wore a new shirt and clean jeans. Everybody called greetings, and the kids pelted him with questions.

Ross shot Jennie a look as if he hoped she would rescue him. *And some things don't change.* She grabbed his hand. "Let's go to my room."

"Ooooo!" Dee crooned. She sang, "Ross is going to Jennie's room! Oooo-oooo! Hey!" That last was a protest as Yolanda sent a gust of wind into her face.

Jennie escorted Ross out of the line of fire and into her room. Once they were alone together, Dee's silly little song replayed in Jennie's head, making her self-conscious. If she felt awkward, Ross had to be petrified.

But he was the one who closed the distance between them. The kiss was satisfyingly long. In the jail, she'd been so overwhelmed with surprise and relief that afterward, she couldn't remember any details. This time, she let herself sink into it, running her fingers through his damp hair. She could feel her own heart beating, and they were pressed so tight together that she thought she could feel his, too.

Oh yes. Some changes were definitely good.

She stepped back, and looked straight into Ross's eyes. Once again she got that image of him falling. But with his kiss still warm on her lips, the memory didn't hurt so much. Maybe she could let it be in the past, because here he was, standing in front of her. Alive.

"Watch this." Ross walked to her bookshelf, pulled out a book, and opened it at random. He read, *"I might as well enquire," replied she, "why with so evident a design of offending and insulting me, you chose to tell me that you liked me against your will, against your reason, and even against your character?"*

He read slowly but fluently. Jennie applauded.

"Voske had me locked in a room with two whole bookcases full of books," Ross explained. "I kept thinking how much you would have loved them. So I read some of them." His gaze dropped to the floor. "I thought maybe...someday...I could tell you the stories. If you wanted."

"Of course I want!" She sat on her bed and patted the coverlet. "There's something I should tell you."

Ross dropped down beside her. She took his good hand in hers, so warm and strong, and stroked up his wrist inside his sleeve, until she hit the taped edges of a bandage.

She pulled her hand back and caressed his palm. Dr. Lee had kept Ross in the surgery for a long time before he went to the council meeting. Afterward, she and Mia had caught him up on what had happened while he'd been gone, but he hadn't said one word about his injuries.

"What did you want to tell me?" he asked.

"I wanted you to know why I avoided you after the battle."

"Mia said you were close to Sera Diaz."

It was still hard to hear Sera's name. "Yeah, but that's only part of it. I was falling to pieces and I didn't think I could tell anyone. Every time I looked at you, I felt like I was back in the battle, when I thought you were dead. When I was in a Ranger training exercise, I actually thought I *was* back in the battle. They declared me unfit for duty."

Ross closed his hand over hers. "I wish you'd told me. I get it. I really do."

"You do?"

He nodded, but didn't elaborate. Some things were not easy to talk about. Maybe they never would be. But she was glad not to feel so alone anymore. She had to make sure she never let herself get that way again.

Jennie tried to remember if she'd left anything out of her confession. She'd promised herself that she'd tell Ross *everything*. "Oh, and I threatened to kill Mr. Vilas."

"Fair's fair." Ross grinned. "He threatened to kill me. A couple times."

Jennie laughed. "I'm doing better now, but I wanted you to know. I guess I was afraid of having everyone…having you…find out that I'm not as strong as I seem."

His fingers tightened over hers, squeezing harder and harder until she could feel the pressure in her bones. "I'm not that strong, either." He was sitting so close to her that she felt his breathing quicken. "I told you Voske was planning to execute me. I didn't tell you he said it would take all day. I was hurt, and scared, and I gave up."

Ross indicated the bandage on his neck. "Voske didn't do that. I tried to kill myself."

Jennie pulled him into her arms and held him tight. "I wish I'd been there for you."

"I don't want anyone to know," Ross said into her shoulder. "I didn't even tell Dr. Lee. Don't tell anyone."

Jennie sat back and peered into his face, then cupped her hands around his cheeks. "*I* won't tell anyone. But I think you should." And when he stiffened, "Not the world. Just Mia."

Ross pulled away. "I told her Voske's guards used her weapon to break my arm, and she started crying. I didn't even get to the hell cells, let alone…" He wrapped his arms around his chest and muttered, "…what happened there."

Hell cells? Jennie shuddered. "Yeah, it'll upset her. But she'll end up a lot more hurt if you start hiding things from her. Besides, this isn't something you should carry alone. I learned that the hard way."

Ross looked down. She watched the long lashes hiding his eyes, and wondered what he was thinking. The turn to his mouth was so unhappy she wanted to pull him tight and kiss him again.

"Maybe you're right," he said at last.

He was tensing up, so she sat back, giving him space. The first time he had kissed her, she'd thought about inviting him to spend the night. But now she knew he wasn't ready.

"Did you have anything planned for the evening?" she asked, to see how he reacted.

"I'm having dinner with Mia and Dr. Lee. Would you like to come?"

Jennie smiled. Definitely not the right time yet. "Another day? Tonight I want to stay with my family."

They kissed once more before he left. She stood by her window until she saw him walking away. Back to Mia. They'd promised not to be jealous of each other, but Jennie was, a little. Not just of whatever Mia and Ross would do tonight, but of the two months they had spent together while Jennie was busy avoiding them both. But she couldn't turn back the clock.

She touched her lips, imagining the warmth of Ross's kiss lingering there. He would be back.

CHAPTER FIFTY-FOUR
LAS ANCLAS
MIA

Mia stood at her window and watched Ross walk away, angrily swiping yet another tear from her cheek. He'd trusted her enough to tell her that whole horrible story about being tortured and trying to kill himself, and had she comforted him? No! She'd cried until *he'd* ended up comforting *her*!

Ross vanished into the surgery, to go sleep in his own room. Alone. Mia kicked a screwdriver across the floor, then flung herself on the bed, beside the engine, and stared miserably up at the ceiling.

The ceiling! After Ross had been locked up for a month, she bet he wouldn't want to sleep under any sort of ceiling. He'd be back in her yard in two minutes.

Oh, why not. She lifted the engine off the bed, gathered up the bedding, and kicked her door open. Ross might as well sleep in comfort. She carried the bedding out to his favorite spot in the yard, surrounded by sheet metal and rusting iron, with an unimpeded view of the starry sky. A huge orange harvest moon rested on top of the stable roof. It was beautiful.

She pulled the sheets and blanket straight and plumped up the pillow. Would Ross like to see the moon's travel? She dragged the bedding around to the best vantage. When she turned to go, he was standing in front of her. Mia jumped.

"I thought you might want to watch the moon set." She indicated the bedding. "I mean, that's why it's positioned that way."

Ross looked down, then back at Mia, then down again. He sat on the bedding, then looked up again. "It's really comfortable." After another pause, he said, "Thanks."

Now that he was sitting there, she longed to lie there next to him. She could cuddle up, and she'd know exactly where he was. If she went back inside, she'd be peeking out every five minutes to make sure no one had kidnapped him.

But he probably wouldn't want her there. Anyone in town could walk by and see them lying there together. No, the sheet metal shielded them, but if anyone walked into the yard, they would see. Anyway, if Ross wanted her there, wouldn't he have asked?

Mia knew he wouldn't ask, regardless of what he wanted. She scowled at him fiercely, trying to read his mind.

"Good night." She started toward the cottage.

"Good night." He sounded wistful.

She spun around and marched back. "Mind if I sleep here with you? I mean, just sleep. Would that be okay?"

Ross pulled her down beside him. "I wanted to ask you. I didn't know if you'd like to."

"It would be so nice if I was telepathic." She settled next to him, and he pulled the blanket over them both.

They kissed for a few minutes, until Ross fell asleep mid-kiss. Mia snuggled close to his warm body and looked up at the stars. When she and Jennie were Dee's age, they used to drag a blanket into Jennie's yard and count shooting stars.

His chest rose and fell softly, his ribs pressing against hers. He was as thin as he'd been when he'd first arrived in Las Anclas, chased by that bounty hunter. Three months of Dad and Jack's cooking, all to vanish after a month of Voske's royal prison.

She peered at the nasty bruising and half-healed cuts on his face. What had Voske done to him? She was sure that Ross hadn't told her half of it, even if he had told her the worst of it.

She'd love to get her hands on that Voske. No, not her hands. Her flamethrower. A crossbow. One of Ross's knives. One of Ross's singing trees. How would Voske like *his* head on a pike? She imagined that, except somehow still alive, so he could see Las Anclas celebrating his defeat.

Ross's breathing sped up. The night was cool, but sweat beaded his face. Pressed so close against him, she felt it when every muscle in his body locked tight.

She rolled away and sat up. "Ross. Ross, wake up."

His eyes flew open, but he didn't seem to see her.

"Ross." Mia leaned forward. "It's okay. You're safe."

He grabbed her hand and hung onto it, then pulled her in close. He was shaking. She tried to wrap every part of herself around him, then worried that it would make him feel trapped. But he didn't pull away.

"Thanks." His voice shook, too. "I was back in the hell cell. I couldn't breathe."

Mia's face was pressed into the side of his head. She kissed him on the ear. "You're safe in Las Anclas. And the hell cells are underwater now, right?"

"Right." Ross let out a long sigh. "Well, they're muddy, anyway."

After everything he'd gone through, he couldn't even get a good night's sleep. Thanks to Voske!

"I want to kill that Voske," Mia said. "I wish I could have rescued you."

"You did rescue me. You sent Kerry."

"Too late! I wanted to search for you immediately. I was sure you'd escaped. But that Preston wouldn't let me."

"You were right," said Ross. "They should have listened to you."

"It was the same when I wanted to let Kerry go. Nobody believed me when I said we should trust her, except Jennie and Yuki. Actually, I don't think Yuki did believe me. I think he helped for a completely different reason." As Mia spoke, years' worth of anger boiled up in her: not only for Ross's sake, but for herself. "I fought in the battle here."

"I remember," Ross said quietly. "You saved my life."

"I thought it would make people see me differently. But it didn't. Once the battle was over, everyone went right back to treating me the same way they always did, as if it had never happened. Nobody takes me seriously about anything but machines."

Ross stroked her hair. "I take you seriously. If you ever need me, I'll back you up."

"Thanks." Mia rested her head on his shoulder, and sighed her anger out. Ross was slowly relaxing as well, she could feel it. She began to enjoy being outside, under the stars, with Ross beside her.

A shooting star blazed across the sky. "Did you see that? There, in the Seven Sisters."

"I always heard that one called the Seven Puppies," Ross said.

"Puppies!"

"The story is, there was a dog who could transform himself into a handsome young man. One day he saw this beautiful woman…"

Mia laughed.

CHAPTER FIFTY-FIVE
LAS ANCLAS
KERRY

"Try it under the window," Kerry said, standing back.

Brisa, Becky, Sujata, and Meredith picked up Kerry's bed and set it under the window.

Meredith flopped onto it. "I like this. Maybe I'll move mine under the window."

Brisa dropped down beside Meredith, followed, more gracefully, by Sujata. Becky snuggled in next to Brisa. Kerry eyed the four girls piled on her bed. It was a sight that would never have been seen in the palace.

"C'mon, Kerry." Brisa shoved Meredith over. "Test it out."

Kerry smiled, aware that she was going through the motions. People—some people—had kindly offered her extra furnishings, and even this room on Singles Row, as if she was going to settle in Las Anclas. They'd done it even after she'd told them she planned to ride out as soon as...well, soon.

"Lie on Brisa, Kerry." Meredith crossed her arms behind her head. "She makes a nice soft pillow."

Kerry hesitated. But why not? She wedged herself into the tiny remaining space, lying mostly on top of Becky, and looked out the single window. It was nothing like the view from her bedroom in the palace, of gardens, woods, and the distant hills. All the south-facing rooms in the adobe bungalow for singles had windows facing a row of vegetable plots, and beyond that, the city wall.

The plain bed had been finished that morning, and smelled like freshly cut wood and varnish. The table, chairs, and clothes trunk were even plainer, and had obviously served at least a generation of Las Anclas families. But people had offered it all freely, without looking over their shoulders.

"I like it here," Kerry said.

"Good job, everybody." Meredith started to applaud, and accidentally elbowed Brisa in the face.

"Ow," Brisa protested, and elbowed Meredith back.

Meredith promptly started a shove fight, tipping Kerry onto the floor.

"Sorry!" rose up in a four-part chorus.

So this was what it was like to have friends. Kerry picked herself up and looked down at them. Then she wondered what her expression had been, because the laughing girls fell silent.

Becky said softly, "Let's let Kerry settle in."

The girls scrambled off the bed and headed for the door.

"See you at Luc's, Princess!" Brisa called.

Kerry grimaced. "Don't call me that."

"As a nickname?" Brisa asked hopefully.

Sujata gave a delicate shudder. "If you insist upon a nickname, Brisa, *I* will think of a better one."

Brisa and Becky were the last to go, their clasped hands swinging between them. Kerry waved, then left the door open to air the room.

Six weeks ago, she'd thought Becky pathetic, Brisa stupid, and both girls weak and sentimental. Now she saw Becky as sweet and thoughtful, and Brisa as playful and fun. It was strange how her perceptions had shifted.

It was even stranger to think as herself as a part of a group, instead of its leader. She could analyze the initial motivations for the girls to be interested in her—Brisa was fascinated by princesses, and Becky had felt sorry for Kerry—but if that was all it was, they should have dropped her once she was out of jail and no longer a princess.

Instead, Becky had introduced Kerry to her friend Sujata, Brisa had introduced Kerry to her friend Meredith, and the next thing Kerry knew, she was designing clothes with Sujata, sparring with Meredith, and dancing at Luc's with them all.

In Gold Point, Kerry had never had girl friends. Now she had these four, and Mia, too. Jennie wasn't a friend, but she was clearly trying to be friend*ly*.

And Ross… Kerry grinned to herself. She'd assumed that the way he'd acted in Gold Point had been because he was a prisoner. But no. He still shied away from crowds and enclosed spaces and being the center of attention, and sudden movements still made him jump as if he'd been stabbed. But now he smiled and even laughed. And of all the teenagers who trained secretly in Sujata's orchard, he was the most fun to spar with.

And they were probably all going to die when Father repaired the damage to Gold Point and set out for revenge with an army at his back.

Maybe she could persuade someone to leave with her, and save at least one life. Kerry sighed. There was a useless, sentimental fantasy. Ross had already said he wouldn't go, and neither would anyone else. It was like the way Father controlled Gold Point: everyone had people they loved too much to leave.

Except for Kerry, who had loved someone and left him anyway. She wished she at least knew if Santiago was all right. But that uncertainty was something she'd have to live with for the rest of her life. However long that was.

Kerry pulled her mind away from that thought. She'd spend another week or so in Las Anclas, enjoying the company and pretending she didn't know the future.

She went to her backpack and took out the four personal possessions she'd brought from Gold Point, apart from her crown. First, her silk pillow, painted in swirls of blue and white, like clouds on a sunny day. She fluffed it up and set it on the patchwork quilt that Mrs. Riley had given her.

Next were two books, one an ancient novel about heroes fighting a war in flying machines, and another, equally ancient, that she'd treasured since she was a little girl, full of color pictures of horses. She set them on a shelf.

Finally, the red and black hanbok Mom had given to her, Kerry's favorite, embroidered with the four-clawed dragon design that only the crown princess could wear. She hung it on the wall across from her bed, where she could see its bright colors.

Had Sean taken anything personal with him when he'd disappeared? She hadn't spotted anything missing when she'd checked his room, but maybe he'd taken something that Kerry had never known was important to him. Out of pure habit she glanced at the open doorway, and asked herself, *Is Sean here?*

He was.

Kerry jumped. "Sean!"

He stepped inside and shut the door. Kerry launched herself across the room, and was locked in a bone-rattling hug. He swung her around in a circle, then set her down, and stepped back.

"You're taller," they said simultaneously, and laughed.

When Sean had left, he'd been sixteen and gawky. Now he was broad in the chest and had shoulders like a blacksmith. But his wide, sweet smile was the same as she remembered.

"Sean, what are you doing here?" she asked. "You can't have been in Las Anclas this whole time!"

"No, of course not," her brother replied. "I would have rescued you. But I didn't know you'd been kidnapped until weeks after it had happened. Then I came straight here—and I missed you by a day."

"But where have *you* been?"

"Catalina. I started off crewing on a fishing boat. Now I'm second mate, and I've got my own little pinnace. I could take you fishing in it. The ocean's beautiful at night."

Kerry could hardly believe it. Sean—here! The last time she'd seen him, he'd had a golden crown atop his dense black curls, with a white silk shirt setting off his deep brown skin. Now he was bareheaded, with his hair in cornrows. His shirt and trousers were undyed cotton. But he'd never been happy when he'd worn his crown, only when he was dressed as plainly as he was now, and off in the desert watching wildlife. He used to do that for hours, long after Kerry had gotten bored.

She smiled back at him. "I'd love to go sailing, but not if we're going to watch jellyfish mating all night."

Sean cracked a laugh. "It's fun. But I'll spare you."

"Why did you leave? I've always wondered."

The humor died out of his face. "From what I've heard, the same reason you decided to break Ross Juarez free."

"You know about that?" Kerry exclaimed. "Oh, of course, you overheard people here talking."

Sean shook his head. "I heard it in Gold Point."

Kerry leaped up and grabbed him. "You were in Gold Point? How's Santiago?"

"He's fine," Sean said quickly. "In fact, Father promoted him to personal bodyguard."

Kerry's legs went wobbly with relief. She sat down hard on the bed.

Sean joined her. "When I heard you'd escaped, I decided to make sure you arrived okay. But I missed you again. By the time I got there, you and Ross Juarez had blown up the dam and disappeared, and half of Gold Point was under six inches of mud." He grinned at her. "You made a much bigger splash when you left than I did. Literally."

Kerry laughed. "So what's happening at—" She stopped herself before she could say the word *home*. When would it stop hurting to think about it?

"It's a mess. No one got killed in the flood, but there were some broken ankles and stuff like that from stumbling around in the dark. And all that water woke up every desert bug, reptile, and amphibian that doesn't hatch or metamorphose or emerge until there's a big rainfall. Gold Point is swarming with creatures I've never even heard of." A familiar enthusiasm sparked Sean's old grin. "It was fascinating. I spotted a yellow frog that had a symbiotic relationship with an armored—"

Kerry whacked him in the ribs. "Forget the zoology lesson. Did you see Father?"

The grin vanished. "I didn't have the nerve to go anywhere near him, but everyone was talking about how furious he was."

"What about Santiago?"

Sean shook his head. "I avoided anyone who might look for me, especially him. He was always good at spotting me. But the gossip is, when he heard that you'd dumped him for that prisoner, he went on this incredible rant about what a selfish, shallow, ruthless, disloyal person you were, and how he was sorry he'd ever laid eyes on you, and he wanted to lead the search party so he could be the one to shoot you dead."

Kerry winced.

"I assume that's what you told him to say," Sean added.

"More or less." She recalled Santiago echoing her words: *I loved you. You broke my heart.*

Sean patted her hand. "He'll be all right. Will you?"

"I miss him," Kerry sighed. "I wanted him to come with me, but he didn't dare. What about my mom? Father didn't blame her, did he?"

"No. He would never do anything to her. The technicians and soldiers and grooms and the guards at the gate got off with reprimands for the rank and file, and a session at the flogging post for patrol captains. The only people he beheaded were the hell cell guards."

Kerry spoke a beat ahead of Sean, quoting Father: "'If too many people bear responsibility to execute them all, select the ones who are most expendable.'"

She'd told Ross no one would die, but she'd known that Father was bound to make an example of *someone.* Still, it could have been much worse. Those guards thought torture was a sport.

Then Kerry remembered how she'd laughed along with them. Had she been the only one who had feigned cruelty to protect herself?

Sean went on, "Father didn't even punish Luis."

"Why would he? Luis followed his orders."

Sean gave her a funny look. "Father told Luis to heal the prisoner?"

"What?" Kerry exclaimed. "He can heal, too?"

"You didn't know that? Yes, he apparently healed Ross accidentally and didn't even realize it had happened until afterward, when everyone was trying to figure out how he'd recovered enough to blow up the dam."

Everything that had perplexed Kerry on that night now made sense.

Sean went on, "Luis healed Father's arm, and Father was so pleased that he appointed him the royal healer." Sean's gaze fell upon her hanbok, with the royal colors. "Have you spoken to Paco?"

"He pretends I don't exist. Have you?"

"I've only seen him from a distance," Sean said. "I know some people here look for me. Scary, isn't it? How much he looks like Father?"

"We all look like Father."

"But there's something else. Something about his eyes... No." Sean shook his head. "I'm not going to guess, and I'm certainly not going to judge. Listen, Kerry, I risked coming into town to ask if you want to move to Catalina with me."

Kerry's breath caught. She could have a family again. Then, reluctantly, she said, "Pru's hawks can't see you, but they can see me. If I go to Catalina, Father will come after me, and then he'll find you. My plan was to head north until I hit territory where no one's even heard of Gold Point."

"Father won't come after anyone," Sean replied. "Word got out about the dam blowing up, and Lake Perris decided it was the perfect time for a revolution."

"What!"

He nodded. "They killed the governor and half the soldiers from Gold Point, chased the rest out, and buried all the heads on their walls in a big ceremony. Father couldn't do a thing about it, since you'd swamped his gunpowder. People are whispering that once more towns get the word, his entire empire will fall apart."

It hadn't occurred to Kerry that what she and Ross did would have any effect outside of Gold Point itself, except to delay Father from attacking Las Anclas. She'd never intended to bring down Father's empire. She could barely even imagine that was possible.

"And that's not all," Sean added. "I spotted Pru on my way to Gold Point, headed in the opposite direction. I would have thought she was spying for Father, but she had two burros loaded down with her stuff." He laughed. "She had a sack stuffed full of silk pillows."

"She took off." It was hard to imagine. Pru had been a fixture in Gold Point for years. "She must have guessed I'd tell Las Anclas about her, and she figured even Father couldn't protect her once her secret was out."

Sean nodded. "A handful of people grabbed their families and ran during the chaos after the dam blew, and I guess she was one of them. Pru always did know what side her bread was buttered on."

More than anything else Sean had said, that made Father's downfall seem real to Kerry. Pru was canny, and she had been happy to work for Father. If even she had abandoned him...

"So," Sean went on, "Want to come to Catalina?"

It was hard to believe that Father wasn't going to appear one morning at the head of an army. But it sounded like he had his hands full—with luck, for years. And who knew what might happen in years?

But it was a fantasy to think that the threat was over forever. Father never forgot a grudge. And if he did come after her, how could she risk drawing his eye to Sean, who had also betrayed and left him? Catalina was the one place where she could never go.

If she stayed in Las Anclas, at least she'd be near him. She was a hero in the town, and if some people still hated her, there was nothing they could do about it.

If she stayed in Las Anclas, she could keep her friends. She could keep her plain little room, with its varnish-smelling furniture. She had her horses, and the sparring group. Maybe she could trade for a rat of her own. It was a life she'd never dreamed of, but it seemed like a good one.

"If I stayed here, would you come back again, with your jellyfish-watching boat?"

"Sure. I've been checking up on the family at Gold Point whenever I had a long enough liberty for the trip inland." Sean flashed his grin. "But now you'll see me. I take it you want to stay in Las Anclas?"

Kerry patted her bed. "Did you see those girls who helped me move my stuff? They're not servants, they're friends!"

Sean nodded vigorously. "That's been one of the best things about Catalina. I couldn't have real friends in Gold Point."

"Is that why you left?" Kerry asked.

He twisted a braid around one finger. "You remember how it was. Father had me spying on people and reporting back to him since I was four! When I was little it was a game, and later it was just how things were. Then Leila died on Opportunity Day, and all Father said was, *Better luck next time.* One day I walked out the gates to watch the bobcats, and I looked back at the latest head that had belonged to someone I'd spied on, and I just kept on walking."

In the distance, the bells rang the evening watch change.

"No one in Las Anclas knows about me, Kerry," said Sean. "I'd like to keep it that way."

"Sure." In a way, she was glad to have Sean all to herself. Everything else had changed, and she'd lost so much. Now she'd have one special thing that was just hers. "When will I see you again?"

"We trade up and down the coast. Whenever I get overnight liberty, I'll turn up."

Another bone-cracking hug, and he was gone.

Kerry closed the door behind her, and went out to meet her friends.

CHAPTER FIFTY-SIX
LAS ANCLAS
YUKI

Yuki stood beneath Paco's window, trying to get up the nerve to knock. It was ridiculous to be more nervous about talking to his boyfriend—his ex-boyfriend—than when he'd risked everything to set Kerry free. But instead of giving him courage, the thought only made him feel foolish as well as anxious.

Kogatana dug her claws into his shoulder and coiled her tail around his throat, chokingly tight. She'd stuck to him like a limpet ever since she'd come back, often giving him reproachful glances from her shiny black eyes. He wished he could let her know that he'd never send her away again.

A roar of laughter rose up from Julio Wolfe's party at the other end of Singles' Row—the party Yuki had slipped round the back to avoid. The entire town had started celebrating that afternoon, when Mr. Preston had announced the news from the Ranger team he'd sent out to confirm Ross's story: not only had the dam come down, but Voske's conquered towns were rebelling, one by one.

Voske was unlikely to attack Las Anclas any time soon, and some thought he'd be lucky to keep his crown. "Or his head," Henry had joked.

Yuki had made up his mind at that moment. Now he had to tell Paco... if Paco was even willing to open the window. They hadn't spoken since Paco had stormed into the jail to break up with him.

His heart pounding, Yuki tapped on the glass. An eternity passed until the curtain twitched aside and Paco's face appeared, barely visible in the dark room. Yuki half-expected him to drop the curtains back down when he saw who it was.

Paco froze, then unlatched the window. "Come in."

Yuki passed Kogatana to Paco, then hoisted himself through the window. Paco retreated into the room, set the rat on the bed, and pulled the cover off the bright-moth cage. In the soft light, Yuki searched Paco's face for clues as to his feelings.

"I'm sorry, Paco."

"Sorry for what?" The light didn't reach his dark eyes.

Yuki didn't want to lie. "Sorry I went behind your back."

Paco sat down on the bed. "Yeah, well, I'm sorry you had to. If you'd told me, I would have stopped it."

"I know." Yuki felt awkward, standing while Paco was sitting, but he couldn't sit on Paco's bed without an invitation.

Paco didn't invite him to sit. "What made you trust Kerry?"

"I didn't. I…" Yuki was certain that the conversation would end then and there if he said, *I couldn't let you kill your own sister.* "I couldn't let her be killed in cold blood."

Paco absently stroked Kogatana's fur. "So she did what my mother did —left Voske. I guess I've got to respect that." Stroke, stroke, his hand worked gently through the rat's gray fur.

"Actually, I'm not sorry for what I did," Yuki admitted. "But I'm sorry it wrecked things between us."

Paco kept petting Kogatana. Yuki hadn't moved from where he stood, up against the window.

Another roar of laughter came from outside. Someone shouted, "Julio! It's past midnight! Some of us have to work in the morning."

"Shut the window, will you?" Paco suggested. "It's getting cold in here."

Yuki latched the window and pulled the curtain.

Paco let out another long breath, then patted the bed. Yuki sat down next to him. He could feel the heat in the air between them—that hadn't changed. But it made what he had to say even harder.

"I'm leaving Las Anclas," Yuki said. "I'm going prospecting."

Paco's hand froze on Kogatana's back. "Seriously? By yourself? When?"

"The day after tomorrow. I wanted to go tomorrow morning, but mom said I had to give everyone a chance to say good-bye."

Unexpectedly, Paco laughed. "She's going to make you sit through an entire day of everyone in town asking nosy questions and giving you advice you don't want, huh?"

"Yeah, I'm really looking forward to it," Yuki said wryly.

"Did you buy a burro? I know you can't afford a horse."

Yuki had braced himself for Paco to be hostile, or, worse, to not even care. But Paco acting like he used to, before everything had gone wrong— before Voske's soldiers had killed his mother—was unexpected, and unexpectedly painful. *This* was what Yuki was leaving behind.

Yuki shook his head. "It'll just be me and Kogatana."

Silence fell, and the question he hadn't asked seemed to hang in the room, glowing like the bright-moth cage: *Will you come with me?*

The silence continued, its own answer: *No.*

"I have to protect the town." Paco's voice was level, neither defensive nor apologetic. "I think I'll get into the Rangers."

"I think you will, too." Yuki tried to phrase the question without mentioning the name *Voske.* "Don't you think the town's safe now, though?"

"Maybe. But I'd never forgive myself if I left, and it wasn't." Paco frowned. "I don't mean you shouldn't go. You *should* go. It's what you've always wanted."

It is, but it's not the only thing, Yuki thought.

If he stayed, maybe he could he patch things up with Paco. If he stayed, he'd still have the sea cave to explore, and maybe the ruined city.

Everything he'd miss if he left popped into his mind: not only people, like Paco, Mom, and Meredith, but Fuego, the beautiful red-gold gelding he could never afford to buy. Hot baths. Books. Luc's. Music.

"I think I've been afraid to leave," Yuki said slowly. "Not afraid of danger—afraid of losing what I have here."

As he said it, he knew it was true. He'd lost his entire world once before, when the *Taka* had been attacked by pirates, and he'd spent years vainly wishing for time to turn backward and change what had already happened. Thanks to Kerry, he now knew that the life of a prince, too, wouldn't have been the life he wanted. He'd have done his duty. But he wouldn't have been happy.

He had to either settle in Las Anclas and call it home, or leave and find a new life of his own making.

"You don't have to go," Paco said.

"I said I was afraid. Not that I don't want to. There's a saying, *Koketsu ni irazunba koji wo ezu.*" Yuki translated, "You have to go into the tiger's cave to catch its cub."

"Nothing ventured, nothing gained? Yeah, you're right." Paco gave him a little smile. "Say it again?"

Yuki repeated the saying, translating each word. With his music-trained memory, Paco caught it on the second repetition. It had been months since Yuki had taught Paco any Japanese, but soon they were having a stilted Japanese conversation on the subject of tigers.

"Are there tigers in the desert?" Paco asked in perfectly accented Japanese. In English, he added softly, "I'll miss you."

Yuki struggled to keep his voice even. "I'll miss you, too. But it's not like we'll never see each other again. I'll come back for a visit in a year or two."

"Or three," said Paco glumly. "Or four."

"Two, maximum," Yuki said firmly. "Anyway, I have to come back: I made a deal with Ross over the sea cave. He can prospect it, but I get half the profits. Would you mind diving it with him? He's a good swimmer, but he's inexperienced."

Paco nodded. "I'll make sure he doesn't drown."

"One more thing." Yuki opened the pouch he wore at his belt, and placed a small statue beside the bright-moth cage. The light of the fluttering moths flickered across the silver dancer, making her seem to breathe. It was the one treasure he'd wrested from the sea cave, almost at the cost of his life. "I'd like you to have this."

"I can't," Paco protested, as Yuki had known he would. "It's too valuable."

"Just keep it for me. You never know what might happen in the desert. It'd be safer with you."

"Well…" Paco looked at the statue, and Yuki wondered if he was remembering how he used to drum for the dancers. How he used to dance himself, making the formal steps and turns of folklorico look relaxed and easy. "All right, then."

Yuki got up. "I should get back home."

Paco caught his hand. "Stay. Just tonight."

Yuki sank back down on to the bed. Paco tossed the cover over the bright-moth cage, darkening the room. Yuki could barely see, but he felt it when Paco pressed his lips against Yuki's.

*

The next morning, Paco walked Yuki to the stables, Kogatana trotting at their heels. He walked with Paco in their old rhythm, matching strides, trying not to think that it would be the last time they did so.

If Yuki stayed in Las Anclas, would that "just tonight" have led to more nights, until they were a couple again? Or had it only happened *because* it was the last time?

Inside the stable, Kerry was grooming her royal horses with an invisible curry comb. They gleamed as if they'd been polished.

"Yuki, I have something for you." Kerry's quick black glance flickered toward Paco, and then the two of them resolutely ignored each other.

"What is it?" Yuki asked.

"Meredith told me you were leaving," Kerry said.

Yuki reminded himself that this was the last time he'd have to put up with everyone discussing his private business. "That's right."

Kerry ran a hand along the bronze mare's shining mane. "I want to give you Tigereye."

"What?" Yuki exclaimed.

In the weeks he'd helped Mrs. Riley at the stables since Kerry had come back, he'd coveted those graceful royal horses, which were faster and smarter—though more temperamental—than the horses of Las Anclas. The thought of owning one took his breath away.

"Her full name is Tennessee Bronze," Kerry said.

Tigereye nuzzled his cheek, her breath hay-sweet and warm.

Yuki stroked her glittering neck, unable to believe that she was really his. "I don't know how to thank you. This is the best gift I've gotten in my entire life. Well, her and Kogatana."

"It was Jennie's idea. But I wanted to give you *something*." To Yuki's surprise, she turned to Paco. "I'm sorry about what I said at the party. I was terrified that I was going to be executed, and I thought an ally might save me."

"An ally? Against Las Anclas?" Paco repeated angrily.

Kerry held up her hands. "I was desperate and I did what I'd been taught to do. Can we start over?"

"I guess," Paco said reluctantly. "I know you could have stayed in Gold Point and let Ross die, if you'd wanted to."

"Don't think that didn't cross my mind," Kerry said. "But I had a promise to keep."

Yuki wondered if Kerry had planned out this entire conversation, and had only been waiting for a chance to have it.

She continued smoothly, "Do you like to ride? Sally could use the exercise." Kerry indicated the slim silver mare.

Paco's face lifted with pleasure, as it used to when he drummed. Then he glanced away. "Maybe later. I'm due on the wall. See you, Yuki. I'm glad you'll have a horse."

Yuki watched Paco leaving, and saw that Kerry did the same. It was strange to see Paco's high cheekbones and sharp chin on a girl's face. Then she turned to him and smiled. The features were the same, but the resemblance was gone.

"I think you and Tigereye will suit each other," Kerry said.

"Oh?"

"She likes wide open spaces. You'll see."

*

Yuki and Kogatana rode out on Tigereye at dawn.

Mom and Meredith came to see him off, of course. Paco and Brisa stood with the rest of Yuki's bow team. And he wasn't surprised to see Mrs. Riley, Jennie, and Ross also waiting at the gate to wave good-bye.

What surprised him was how many others were there, too: a handful of nosy gawkers, which was to be expected, but mostly people he knew and liked. All the Rileys were there. So were Trainer Koslova and Trainer Crow, along with their rats. So were Mia, Dr. Lee, Indra, Becky, Sheriff Crow, Jack from the saloon, and even Kerry. There were old schoolmates, guys he'd dated, people he knew from patrol and sentry duty, and the entire Old Town Band.

Yuki hadn't realized that he'd gotten close, at least a little bit, to so many people. He blinked hard, his throat unexpectedly tight. Then he raised a hand in farewell and rode toward the gates.

A chorus of "Good-bye!" and "Make some good finds!" rose up.

"Bring back a tiger cub!" Paco shouted in Japanese.

"You *better* come back!" Meredith yelled, and fiercely scrubbed her eyes.

Yuki rode through the gates, and left the walls of Las Anclas behind him.

He nudged Tigereye with his knee, and she set off in a gallop, her flying mane glittering in the sun. She moved like an extension of his own body, fast as a gale. Kogatana squeaked in excitement.

Yuki laughed aloud with the sheer joy of it. As they sped across the sands, all his sadness and regret and loneliness fell away, like barnacles scraped off the hull of a ship before it could set sail. The desert plains rolled out before him like the open sea, and the very air he breathed seemed full of endless possibilities.

CHAPTER FIFTY-SEVEN
LAS ANCLAS
ROSS

Ross walked through the back gate, with Mia and Jennie at his side. The girls each held a glass lamp filled with bright-moths, Jennie's all gold, and Mia's a rainbow mix of colors. The setting sun burned red over the cornfields, and flashes of crystalline scarlet and black overlaid his vision. Chimes rang out in chorus, each one clear and distinct.

But even more distracting than sight and sound, the singing trees sent him emotions: from his own crimson tree, curiosity and the desire to have him near; from the obsidian grove, hatred and rage, fear and pain, shock and disbelief and denial...

"Ross!"

His nerves jolted. The link with the trees snapped, dropping him back into reality.

Mr. Preston had climbed down from the wall. Mia put a hand on Ross's back, and Jennie stepped forward protectively.

Mr. Preston raised his eyebrows. "Stand down, Jennie. I already gave you all permission to stay out past the gates closing."

Jennie didn't give an inch of ground. Ross stopped himself from getting into a defensive stance, but every muscle in his body longed to do so. Every time he saw the man, he thought of how Mr. Preston had sent the bounty hunter to kill him.

"Ross, I'm not going to stop you from doing..." Mr. Preston's mouth twitched, the way it always did when he mentioned Change powers. "... whatever it is you mean to do, which I can't say I fully understand. I just wanted to remind you to be back by midnight. If you're not, I'll send a search party."

"We'll be back on time," Ross promised him.

He hurried toward the cornfields, the girls matching his pace. He wished he could have simply climbed the wall. But he hadn't wanted to go alone, and he couldn't risk Mia and Jennie getting in even more trouble for his sake.

"I don't fully understand it, either," Jennie admitted. "Do the singing trees trap the souls of the people they kill?" She was so close to Ross that he felt her shudder.

"No, I'm sure they don't." He struggled to put into words what he felt and understood. "A soul is the whole person, right? What's in the singing trees is everything the person was thinking and feeling in the minute or so it took them to die, before it becomes something else—the tree."

"Like a footprint?" Mia suggested, stamping on the damp earth. "It's the imprint of a boot, not the boot itself."

Ross nodded. "The tree that grew from my blood wanted to communicate with me. The trees that grew from the soldiers I killed want something from me, too. I thought at first that they wanted to kill me…"

The sound of shattering glass rang sharply in his mind. He flinched, then spoke louder to drown it out, "…and they do, but I have something else to offer them."

He could see the jagged spires and shards of black now, rising above the corn and stabbing at the sky.

Ross turned to the girls. "Stay here, okay? No matter what happens, don't run in to rescue me unless I say it's safe."

They glanced at each other, then reluctantly nodded. He walked on, trying to draw courage from the knowledge that he wasn't alone.

He stopped out of range of the crystal shards, fear gnawing at his belly. But it felt right to come and face the obsidian trees. After all, he had created them. He had killed all those people. It didn't make a difference to them how justified he'd been.

His hand drifted upward, rubbing his neck. He had no feeling in the scars themselves, only on the flesh beneath, as if he was pressing down on a fingernail. The imprints of Luis's fingers remained as shiny pink-white scar tissue. When he had to deal with people he didn't know well, their gaze kept drifting to his throat.

Gold Point had left its mark on him.

Ross closed his eyes. The concrete wall in his mind was crumbling, pierced through by sharp black branches and roots. The anger of the obsidian trees clawed at him. Ross hurriedly rebuilt the wall, thicker than ever, though he knew it wouldn't hold long.

Then he cracked open the steel door. Before the trees could wedge it farther open, to attack him with a barrage of fear and pain, he sent them an image of his own:

The broad main street of Gold Point, lined with shops, and all the people turning to look at him.

That caught the attention of the obsidian trees. One nudged at it curiously, trying to get a closer look at the woman floating a few inches above the ground. Ross tried to remember her as vividly as he could: her soundless steps, the green scarf fluttering around her neck, her bright smile.

He offered that picture to the tree, and received a flurry of images of the same woman in return: asleep in mid-air above the bed, laughing and gesturing with a forkful of salad, standing with her eyes closed and her face tipped back, waiting for a kiss. Whoever the woman had been, whoever the soldier had been who had died to create that obsidian tree, they had loved each other.

The other trees pressed eagerly at Ross's mind, throwing images and feelings at him, far more than he could take in. He was caught in a storm, buffeted by a stream of memories. Then he spotted one he recognized: a young man with clipped black hair, sitting back to tell a story.

Ross grabbed at it like a lifeline, pushing the other images aside. He pictured Santiago with his hands spread over a glowing rock, Santiago winking at Kerry, Santiago playfully knuckling his little cousin's head. Ross focused on those memories, in as much detail as he could bring up, and felt the satisfaction of the tree.

He recalled Gold Point for the black trees until every one of them had found something that matched one of their memories, whether it was a person or a place or merely the trumpet call that summoned the soldiers to their next shift.

Then he showed them himself, walking forward and opening his mind to them, and he showed them his concrete wall, with the trees waiting patiently on the other side, not trying to break through.

Chimes rang out in an eager note, and the black roots and branches withdrew from his wall. The deal was accepted.

Ross closed the steel door.

He was back in his body, dizzy and disoriented. It was pitch-black... no, his eyes were closed. He forced them open. He found himself on his knees in the dirt, leaning against one of the obsidian trees.

By the light of the moon and lamps, he saw Mia and Jennie standing out of range, the lines of their bodies rigid with tension. Ross wanted to go to them, but the crystal tree was the only thing keeping him upright.

"You can come here now," he called. "They won't hurt you."

Mia immediately ran toward him, the lamp swinging in her hand. Jennie hung back, eyeing the shard-filled seed-pods, then slowly followed. He didn't blame her, remembering how terrifying it had been the first time he'd deliberately approached a singing tree. He couldn't imagine how much courage it must have taken for Mia to get within range that first time, when she hadn't known whether or not it would kill her.

Mia sank down beside him and put her arm around his shoulders. "Did it work? It worked, right? How do you feel?"

"It worked. I'm okay. Tired." His head ached fiercely.

Jennie knelt down, holding up her lamp. The bright-moths' wings flared as her hand began to tremble. "There's blood all over your face."

He touched his cheek. He'd cut himself on a razor-sharp ridge on the black tree's trunk. His face was wet with blood and tears.

Ross caught her hand. "I'm all right, Jennie. Really, I am."

Jennie gave him a doubtful glance, then her fingers relaxed in his. "Standing there watching you was one of the hardest things I've ever done. But Mia said you knew what you were doing, so I had to trust her."

"What did you say to the trees?" Mia asked curiously. "You never did tell us exactly what you meant to do."

Every time he'd thought of explaining, the words had stuck in his throat. He swallowed and tried again.

"The singing trees at Gold Point didn't only remember fear and pain. That was… on top, I guess. But beneath that, there were other memories. Places they wanted to be, things they wished they'd done. But mostly, they remembered people."

That was the easy part. He could leave it at that, and the girls would understand. But that wasn't what had given him the idea.

"When I thought I was dying. In the hell cell. I remembered us sitting on my bed, looking up at the stars." Ross made himself meet Mia and Jennie's eyes. "I thought of the people I loved."

Mia squeezed his shoulder. Jennie lowered her head until their cheeks were pressed together.

"That's the deal I made with the trees," Ross went on. "They stop sending me nightmares and trying to force their way into my mind, and I come out here sometimes and show them my memories of Gold Point."

"And of the people *they* loved." Jennie gave a nervous glance up at the canopy of crystal leaves and branches. "I know they're not really the souls of the dead… but could you give them a message from me?"

"What's the message?" Ross asked.

Jennie gave a rueful chuckle. "I don't know yet. I just know I'd like to say *something*. Maybe I'll know what by the next time you come."

"I know what you mean," Ross replied. "Well… I'm not sorry for what I did. It was the only way to save the town. I guess I'm sorry I had to. I wanted to say something, too."

Who had that soldier been, whose dying thoughts had been of Santiago? Some family member or close friend, Ross was sure; the emotions hadn't been romantic. In all that time and talking, Santiago had never breathed a word of it.

"Can you walk, Ross?" Mia asked. "We've been here for hours. I'd hate to run into Mr. Preston's search party."

Ross took Mia and Jennie's hands, and they helped him to his feet. "Let's go home," he said.

*

AUTHORS' NOTE

Thank you for reading *Hostage*. It is the second in the *Change* series. In order, the books are Stranger, *Hostage, Rebel,* and *Traitor.* If you'd like to be alerted by email when new books in the series are released, please visit **http://eepurl.com/Tzv25** to be added to the mailing list.

Please consider writing a review of this book. We appreciate all reviews, whether positive or negative.

Rachel Manija Brown (www.rachelmanijabrown.com) is the author of *All the Fishes Come Home to Roost: An American Misfit in India.* She works as a therapist, specializing in the treatment of PTSD (post-traumatic stress disorder).

Sherwood Smith (www.sherwoodsmith.net) is the author of many fantasy novels for teenagers and adults, including *Crown Duel* and the Mythopoeic Award Finalist *The Spy Princess.*

They both live in Southern California

ABOUT BOOK VIEW CAFE

Book View Café (BVC) is an author-owned cooperative of over fifty professional writers, publishing in a variety of genres including fantasy, romance, mystery, and science fiction.

Our authors include New York Times and USA Today bestsellers; Nebula, Hugo, and Philip K. Dick Award winners; World Fantasy and Rita Award nominees; and winners and nominees of many other publishing awards.

BVC returns 95% of the profit on each book directly to the author.

CPSIA information can be obtained
at www.ICGtesting.com
Printed in the USA
LVOW12s1138300516
490465LV00007BA/928/P